PRAISE FOR
THE BRIDE'S KIMONO

"Brimming equally with Japanese cultural
lore and with Rei's sharp comments on
love, money, death and silk."
S.J. Rozan, author of *Reflecting the Sky*

"The cross-cultural suspense story is as active
as the traffic pattern at Dupont Circle . . .
Japanese pop culture references, style, intrigue
and the quick pace of *The Bride's Kimono*
combine . . . to attract hip readers."
Daily Press (Virginia)

"Astute character development and
fascinating use of Japanese history."
Booklist

"*The Bride's Kimono* takes the reader along
on another humor-filled thrill ride with a
heroine for the new age, Rei Shimura, the
Japanese-American antiques dealer-cum-sleuth
who must navigate between two worlds and
two lovers—and around a corpse—as she
solves the mystery of a stolen antiquity."
Stephen Horn, author of the
New York Times bestseller *In Her Defense*

Also by Sujata Massey

THE FLOATING GIRL
THE FLOWER MASTER
ZEN ATTITUDE
THE SALARYMAN'S WIFE

Coming soon in hardcover

THE DAIMYO'S DAUGHTER

SUJATA MASSEY

THE BRIDE'S KIMONO

AVON BOOKS
An Imprint of HarperCollinsPublishers

This is a work of fiction. Names, characters, places, and incidents are products of the author's imagination or are used fictitiously and are not to be construed as real. Any resemblance to actual events, locales, organizations, or persons, living or dead, is entirely coincidental.

AVON BOOKS
An Imprint of HarperCollins*Publishers*
10 East 53rd Street
New York, New York 10022-5299

Copyright © 2001 by Sujata Massey
ISBN: 0-06-103115-1
www.avonmystery.com

First Avon Books paperback printing: October 2002
First HarperCollins hardcover printing: September 2001

Acknowledgments

My heartfelt gratitude goes out to the true cast of characters who helped me sew up *The Bride's Kimono*! First, I'm deeply grateful to Claudia Brittenham, assistant curator of the Eastern Hemisphere Collections at the Textile Museum in Washington, D.C., who taught me so much about the history of kimono, as well as to her colleague Rachel Shabica, the museum's assistant registrar. I am similarly thrilled to have had Joan Elisabeth Reid, chief registrar of the Walters Art Museum, teach me so much about the world of fine-art couriers.

I learned what it feels like to wear kimono from Shizumi Shigeto Manale, the dancer and kimono collector, and Norie Watanuki, a professional kimono dresser. My kimono knowledge was also expanded through the terrific book *Kimono: Fashioning Culture*, by Liza Dalby, and a Ph.D. thesis by Manami Suga.

Mr. Shimuzu of the Office of the Japanese Consul was extremely helpful in explaining matters relating to missing persons—thanks for letting me into the embassy, too! Also in Washington, I thank Phyllis Richman, the wonderful mystery author and retired food critic, for her restaurant tips. More gastronomic thank-yous to Evan Reynolds, chief concierge for the Hotel Sofitel, and Janet Staihar, who represents Café

Milano in Georgetown. For excellent explanations of police procedure, I'm grateful to Officer Julie Hersey in Fairfax County, Virginia, and Officer Chris Myers in Troy, New York.

As always, Mary Sugiyama, the retired executive director of the North America branch of the Sogetsu School of *ikebana*, provided key introductions and advice. Rei's sound track of Japanese and American pop music was suggested by the pop-music critic J. D. Considine and by Kristin Weisman, the coolest college student in Baltimore.

I also thank Mari Miyake, Chris Belton, and Mark Schreiber for answering my questions about Japanese culture, and Susanne Trowbridge for continuing good advice and maintaining my author Web site. I thank Marcia Talley, Karen Diegmueller, John Mann, Janice McLane, Susan Shorr, Joshua Wolf, Rufus Juskus, Sandy Fleming, Meg Tipper, Anita Sherman, and Lalita Noronha, all great writers themselves, for coaxing the book along. And finally, to my family in New York— my agent, Ellen Geiger, and editor, Carolyn Marino— and the family at home—Tony and Pia Massey—I continue to feel blessed to have you in my life.

And to my readers here and abroad—don't be strangers. You can drop me a line through my Web site, www.sujatamassey.com/sujata

Sujata Massey

Cast of Characters

REI SHIMURA, the Tokyo-based daughter of a cross-cultural couple, TOSHIRO and CATHERINE SHIMURA of San Francisco. Toshiro's sister-in-law, NORIE SHIMURA, watches out for Rei.

RICHARD RANDALL, an English teacher living in Japan who is Rei's best friend.

TAKEO KAYAMA, the Tokyo heartthrob who replaced Rei's ex-boyfriend, HUGH GLENDINNING.

ALLISON POWELL, curator of the Museum of Asian Arts in Washington, D.C.

JAMIE STEVENSON, conservator at the Museum of Asian Arts.

MR. SHIMA, registrar of the Morioka Museum in Tokyo, who works closely with textile curator, MR. NISHIO. Both are supervised by the museum's director, MR. ITO.

KOICHI OTANI, a Kawasaki businessman who is a descendant of an important Osaka tea merchant.

DICK JEMSHAW, chair of the advisory committee at the Museum of Asian Arts.

MRS. CHIYODA, director of See America Travel.

BRIAN HUNTER, night manager at the Washington Suites hotel.

MARK LEESE, security chief at the Washington Suites.

HANA MATSURA, office lady with a yen for shopping. She is traveling with a friend from work named KYOKO OMORI.

YOSHIKI "YOSHI" WATANABE, Hana's fiancé.

JAMES HARRIS, homicide detective who works in cooperation with LILY GARCIA, a patrol officer.

THE BRIDE'S KIMONO

1

For most people, a telephone ringing in the middle of the night is a bad omen.

In my case, it is business as usual. The caller could be an overseas client ignorant of the time difference between New York and Japan, or he could be my best friend, Richard Randall, stranded after the subway's close and in need of a place to crash. There is always a reason to fumble for the phone sandwiched between my futon and the old lacquered tray that serves as my night-stand.

"Rei Shimura Antiques," I croaked, unsure if I was awake or still dreaming.

"Is this Rei?" The voice on the other end sounded like my mother's, but she should have known about the time difference.

"Yes, Mom." I sighed heavily, trying to give her the message that I'd been asleep.

"Actually, I'm not your mother—"

"Oh, I'm sorry. I didn't catch your name." What I had caught on to was that I'd been fooled by the super-modulated, almost English, but really American accent. Flowing into my eardrum at two-forty in the Tokyo morning, it rang with a surreal clarity.

"My name is Allison Powell. I'm the textile curator at

the Museum of Asian Arts in Washington, D.C. I don't know if you've heard of us."

"Of course I have," I said, coming fully awake. I'd made a few visits to the museum near Embassy Row when I was a college student. I remembered the charming black-and-white marble-tiled foyer and a pleasant collection of Utamaro woodblock prints on the walls. There were other wonderful Asian antiquities, too: Chinese terra-cotta figures, Korean celadon-glazed pots, and Kashmiri shawls. It was the kind of place that had served as inspiration for my own fledgling business in Japanese antiques.

"Can you give me a few minutes? I have a proposition for you."

I had a suspicion that all Allison wanted was a guided tour on her next trip to Japan. The previous month an unknown Los Angeles woman had landed on my doorstep and asked me to escort her round-trip to Kyoto—going Dutch, of course.

Trying not to sound too rude, I said, "Well, let me guess. You're coming to Japan and need to be shown around? I can recommend a wonderful English-speaking guide—"

"No, I actually want to give *you* the chance to take a trip," Allison said brightly. "You see, we are about to launch an exhibit on Edo-period kimono. I know it's short notice, but I want you to join us for the opening festivities a month from today."

"Are you sure that my mother didn't put you up to this?" I was suspicious, because my mother had been badgering me to come home to the United States to visit her and my father for the last year.

"I don't know your mother, but I do know about your expertise in Japanese textiles."

"Thank you," I said, still feeling paranoid. "I'm wondering who gave you my personal phone number, because it wasn't in any of my articles."

"A member of our advisory committee had the information. I do apologize for the short notice, Rei. We were supposed to have a speaker from the Morioka Museum, but he canceled at the last minute, so that's why we're so desperate to get someone like you. We can pay an honorarium, per diem, and your travel expenses."

"Oh, really?" So I was a *second* choice. Still, I might as well hear about the money.

"Three thousand is what we were going to pay Mr. Nishio," Allison purred.

"That's barely going to cover the cost of a night in a place like D.C.—" Three thousand yen was about thirty dollars.

"Well, three thousand dollars is a bit higher than what an American courier would typically get for a ten-day visit. However, I know you're not on salary from a Japanese museum, so I could see if I can swing an extra five hundred. Would that suit?"

She'd been thinking in *dollars,* not yen. I said, "I don't understand. What is the money supposed to take care of?"

"Seven days' worth of hotel, food, city transportation, and incidentals—we budgeted that at two thousand and were planning to give a thousand dollars in honorarium for two brief talks on kimono of the late Edo period. The plane tickets will be arranged out of a separate budget—"

"I can do that for you," I said quickly. I knew I could get a much cheaper round-trip flight through my Tokyo connections.

"You could do that and keep the difference, if there's any, as long as you fly business when you're carrying the kimono. Economy class on the way back is fine. You see, the kimono will stay in the U.S. with us for three months. At the end of it, we could possibly hire you again to do a pickup of the goods, if you're interested . . ."

Allison chattered on, but I was busy making my own happy, rapid calculations. Not even factoring in airfare, I was being offered a budget of $500 a day. It was an outrageous amount. I could do the Washington gig and profit.

"I'm going to have to check my calendar," I said, snapping on the electrified antique lantern next to my bed. "Why don't I write down your phone number right now, just in case we get disconnected—" *Or if I wake up and worry this was a dream.*

"Certainly." Allison rattled off a number with a 202 area code, then gave me her fax number and an e-mail address.

"Um, I don't e-mail."

There was a pause. "No e-mail?"

"E-mail came to Japan a little later than in the States. I haven't signed up yet." The truth was, Internet access in Japan was much more expensive than in the U.S., and the idea of communicating by e-mail, rather than by voice or letter, made me uncomfortable. It all seemed so—temporary. My boyfriend, Takeo, swore by it—he spent a couple of hours a day with his laptop, but he couldn't get me to do more than glance at the thing.

"You sound like a real antiquarian." Allison laughed lightly. "Never mind, I'll send things to you the old-fashioned way. I think I have your fax number already." She rattled it off, startling me. I couldn't afford to advertise my antique shopping business in any international arts journals, so I could only assume Allison had a network of excellent contacts in Japan.

After hanging up, I was too excited to go right back to sleep, so I bounded out of bed to make a cup of chamomile tea. If I could get by spending only $500 for the week—rather than per day—I could bring back $3,000 to put in the bank. My savings account was quite low, because in the past year, I'd lost the steady income I'd had from writing an arts-and-antiques column for the *Gaijin Times*. I needed to cobble together all kinds of odd, antiques-related work in order to make my rent. Traveling overseas and speaking about Japanese antiques was something I'd never done—and I had to admit, despite my being the museum's second choice, this would be a great boon.

I finally went back to bed and, two hours later, woke again when the fax machine in the corner of my bedroom started grunting. Allison had been true to her word and had sent a proposed agenda for my visit, as well as a contact name and number at the Morioka Museum in West Tokyo, which, the fax explained, was the institution that owned the kimono that I'd be carrying with me.

I blinked and read the line again. That's right, she'd said very quickly when she was talking about timing that I needed to come early so that the kimono could be installed. She wanted me not only to speak, but to bring a small collection of Edo-period kimono on the plane. That's why I was flying business class to America, and economy on the way back.

I knew that the transportation of museum pieces was something that took place daily at airports around the world—but I'd never done it. Would the Japanese museum trust me?

Looking into the mirror at my tousled early-morning appearance, I shook my head. No. Not this shaggy-haired, almond-eyed American citizen who had been around a few too many dead bodies. Add in the fact that I was twenty-eight and unattached: a rootless, untrustworthy woman who needed a cosigner for every financial or real-estate move she made. Allison Powell might be willing to give me a chance, but she didn't know my full story the way people in Japan did. If she had known, she wouldn't have called.

2

"Honey, I wouldn't trust you to carry my favorite vintage Levi's out of my apartment. And you're saying that you're going to carry a collection of antique kimonos out of the country?" Richard Randall, the twenty-five-year-old Canadian who was my best friend in Tokyo, shook his head as he stirred sugar into a tiny cup of coffee.

"'Kimono' is the preferred form of the plural for scholars," I said frostily. We were at Appetito, my favorite *sanduitto*—the Japanese interpretation of sandwich shop. Lunch together at Appetito had become a Friday tradition because Richard had a shorter teaching day at It's Happening! Language School, where he was a full-time English teacher.

"Kimono, then. Whatever! You aren't going anywhere with them, babe."

"I suppose you're right. Well, it was a nice fantasy while it lasted." I was depressed that Richard also agreed that I'd not be able to get antiques out of Japan. In the last few days, I'd worked myself into a frenzy of wanting to go. Looking at the odd little pastry called a "cheezu bagel" sitting on my lunch tray, I added, "I'm dying for an American bagel. Not to mention real cheese. Do you know how tired I am of going to overpriced foreigner supermarkets here and finding nothing but Kraft singles?"

"You *are* a Kraft single," Richard cackled. "That's the problem. Who would trust a young single woman without Japanese citizenship to be responsible for Japanese cultural treasures? And why has the American museum asked you instead of someone from the Morioka to carry the goods? It all sounds fishy."

"The Morioka guy said he couldn't possibly travel, so the American museum is desperate. They want certain kimono from that museum. It would be difficult— from a manners standpoint—to ask a Japanese textile curator from a different museum to carry things from the Morioka. Anyway, that's my guess. Maybe I'll find out more today." I was scheduled to be at the Morioka Museum in an hour and a half for an interview with the museum's director, its textile curator, and its registrar.

"But you've never worked at a museum," Richard said.

"Allison told me I've got a reputation for my knowledge of Japanese textiles. If it's really true that I'm a known person, the people at the Morioka might have a favorable impression of me already."

"Come on, girlfriend. The only reputation you have is for making it into tabloids."

"Those pictures were taken just because of Takeo," I protested. For the last half year, I'd been dating a rather dashing man my age named Takeo Kayama. Takeo was an odd sort, spending his days mulling over the rehabilitation of historic Japanese houses and advising various ecology groups. Because Takeo was the son of a famous flower-arranging-school headmaster, his moves were reported with some interest, especially when he did bizarre things like show up for a black-tie flower-arranging gala wearing jeans and a Greenpeace T-shirt.

I hadn't cared about what Takeo wore that night, but I was mortified when our long good-night kiss at a taxi stand wound up being circulated to a million readers. Since then, Takeo and I hadn't dared to go out together in public. Now we spent most of our time together at his country house, doing about the only thing possible in a place without a television set.

"Ha. I wonder if they'll do an Internet search on you and come up with pictures of the boyfriend before him."

"Don't remind me." I didn't want to recall Hugh Glendinning, the Scottish lawyer who'd walked out of my life a little more than a year ago. When Takeo had come along, I'd decided that it was in my best interest to get involved with a Japanese man. Who else could I count on to want to live in my favorite city with me? Not that Takeo and I had reached the point of living *together,* or getting married. Takeo came from a prominent family, and I suspected that it would look better to his father if I were on firmer financial footing before we got really serious.

Feeling invigorated by thoughts of how powerful an alliance with a Japanese museum might be for my career, I parted with my best friend and walked to my appointment. Twenty minutes later I'd made my way through the boutique-lined streets of Omote-Sando and arrived at the entrance to the Morioka Museum, a small, elegant stucco building that had survived the World War II bombs and been home, for the last thirty years, to many of Japan's great textile treasures.

A guard showed me down a hall and into the reception room of the director's office. The room was decorated with framed posters of the museum's past exhibitions. Its furniture was modern rosewood: a matching group of four chairs, each with a tiny table in front of it. Three

of the chairs faced one. I could tell right away where I
was supposed to sit.

Mr. Shima, the museum's registrar, urged me to sit
down right away, but I knew better: I shouldn't appear
to make myself comfortable until his boss had come. I
wondered how much he really knew about textiles,
judging from the boring gray wool-blend suit that he'd
chosen to wear. It was interesting that the Morioka had
a registrar, an administrative position that involved
keeping a careful tally of the museum's holdings. Most
American museums had them, but in Japan, the job was
still fairly rare; the Morioka obviously took its collections quite seriously to have established the office of
registrar. I thought it was interesting, too, that Mr.
Shima didn't have the stereotyped geeky museum-
employee appearance. He was in his mid-forties and
looked fit. His hair was cut short in a fashionable style.
His age meant that he was probably married, but I
wouldn't be surprised if he went to hostess bars or had
a girlfriend on the side, from the way he had checked
me out when I'd had to bend over for a second to get
my business cards out of my backpack.

I was actually quite modestly dressed. I'd decided
that to subtly show my passion for Japanese textiles, I
would wear one. Thus I had layered an early-twentieth-
century *haori* coat patterned with pink and orange *ikat*
arrows over a simple black dress that went right to the
knee. It seemed a better option than a skirted suit, not
to mention that my suits were all out of style—the
early-1990s Talbots vintage.

I bowed deeply when Mr. Shima introduced me to his
boss, Mr. Ito. The museum's director was as round as a
Buddha, an interesting effect with a salaryman-blue suit
stretched over his girth. It was hard to assign an age to the
man, but I guessed that he was in his sixties. I couldn't

sense how he felt about meeting me, so I trotted out my Japanese etiquette again and apologized profusely for taking him away from his management concerns.

Mr. Nishio, the textile curator who was supposed to have traveled to the U.S., swept in five minutes later. He made brief apologies to both Mr. Shima and Mr. Ito before bowing to me in a slight movement that didn't communicate much respect. He seemed to be studying my clothing with an incredulous expression. Now I wished I had dressed more conservatively. Mr. Nishio might think that a woman who'd wear an antique *haori* with impunity would take it upon herself to slip into one of their antique kimono when nobody was looking.

I handed Mr. Nishio my business card, just as I'd handed cards to the two other men, but instead of reading it, he stuffed it into his pocket like a gum wrapper he would later discard.

Well, Mr. Nishio wasn't the big boss, I told myself. He might be tense because he hadn't really wanted to cancel his trip to Washington, D.C. People usually relished opportunities to shop abroad and buy luxury goods, like the Hermès tie he was wearing, for a lower price than in Japan.

We finally sat down, the three of them in the row of chairs facing me, as I'd expected. I sat on the lone chair on the west side of the table, pulling at the edge of my *haori* coat to cover the slight bit of thigh that was exposed. An office lady my age wafted in with a trayful of small cups of green tea. She served me first, as was customary since I was a guest, but I was careful not to sip before the men did.

"So you would like to take Nishio-san's place as the lecturer in Washington," Mr. Shima, the registrar, said. The way he phrased it let me know he was already offended at the prospect of my going to Washington.

"I'm not trying to take his place, exactly. I was told that he could not travel," I said.

"Actually, we were both to have traveled together," Mr. Shima said. "As registrar, I am accountable for the safety of our possessions. Nishio-san is the textile curator, with a subspecialty in traditional religious garments. We traveled together four years earlier to bring some altar cloths for an exhibition at the Museum of Asian Arts."

"Ah, what a beautiful exhibition that must have been. I will do my best to follow you. You may have heard of my specialty in Japanese antique furniture, but I did write a paper on kimono while in the master's program at the University of California at Berkeley."

"So you're a Californian?" The question came from Mr. Ito.

"I was born there, but my father's from Yokohama," I said, as always trying to qualify myself as Japanese.

"So you don't really know Washington, D.C." Mr. Ito's voice was flat.

I'd stressed the wrong part of my identity. Now I quickly said, "I do! As an undergraduate, I visited the Museum of Asian Arts to do research. And my mother's family is in the area—"

"How well do you know the staff?" Mr. Ito asked pointedly.

Damn it, I shouldn't have mentioned my mother. Too unprofessional. In a more subdued voice, I said, "I have spoken several times with Powell-san, and I think we have a good working relationship."

"Powell-san mentioned that you plan to remove some treasures from our collection to exhibit in Washington." Mr. Shima spoke up.

"I have been requested by the Asian Arts Museum to bring some items, yes." I fumbled for a rejoinder and came up with, "I understand that you had already approved a specific group of textiles that could travel."

"This is a very last-minute request for a courier. That makes it . . . difficult," Mr. Shima said, looking sideways at his boss, Mr. Ito.

Aha. Now I sensed what was going on. The museum's administration had decided against participating in the Museum of Asian Arts exhibit. Mr. Ito, the museum director, was the good cop, Mr. Shima was the bad one, and Mr. Nishio was the mute. The important thing was, they were all against me.

I fixed my attention on all three men and said: "As someone who grew up in the United States, I would like to explain something about the nature of American museum culture. American museums promote their programs many months in advance. The highlights of the exhibits are described in magazines and newspapers. Powell-san has planned an opening reception for six hundred guests—including high Japanese government dignitaries from the Japanese embassy. She believes up to ten thousand visitors will come to admire the kimono during their three-month exhibition. The visitors hope to see the treasures of the Morioka. If you withdraw, the American museum may be so injured by loss of status that it will not recover."

"You really think . . . our *kosode* will be the highlight?" Mr. Ito said, after a pause.

"Absolutely! The centerpiece! And the talk I'll give—why, I'll go beyond discussing just the textiles you've brought, but bring attention to the importance of the Morioka as Japan's leading textile museum."

I sensed I was gaining ground until Mr. Nishio finally spoke. "I understand you have a good feeling for American museums, even though you've never worked in one. But surely you must admit that it is unusual for the museum to ask a freelance antiques buyer—someone who doesn't have her own shop, not to mention museum ties here—to be the speaker."

Smiling apologetically, I said, "I know that I am young and not as experienced as you. I imagine they chose me in part for my bilingual ability."

"What makes you think there are no skilled English speakers here?" Mr. Shima demanded.

It was the Morioka's policy to hire only native Japanese; I was told that when I was turned down for an internship four years ago. But I couldn't say that; it was too combative. Instead, I widened my eyes and said, "I understand Mr. Nishio was the first choice, but apparently he told them that he could not go?"

Mr. Ito shot a surprised look at Mr. Shima, and Mr. Nishio looked down at the floor.

Mr. Shima said, "That's right. He is needed here to do work on our next exhibition, and to oversee some of my work during my vacation. I'm very sorry that I must go—"

"Completely understandable," Mr. Ito said in a brisk voice. "Shima-san has not taken a day off in five years. The Japanese government has asked managers to encourage all employees to take their vacation times so they will not die of heart attacks from overworking."

Mr. Shima coughed. "I feel guilty about the loss of service to my museum, as well as the American museum being inconvenienced. Perhaps we should present the prospect of Miss Shimura's travel plan at our committee next week."

Enough of all the fake apologies. I looked straight at each man again and said, "The problem is that I'm scheduled to travel twenty days from now. If you're not interested in having your kimono included, I must warn Miss Powell so she may organize with another museum." This was a bluff, because I knew Allison wanted kimono only from the Morioka—and it would be impossible to organize a kimono loan elsewhere.

There was silence, and I wondered if I'd gone too far.

"Regarding the Asian Arts Museum travel plan, we will try to give an answer as soon as possible," Mr. Ito said. "But please understand that Japanese museums make plans carefully."

"American ones do, too," I said. "This exhibit was two years in the making. It's sad that because of some last-minute employee-scheduling conflict, the centerpiece might be missing."

We all said a few more things, none of them constructive. I left the museum with nothing but Mr. Ito's hollow promise that one of his men would call me. Yeah, sure. I'd heard that one before.

3

"So, how much do you think it would cost me to have a sex change?" I asked Takeo Kayama, from my position curled up near the space heater in the traditional living room of his country house in Hayama the next evening. We had been eating our supper of an octopus-and-corn pizza on a short-legged *kotatsu* table that had a tiny heater underneath it, to warm our feet. There was nothing else in the room except for the *zabuton* cushions we sat on and a casual arrangement of pampas grass and bittersweet in a vase in the room's ceremonial alcove.

"Well, you'd lose the chance to sleep with me," said Takeo. He was lounging on the *tatami*-mat floor looking like a handsome cat burglar in his black cashmere turtleneck and jeans. The only thing marring his elegant appearance was a pair of thick ragg wool socks on his feet, necessary protection against the cold.

"Now, if I were a Japanese man, the Morioka Museum would without question let me take the kimono to America. I wouldn't have lost a night of sleep worrying." I didn't think I'd get much more sleep at Takeo's place. The *shoji* screens were rattling fiercely from the strong winds that went with the onset of typhoon season.

"I'm glad you're not going to America. I'd rather have you around here." Takeo smiled lazily at me, and pulled me against his body.

"Well, what if I *do* get permission to go? Would you come with me? It would be about a week to ten days." I knew that he'd be free, because Takeo didn't really have a job. He sat on a few environmental organizations' boards, worked on and off on the restoration of his family's country house, and arranged flowers and gardened.

"I haven't been back to the U.S. since I graduated from Santa Cruz. What was that, six years ago?"

"Well, maybe it's time. You could come to California with me when I'm visiting my parents at the tail end of the trip. Before that, you'd be in Washington, D.C., the nation's capital—there's an arboretum and a botanical garden you might like."

Takeo snorted. "I can't think of worse torture than going back to the country where ketchup is a vegetable and anyone can buy a gun. I don't like the thought of you being anywhere outside the museum, your hotel, and your parents' place. It's simply too dangerous."

"Okay," I said, "I disinvite you, then—if 'disinvite' is a word. I've been away from my own country so long I've practically forgotten the language." I rolled away from him, and waited for him to come after me. He didn't, so I spoke again. "You know, Takeo, what you say about the world being dangerous bothers me. I miss going out. I can hardly remember the last time we went to the Kabuki theater or saw a foreign film at the Yebisu Garden Cinema or even had dinner at Aunt Norie's house—"

"Everything you mention relates to consumption. You want to go places and spend money."

"Not at my aunt's."

"Well, we've got to take her some kind of gourmet gift."

"I always buy the gift," I said pointedly.

"I wish you wouldn't harp on this. When we started seeing each other, I was impressed because you seemed to be the one woman who didn't want things from me. Now you want to trot me out everywhere like a showpiece."

"So you think I'm causing the tabloid problems? Actually, if you hadn't been so overly passionate with me on the street, we wouldn't have been photographed."

"It bothers me that you believe the tabloid invasion came about because of me. I think *you* are the one they're really interested in."

"Me? The daughter of a little-known interior decorator and a professor of psychiatry? I'm hardly as fascinating as the young heir to the eighth-richest man in Japan." I could have bitten my tongue after the words came out, because I didn't mean to rub Takeo's father in his face.

"Your parents don't matter, but *you* do," Takeo accused. "For the last two years the papers have been full of tiny but perfectly placed mentions of Rei Shimura. You've helped the police solve murders, you've rescued long-lost historic treasures, and you'd go dancing every night if the clubs you favored didn't keep getting raided."

"If that's supposed to be a compliment, I'm not taking it," I said tightly. "In fact, I'm not going to stay here. There are still a couple of trains back to the city tonight."

Takeo shrugged. "It's your choice."

"Thanks for the pizza and your extreme kindness." I used the super-polite Japanese phrase with deep sarcasm. I'd expected to be defeated by the men at the Morioka, but not by the boyfriend who'd been intimate with me an hour earlier. The trickling, sinking feeling I had as I left Takeo's house that night was not a good one.

The next week, I heard nothing from Takeo, even though I'd called to leave a message, and nothing from the museum. Thursday evening I went to have dinner with my aunt Norie, and she spent half the time trying to figure out why Takeo wasn't with me. I couldn't possibly tell her that he'd rather just have sex with me in his house than eat *shabu-shabu* with all of us.

On Friday morning, my telephone finally rang. Mr. Shima told me the museum's high committee had ruled that I could carry seven robes to the Museum of Asian Arts—not the original eight, because upon recent examination, one was deemed too fragile.

I hung up the phone and screamed. I'd won! Even though I could take only seven robes instead of eight, I was back to Washington on $500 a day.

I returned to the Morioka the following Monday to look at the kimono. Mr. Shima met me with a weak smile.

"Shimura-san, I'm pleased that we can allow you to carry the collection of *kosode*."

"I am, too. Thank you for your generous consideration," I said, wondering if Mr. Shima was really glad or employing *tatamae*—the surface courtesy that made Japanese social encounters as smooth as raked sand in a Zen garden. Some foreigners railed against *tatamae*: they called it phony and insincere. I thought *tatamae* prevented fights and ugly situations, and it also enabled people who had disagreed to find their way to compromise and take care of business as needed.

Mr. Nishio still didn't look happy to see me. Silently,

he slipped on a pair of spotless cotton gloves and opened a long acid-free cardboard box. He withdrew a flat rectangle wrapped in tissue paper: the identical manner in which my aunt and I stored our own kimono. The acid-free tissue paper, as well as a stronger external rice-paper wrapper, protected against the pervasive moisture in Japanese air, although I also imagined that the museum's storage was climate-controlled.

Mr. Nishio unfolded the kimono and laid it out on a long table covered by a clean muslin cloth. The garment was a dramatic red silk *furisode,* the name for any woman's kimono that had very long sleeves. The kimono had been decorated with an elegant design of palace curtains, clouds, and fans using *shibori* and *yuzen* dyeing techniques, appliqué, and silk thread and metallic thread embroidery. Its style was exuberant and exquisite all at once.

"This kimono has not seen light for more than thirty years," Mr. Shima commented. "I'm pleased to see that its condition has stayed constant. We have a climate-controlled storage, of course, but one always worries."

"What an outstanding example of Edo-period design." I stretched out my hand toward a sleeve, then pulled it back. What was I doing, trying to touch a museum object that was so fragile?

"Don't touch without gloves," Mr. Nishio said sharply.

"Actually, she will need to touch when she hands the items over," Mr. Shima said in an almost apologetic voice to his colleague. "Why don't we give her a pair of gloves?"

"Are you sure? Thanks," I said, putting on the gloves and lightly touching the embroidery. "I've never seen one so lovely as this. The embroidery is completely intact, and the design is so bold—that's *nuishime shi-*

bori," I said, mentioning a style of tie-dyeing that became very popular during the Edo period.

"The tie-dyeing techniques are *kanoko* and *nuishime shibori*," Mr. Shima said. "Now Nishio-san will show you our technique for refolding the kimono; we fold sleeves in the opposite direction, using acid-free tissue paper as cushioning in order to avoid degradation of the fibers. You will need to do this in case you are asked to unfold some of the robes at customs."

Moving slowly and deliberately, reminding me of a Noh theater actor, Mr. Nishio refolded the kimono and set it aside.

"Time for number two," Mr. Shima said cheerily.

This kimono was what was classified as *kosode,* a shorter-sleeved robe befitting a more mature woman than the red *furisode.* It was adorned with a graceful pattern of orchids covered with small drifts of snow, using a stunning combination of two styles of *shibori* tie-dyeing, and silk thread and metallic thread embroidery.

The third kimono was actually a *juban,* an underjacket worn by men and women. This one was a creamy silk decorated with a pattern of books. "A woman's *juban,*" I said. "Not many have survived, so this is really special. First half of the nineteenth century?"

"Why do you think that it belonged to a woman?" Mr. Shima asked me.

I didn't have a good answer for this, because although the books on the robe were dyed in attractive greens and purples, these colors could be worn by men as well as women. "The writing on the kimono is in *hiragana*. In the Edo period, not all women read *kanji* characters."

Mr. Nishio cleared his throat and said, "This *juban,* and the orchid-patterned kimono, were worn by Ryohei Tokugawa's wife."

I knew, of course, about the Tokugawa clan, which was the last family dynasty that ruled Japan as Shoguns. But I hadn't heard of Ryohei Tokugawa. There was no point in hiding my ignorance. "Are you talking about one of the Shogun's relations?"

"Yes, a cousin to Yoshinobu—the last Shogun," Mr. Nishio added pointedly, as if I might not know.

"Do you have a lot of Ryohei's wife's clothing?"

"Some of it. Many kimono were given away to her courtiers. We have a full description in this diary photocopy we have prepared for you."

Photocopies that I'd have to have translated because my *kanji* knowledge was so poor, I thought ruefully. "If it's not too much trouble—could you talk about this as we go along?"

"Yes, please tell her. The lecture will only go more smoothly," Mr. Shima said to his colleague.

In a halting voice, as if he really couldn't bear to share any secrets with me, Mr. Nishio talked. He showed me the various tiny places that showed signs of age and fragility on a formal black kimono with the Tokugawa crest, and the ancient soy-sauce stain on a girl-child's kimono that was embroidered with cherry blossoms. It was believed that the girl who'd worn the kimono might have been the child of Ryohei and his wife.

We moved on from the Tokugawa kimono to some others, which, I found to my surprise, were even lovelier. I sighed over a cool blue *furisode* patterned with images of palace curtains, and another striking long-sleeved robe dyed and embroidered with streams, flowers, and pavilions upon which rested bamboo cages holding crickets—the era's favorite musical performers. Mr. Nishio said that these kimono came from the same source—a tea merchant's wife who was alive at the same time as Mrs. Ryohei Tokugawa.

It seemed bizarre to me that the more splendid kimono belonged to a tea merchant's wife, not to the wife who was part of the Shogun's family. I wanted to get the translations of the photocopies done so I could read them for myself.

"Do you know the tea merchant's name?" I asked.

"Otani." Mr. Shima mentioned one of the most common names in Japan. "The Otani heirs donated quite a collection, including a splendid *uchikake* we can guess Mrs. Otani wore at her own wedding."

"What a gorgeous piece that must be," I said, wanting to hear more.

"Yes. The Otanis became poor during the war, so they sold their collection of family textiles to an American officer living here during the occupation years. That American sold the kimono to our museum in the 1960s."

I paused. An idea was growing, but I was hesitant to express the whole thing before I'd thought it through. "If it's not too much trouble, I would like to see the rest of the Otani collection. I'd like to learn as much as I can before speaking to Americans about your holdings."

Mr. Shima raised his eyebrows. "It would be easier for the library staff to show you the slides first; then, if you're still interested, I shall bring the robe."

"That sounds fine." I was glad for the chance to study something on my own, without either of the men standing like a black cloud over my shoulder.

Inside the museum's small library, a studious-looking young woman brought slides and accompanying notes to me within a few minutes. Since everything was all written in Japanese, I did what I always do in such situations: photocopy, and arrange for translation later, on my own time. The slides were easier for me to appreciate. The tea merchant's family had a vast assortment of kimono that seemed to range in age from early nineteenth century to the 1920s. It was the early-nineteenth-century robes that I was interested in, and as I'd suspected, a number of them had images that would have been appropriate for a courtesan to wear: in addition to exquisite florals, there were vistas of teahouses and symbols of an incense-smelling game. These were not the kimono of a typical housewife—not even a rich one. I had a sense of the kind of woman they might have belonged to, but it would take a bit of independent research before I could confirm this fact for myself.

The last slide I looked at was that of the *uchikake* I'd heard about. It was a scarlet silk satin robe decorated with pairs of mandarin ducks diving through a pond that rippled with tie-dyed *shibori* droplets of water. Blossoming cherry trees created with meticulous embroidery added to the charming picture. This kimono was not as grandly decadent as some Mr. Shima had shown me, but it was sweet, romantic, and amusing. It would serve beautifully as the highlight for my talk.

"Mr. Shima says for you to return to the conference room. He has retrieved the *uchikake* you were waiting to view," the library clerk said after I'd been looking at things for about a half hour.

So he'd done it himself, and not waited for Mr. Nishio. That was kind, I thought, hurrying back to the office.

Mr. Shima already had the bridal kimono spread out on the table when I went in. I saw him before he saw me; he was bent over, studying the fabric. I could see tension on his face for the first time that day, and a ripple of nervousness went through me. Maybe the kimono was damaged or fragile. Every single stain, break in a fiber, loose stitch, crease, spot, snag, or tear would be documented—and I'd be responsible to see that there was not a single bit of extra damage. If the kimono was in bad shape to begin with, it would make the likelihood of my getting to travel with it quite slim.

I coughed slightly so he would know I was there.

"Here you are, Miss Shimura. Interesting—I haven't looked at this robe for quite a few years."

I stood next to him and gazed down. Examining the robe in full, I could appreciate the details even more. The ducks were diving, playing, and flying over the water—almost all of them in pairs. Now I remembered the significance of mandarin ducks: they were symbols of marriage. That, paired with the good luck present in the cherry blossoms, made this a very auspicious robe for a woman to wear at a wedding. The condition looked excellent—colors were faded, here and there, but the stitches looked intact, and I didn't see stains or any other obvious signs of damage.

"It's very special," I said. "It gives me a feeling for the romanticism, and the joy the woman marrying the tea merchant must have felt when she wore it."

"We really can guess nothing of emotion," Mr. Shima said. "And in my opinion, it's a fine example, but not nearly as fine as some of the other garments."

"You know so much about textiles themselves, Shima-san. You could be more than a registrar, *neh*? Perhaps a museum director, someday," I said, flattering him. It was true that he was more forthcoming, and perhaps even more knowledgeable, about textiles than Mr. Nishio.

"It is kind of you to say, but my training is incomplete in that area," he answered, but I could see he'd been pleased by my compliment.

"I'm sure you've also noticed that an *uchikake* is the one thing that's missing from the group of kimono I'll take to America. If I could bring this bridal kimono, it would perfectly illustrate the life cycle of a family of women in Edo-period Japan."

Mr. Shima looked at me as if I'd said something shocking. "But the Museum of Asian Arts didn't request it."

"They did not understand the connection," I said. Realizing that I sounded perhaps too proud of my own scholarly abilities, I amended my words quickly. "What I mean to say is, they did not have the opportunity to sit with you, and learn from your scholarship the intricate histories of the garments. You've opened a special world to me, and for this, I am truly grateful." I ended with a little bob of my head as an expression of a formal bow, without seeming too over-the-top.

Mr. Shima was silent for a minute and then sighed. "Well, I suppose I can give permission. After all, they were expecting eight robes, and we cut the total to seven. There is room in the box."

"Thank you," I said fervently. "This will be so appreciated by the audience there. It will allow me to give a talk that has some real substance."

Mr. Shima took a piece of stationery from the table, and on it wrote the *uchikake*'s item number and a few lines of Japanese. I imagined they were a description of the item, because I recognized the *kanji* characters for "Edo period," "red," and "duck." Then he marked the paper with his personal seal and stapled it to the loan slip.

"I hope the museum will appreciate it as much as you. May I tell you something personal, Miss Shimura?" Mr. Shima said.

I nodded, unsure of what was coming.

"I did not believe you had any knowledge of historic textiles when you first approached the museum. But now I've seen you have studied, and even more impor-

tantly, you have an appreciation for these antique robes.
I am pleasantly surprised, but I think things may work
out well for everyone concerned."

I wanted to hug him, but that would have been out of
line.

I bowed deeply instead.

4

The last days dwindled as I worked on my research into the Tokugawa and Otani kimono and double-checked the itinerary that Mr. Shima at the Morioka organized for me. I would be flying All Nippon Airways to Washington in a business-class seat, with a second seat next to me reserved for the two boxes of kimono, since the museum did not approve of the climate, or the security, of any jet's baggage compartment. I'd found the cheap price on two business tickets through a ticket wholesaler who did a lot of business with Richard Randall's language-school students.

Part of the cheap airfare deal included a choice of a few hotels; I went with the cheapest one, called the Washington Suites. The air-hotel package included a handful of coupons to use at a nearby shopping mall. I decided to budget $500 for shoes and clothing, things I could barely afford to buy in Japan. I made up a shopping list for America: running shoes, black everyday pumps, black evening pumps, strappy sandals. I also longed for a suit that was current. I'd probably have done better if I'd had such a suit when I went to visit the Otani family, whom I'd finally tracked down living in a spacious house in the suburbs of Kawasaki.

"So pleased to meet you," Koichi Otani, the silver-haired patriarch of the family, had said, glancing skeptically over me in the favorite *haori* coat I'd chosen again to wear with my basic black dress.

"I'm very glad to meet you," I said, following him into a pristine all-white living room. I stuck out like a pink-and-red arrow—but an arrow without a real direction, I thought to myself. I sensed he had information that could help me learn about the kimono collection's history, but I had no idea how to proceed. Blandly, I said, "I was so impressed with the collection that your family once owned."

"Do you think it's worth more than we sold it for?" Mr. Otani asked. He was an ex-stockbroker, I'd found out when I'd called after having traced him through the Japanese government's notoriously accurate family registry. I'd been thrilled with the details of what he'd told me over the phone—that the kimono collection was chiefly made up of garments worn by his great-great-great-grandmother, who had been named Ai, and married into the Otani family in 1850.

"I'm almost certain it is. Is there a record of what the American officer paid your father for the kimono in 1948?" I asked.

"He didn't pay with money, just rice and charcoal. He gave enough to last one winter."

I flushed, feeling guilty about the acquisitive nature of Americans abroad. After all, when I shopped at the Tokyo flea markets, I tried to get the best deal for myself. That's what the officer had done. "I've only seen four of the kimono that belonged to Ai. The three that were formally appraised were valued together at a little over twenty million yen." Two hundred thousand dollars, that was.

"Ah. I believe my father gave a total of fifteen kimono. What a great value he gave away. The house was pleasantly warm that winter, though, I remember. That's all that matters, isn't it?" He smiled, but his eyes remained sad.

Things were going to be difficult. I began, "Um, Mr. Otani, I wanted to say . . . in looking at the kimono that were worn by your great-great-great-grandmother, a few questions come to mind. They are so lavish and exquisite . . . especially the ones with longer sleeves, which were worn before Ai-san married. The themes are also very splendid. I don't know if you've seen these kimono?"

"They were always wrapped up in rice paper and stacked in a *tansu* in the family storehouse. I was a small boy. I wasn't interested."

"The themes deal with court life. It makes me wonder whether you know anything about what Ai-san did before she got married."

"What she *did*? Young ladies of the day did not have careers. It's not like the women's liberation of today."

"In those days, some women who worked as—courtesans." I settled on that word because it was milder than "prostitutes." "Some women lived in the Yoshiwara Pleasure Quarter, and some were in the court of Tokugawa Shogun."

"Are you saying—are you saying that my great-great-great-grandfather married a prostitute?" Mr. Otani sank down on a white velour-covered chair, leaving me standing awkwardly in front of him.

"It could be, of course, that Ai-san was just a wealthy girl who preferred kimono with themes that were also popular in the floating world—" I sputtered a bit in my haste to save the situation.

Mr. Otani shook his head. "We're Osaka people. It's impossible that my ancestor was in Yoshiwara, or the Shogun's court."

"Very well," I said, realizing the door had been closed. "I'm very excited about the kimono. As I told you on the phone, your family's kimono were sought out by a top American museum because they are so splendid."

"Don't call them my family's kimono," Mr. Otani snapped. "They belonged to a Lieutenant Commander Ashburn. He's the one who made the profit."

"If it's any consolation, in the sixties he couldn't have possibly gotten what they're worth now," I said.

"He received more than a winter's worth of coal, I imagine."

I couldn't disagree.

Mr. Otani never came through with more information about Ai, but then, I hadn't thought he really would. Maybe I'd been crazy to try to find out more about the Otani kimono. The truth was, I had precious little about their history on paper from the Morioka Museum, even after I'd pored over the translated documents I'd been given. I might be able to do a little research in Washington, at the Textile Museum or the Smithsonian Institutions. At the moment my most serious task was getting all the kimono out of Japan without losing my cool.

The morning of my departure, I went to the Morioka Museum to pick up the two five-foot-long acid-free cardboard boxes packed with kimono. Mr. Shima had already gone away on his vacation, so Mr. Nishio was the one who opened the boxes with me for the final condition analysis and count. Watching alongside us was a man called Mr. Morita in a plain gray suit. He was the customs broker, a representative of Nippon Shipping, who would escort me all the way from the museum to

Narita Airport, where he would present the proper papers to the customs officials and watch me until I boarded the plane.

"At the museum, you must check the number of kimono again. Don't forget!" Mr. Nishio added the last as an order in an impolite verb form—something he must have been sure I'd be offended by.

"I won't. I feel very fortunate for this opportunity," I said, although I knew quite well that he had nothing to do with the decision for me to leave.

"You have a very serious responsibility. I see that Shima-san has substituted a wedding kimono for the other one originally on the loan receipt. I'm a little concerned about it," Mr. Nishio added, mainly addressing Mr. Morita, the customs broker. Mr. Morita shook his head, muttered something under his breath, and looked unhappy.

If only I could read the Japanese paper that Mr. Shima had given me. I was beginning to get the idea that Mr. Nishio wanted to screw up my trip in any way possible. I stuck to my guns and said, "I've got Mr. Shima's seal on a document approving the loan. Please don't worry. I'll treat this kimono with the same care as the others."

Mr. Nishio didn't wish me bon voyage, so I didn't say much more to him when I left. Because the customs broker was involved, we went by a private limousine. This was an uncommonly luxurious—though not necessarily speedy—way of leaving Tokyo. As we rode along, Mr. Morita snored. I wondered whether it was Mr. Nishio's idea that I be so closely supervised by the customs broker. I supposed I should feel glad to have an extra person to help me get two five-foot-long boxes to the airport, but Mr. Morita hadn't been particularly helpful getting the luggage into the car. The taxi driver loaded my luggage in the car's trunk while I had to fit the two giant boxes, and myself, in the backseat. The customs broker sat up front and, once the car was on the move, shut his eyes and went to sleep, as if he were a salaryman on the Tokyo subway.

After an hour, the car had made it out of the city and into the Japanese farmland that surrounded Narita. Mid-autumn in Japan meant that dark orange persimmons were bobbing from trees, and the air smelled deliciously of roasted sweet potatoes and chestnuts. It was hard to leave this world, even for a week. In Japan, one felt the seasons so strongly; persimmons were celebrated as gladly as cherry blossoms. In America, seasonal decorations meant Christmas lights going up sometime around Halloween.

To my surprise, Mr. Morita woke up promptly as we took the freeway exit for Narita Airport, and turned into a considerably more active man. He loaded the boxes onto a cart and let me follow carrying my luggage as we navigated our way through the packed terrain of Narita's old terminal. When we had to pass the boxes through a metal detector, and the guard manning it asked for one of the boxes to be opened for direct inspection, Mr. Morita said a few quiet words and we were waved through. Good. Even though I'd been instructed how to refold the kimono and retape the box, I didn't want to do it in front of an audience of thousands.

Now the boxes were cleared and we were off to check in at See America Travel, the tour group that had disbursed my airline tickets. Its counter was decorated with tiny American flags and cardboard cutouts of the Washington Monument, the Lincoln Memorial, and the famous Hollywood sign. Hollywood? I guessed some of their travelers would be stopping in Los Angeles. Maybe that was why the agency had been so flexible about my adding a stop in California on the way home. I was going to fly for free to Los Angeles, and after that, it would be up to me to pay the added airfare for a commuter flight to San Francisco.

A man in a red blazer carrying the travel-agency flag told me that I had to give up my luggage trolley, since it was taking up too much room. Mr. Morita wordlessly complied, but I was annoyed because I'd been balancing the boxes on top of the suitcases while I was waiting, which was a nice break after having carried them so long.

"I have a rather large number of small pieces," I said. "I have to keep them together and off the ground. It's a special circumstance."

The man frowned. "In the literature all customers were sent, we explain the luggage limit is two pieces to check in the baggage compartment, plus a carry-on to bring on the plane. You have three carry-on items and only one suitcase for the baggage compartment. That's not allowed."

"I bought an extra ticket," I said, waving it at him. But it wasn't until Mr. Morita introduced himself that the travel-agency man quieted down and agreed I could take everything on board. I supposed I should have been grateful to have Mr. Morita there, but I found it was only making me annoyed. I was used to taking care of myself, fighting my own battles. What was happening to me was only feeding into my new theory that single women in Japan received less respect than anyone else.

Unwilling to give things up to Mr. Morita, I tried to balance the two huge boxes atop my slim suitcase, but one fell off.

"Careful," a husky male voice said. Before I had time to snap at the new chauvinist in my life, I realized that my box had been caught by a good-looking young guy who looked very much like Takeo Kayama.

It *was* Takeo. He handed the box back to me with a smile.

"How'd you know I'd be here?" I said, after reassuring Mr. Morita that Takeo was not a robber.

"I telephoned your friend Richard. I would have driven you in, if you'd wanted it."

"How thoughtful of you." I was stunned that Takeo had come all the way to the airport. Narita was about a two-hour drive from the city, and it was a tough drive filled with traffic, lane changes, and tension.

"Well, let me hold the boxes while you wait."

"I better not," I said, seeing Mr. Morita looking unhappily at the two of us. I didn't want him reporting back to the Morioka that the courier was a social butterfly.

"I came because I want you to have a good trip, and to come back to me safely. I've got a little present for you. Can you reach in my pocket?"

"Okay," I said, handing the boxes to Mr. Morita and mumbling, "This is a friend of mine; can you hold my place in line for a minute?"

Before Mr. Morita could protest, I stepped a few paces away from him and the line. I didn't want whatever Takeo was giving me to be noticed by everyone. Keeping my eyes on Mr. Morita, I reached into the pocket of Takeo's baggy jean jacket and pulled out a small box exquisitely wrapped in green *washi* paper—green, the color signifying a gift from the heart.

"Oh, my," I said in English, forgetting myself for a minute. Then I switched back to Japanese. "Should I wait to open this when we have a little more privacy? Say, downstairs in the lounge?"

"They only allow passengers downstairs," Takeo said. "Just open it now."

I unwrapped the paper with suddenly clumsy fingers.

This was the moment for which my aunt had been waiting but that I wasn't sure I really wanted.

The box underneath the paper was small and black and made of wood—not velvet, as you'd expect for a jewelry box. Trust Takeo to find an organic material, I thought, looking at him shyly.

"You seem nervous," Takeo said.

"I am," I said. "I have to say, the timing is a bit odd."

"I wanted you to have this before you left."

I opened the box and stared down at a small, rectangular piece of red brocade embroidered in gold. Slightly confused, I wondered if this was the padding that the ring sat on. With careful fingers, I picked up the small piece of fabric and heard the jingling sound of a tiny bell. I turned the fabric over and saw, in gold, the embroidered phrase SAFETY TRAVEL.

"It's a safety amulet for your trip," Takeo said. "I always carry one during plane travel. In fact, this belonged to me. But now it's yours."

"Thank you," I said faintly. I had been incredibly naive to think, for the space of a few seconds, that Takeo wanted to marry me.

"You're very welcome. Hey, the clerk is ready for the boxes. You'd better go back to that unpleasant man holding them. I've got to run, because I'm parked illegally. Give a great talk, have a great time, and don't forget me." Takeo blew a kiss, and then was gone.

Why had I thought Takeo was giving me a ring? He'd never said that he loved me. For that matter, I hadn't said this to him, either. I wasn't sure how I felt, especially now. All I knew was that I hoped I wasn't becoming as conventional as the stereotyped office lady with hopes of a wedding at the Prince Hotel and a honeymoon in Guam.

I shuddered as I gave Mr. Morita my carry-on to hold as we both went downstairs to pay departure tax and pass through customs. The process was as smooth as silk. Mr. Morita presented the papers from the Morioka, and the customs official greeted him, if not as an old friend, at least as a business acquaintance who he knew and trusted. The papers were stamped, and Mr. Morita zipped them carefully into the outer pocket of my carry-on bag, for me to present at Dulles Airport customs when I arrived. That was it.

As we waited in the airline's lounge for the plane to board, Mr. Morita acknowledged that the seats I'd booked in the 747's upper compartment were a good out-of-the-way place to sit. He reminded me not to tell anyone what I was carrying. If a flight attendant challenged the fact that I had the boxes seat-belted into the seat next to me, I was to present her with a letter explaining the importance of my mission. This way I would not have to speak, and nobody would overhear anything about the items I was carrying.

When the call came in the passenger lounge for the preboarding of small children or those needing special assistance, I rose to my feet and bid the customs broker good-bye. As I walked down the runway, I realized that it had been over a year since I'd last been on a plane. A smell of plane air—a mixture of new-car scent mixed with fuel and something stale and indescribably unpleasant—wafted out to me.

"Do you need help taking your carry-ons upstairs?" a flight attendant asked instantly upon seeing me laboring under the two boxes and backpack.

"I'd better not," I said, climbing the spiral staircase precariously with the two boxes in my arms. I knew that I couldn't let anyone else hold the boxes. The brief episode with Takeo had made Mr. Morita frown. I hoped he wouldn't repeat the story about Takeo touching the box to Mr. Nishio.

When I was safely at the top, I found my two seats. I stacked the boxes in the seat by the window, wrapping a seat belt around them so they sat up straight and securely. Then I began rifling through my backpack for my lecture notes. If I got tired of practicing my talk, I would read my dog-eared copy of *The Makioka Sisters*. I'd finally finished *Tale of the Genji* and had moved on to this classic early-twentieth-century novel about an Osaka family's four daughters, two of whom were married and respectable and two others who were in need of suitable partners. The subtle humor and domestic details in this book were delicious, but it was still a dense, slow read.

"You're in my seat." The words were spoken slowly and spaced apart, as if the talker, speaking American English, thought I wouldn't understand. I looked up at one of the American men with marine haircuts that I'd seen at the departure gate.

"I believe this is *my* seat," I replied politely in English. "I bet you're in the row ahead of me. It's sometimes hard to match the numbers overhead with the seats below, isn't it?"

"I don't think so. I'm 28A." He stared me down in a belligerent way. Somehow, a name flashed into my mind—Lieutenant Commander Ashburton. The American who'd tricked the Otani family into giving him a superb kimono collection for a winter's worth of rice and coal.

"That's my seat number as well. Hmm, the airlines must have made a mistake." I was still trying to keep things harmonious; how Japanese I'd become.

"Can I see your ticket?" he demanded. I sighed heavily and fished around in the outer pocket of my backpack to find my boarding pass. Yes, it said 28A. I handed it to him, and his jaw began working.

"Damn it," he said. "If I don't get out of this country within an hour, I'm going to go nuts."

"Don't worry. I overheard that the flight isn't that crowded."

"Yeah, but I want this seat. I used to fly fighter planes. I like being up high. Tell you what—why don't you take the seat next to me? Then you can work it out with whoever else might come along."

I was losing my patience. I said, "Actually, I'm booked in these two seats."

"Whaddaya mean, booked into two seats?"

"I have the seat that I'm in, and the boxes are riding in the window seat."

"I thought all baggage had to be safely stowed underneath the seat or in the overhead compartment. FAA regulations!" he added nastily.

I wasn't going to explain that I was a fine-art courier to the man; he was probably the kind of person that museum people worried about. I pressed the bell for a flight attendant, and the woman who had helped me with the boxes came halfway up the stairs.

"Hello," I called out to her. "There seems to be a mix-up with our seat assignments."

"She's in my seat," the military man said. "I got assigned 28A, and I need to stay here. I used to fly fighter planes and I like being up high."

"Well, I paid for two seats to be together because of my special baggage." I handed her the letter Mr. Morita had given me.

The flight attendant read the note and looked anxiously at me. "Madam, I understand your need for two seats, and the flight's not completely full. Let me find another seat for you, please."

I spoke to her in Japanese, keeping my tone light and pleasant so the man would have no idea of what was going on. "Why would you suggest moving me and my boxes—two seats' worth of travelers—and leave him behind with an empty seat next to him? You'll have to do much more work. I was in the seat first, anyway. Remember how much trouble it was to move all the boxes up here? The gentleman is the one who should move."

"Madam, I can tell from your ticket that you booked with See America Travel. Most of the tour group is sitting below. I'd like to find two seats for you there, among the ladies, who are very pleasant. Please wait just a moment while I clear two seats for you. Miss Kimi, please give both customers a glass of Dom Pérignon."

"I don't want champagne," I said. "All I want is a seat for myself and for my boxes."

"Shh, shh. We'll take care of you." Kimi lifted the boxes out of my arms and set them securely atop a cart. I kept my eyes on them until the lead flight attendant returned. She was smiling at me.

"There is room for you in the central cabin," she said. "One of the passengers has volunteered to move so that your boxes can have the window seat. The center seat was open anyway, so you can sit there."

"Is it business class?" I asked pointedly.

"No, but I'm so sorry about everything, I can give you a coupon entitling you to an upgrade to business on your return trip—that was supposed to be economy, *neh*?"

I felt jerked around, but at the same time I was glad to be getting away from the man; I wouldn't be able to close my eyes for a minute with him next to me and my precious boxes. Especially after knowing what had happened to the Otani kimono collection, thanks to an enterprising military man.

Downstairs in the main cabin, most of the passengers had their eyes shut and were sleeping. It was just like the Tokyo subway. The flight attendant pointed to the area where she hoped to place me. As she'd promised, the center and window seat next to a young woman were free. I'd noticed her when we were checking in, because she'd had a Walkman on, and her eyes were closed as if in rapture. Her hair was obviously dyed, a chestnut brown a few shades lighter than my natural brownish-black color. The woman's eyes were circled with eerie, glittery eye shadow that gave her the look of a raccoon—a rather trendy look for teens and young twenty-somethings. I'd seen the look on members of Morning Musume, a popular all-girl singing group whose CD case she was opening up as I squeezed past her with the boxes to sit down.

When I'd gotten settled and the flight attendant had left, the girl turned to me. "Are you on the See America shopping tour?"

"Yes. There was a mix-up about the seats. I hope you don't mind my coming in next to you."

"It doesn't matter. My friend from the office who came with me got to go into first class, where the food's supposed to be really good. And maybe she'll pick up a rich businessman, too—she could use some company!"

"Oh, really?" I laughed uneasily.

"Yeah. By the way, my name is Hana Matsura. What's yours?"

"Rei Shimura. Thank you so much for letting me come into this row, Matsura-san. You gave up space to have me here; I feel like I owe you a glass of wine."

"Call me Hana. That's what they do in America, right? Everyone calls by the first names. And I already have a drink." Hana grinned, toasting me with the half-full glass of red wine that had been on her tray. "Should I call the hostess to get you a glass?"

"No, I'll just get some when they serve dinner."

"What's in the boxes?" Hana looked eagerly at the stack on the window seat.

"Just some souvenirs for my family."

"They're such nice, big boxes. I guess you can use them to bring home any extra clothes that don't fit in your luggage."

"Yes," I answered, thinking this girl was exactly the kind of person Takeo couldn't stand. "I take it that you're going to spend a lot of time at the Nation's Place mall?"

"I am. It's my last trip before my wedding next month."

"Congratulations. What a happy time it must be," I said, thinking that the last thing I'd want to do is take a transatlantic trip before a wedding. It seemed like a stressful, tiring action.

"I never thought I'd find a man like my fiancé."

Again, a reference to men. I knew she wanted to keep talking, so I said, "What is he like?"

"Well, Yoshiki is about five feet ten inches tall, and he has very nice hazel eyes—about the color of my hair, actually. He grew up in Yokohama, like I did, and he went to Keio University. He's been at Sony in the marketing department ever since college graduation. He likes to drive cars, watch television, and sing karaoke in his free time."

"Does he like international travel, too?"

"Yes, but I wouldn't want him along on this trip. I've only known him a few months."

"And you just decided to get married?"

"No, we made the plan the third time we met. Our marriage is *o-miai*, if you hadn't already guessed."

She was talking about arranged marriage. While plenty of people in Japan had love marriages, unions arranged by parents or professional matchmakers were still popular. I couldn't quite understand it.

"You look so modern and with it," I said, gesturing toward her brilliant makeup. "I'm surprised you'd agree to o-*miai*."

"It's boring at my company. Marriage will give me the freedom to do whatever I like when Yoshi is not eating or sleeping."

"Are you going to live with your in-laws?" I asked, thinking to myself that her plan might not be so appealing to the older generation.

"No. Yoshi has been with his company eight years now, so he's got a decent salary. We're going to buy an apartment. I'm so excited about that! I can see it in my mind—a tall white building, a high-class one, where nobody can hang out shabby futons. I'll have lots of windows and an all-white interior. Everything new."

"Maybe you can buy a nice white wedding dress while you're in the States," I said.

"I don't need to. I'm renting all that stuff. What I'm going to buy in Washington are purses and shoes. Accessories are the most important investment a woman can make."

"I never thought of accessories as investments," I mused. So this was what was driving Japanese women to shop so hard—a dream of private investment. A way to achieve power when nobody took them seriously.

"Accessories are important," Hana said firmly. "But don't worry, I won't be working too hard at shopping. I also will find a playboy. Hopefully one in Washington, and one in Los Angeles—we are stopping there for shopping on the way back."

I was confused again. "You mean . . . you're looking for a magazine to bring back to your boyfriend?"

"I'm looking for a guy to sleep with. You know, my last fling before I get married." She laughed at my expression. "What do you think our fathers and bosses are doing on their business trips to Thailand? They're looking at more than their companies' factories. If men can stretch their wings, why can't women?"

"But you found someone to *marry*. How good can it feel to have sex without emotion?" I was thinking about how things had gotten with Takeo lately.

Hana smiled at me. "Don't worry about me. You are a good girl, aren't you? I can tell by the way you're taking such special care of your parents' presents."

My back prickled at her mention of my packages. Was I just being paranoid?

"What are you thinking about?" Hana asked.

"Oh, just that you're funny and not at all shy," I said quickly. "You'll do well on this trip to America."

"I speak English, too. Want to hear? 'Hello, sexy. Your place or mine?'" Hana yawned and stood up. "I'm going to the toilet anyway. Wine runs right through me."

She wandered off, and I opened my notebooks and began the task of running through the translated notes about the kimono. They were all about thread content; not the information that I thought would really interest people. I would keep my fingers crossed that at the museum libraries in Washington, I might locate sources of information about the lives of Tokugawa women and Ai Otani.

"Still working on your papers?" Hana asked when she came back.

"Mmm-hmm," I said, closing up the work I was doing.

"What's your job, by the way?" she asked, sounding casual. It was a personal question, though; people didn't ask such things upon first meetings in Japan. They relied on learning the truth through a business card.

"I deal in clothing," I said, thinking that that word was less provocative than "antiques."

"Wow! Are you a department-store buyer? Will you buy clothes wholesale in the U.S. to sell back in Japan?"

"No. I'm doing—research."

"That's still cool. Do you work for a store or a private company?" Hana asked, settling back down into her seat.

"I'm self-employed."

Hana moaned in a theatrical way. "You don't have a boss, you don't live with your parents, and nobody's making you get married. You're lucky to have such a life."

"Well, I'm not being supported by anyone, so I have to take whatever work comes my way," I said. "Also, this kind of profession doesn't look good to the authorities. It's very hard for me to get any kind of bank loans."

"Nevertheless, I'd trade my life for yours anytime," Hana said, and I realized now that the reason she'd been sounding so dramatic was that she was drunk. There were two empty mini-bottles on her tray.

I wasn't going to get any more work done right now, but I was betting that I would be able to finish up later, after Hana had fallen into a wine-induced slumber. "So," I asked, smiling at her, "if you were your own boss, what would you do?"

"I'd have my own karaoke box," she said. "You know, those little booths that you rent out to people who want to sing with friends."

"What a fun idea," I said, unable to hide a shudder. I

couldn't carry a tune, so I was perpetually trying to avoid the chance to sing in front of friends or colleagues in Tokyo's many karaoke bars and karaoke boxes. "So, what does Yoshi think about you working after marriage?"

Hana bit her lip, smearing purplish lipstick over her teeth. "Um, we haven't discussed it beyond what date I should quit. Three weeks before the wedding, I said. After that, I'll stay home. I'm sure that's what he wants."

Despite Hana's talk about wanting to be a self-employed karaoke entrepreneur, I was getting the feeling that she wasn't very serious about it. She was a party girl, pure and simple. I said, "Well, you'd be surprised what men might think. You should talk about it with him. I guess you'll have more time for that after marriage."

"He's not much of a talker," Hana said. "Can you give me some advice? What should I say to the men in America if I want to meet them for a short experience?"

"I don't know. I think they'll be surprised. Usually, if American women want to have a fling before they get married, they go to see men dance or they go have some nice beauty treatments with their girlfriends at a spa—"

"I like beauty treatments, too. What's that cool brown lipstick you're wearing?"

"Actually, it's an American brand called MAC," I said, surprised there was something about my own simple makeup style that would appeal to Hana. "I'm sure you can find it at the mall. I'm going to stock up, too."

"Thanks for the tip. Hey, do you want to go to the spa at the mall and have a makeover with me?"

"My work schedule is extremely demanding. Why don't you go with your girlfriend?"

"We had a little argument earlier today. Actually, that's the reason she was willing to change seats with you. Even though Kyoko and I both work as office ladies at the same place, I don't think we'll be socializing much on this tour."

Hana sounded so downcast that I took pity on her. I said, "I'm sure we can get over there for a little time together. I need to buy some shoes."

"Shoes! Me, too. What do you think about Nordstrom versus Saks?"

The flight attendants called for everyone to put down their shades, but it was still hard for me to sleep. Hana didn't have a problem, though. She snored delicately, her small chest rising and falling with every breath. She really was a pretty young woman, though I didn't like the fact that she'd dyed her hair.

I closed my eyes, and my worries about Hana turned into worries about the kimono lectures. I thought more about the information gap—that I'd have to explain why I was showing such splendid kimono worn by a tea merchant's wife during a time that the Shogun didn't allow commoners to dress better than aristocrats did. I drifted off, laying my head against the boxes strapped in the window seat. This way, if anyone tried to take them, I'd feel it.

When I awoke, the flight attendants were serving dinner. I finally had a little wine with my meal, seeing how well it had made Hana sleep. We chatted a little more during supper, and then we both must have gone to sleep. The next thing I knew I was feeling a series of hard bumps. We'd touched down at Dulles Airport in Virginia. I was back on home ground.

5

Just as at Narita Airport, the ritual at Dulles Airport's customs went off without a hitch. As I entered the area, I saw all the different customs booths ahead of me, but next to one stood a thin woman holding a sign that read REI SHIMURA. She had to be the customs broker waiting for me. I got into the line heading her way, and when I reached the agent, I handed over my passport and the papers and identified myself to her in a low voice. She nodded at me and pulled out her own set of papers for the customs official. Everything was in order, so he waved us on. I reset my watch two hours back; it was two o'clock in the afternoon, and still Monday, since I'd traveled back across the international date line.

I exited customs and followed the red, white, and blue flag to where See America Travel had assembled, with the female customs broker in my wake.

"Where are you going?" asked the woman.

"I heard there's a free shuttle to the hotel, provided by See America Travel." I could see the tour group leader, a middle-aged lady holding the tour's official flag, surrounded by a growing number of office-lady travelers.

"Are you a first-time courier?"

I nodded, feeling a flush of embarrassment.

"That must be why you don't know about the transport. I'm Joan Forster of Fine Arts International." She reached into a Coach handbag and took out a business card, as well as a driver's license, as well as an employee ID with photograph.

"Okay, Miss Forster, I see you're who you say you are," I said, examining the ID pieces as best I could from behind the two boxes I was carrying.

"Joan, please. You're back in America, remember?" She cracked a smile that vanished as quickly as it had appeared. "Now, Allison at the Museum of Asian Arts should have explained that you are to proceed directly to the museum to have the packages checked in. I know you must be tired, and we have about an hour of travel ahead of us. But the legal agreement stipulates we must bring the boxes immediately to the museum, where Allison is waiting. After that, I'll say good-bye to you and have the limo take you to your hotel."

"I see," I said, understanding the logic of what she was saying but still feeling a bit nervous about going into a private car. "Do you mind . . . if I just stop at a phone booth to call Allison first?"

"Of course. If you like, you can use my cell phone," Joan Forster said dryly.

The truth was, I didn't have any American coins yet. I took the Nokia she handed me and dialed the museum's main number, followed by Allison's extension. I recognized her voice when she picked up on the second ring.

"It's Rei Shimura. I'm here at Dulles and was met by Joan Forster. I'm calling to check that you want me to travel in a limousine Joan brought. I wasn't expecting such—generosity," I said quickly, trying to make it seem as if I wasn't so distrustful of Joan. But I had to know.

"Yes, it's all part of the package deal. It went smoothly at customs, then? You didn't have to open anything?"

"No. Will we be doing all the examination of the textiles this afternoon?"

"No, we'll do the examination tomorrow morning. That is, if you're not too tired."

I assured her that I wasn't, and I hung up and handed the phone back to Joan.

"You're doing a good job to be so cautious," she said. "Come on, our guy's waiting at the curb."

The car was an unmarked black Toyota Camry; I had the back with the boxes, while Joan sat up front with the driver, a man in a dull brown suit. When the vehicle started up, I forgot about them and stared out the window. My first view of America in two years, and it was of a part of the country I hadn't seen for six years. We were on a toll road that was relatively empty in the direction we were moving in—though the other side was packed with an unmoving line of cars. On either side of the freeway there was an imposing array of shiny sterile buildings. So this was the new suburban landscape. I was glad we were going to get out of it fast and into the city.

We hit some traffic as we entered Washington, D.C., so it was an hour and a half until we reached Kalorama, the elegant Northwest neighborhood of diplomatic residences and homes of the rich where the Museum of Asian Arts was located, along with a number of other small museums like the Textile Museum, the Woodrow Wilson House, and the Phillips Gallery. I didn't look too closely, because my tired eyelids kept closing. The car pulled into a circular driveway outside a large brick town house and stopped.

"Here we are," Joan said, and she sprang out and opened the door for me. "You can carry the boxes in, and I'll carry in your personal luggage if you don't feel comfortable having it stay with the driver for the time that we'll be inside."

"Just my backpack," I said, taking my first real footsteps on Washington soil. Pebbles, to be exact—the driveway in front of the museum had been paved with the kind of river stones that were popular in Japan.

Joan walked straight into the lobby, and I followed her, carrying the boxes. I recognized immediately the hall laid with black-and-white tiles: this was the museum I'd visited so enjoyably when I was in college.

"Joan Forster, Fine Arts International—" Joan again whipped out her identification pieces for a guard standing in the lobby.

"Of course. I'm Major Andrews. And this is the courier we've been expecting?" The guard, an older Caucasian man with silver hair and a trim frame, smiled at both of us. "Come into the lobby and have a seat while I call Allison."

I barely had time to sit down on a bench upholstered in Indian sari silk before a tall woman came rapidly down the staircase.

"Joan, thanks for another job well done. And Rei! You look utterly exhausted. I promise to keep you only half a minute."

I looked into the beaming face of a woman in her fifties with blond hair held back with a velvet headband. Allison Powell was a lot the way I expected, though she was a touch heavy for someone who sounded like one of my mother's tennis league friends. It didn't matter. She carried the weight well, dressed in a stylish black tunic and matching slacks.

"Here's all the paperwork. We'll take the courier back to her hotel." Joan handed Allison a sheaf of documents.

"Very good. Where are you staying?" Allison turned her smile on me.

"It's called the Washington Suites."

"Washington Suites? I've never heard of that one. Most of our visitors stay at the Sofitel, just a few blocks away."

"We know the Washington Suites," Joan said. "It's a budget place close to Dulles."

"But Dulles Airport is in Northern Virginia!" I said.

"Yes, that's where the hotel is located. Haley Heights, Virginia."

No wonder the price was so cheap. I cursed Richard for his savvy travel tip; he'd been more interested in having me close to a shopping mall than to the place where I'd be working.

"Never mind, you'll find your way in to us," Allison said. "Now, let me sign these papers for you, Rei, and be sure to keep them with your valuables. I'll see you tomorrow around ten. Again, I'm glad you're here, and I offer you congratulations on a courier job well done."

I was handed back the papers, and next thing I knew, Joan was waving good-bye to me and I was in the limousine heading out of the city. I closed my eyes, finally able to relax. The boxes had been delivered. Now I could really sleep.

The limousine stopped almost two hours later at the Washington Suites, time that had passed with excruciating slowness because of the long lines of unmoving traffic around us. I was so relieved when I reached the hotel that I was almost ready to overlook the fact that it looked like a cheaper version of a Days Inn. The parking lot full of tourist buses and minivans with out-of-state plates furthered my impression I was not in a place where I'd be pampered. At least the Japanese office ladies would be there to add a bit of class to the place.

I thanked the driver for the ride and lugged my back-pack and suitcase into the lobby, which was deserted. Apparently all the See America Travel tourists had checked in. A key card to Room 410, as well as a lengthy, unintelligible note in Japanese from Mrs. Chiyoda, proprietor of See America Travel, were waiting for me at the front desk.

I got myself into the elevator and up to a room that seemed palatial to me. Two double-sized beds and a bathroom with a walk-in shower and a tub—that definitely made up for the hotel's disappointing exterior. I hadn't seen such luxury for a while. I crawled into bed, trying not to notice the ugly faux-pastoral painting over it or the scratchy polyester-blend sheets. These were minor in comparison to the plumbing and the space.

I shut out the light, aware that in the hallway, some sort of a party was in progress. It was somebody screaming the word *Chippenderu! Chippenderu!*

I stuck my head out into the hall. "Um, I'm sorry to bother you, but I'm trying to sleep."

Hana, the girl who'd sat next to me on the plane, was pouring champagne for a small circle of women. She looked over at me and grinned. "Sorry to bother you, Rei-san. We'll go into our room now. We got excited because there is a paper in our room promising every guest a chance to reproduce with *Chippenderu* dancers!"

"What?" I went back into my room and grabbed the vinyl-coated guest information folio. I flipped through it, and pretty soon I saw what Hana had misread.

"They're talking about the furniture style, Hana."

"Heh?"

"The chairs. The brochure here says every guest room

has reproduction Chippendale furnishings. They don't
mean dancers. Here, let me show you." I waved Hana
and her friend into my doorway and pointed to the ma-
hogany-stained console table, desk, and chair. All had
the signature curvy Chippendale styling, though they
looked as if they'd been slapped together quickly in
North Carolina last year instead of in England 250
years ago.

"*Baka, ne!*" Hana groaned. In Japanese, that was the
way a woman said "damn." Then she and her friends
laughed even more loudly than before.

My body told me I'd been sleeping for only a few
hours, but the clock radio set to an alternative rock station went off at six A.M. I got up and did a few prerun-
ning stretches to Cibo Matto's upbeat song "Working
for Vacation," before remembering that I hadn't
brought my Asics. One of the missions of the trip was
to buy new running shoes at a good price to take back
to Japan.

Instead of pushing my body, I rewarded it with a
long, hot shower. During my years in Japan, I'd grown
weary of the handheld shower attachment in my bathroom, so the hotel shower's stationary head was a special treat. I washed my hair using a tiny sample of a
eucalyptus-scented shampoo and conditioner that
seemed so much more exotic than my flowery-smelling
Kanebo brand. After toweling off, I continued my
grooming frenzy by actually blow-drying my hair, putting on eye makeup, and using the hotel's tiny iron and
board to iron the microscopic wrinkles out of my
slacks. There was even a tiny coffeemaker that I used to
brew a cup of Folger's.

My grooming and coffee drinking had been fun, but

it was eight o'clock by the time I left the room. In the sun-filled lobby, Mrs. Chiyoda of See America Tours was up and talking with the concierge, a young woman with a brown cardboard coffee cup in her hand. The cup read STARBUCKS, which seemed a fanciful, almost Japanese-designed name; I liked it. But she had an anxious expression on her face, and as I got closer, I understood she was having a difficult conversation with Mrs. Chiyoda. "You *know* we can only provide two bus runs an hour," the concierge was saying to Mrs. Chiyoda. With her free hand, she held up two fingers, as if she thought Mrs. Chiyoda didn't understand English. "Two buses. It cannot change."

"Excuse me for interrupting, but I have a quick question about transportation—" "There are two bus runs an hour," the concierge repeated.

"No, I'm not interested in the mall," I said. "I have to go into D.C. Can you call a taxi for me?"

"You want to take a taxi into the District during rush hour?" The concierge shook her head. "That'll be almost a two-hour trip, depending on where you're going. Washington Flyer is the only cab company in this area, and they charge over forty-five dollars for a trip to the District. One-way and that's without the meter ticking up extra costs for waiting in traffic."

At that rate, I'd go through my budget in six days and save nothing. "Can you suggest any other way for me to reach the Kalorama area?"

"Why don't you take the Metro? It's about thirty-five minutes from West Falls Church Station to Dupont Circle. You're going to have to change at Metro Center, but that's easy. After that, depending on where you're going in Kalorama, it's about a fifteen-minute walk."

"Public transportation is not safe," Mrs. Chiyoda muttered in Japanese to me. "And don't go walking in the city. You could be mugged. I wrote that to you in the note I left with your key, since you missed our tour orientation in the lobby yesterday afternoon."

"Sorry about that," I said, thinking happily about the subway. How had I forgotten Washington had the Metro system? I'd used it a few times to get around when I was visiting the city with college friends. This would be perfect for my budget.

Out of the corner of my eye, I saw a woman emerge from the hotel's restaurant and amble toward us. It was Hana, dressed in a pair of black leather jeans and a T-shirt that could only have been made in Asia. The English lettering across Hana's chest read: PRETTY LITTLE BUMBLE. SINCE 1987. There was an appliqué design of a bee pollinating a flower. Although *hana* meant "flower" in Japanese, it was easier to picture her as the bee, given what she had told me about her romantic aspirations while in the United States. Hana had a black quilted coat slung over her arm, and atop her head was a red cowboy hat that matched the color of the tiny Kate Spade canvas handbag swinging from her hand.

"What about our makeovers? Shall we do it this morning?" Hana called out.

"I wish I could, but I have business in the city." I smiled at her, unable to resist her sweet enthusiasm, then turned to the concierge again with my dreary question. "How can I get to the Metro station?"

"Well, as I've been saying, we have a shuttle bus that runs to the Metro station and the mall twice an hour, but it just left. You could either walk or take a taxi. It's about a mile from here."

"Oh. Will I see you again?" Hana asked plaintively.

"Of course. I'm sure I'll be back by four."

"Can you meet me in the bar at four-thirty? We can go to happy hour somewhere?"

"Yes, happy hour is a tour option," Mrs. Chiyoda cut in. "But please sign up in advance, *neh*?"

"Let's find a bar that's not connected to the tour," I said to Hana. "*Ja, mata!* See you later."

"See you later, alligator!" Hana replied, waving her handbag at me.

6

I found a taxi parked outside the hotel entrance. Five dollars to ride three minutes was an outrage, but at least I was on my way. In the light of day, I could see the landscape around me was even worse than what I'd seen in the evening. There were large plastic signs for steakhouses and massage parlors interspersed with office buildings. We passed a residential area completely made up of large new houses covered with aluminum siding. There were no trees.

The West Falls Church Metro Station looked about ten years old—big, brown, and boxy like everything else around the area. I had to admit I liked being able to ride an escalator down to the platform—in Tokyo subway stations, there were very few escalators. I spent a few dollars to buy a fare card I could use to get home, and I picked up a map to study during the ride into the city.

We were far enough out in the suburbs that the train was still not crowded when I boarded. I sat, marveling at the people around me. The houses in northern Virginia might have been homogeneous, but the people who lived in them weren't. I was surrounded by every imaginable gradation of skin hue, and hair that ranged from ramrod straight East Asian to dyed purple to dreadlocks.

Following the concierge's advice, I changed trains to the Red Line at a stop called Metro Center. Here the crowds were larger, and I had to squeeze my way up a short flight of stairs to the platform where Red Line trains ran. As I waited, I glanced at a giant television screen hanging over the platform. The screen said: METRO POLICE FOLLOW ZERO TOLERANCE AND DO NOT ISSUE WARNINGS BEFORE MAKING ARRESTS. I'd never heard of any ideology called Zero Tolerance. It seemed strange that police would advertise the fact that they were intolerant. What had happened in the years since I'd been away from America? In Japan, there were TV screens over train platforms, too, but their purpose was not to scare commuters, just to announce the trains and their destinations.

I made it onto the train without incident and got out two stops later at Dupont Circle without having witnessed any crimes. Still, the warnings on the TV screen made me feel relieved that I hadn't had to carry the kimono with me on the Metro. They were safe with Allison Powell, and I'd be seeing them again in a few minutes' time.

From Dupont Circle, I took a very long and steep escalator upward to Connecticut Avenue, which was jammed with every sort of store imaginable: bookstores, cafés, boutiques, art galleries. There was even a large store with a green awning that read STARBUCKS, the brand of coffee the hotel concierge had been drinking. Now I recalled that I had seen Starbucks in Japan, but I always figured it was too expensive to go in.

I turned my attention from the pleasant window scene of people drinking coffee and reading newspapers, in order to concentrate on finding Florida Avenue, where I needed to take a left. From Florida Avenue it was a short jog onto S Street, and then I was in the

Kalorama neighborhood, full of majestic early-twentieth-century town houses and tall, old trees in lush fall colors. Many of the houses seemed to have been converted into embassies or diplomatic residences; I could tell from the flags flying over porticoes and the people standing outside who looked like guards.

As I passed the embassy of Pakistan, I smiled at the mustachioed man pacing back and forth before the entrance, but he didn't break his intense gaze. He was obviously keeping a lookout for terrorists. I hadn't thought I looked like one. I was wearing sleek black Japanese pants that ended a few fashionable inches above my ankles, and black suede platform shoes. On top I wore a black-and-green bouclé St. John jacket my mother had handed down to me. The jacket was a little warm for the temperature, which was in the sixties, but I thought it was very lady-like—just right for the first meeting with Allison Powell.

I recognized the Museum of Asian Arts' handsome brick town house from the night before. It was five to ten, so the huge mahogany door was still locked. Remembering what Joan had done the previous evening, I rang a buzzer and rapped hard on the brass knocker. After a minute, I saw a beefy pink face appear in one of the long leaded-glass windows that flanked the door.

"Are you expected?" the man asked. He was a different guard from the previous evening.

"Yes, I'm Rei Shimura, here to see Ms. Powell—"

Before I could finish, I could hear the man sliding the door's bolt. "Fine. You can wait here and I'll call her."

"How was the ride in?" Allison called as she came downstairs.

"The Metro was great. From my experience in the limo last night, I get the feeling that driving around here is a nightmare."

"Yes, yes, especially on the Beltway, the highway that

circles the city. How's your hotel?" As she spoke, Allison beckoned me to follow her up the curving staircase to an area that was off-limits to the public. I assumed this was where the administrative offices were.

"Well, I'd hoped the Washington Suites was in the District, but aside from that disappointment, it's fine. There's a lot more greenery outside the Beltway." Not to mention Kentucky Fried Chicken, McDonald's, and Chi-Chi's.

"Well, I can understand you putting your heart and curiosity into travel." Allison sighed heavily. "I used to travel all the time, but I don't anymore. It's my job to stay here, take care of the textiles. In fact, we may as well get on with the routine of inspecting the kimono."

"By the way, I don't know if they told you that at the last minute they decided one of the kimono was too fragile to travel," I said. "We made what I think is an excellent substitution."

"No, they didn't tell me anything; communication has always been a sore point between Mr. Nishio and myself, which is why I was relieved to get you as the go-between. Well, let's open up what you've brought. The faster we get it all unpacked and documented, the quicker we can get it in the freezer."

"Excuse me? Did you say the kimono would be frozen?"

"Yes. Jamie, who is our conservator, freezes every incoming textile for forty-eight hours, and then we gently vacuum it. The process usually kills any insects that might be present in the fabric." As I gaped, she added, "We do this for *everything*. Not just items from overseas."

"Do you think the Morioka Museum people approve of this technique? They're awfully particular."

"I know, low light, controlled humidity, all that. We

had to explain about the freezing a few years ago when Mr. Nishio and Mr. Shima came over with some other kimono. They understood. Anyway, our procedures were spelled out on the loan receipt. I assume they signed it and you've brought it with you?"

"Of course." I handed her the envelope stuffed with documents as I began to open the boxes that she'd placed on a long table in her office. Wearing the cloth gloves that I'd brought from Japan, I showed Allison all Ai Otani's *furisode* and the wedding kimono, and then brought out the kimono belonging to Mrs. Tokugawa and her daughter.

"So whose daughter was she really?" Allison raised her perfectly plucked eyebrows. "One never really knows, with these extended families and courtesan situations in old Japan. Maybe you've brought clothing that's evidence of an early-nineteenth-century love triangle."

"You and I might call it that, but the Japanese wouldn't." I perked up at her reaction, because I believed that clothes with an exciting personal story behind them would be good for the lecture. "I have a feeling there's an interesting social history behind Ai Otani's kimono, but the problem was, I didn't find out much before I left Japan. I was thinking of going to the Smithsonian Institutions to do some research—"

"We have more on Japanese textiles than they do," Allison said swiftly, and I realized I'd offended her.

After we'd both looked at the garments, I began to explain the kind of lectures I hoped to present. I asked, "Can you lend me a mannequin to dress while I give the lecture? I know you plan to hang the kimono that I brought, but if you can lend me a kimono from your collection, I could demonstrate kimono dressing for the audience."

"Don't tell me you can tie an *obi* in one of those huge butterfly bows?"

"Sure I can. I studied kimono dressing for a year at an academy in Tokyo. I can dress myself, too."

"Fabulous. Wearing a kimono, you'll be much more attractive than that stiff old Mr. Nishio could ever be. He was here once and he wore a very drab suit."

"Did the Morioka ever tell you why Mr. Nishio couldn't come?"

"They said something about needing to cover for another employee who'd be away on vacation. They were so terribly vague, and I couldn't get anything more out of them. Did you hear something else?" She looked as if she'd pounce on me if I had.

"No, I didn't. And I'm going to have to disappoint you about my wearing a kimono. I didn't bring any of my own kimono to wear, just a suit for the daytime lecture and a little black dress for the VIP reception."

"Oh, that won't work at all." Allison clucked her tongue. "The reason I wanted a young Japanese woman lecturer is that you can actually *be* what you're talking about. Could you borrow a kimono from a relative?"

So she wanted me to present the stereotyped image of a proper Japanese lady—even though it was the twenty-first century, and only a small fraction of Japanese women wore kimono. Now I was starting to realize what I was being paid for. And if I wanted the money, I had to be agreeable. "I'll check if I can have something sent from Japan. But it will take at least two days to get here, even with express mail."

"Since the party's in two days, you'd better call right away," Allison said. "Please use my phone; we'll happily take care of the long-distance charges, too. I'll just call Jamie to check the condition of the kimono herself before putting them in the freezer."

It was almost midnight in Japan, but that was no deterrent to telephoning. Everyone there seemed to stay up past midnight. Since there was a strong chance my friend Richard hadn't made it home from the clubs yet, I decided to try my aunt Norie. She would be more reliable at putting together a kimono outfit that matched, and getting it quickly into the mail.

"Hai?" Yes, my aunt answered on the second ring.

"I hope I'm not waking you." I explained the situation, including that I would reimburse her for all the overnight mailing charges.

"What a lovely idea for you to dress in a kimono! But why don't you wear some of my kimono? I have more than fifty resting in perfect condition in my *tansu*. Some of them haven't been worn since I was a young woman, and the colors are just right for you—splendid purples and greens and reds. I have *obi,* underrobes, petticoats, everything you need. I think you left a pair of *zori* here after a tea party last summer. If they don't match the kimono that I choose, I'll buy you new ones. I remember you take the largest size." My aunt sounded as if she were rummaging through her *tansu* full of kimono as we spoke.

I paused, deciding. My kimono collection dated primarily from the 1920s; all were historically interesting. However, these kimono had mostly been bought without coordinating sashes. When I wore them in public, with the various *obi* I'd bought at the flea markets, I'd occasionally get compliments on the rare mix of fibers and patterns, but I knew the Japanese thought my kimono were extremely odd. Buying a new set with everything coordinating cost upwards of $12,000, which was out of the question for my budget.

"That is really, really kind of you," I said to my aunt. "If it's not too much hassle, could you send me more than one kimono, just to be sure I have a backup? I'll pay whatever it costs for overnight shipment, plus insurance. And please be sure that what you send is formal—"

"Rei-chan, do not have a moment of worry. I even own a few *uchikake* robes formal enough for you to wear for your wedding with Takeo Kayama."

"Um, isn't it best to tap a stone bridge before crossing it?" I reminded my aunt of the popular proverb that urged Japanese to proceed with caution.

"Flowers on a high peak are still nice to pick," Norie said, answering me with a favorite of her own. "Dearest niece, don't imagine for a minute that I'll send you a wedding kimono. Instead, I'll send you three long-sleeved robes—*furisode*—suitable for formal occasions. How I wish I could see you dress like this more often, Rei-chan. Please have someone take a photograph, *neh?*"

We ironed out a few more details, and I was glad my aunt had offered to send three instead of two—this way, I would have a really good choice. When I hung up Allison Powell looked me over with a hard eye and said, "Your Japanese is excellent. Jamie had said the advisory committee member who recommended you told her you were fluent, but I know, from experience, that résumés often stretch the truth."

"Do you speak Japanese?" I wondered how much she'd understood of my talk with my aunt.

"Oh, just enough to say hello to the ambassador. Which reminds me. In his entourage, there are a number of people who are less comfortable with English, so it would be lovely if you could speak both languages during your presentation."

"I'd be happy to do that."

The museum's conservator, Jamie, turned out to be a strikingly pretty young woman with close-cropped blond hair. She was wearing a square-necked plain black cashmere sweater with a matching skirt that showed off her flat stomach. What looked like Wolfords stockings covered her long slender legs—I was instantly jealous, because I knew the hosiery alone probably cost fifty dollars.

As if unaware of my inspection, Jamie looked over the kimono that I'd brought, then read the loan receipt.

"That bridal kimono you brought—it's not on the loan receipt," she said, sounding triumphant.

"I know that," I said. "I already explained to Allison that one of the original kimono she wanted couldn't be released, so I picked another one that worked in beautifully with the talk."

"I don't think John would like it," Jamie said to Allison.

Allison made a slight face. "I know what you mean."

"Who's John?" I asked.

"Our registrar," Allison said. "He's a real stickler for details. He's not here right now—he's traveling with some ceramics that we're lending to the Los Angeles County Museum of Art."

"I don't see how he'd let us take the bride's kimono," Jamie said, looking nervously at Allison. "Since it isn't listed on the loan receipt, it isn't insured. Secondly, there already is our own bride's *uchikake* hanging in the exhibition."

"Is it as old, and artistically significant, as the one that I brought?" I asked, put out that this young woman was ruining my plans.

"Come see," Allison said, leading both of us downstairs into a gallery where fifteen kimono from the museum's own collection were hanging. "I neglected to tell you that we have our own Edo-period *uchikake* on display, along with the white kimono that goes underneath, the headdress and *obi,* and other accessories. It's a complete set—really an important part of the show."

I examined the museum's bridal kimono. It was of heavy cream silk, patterned with wild ginger, clouds, and *kanji* characters; I couldn't read the characters, but I guessed they were auspicious. It was a great kimono, and it had the bonus of all the matching pieces.

"What a lovely kimono," I said, looking levelly at Jamie, who had made all the trouble for me. "I understand your position, but it puts me in a rather awkward situation. If I'm forced to take this *uchikake* back to Japan with me in ten days, we'll have to pay for customs brokers all over again, not to mention that the Morioka people would be upset about the rejection of one of their treasures."

"Since John isn't here to give us advice, you'd better take custody of it, Rei. You find a safe place for the *uchikake* for the duration of the exhibition, and then we'll put it back in the box with the others in three months' time and courier it back to the Morioka."

I held up a cautionary hand. "The only place that I'd feel safe about is this museum. Freeze it if you must. It really should stay here."

"The problem is, to put something in storage, it's got to have a number corresponding with our own collection or that was marked on the approved loan receipt. Our lawyers would go bonkers if I did anything that violated the insurance policy," Allison replied, with a little laugh. It was as if she expected me to laugh along with her, but I was too frustrated to do that.

"I'm sorry we can't show it, seeing that you went to all the trouble . . ." Jamie's voice trailed off awkwardly as she handed me an empty kimono box. The message was clear; I was to fold the bride's kimono and put it back inside.

I did just that, carefully tying the kimono's rice-paper wrapper and slipping the soft rectangle in the box. I taped the lid down again.

"It's almost noon, so I think we should go up to the museum restaurant for lunch before the crowds get there. Your kimono will be safe here," Allison said. "I'll lock the door."

I shook my head. "If it's not going into storage here, I've got to keep my eyes on it at all times."

"Fine. But it's rather large."

I made an executive decision. "Do you have a shopping bag that I could borrow? I'll just shift the kimono into that, for the time being."

I would do without the box because I thought it was most important that I conceal what I was carrying. I was looking forward to getting back to the hotel, where I would put the kimono into a safe-deposit box until I could reach the Morioka people to ask them what they wanted me to do about its storage. I didn't relish the thought of talking to Mr. Nishio, who hadn't wanted me to take the bride's kimono at all.

My worries about the kimono receded a bit when we entered the museum's restaurant. The walls were covered in rice paper painted with a faint wash of orange, and over that were stamped gilded *kanji* characters. The tables were made of a glossy, polished pine that was similar to what you'd see in Japan, but the chairs were cushioned in Chinese red, and there were Indonesian cabinets and Indian bronze statues here and there. The name of the restaurant was inscribed in a vaguely Japanese calligraphic style on the menu: *Pan Asia*. Its offerings were all Asian-European combinations, a style of cooking, I knew, that had been popular in the United States even before I'd left for Japan.

Since the meal was on the house—and also, since I was peeved by the rejection of the bridal kimono—I decided to order three courses. Recalling my last lunch at Appetito with the inadequate cheese bagel, I ordered the eggplant and feta cheese as my appetizer. For the entrée, I decided against fish—I could eat that all I wanted in Japan—in favor of a leek, portobello mushroom, and tomato risotto. I recalled that American etiquette required me to wait with my dessert order until the main courses had been finished, but I made a silent commitment to the Valrhona chocolate bread pudding, and a cappuccino to get me home.

Allison ordered just as much food as I did, plus a bottle of Pacific Rim Riesling for the table. Jamie stuck to hot-and-sour soup and iced tea. I felt a little vulgar digging into my cheesy eggplant as she sat with her hands folded on the table, staring. It wasn't my fault if she had an eating disorder, I thought as my taste buds were caressed by the sensuous, salty cheese that I'd missed.

"Cheers. To a successful exhibition." Allison raised her glass toward me and, after we'd all toasted, began a serious discussion about the opening reception.

"The first night is the most complicated, because we have the large VIP crowd and they've got to be fed," Allison told me. "We're having a typical Japanese buffet—sushi, sesame noodles, grilled fish. I hope our Japanese guests will find it aesthetically pleasing. I know from my own visits to Japan that there's a difference between the way food looks there and here."

"Well, if this restaurant is handling the order, it will look and taste terrific." I watched happily as a waiter whisked away my empty appetizer plate and replaced it with a large shallow bowl of pale pink risotto. On the side was an assortment of crusty rolls and a crock of blue-cheese butter. Heaven. I'd go back to Japan a few pounds heavier but with great food memories.

"Yes, it's a good restaurant, so it's very popular with the embassy people, European as well as Asian. In fact, we have invited quite a few Europeans to join our advisory committee recently. Jamie, wasn't it a European who recommended Rei to you?"

I wasn't particularly interested in Europeans, but I seized on Allison's mention of aesthetics to ask about something that had been on my mind all morning: her lukewarm reaction to my idea of demonstrating kimono dressing to the audience.

To my surprise, it was Jamie who spoke first. "I think our visitors would be fascinated to watch a kimono being put on. I mean, I know enough to drape a T-bar hanger with a kimono, but I can't say that I've ever wrapped and tied a kimono. I'd like to know how it works."

"I'd be happy to show you beforehand—that is, if you have time," I said to Jamie, wary of her enthusiasm. It had seemed that she wanted me to fail in front of her boss; why was she making nice with me now?

"Rei can wrap a kimono for the lecture that is open to the public, but for the talk with the consulate people present, that wouldn't be appropriate," Allison said. "They already know how to wear kimono. It would be old hat, so to speak."

"I understand," I said. Allison did have a point. Kimono dressing would awe Americans with its novelty but bore those who did it on a regular basis. Also, there was the chance that I'd screw up under pressure in front of the Japanese, who were experts.

I was the only one to order dessert, so I was surprised when the waiter brought three forks. I'd forgotten about the ridiculous American custom of collectively shared desserts. Allison just took a bite, but Jamie, no doubt starving after her spartan entree, ate more than half. In the end, I was left with considerably less chocolate than I'd hoped for. Still, I'd accomplished something—wine, cheese, and chocolate all at the same meal, and I wasn't paying.

"Thanks for a delightful lunch." I watched Allison sign the bill. "And you're right—my jet lag has hit. But what a way to go."

"Before you go, let's stop at the table by the entrance. I see that Dick Jemshaw is having lunch with someone. I'm sure he'd love to meet you," Allison purred, getting to her feet. She was like my mother: a wheeler-dealer, always putting people together.

"I don't know if Rei really has time for that," Jamie said.

I shot a look at her. Did she really understand how badly my jet lag had hit me—or was she jealous that I, someone close to her age, was being put in a special light while she toiled as an assistant?

"Dick's also a very good person to know—he's chair of our advisory committee," Allison said as she placed her hand in the small of my back and propelled me across the room. I'd forgotten how physical Westerners could be.

"Dick's the one with no hair," Jamie whispered.

I looked at Jamie, realizing that the wine had gone to her head. Perhaps that was why she was nervous about approaching the table.

"I think the man with him is called Glen something," Allison murmured. "I don't have as much contact with the advisory committee as Jamie does."

"He's a lawyer," Jamie said.

"Oh, really?" I said. This Glen might be the genius who was keeping my bridal kimono from being allowed into storage. If the moment was right, I could perhaps say something about how much the kimono needed to go into storage.

They were seated very close to the museum's entrance: the balding man, as Jamie had said, and his companion. From the direction from which we were coming, all I could see was the companion's thick reddish-blond hair—a color I hadn't seen for a while.

"My favorite ladies!" The man who had to be Dick Jemshaw raised a hand in greeting.

"What perfect timing, Dick," Allison said. "I've got the lady you've been waiting to meet. Here's our kimono lecturer, Rei Shimura."

Jamie stepped aside, so I came face-to-face with the smiling, round-faced Dick Jemshaw. Instinctively, I started to bow, but stopped myself before my head reached the fifteen-degree mark. I wasn't in Japan anymore.

"I'm very happy to meet you," I said, trying to catch a glimpse of the companion, who hadn't turned around to greet us. From the back, he looked pretty attractive. I liked the athletic shoulders and the fiber mix of the suit jacket. Being a textile buff, I could tell a true mix of silk and worsted wool at twenty paces.

Dick Jemshaw was doing something weird to the fleshiest part of my palm with his finger: a stroking and tickling all at once. "You know, Rei, Japan is my favorite country."

"How—nice," I said, trying to discreetly withdraw my hand. I wanted to wash it.

"We had a real problem with that Japanese fellow canceling. I know I can speak for the whole museum when I express my gratitude for your help at the eleventh hour."

"It's my pleasure, believe me," I said, slipping my hand out of his grasp.

"Terrific. Now, let me introduce you to a guy who has actually worked in Japan before he joined our board. Come on, Hugh, put that menu down."

I had an odd feeling just before Dick's well-built dining partner turned to face me. It was more than the hair and the broad shoulders—it was the suit. I knew that suit—it was an Issey Miyake I'd helped my ex-boyfriend buy at Mitsukoshi's flagship store on the Ginza.

The man turned around in his seat to look at me. His cool green eyes held no emotion, and he made no move to take my hand. "It's great to meet you. I'm Hugh Glendinning."

I didn't answer. I couldn't believe what was happening.

"Rei, I've been trying to tell Hugh that he should cancel his meeting Wednesday night to make the preview. He's done so much on the advisory committee, it would be a shame to miss the party. Maybe you can talk him into it, seeing as you came all the way from Japan—"

"I said I'd try to make it, but my schedule at the firm has been insane." Hugh Glendinning still had the same soft Scottish burr, but it was subtly overlaid with an American flatness that he must have acquired recently.

"Rei? Are you all right!" I heard Jamie's whisper in my ear, but I was still too shocked to speak. Hugh had introduced himself to me! Granted, my hair had grown out; it was blunt-cut and hung halfway to my shoulders. But it had been only a year since we'd last seen each other, and he'd heard my name. He was pretending that he didn't know me? Or was I that forgettable?

"So what are you going to do, Rei? Make me your test audience. What are you going to teach me about kimono that I don't already know?" Dick Jemshaw was trying to engage me, but at a moment like this, I had no patience—just irritation.

"I guess I'll put the kimono on—and then I'll take it off," I said crisply.

"Hey, that sounds like a winning game plan! What do you say to that, Hugh?"

Hugh didn't respond—he was coughing into a napkin.

"She's only joking," Allison said sharply, giving me an elbow. I'd gotten out of line.

"What I'm talking about is dressing a mannequin, and I'll actually be doing it for the public lecture," I said, but from the wolfish grin on Dick Jemshaw's face, I could tell that my explanation hadn't helped.

"Good to meet you," Hugh said, and turned back to his plate.

"Dick Jemshaw's a real ladies' man. You shouldn't rev him up like that!" Allison whispered in my ear as we walked toward the exit together.

"I'm sure it was just a misunderstanding," Jamie said, sounding anxious.

"I'm not used to speaking English," I apologized. "And like I said, I'm feeling jet-lagged. You were right about it hitting in the afternoon."

"I see. Well, get your rest because there are plenty more people to meet in the next couple of days. I'd like to see you tomorrow afternoon to go over the outlines of your lectures."

She'd not spoken before about my needing to have the lectures preapproved. This must mean she didn't trust me anymore.

"Fine," I said without arguing. At the moment I wanted nothing more than to collapse on my futon at home in Tokyo, where the days started and ended at the proper times, and complicated feelings were buried beneath the surface of my busy life. But there was no cozy, low futon waiting in Northern Virginia—just a queen-sized bed with poly-cotton sheets.

"You forgot something." A man's voice spoke, and I turned quickly, hoping that Hugh had come after me to beg my forgiveness. But instead, it was the waiter, handing Allison the museum shopping bag. Oh, God. In my confusion over seeing Hugh, I'd dropped the Morioka's treasured bridal kimono.

Allison handed the bag to me with a slight frown, and I thanked the waiter profusely.

"Here," I said, stuffing a five-dollar bill into his hand. A small tip was the least I could give him for providing the only saving grace to a truly terrible day.

7

At four-thirty I was on my second glass of Chardonnay in Revolutionary Idea, the Washington Suites' cocktail lounge. I'd spent some time before that at the front desk, where it was explained to me that the safe-deposit boxes were only eighteen-by-ten-by-six, so my kimono wouldn't fit. Now I was drowning my sorrows at a small table with the kimono in its bag at my side. How much it had cost me already was pathetic—fifty dollars for a cab ride from D.C., since I was paranoid about having the kimono stolen out of my arms on the Metro.

Wine was so cheap here—just three-fifty a glass, instead of the ten or so it cost in Tokyo. Right now, it was just what I needed. It softened things, made me feel cozy and safe. I told myself that no matter how many things had gone wrong, it was good that I'd come to America. My brief fit of inappropriate behavior in front of Hugh, Dick Jemshaw, Allison, and Jamie was an isolated incident. It wouldn't be repeated.

I sipped the oaky-tasting yellow wine, recalling the last intelligence I'd had on Hugh. It had been on the party page of *Tatler*, an English glossy that one of my *gaijin* friends had brandished at a meeting of my *kanji* study group. In the top left photo, Hugh was looking fabulous, as was his companion, Fiona Something-

Double-Barreled. The two were at a shooting party at a castle in Scotland. He was back on his turf, with a tall woman with the same color of hair and skin: his kind. Nothing like me.

I wondered what he'd think now, seeing the bar around me filled with tired but happy Japanese women just returned from their shopping expedition. Their interest chiefly seemed to be opening their shopping bags and displaying goods to each other. Words floated back to me—"Gucci," "Nike," "Rough-Roaring."

Rough-Roaring, Rough-Roaring. I hadn't heard that brand before. I drank another inch of my wine and decided they were talking about Ralph Lauren.

A Japanese girl with dyed hair wavered across the room, going up to the bar with an empty glass. It wasn't Hana, but I thought of her now, and how she'd asked me to meet her. She'd been so insistent about wanting to meet at four-thirty, but she hadn't come. I considered whether she'd gone instead to my room to find me.

I got to my feet, picked up my shopping bag, and proceeded more or less steadily out to the lobby, where I asked the front-desk manager if anyone had left a message for me. "It should all be in the voice mail on your telephone. Go upstairs and dial three."

So impolite—not a please or thank-you in the exchange, I thought with annoyance as I headed upstairs. I was even more cranky when my key card didn't work in the door. So much for high-tech gadgets. I went downstairs again.

"Do you have ID?" demanded the front-desk clerk, who wore a nametag that said I'M JULIE! ASK ME ANYTHING.

Didn't Julie remember that I was the one who'd just asked about phone messages? Feeling annoyed, I dug about in my wallet. I had left my passport for safekeeping in my room, so all I had was an outdated California driver's license, which the clerk frowned at.

"Shouldn't you have a Japanese license?"

"I'm an American citizen, okay?" I was just drunk enough to raise my voice in a manner that made the Japanese girls waiting behind me take a second look.

"Okay, Ms. Shy-mure. I'll recode your key card, and that should take care of the problem." The unfriendly Julie picked up the key card and did something to it with a small machine behind the counter.

The recoded key card worked in my door, but I was still ticked off. I slammed the door and zipped the bag containing the kimono into one of my empty suitcases, padlocked it, and put it in the closet. Then I checked the phone. The message light was blinking, and after I made a circuitous trip into the voice-mail system, I learned that my mother had called me once and my father twice.

I hung up and swallowed a couple of Aleve tablets with two glasses of water—my favorite hangover preventive—and lay down. Fully dressed, I fell into the kind of sleep that comes when one is too disoriented to settle down comfortably. After what seemed like a few minutes, a ringing sound started. I struggled for the phone, but it turned out that I'd left it off the hook. The ringing sound was at the door.

I groggily opened the door to a young Japanese woman who looked much like the other women I'd seen drinking downstairs but was very tense. She had a page-boy hairstyle that swung over her face when she bowed.

"Please forgive me for disturbing you. Aren't you Rei Shimura?" After I nodded, she said, "Oh, how lucky I found you. The lady at the front desk wouldn't tell me your room number. She would only give the telephone number, and that was unfortunately engaged."

"So how did you find me?" I asked.

"Hana-chan had written your room number on a paper in our room. It took me a while to find, but at last I did."

"Oh," I said, finally making sense of this woman, who had referred to Hana Matsura using the familiar, affectionate "chan" suffix. "You must be Hana's roommate, the one who so kindly changed seats so I could have a place with my luggage."

She ducked her head and smiled. "Yes. I'm Kyoko Omori. I know Hana-chan enjoyed that time with you. She said you were a nice new friend. That's why I thought you might know where she is."

"I'm afraid that I can't help you. Hana said she would meet me at the hotel at four-thirty, and I've been here since four without seeing her."

"How strange. She agreed to meet me at the mall's shuttle stop at four, and she wasn't there. I'm worried now because the last shuttle bus came back, and she wasn't aboard."

Suddenly I understood Kyoko's fear. So many Japanese tourists thought that stepping outside the group was dangerous. Hana's missing the shuttle—even though the mall was just a few minutes away—represented the worst of the unknown.

"How well were you and Hana getting along today?" I asked.

"Fine, of course!"

"I don't mean to be rude, but she did say you had a small argument yesterday."

"She did?" Kyoko put a hand over her mouth. "Oh, I'm embarrassed now."

"She said something to me about wanting to spend some time privately with American . . . friends." I used a euphemism because I wasn't sure how much Hana had told Kyoko, and Kyoko seemed to be rather innocent.

"She has no friends here," Kyoko said sharply. "She wanted to find boyfriends. I think everyone knew that plan except for her fiancé."

So Kyoko had the same opinion of the plan that I did. I said, "I can understand you being worried, but I think we should just give her some time."

"Rei-san, would you be brave enough to take a taxi with me there? Just to check if she is enjoying a dinner or dancing—I'd be so much more comfortable knowing."

So this was what she'd wanted from me all along—but had not said immediately. Maybe she couldn't stand it that Hana might have a good time without her. Raising a flag of worry was one way to be invited along to a place where she hadn't been asked.

"I'm actually rather tired," I said to Kyoko.

"Oh." Her face clouded. "Yes of course. Well, I'll see you later."

"I'll look for you in the lobby tomorrow morning," I said, trying to close the door without seeming un-friendly.

"We are all leaving early for a shopping trip to another mall called Potomac Mills. That's why I'm wor-ried. If Hana-chan is not in the lobby at eight, she'll miss that trip."

I sighed, sensing how extremely worried Kyoko was. "Okay. I can spend, oh, I don't know, an hour with you for a quick run around the mall. But after that, I absolutely have to come back. I'm very, very tired."

"Thank you for your kindness, Rei-san! I will not forget it."

Another taxi ride, because the shuttles had stopped running. It was just five minutes until I saw the Nation's Place mall. At first glance, it didn't look that immense, but as the driver rounded a corner, I saw how it stretched on and on. The mall had been designed to re-sembled a big white gift box, with ribs of shining golden lights where a ribbon would go. There was a dramatic conflagration of lights on top of the mall that looked like a gift bow.

"*Sugoi*," Kyoko murmured, her first words since we'd gotten into the cab.

I smiled to myself. *Sugoi* was a Japanese adjective that could be used in two ways—to say "fabulous" or "frightening." Kyoko might like the way the mall looked at night, but I thought it was monstrous, both for its aes-thetics and size. The thought of running through the mall in an hour now seemed an impossibility.

"Which entrance would you like?" the driver asked.

"I'm not sure," I said. "Are the bars and restaurants all in one area?"

"Certainly. They're mostly through the New York en-trance, and on the second floor. Shall I take you there?"

"Please. And, um, can you tell me if there's a place in-side that's known for its singles scene?"

"Japanese ladies like Rough Rolling and the Hard Rock Café. They like to see the men wearing the blue jeans and tattoos," the driver added, a bit unnecessarily.

How appetizing, I thought as I walked through the mall's doors with Kyoko. And how stupid I was to let a woman I hardly knew drag me off to a shopping mall in search of someone who was having a good time by her-self.

"This doesn't make sense," Kyoko said after studying the big, bright mall map close to the doors we'd just passed through. "I cannot seem to find Rough Rolling. Maybe it is my poor English."

Taking the hint, I stepped up to look. "You probably didn't see it because it's on the second floor. See? We take the escalator and it's right next to Austin Grill." There were about two dozen bars and restaurants along the second floor—I'd poke my head in the likely ones, as quickly as I could. Hana, with her dyed hair and makeup, would stand out.

By looking at restaurants and nightclubs, we were just circling the tip of the iceberg. The map showed a dizzying list of shops on its two floors; some shops had names that I'd grown up with, and others were completely unfamiliar. Banana Republic, Guess?, J.Crew, and Talbots were old familiars. Oilily and Anthropologie were new to me.

I grabbed Kyoko's wrist when we got off the escalator on the second floor. The nightclub area was so crowded that I was afraid I'd lose her. Waiting lines snaked down the mall's marble hallway, where bouncers studiously examined driver's licenses and the faces of young people holding them.

"Let's go in the Mexican place first." How I'd missed Mexican food. I stepped right up to the hostess's station and told her I just needed to quickly survey the area for a friend.

"Fine," she said, not even looking up from the list of waiting customers. Kyoko and I walked through the restaurant's smoky bar. People of all ages were drinking, smoking, and tossing tortilla chips at each other. No Hana.

We went to the next stop, Rough Rolling, which had a black metal-and-steel design theme. I couldn't see past the bouncer standing in front of a mesh door with his arms folded. Behind the door was the discordant sound of heavy metal music. A long line of young people wearing black leather waited. We managed to convince the bartender to let us in for a minute, but there was no girl in a red cowboy hat, black leather jeans, and a T-shirt with a bumblebee.

An hour later we'd been through all the bars. Hana wasn't around, and none of the hosts remembered seeing a young Japanese woman with artificially brown hair, a red cowboy hat, and black leather pants. I told Kyoko I was going home, and she was welcome to come with me. She agreed, looking sadder than ever.

In the cab, I looked at Kyoko, and her face was in her hands. She was crying.

"Come on, it's going to be all right, Kyoko-san." I felt guilty for my earlier feeling of being tired of Kyoko's stress.

"But what if she stays out all night? We're supposed to go to Potomac Mills, where I know that Hana wanted to purchase some household goods. If she hasn't returned by eight in the morning, she'll lose her chance!"

"She'll come back," I said wearily to Kyoko. "I promise you, she'll come back."

8

In my hotel room, the telephone's message light was blinking. My parents had called again. I decided I'd better call them immediately, tired as I was. If I didn't make a preemptive strike, they were liable to call me back when I'd fallen asleep.

"So you were out this evening? Were you having dinner with friends?" my father asked after he picked up the phone in San Francisco.

"No. There's a Japanese tour group staying here, and one of the tourists needed help with something, so I took her to the shopping mall. How are you two?" I tried to change the subject, because I didn't want to have to explain more about Hana.

"Oh, we're looking forward to your visit! Have you gotten your tickets yet?" My mother had gotten on another phone to join the conversation.

"I'm afraid I haven't had time. Let's see, we were talking about me coming on Saturday, right?"

"We'd hoped for earlier, but Saturday is fine," my father said. "I'm very proud that you're doing those lectures at the museum. You must give that job your full attention."

We said good night. I snapped off the light, checked

my alarm clock, and had snuggled down to sleep in the hotel bed when my doorbell rang.

The peephole was too high for me, so I called out, "Who is it?"

There was no reply. Probably Kyoko hadn't understood my English. I knew it could only be her, at this hour. I unlocked the door and opened it with the chain on.

In the two inches of space, I saw a sliver of reddish-gold hair, ruddy skin, and one green eye looking right at me.

I slammed the door shut, but Hugh Glendinning pushed it back open.

"Thank God I found you. Give me a chance to speak, Rei. Please."

"Apparently, you don't want to know me anymore. Well, I feel the same way, so just leave!" He'd caught me off guard, and I couldn't check my emotions.

"Shhh," he whispered. "Do you want the whole hotel to hear you? Just let me in for a minute."

"How did you get my room number?" I didn't think I'd told Allison or Jamie.

"I asked this Japanese girl peeking out of her room down the hall if she knew you. I thought, if there was a single Japanese person in the hotel, you'd most likely have befriended her."

"Gee, that really narrows it down, given that I'm in the thick of an OL tour group. I was just out at the mall trying to find one who's missing. Actually, I'm rather tired from a fruitless search, so I'll say good riddance, I mean good night—"

"I'm not leaving. I've waited too long to see you."

I looked at Hugh, and realized two things: first, that he would stay until the hotel's security threw him out, and second, that he'd said something rather strange.

He'd waited to see me. What did that mean? He'd been out of communication with me for the last year, so I couldn't imagine the excuse. I also knew I'd never get to sleep if I didn't hear it. After a few seconds of deliberation, I unchained the door.

Hugh strode into my room, taking in the rumpled bed and faux-antique furniture with a slight wrinkle of his beautiful, beaky nose. After a moment he made as if he would sit down on the room's only chair, which was hung with the underwear and stockings I planned to wear the next day. I stopped him.

"It's too crowded in here. Let me, um, get dressed, and we can go downstairs." I turned my back on him, as if that would give me more privacy, and pulled on a pair of ancient jeans under my ancient Lanz flannel nightgown. Then I realized I was going to have to do something about my top part, so I slunk into my bathroom, shut the door halfway so I could keep an eye on what he was doing in my room, and put on the blouse I'd worn earlier. I slid my feet into my Hello Kitty sandals and quickly brushed my hair.

"There's a lounge downstairs," Hugh said. "It doesn't look great, but I think it would serve the purpose."

"I was there earlier. They have good prices on wine by the glass." I realized after I'd said it that I didn't want any more wine. I didn't want to be any fuzzier than I already was.

Hugh made a beeline for the table where I'd lounged miserably by myself during the afternoon. He settled down in a wing chair upholstered with what looked like plane-seat fabric. I took the chair across from it.

"It took me hours of calling around to find you were here," Hugh said as we sat down. "I'm surprised that you chose to stay smack in the middle of nowhere. You used to be such a downtown girl."

"You could have asked Allison where I was staying."

Hugh shook his head. "I can't let them know that I know you. That was the whole problem at lunch today. Thank God you understood and went along."

"Believe me, the last thing I want to offer you is understanding," I snapped. "At the restaurant I clammed up because I was confused—and more than a little hurt. I couldn't believe you had forgotten me so quickly. But then again, I should have known. I haven't heard a peep from you in eleven months."

Hugh moved forward and reached toward me. When I turned my palm outward, he stopped. "All right, I'd better start the explanation by saying that I feel bad about being out of touch. That's why I arranged for you to come to the museum."

"No!" I was paralyzed with horror. "I thought they really wanted me. So how did it happen—did you *pay* them or something?"

"It's nothing like that. I've been in Washington for the last seven months, and in a fit of boredom, I agreed to join a committee at the museum. And I've . . . well, I've been thinking of you. A couple of months ago, I overheard that they needed a replacement speaker for the kimono opening. I gave your name to someone who knows Allison's assistant without saying that I knew you personally."

"How could you?" I breathed. "Do you know how that makes me feel? I would never have taken crumbs from you. Now I'm going to have to *leave*. No doubt I'll have to reimburse them, out of my own pocket, for the plane and hotel."

"That would be rash, especially seeing as the events around your visit will be listed in *The Washington Post* tomorrow. Please stay the week at least. I think it will genuinely help your career."

"You couldn't have done this because you cared about me. If you cared, you would have stayed with me in Japan."

"I wanted to be with you, but not in Japan. Remember?" Hugh said softly.

"I recall a certain political agenda was more important to you than anything," I said, remembering how Hugh had left shortly after the citizens of Scotland had gotten the right to govern themselves. The new parliament needed legal advisers, and Hugh was eager to be one.

"Well, devolution isn't going smoothly," Hugh said. "With the style of decision making that we Scots have—let's say a bit argumentative—there is no clear path. I dragged myself all over the country trying to broker agreements between people. The more I looked into things, the more I began to question what we were doing. I mean, Scotland's gained the right to make decisions that England can't. Even though I'm a nationalist, I see that as being unfair. That kind of unfairness can lead to trouble."

"So you were busy worrying, hmm? Too busy to even let me know you'd dumped me."

"You're the one who wouldn't marry me." Hugh kept his eyes on me, and now it was my turn to blush.

"Okay, I admit I've been indecisive, but I still wanted . . . not to lose contact. But you stopped writing, and your phone was disconnected. No further information available, the British Telecom operator told me."

Hugh bit his lip. "Sorry. Why didn't you do a Web search? It's easy to find my e-mail address—"

"I don't believe in e-mail!" I bleated so loudly that the people at the next table turned to frown.

A waitress approached us with an expectant expression. I ordered mineral water, and Hugh tea.

When the waitress left, I said, "How can you stand tea in America?"

"What option do I have?" Hugh sounded bleak. "Anyway, let me try to explain why I—did the cowardly thing. When I got to Scotland, I fell into my old ways with my friends from university. I found I was drinking with them for hours every evening, and going to raucous house parties on weekends in the Highlands. I drank too much, and during this time, I began to transfer the idea of Scotland breaking from England to my own life and to my breaking from you. There were too many memories of you that hurt—I wanted to stop remembering."

I stared with concentration at the tablecloth, not sure whether I felt more wounded or disgusted. So, without me, Hugh had dissolved into a frat boy—or whatever they called them in the U.K.

"Tell me about the Honorable Fiona," I said, looking up at last.

Hugh appeared startled. "How do you know about her?"

"Someone showed me a *Tatler* with your photo in it."

"A rotten photo." He wrinkled his beautiful nose again, and suddenly I wanted to punch it. "There's not much I can say about her. She's the daughter of a lord and considers giving and attending parties a proper career. My friends said this was the one to build my life with, but I saw after about a month that she drank even harder than I did—she was an alcoholic. The situation was so . . . difficult. I couldn't just drop her and go on with my work—she was the powerful one. She turned people against me."

"Poor Hugh," I said sarcastically.

"Yeah, right. I finally made a call to a headhunter. I said I wanted to get the hell out of the U.K., but I wanted to go to an English-speaking country. I've been working here since January, and while I can't say I love your country, it's made me a new man. I work just fifty hours a week doing international contracts, the thing I can do in my sleep. On Saturdays and Sundays I play rugby on the Washington Mall with a bunch of guys from all over the world who are slowly making a better player of me. I sometimes go to museums. Half the time I'm there, I hear your voice commenting alongside me 'classic vegetable dyes,' or, 'typical example of Gifu-prefecture lacquer,' bits like that."

I smiled sourly. "I thought you hated museums."

"Untrue! I like the Museum of Asian Arts because it reminds me of everything I lost when I left Japan."

"You could have taken your furniture. You made me sell it."

"That's not what I'm talking about. There's too much that reminds me of you. I thought if I saw you again in the flesh, the dream might stop." When I looked blank, he said, "I sometimes dream about you at night. It's the same dream. I hate it."

"What's the dream?" I asked.

"Well, it's as if I'm watching you through a glass window somewhere, and you don't look like yourself because you're wearing a stiff white kimono with a bizarre headpiece—not a veil, but kind of a tall stiff white hat. I don't know where I came up with this idea. It's not like the kimono outfits most Japanese ladies wear."

"You and I once watched a bride getting married at the shrine in Kamakura. The robe sounds right, and the hat is actually quite interesting; it's supposed to symbolically hide a woman's metaphorical horns from her forthcoming husband."

"You mean the Japanese think women are devils?"

"Never mind that. You're the one who was scared of commitment, and this dream is just reminding you—"

"I don't think so," Hugh said. "In this dream, you look straight at me, and then you deliberately walk away toward a man dressed in black. I *know* this bloke is wrong for you, and I call out to say that, but you don't understand English anymore. Only Japanese."

"Bridegrooms wear black kimono," I said.

"Don't tell me—" Hugh's gaze shot to my left hand, which was bare of everything except the old yin-yang ring I always wore.

"I'm not," I said tightly. It wasn't the complete truth, of course. I should have said that I was involved with Takeo. When Hugh had mentioned the man in black, it was as if the painting hanging behind the bar of a nineteenth-century white gentleman looking over his Tidewater plantation had been transformed into a Fujicolor print of Takeo in his favorite black jeans and T-shirt. For better or worse, he was still my boyfriend. And I was sure that he hadn't given me his safety travel charm in order for me to spend time in a hotel lounge with my ex-lover.

"What is it?" Hugh asked, as if he could read my distress.

"Here's what I think: you knew I was bringing kimono, so you dreamed about me wearing one. And interestingly, Allison wants me to wear one for the lecture. Not that I want you to see it. I don't want you to be there."

"But I wouldn't miss you for the world!"

I laughed shortly. "Actually, you put the world quite a bit ahead of me. In fact, your excuse for going incommunicado was so—pathetic—that I believe it's actually true. I'm going to go up to my room now, and please do as you originally promised: stay away from both lectures."

"But I want to see you speak! I only said I couldn't go because I didn't want the others to think I was too eager."

"Please don't come. I don't want to see you there and mix up what I'm saying, like I did today at lunch—"

"You still must care," Hugh said, leaning forward.

"No!" I exploded, causing the same nosy table of guests to turn. More quietly, I repeated, "No. The problems we had before will never go away. You know what they say about east is east, and west is west."

"That's a cliché," Hugh said. "I would have thought better of you."

"I'm glad you're disappointed. That makes it easier to leave." I stood up and took the key card out of my jeans pocket.

"I don't believe you," he said. "I'll see you tomorrow. Call me and we'll set up a time." He pulled out a business card. "It's got home, work, and my mobile numbers on it. I swear they're all in operation."

The "no" I wanted to say was sticking in my throat, so I looked at him one last time and walked away, ignoring the card lying on the table. Hugh didn't come after me.

Upstairs, I found I couldn't get the key card to work in my door. So much for forty-dollar-a-night hotel deals. Once again, I slunk downstairs, hoping I wouldn't run into Hugh. From the hotel's front desk, I could see that he'd left the table where we'd sat together. Just my glass, Hugh's teacup, a few dollar bills, and his business card remained. Since Hugh wasn't there to see me do it, I scurried in and picked up the business card. I was curious about where he worked, I told myself. That was all.

I went back to the reception desk, where I saw that the desk clerk was different from the previous evening.

I was faced with a slight young man with a wispy goatee, which was ironically perfect with his mock-colonial American uniform.

"My key card doesn't work—Brian," I added after reading the name on his badge. It was so odd, this custom of Americans offering up first names instead of second names. I guessed it was supposed to foster friendly feelings, but at this point, I was not in the mood.

"Oh, yeah? There's been a lot of that with this group," he said.

"You mean—because we're Japanese we don't know how to open doors?"

"I dunno, ma'am. I just work here at night. What's your room number?"

"Four-ten."

"Name?"

"Rei Shimura." Brian recoded my key card without asking for ID, which was lucky because my wallet was in my room. I said thank you and went off.

What would Hana do in my situation? I wondered as I got dressed for bed again. She was interested in sleeping with a sexy stranger. I had one who was perfect for her. Ha.

I wasn't sure what Hugh really wanted from me. Letting him reenter my life, after having felt so embarrassingly rejected, would salvage my bruised ego—but was unfair to Takeo. Also, the way Hugh had compared me to England, the mother country he resented, was just too Freudian for my taste. Or was it Jungian? I would ask my father his opinion of the metaphor if it were not actually happening to me.

As I went to hang up my jeans in the closet, my eyes fell on the suitcase where I'd put the kimono. My suitcase really wasn't a safe place for long-term storage. If I still had a bank account in America, I could have taken the kimono there for storage in a safe-deposit box. I wondered if Allison could do that for me.

I unzipped my suitcase and moved aside the clothes I hadn't yet had time to put away. The whole suitcase seemed messier—but somehow less crowded.

Once I got to the bottom, I knew why.

The bride's kimono was gone.

9

I did the illogical thing first—yanked open the door and stared down the hall, wanting a glimpse of the thief. Nobody was there, of course. I went back in my room and sat down on my unmade bed, trying to recall the last time I'd checked on the safety of the kimono. I'd carried the bag up to my room around four-thirty and placed it in the suitcase. The door had always been locked, but I'd left the room twice: initially, to help Kyoko Omori look for Hana at the mall, and, in the last half hour, when I'd been with Hugh in the hotel lounge.

I put my head in my hands, thinking. The thief had probably not stopped at the kimono but gone into my valuables, too. My money and credit cards were in my backpack, but I'd left my passport, airline tickets, and pearl earrings in my underwear drawer. With a feeling of dread, I opened the drawer and shuffled my hands through the practical Jockey cottons and a few silk lingerie sets that matched—those given to me by Hugh, of course, and not Takeo, because he didn't like shopping. I tossed the contents of the entire drawer on the floor and found that the pearls were still in their purple velvet case. Still, my passport and tickets were gone.

I was filled with a sense of anger as I began to search more slowly. My clothes were there—was that a damning statement about how out of fashion they were?—as well as *Stereotype A,* the Cibo Matto cassette, plus my Sony Walkman, and my lecture notes. The folder with the insurance information and agreement I'd signed with the Morioka was still around.

Fifteen minutes had passed since I'd entered the room and discovered the burglary. It was high time that I called hotel security. It turned out the hotel's security officer was off on break, so I wound up speaking to the young man with the goatee at the reception desk.

"We'll get back to ya," he said after I'd told him that a kimono, passport, and plane tickets had vanished from my room.

"What do you mean by that? I need to talk to the police right away. If this robbery occurred tonight the thief might still be in the building!"

"Security will help you with that. Just hold on till they call you back."

A minute after I hung up, my phone rang. I picked it up, hoping for a mature and competent security officer, but got Hugh instead.

"I don't mean to be a bother, but I had to talk to you again. Please listen to me, Rei—if only you'd give me another chance—"

"I don't have time to listen to you! Something terrible has happened."

"Did that missing office lady you were looking for come to harm?" Hugh asked instantly.

I felt embarrassed, because I hadn't thought about Hana at all—I'd been too consumed with my own calamity. "I don't know anything about Hana, but my kimono's gone. I mean, the Morioka Museum's bride's kimono. It was in my room, but now it's not."

"Are you sure it's not misplaced?"

"Of course I'm sure! I had it locked inside my suit-case, not that the lock was that tough to break, and my passport and plane tickets are gone as well, from my drawer. I was such an idiot to leave the kimono for even a minute. But I thought it would be safer in the hotel than if I carried it around the city. I was so wrong."

"Have the police shown up yet?"

"No. I haven't even seen a security officer yet, and from what the front desk told me, they can't guarantee the safety of objects kept in rooms."

"How much insurance coverage do you have?"

"I'm not sure exactly. I added the bridal kimono at the last minute to a group of kimono approved by the Morioka. I don't have a formal appraisal of the bridal kimono as I did for the others."

Hugh clicked his tongue and said, "That doesn't sound good."

"I don't see why. Mr. Shima, the registrar, gave me a document in Japanese, which I signed. That must cover it—"

"What does the document say exactly?"

"I don't know," I confessed. "I couldn't read the *kanji*."

"You mean . . . you signed a document that you couldn't read?"

"It was a touchy situation. I didn't want to *seem* stu-pid." Instead, I'd acted that way.

"Okay, what you need to do right away is to get someone you trust to make a translation for you. I'll turn around at the next exit and be back to help you make heads or tails out of it. That is, if you'll let me."

"I'll let you," I said grumpily. Hugh, for all his faults, was the closest I had to a friend in Washington, D.C. I knew that he might lead me astray on matters of the heart, but never on anything that had to do with the law.

A shower of knocks landed on my door. "Security! Open up!"

"What's going on?" Hugh asked.

"It's the hotel security."

"Try not to talk to them either until we've figured out the insurance policy. I don't want you to accidentally say something that voids the contract."

"Oh, no!" I hadn't thought of anything like that.

"You okay in there? Open up!" the man, who had a sonorous deep voice that reminded me of Barry White, bellowed from behind the hollow-core door. God, if I could hear him so clearly he could probably hear me as well talking to Hugh.

"Hold them off as best you can. I'll be with you within the half hour." Hugh hung up just as the security officer broke the chain on the door. Now the door banged open, ricocheting off a Dolley Madison portrait hanging on the wall.

"No!" I screamed as a huge cinnamon-colored man wearing a blue blazer embroidered with the word SECURITY stormed into the room. He held out a massive gray handgun and made sweeping movements from right to left. The whole thing would have seemed silly if I hadn't known the gun was real. I hated guns.

"Mark Leese, hotel security. I heard you talking to someone. Who else is here?"

"Nobody. I was on the phone." I kept my eyes on the gun. "Can you put that away? It makes me nervous."

"Surely, ma'am. Didn't mean to scare you." Mr. Leese pushed aside the lapel of his blazer and slipped the gun into a holster. He took a small notepad and pen out of his blazer pocket and sat down at the room's desk.

"Your full name, please?"

"Rei Shimura. But can't you just concentrate on hunting for the thief right now? There's a good chance he's still in the building."

"I've got to take a statement before I start any so-called hunt."

"Regarding the statement, I think I'd better wait till my attorney arrives to make it."

"Didn't you tell young Brian at the front desk you wanted to file a theft complaint?" Mark Leese frowned at me.

"Yes, I did that," I admitted.

"Well, hold all the attorney crap and give me your complaint, then. I got two more hours of shift tonight. I can't pussyfoot around."

"I'm part of the Japanese tour group. I'm not used to burglaries or guns and—and this kind of treatment."

Mr. Leese's voice softened and slowed as he said, "I apologize, miss. I didn't know you were part of the tour group—I thought you were American! Did you call the tour director yet?"

"No." The thought of contacting Mrs. Chiyoda hadn't crossed my mind.

"Okay. While we wait for your . . . *attorney*"—he raised his eyebrows at the word—"I'd like to get started checking for the stuff with the assistance of our house-keeping department. The front desk manager said you're missing a bathrobe, a passport, and plane tickets. Is that right?"

"Not a bathrobe! A kimono is a fancy-dress garment made of silk, and this one was old. Even more valuable."

"Well, most people would be more concerned about their passport, and tickets. There's a government office downtown that can issue your new passport—all you have to do is report the loss. And if you came in on All

Nippon Airways with the tour group, you won't have a problem getting your ticket reissued. It's a hassle, but not impossible."

As soon as he'd left me alone, I found the Japanese documents the Morioka Museum had asked me to sign. I tiptoed down the hall to Kyoko's room and knocked lightly on the door.

Kyoko was still wearing the street clothes I'd seen her in earlier. She was in the midst of hanging up clothes that I guessed she'd bought when she was at the mall earlier in the day.

"I'm sorry to bother you," I began. "I've got a problem. It would be so kind if you could translate a Japanese letter I have with me."

"You received a letter from Japan, Rei-san?" Kyoko sounded curious.

"I brought it with me. It relates to travel insurance on some goods—at least, I think so. My *kanji* ability is rather poor." I handed the letter to Kyoko, and she scanned it with a bemused expression.

"Oh, this is about kimono! Hana told me you worked with clothing design or something like that. But I didn't know—something as typically Japanese as kimono!"

Kyoko was reacting in such a strangely gushy way that my radar snapped on. I'd never thought she could be a thief, but maybe . . . as she read through the document, I glanced around her room. I didn't see my kimono, but still, I wasn't reassured.

At last Kyoko spoke. "This is a simple description of item number 1866 from the Morioka Museum. Shall I summarize what it says?"

"I'd rather hear it word by word. I'll write it all

down," I said, grabbing a pad of hotel stationery off the top of the desk, as well as a cheap ballpoint pen stamped with the hotel's name.

Kyoko went back and read the letter verbatim. I copied it in Japanese, and after that asked her to clarify a few vocabulary words that I'd never heard. At the end of it, I had to conclude that, as Kyoko said, it was just a description of the bride's kimono. There didn't seem to be anything that sounded like promises, or restrictions, relating to travel insurance.

"Thanks so much, Kyoko-san," I said, gathering up my things to leave.

"Rei-san, why do you have this letter? You don't work for a museum, do you?"

I weighed the pros and cons of disclosure. I wanted my problem to remain private; however, Kyoko had been staying close enough to my room that she might have heard or seen something. "I was carrying the bridal kimono from the Japanese museum to the one in America where I'm giving a lecture. There was a legal problem, so I couldn't put the kimono in the American museum. Sometime, either yesterday evening or today, the kimono was stolen from my room."

"How terrible! Oh, what are you going to do?"

I let out a gusty breath. "I don't know. I'm hoping that hotel security or the police can catch the person who took it. I can't possibly replace it because it was a one-of-a-kind antique."

"Oh, my. Losing something so special—it's almost as awful as my losing my friend."

We sat in silence for a minute. I was thinking of the two, Hana and the bridal kimono, as victims with a lot in common. Both had come over on the same flight. But while Hana was missing for the night, I knew that my kimono had to be gone for good.

"Hana-chan said you must be rich, but I guess you really aren't."

"She was the one with a status handbag and shoes," I said, feeling irritated. "Why did she think I was rich?"

"You were carrying boxes so special they had their own plane seat. Hana said she didn't believe they were souvenirs because they were so huge—and besides, nobody gives souvenirs to their parents, just to colleagues, friends, and neighbors."

"How stupid," I muttered. I'd forgotten about the nuances of Japanese gift giving when I'd told that casual lie. The conversation with Hana on the plane played out again in my head.

"What's wrong, Rei-san? You look as if you are feeling very ill."

"I'm—I'm just thinking." I sat on Hana's bed, staring at Kyoko, an uneasy feeling growing. Hana had said that she was getting married because she didn't have other choices. She'd confided to me her dream of owning a karaoke bar. She said she couldn't do it because of money, and the societal pressures of being a wife.

"Did Hana ever talk to you about wanting to open a karaoke bar?" I asked.

"Karaoke box," Kyoko corrected me. "A box is smaller than a bar. It's a tiny place where you can go with a few friends to sing and have it recorded. But she's not going to open a box—she's getting married."

"How much do you think it would cost to get a business like that going?"

"Not so much—I guess it all depends on location. What are you thinking, Rei-san?"

If Hana had the bridal kimono and could sell it for even a fraction of what it was worth, she'd have a karaoke box's rent covered for at least a few years. And if she opened her business in a small town or city in

Japan, she could get away from the pressure of her parents. And I wouldn't find her.

No, I told myself.

Hana couldn't have the knowledge and guts to pull off such a scam, I told myself. Office ladies might play fast and loose with their money and with men, but they didn't indulge in truly criminal activities—or so I'd thought.

10

I said a quick good-bye to Kyoko. As I emerged from her room, I caught sight of Hugh standing thirty feet down the hall, knocking loudly on my door.

Kyoko saw him, too, and tugged me back into the room.

"What is it?" I asked her.

"That man! He could be the thief. I saw him here earlier. He said he was your friend, so I told him your room number. I'm very, very sorry—"

"It's all right. Actually, he's my lawyer. He's going to help with the kimono problem."

We parted again, and I hurried down the hall to Hugh, shushing him. It was late, and I didn't want to wake the whole hallway of sleeping office ladies.

"Thank God you showed up, Rei. I was beginning to think *you'd* been stolen."

"No, I'd just taken your suggestion and gotten some quick help with a translation from my friend Kyoko. I think you might have met her when she gave you directions to my room earlier this evening."

"Whoever it was seemed very timid, and rather sad—"

"Yes, for a good reason. Her friend is missing, as I mentioned earlier." I opened my door with the key card and sat down cross-legged on my bed, working out a quick written translation of the Japanese sentences Kyoko had told me. I handed it to Hugh to read, and when he was through, he shook his head.

"There's no mention of insurance here. Do you have any document mentioning insurance?"

"Just the loan receipt, and as I told you before, the bride's kimono isn't listed on it."

"Who knew you had the kimono in your room?"

"Allison and Jamie at the museum knew. I don't know whether they told anyone else. Although when we saw each other at Pan Asia, I almost forgot about the bag holding the kimono. It could be that Dick Jemshaw looked in the bag and got interested."

"I don't think so," Hugh said. "I was the one who picked up the bag and gave it to the maître d'. I watched him take it straight to you. Besides, I can't imagine why you think a chairman of the advisory committee would want to nick a kimono. A hotel employee is more likely, I'd think."

"Perhaps," I said slowly. "There was a young female manager at the front desk who knew that I needed a safety-deposit box. When she brought the box out, I asked if she had anything larger available. She didn't, so I went away. I guess I was pretty stupid to leave such a big gaping clue."

"Don't blame yourself." Hugh came over to the bed and sat down next to me. He put a hand on my shoulder and squeezed it. "If anything, it's my fault. I'm the one who lured you from your room. If the theft happened when we were talking downstairs, I'll never forgive myself."

"It could also have happened when I was at the mall a few hours ago," I said. "I just learned that the girl I was looking for there—Hana Matsura—had told her roommate, Kyoko, that I had something of value in the boxes."

"What? How would she know?"

"Hana figured it out because we'd sat together on the plane and she saw the way I handled the boxes. I guess I just was not an experienced enough courier to be properly subtle. Anyway, who knows how many people Hana told about me and my mysterious boxes, or if she decided to hunt for the boxes herself? Supposedly she's out tonight looking for a one-night stand. I wonder if that's really true."

Hugh shook his head. "I can't even get you to drink tea with me. And you say a nice Japanese girl would want to find a one-night stand in a place where she knows no one?"

"She told me that she wanted to find a quote-unquote playboy. She planned to have a wild fling in another country, and then she'd go back to a regular life. I'm sure it's a concept you can understand—"

"You were no more a fling for me than I was for you," Hugh said tightly. "At least, that's what I hope."

I wouldn't give Hugh the gratification of a true confession. Instead, I said, "Well, back to the point of Hana. I think she could have gotten in my room to snoop around if she were able to get her room's key card recoded to enter mine. To get the key card working, all she would really have to do was say that she was me."

"But would the hotel believe it?"

"Sure. Hana is just a bit taller than I, and her hair is dyed close to my color. She's a friendly, well-spoken girl. Why would they suspect anything bad of her?"

"You do," Hugh said.

"I know it sounds crazy, but I can't rule it out. I've got to call the security officer to come back. Tell me if there's anything I shouldn't say, all right?" By now, I was feeling pretty grumpy.

"Well, you have nothing to offer in English that could show him that the bride's kimono exists. You'll have to convince him, somehow, that you lost it, and offer to have the museum people back up your story tomorrow with a phone call. I think the important thing is to get them moving on figuring out who of the hotel staff were around tonight and any unusual goings-on, during the times you were out of your room. I don't suggest you say *anything* about your idea that Hana Matsura committed theft. She could call your assumptions libelous, if she comes back tomorrow morning and gets hassled by hotel security or the cops. If she doesn't come back, well, that's a different story." Hugh paused. "How much talking do you want me to do?"

"None," I said. "I mean, if I need your help, I'll ask. But this is my loss. I think I should describe it to them myself."

When Mark Leese arrived, he wasn't alone—he'd brought the hotel's young night manager, Brian Hunter, and Mrs. Chiyoda, who was wearing a terrycloth bathrobe and a very annoyed expression. It softened slightly when she looked at Hugh—apparently, she liked a good-looking man, and Hugh obliged with a faint ducking of his head.

"I was woken with the story you're missing an item. My tourists have never before reported such a problem," Mrs. Chiyoda said, her eyes moving between us—as if she trusted neither.

"My lawyer, Mr. Hugh Glendinning, came to assist me because this is such a serious problem." I switched to Japanese and outlined to Mrs. Chiyoda the loss of the kimono, and the fact that some people had knowledge of the valuables I was carrying.

"Well, I knew, too!" Mrs. Chiyoda said. "You reserved a seat for some boxes. Spending extra money that way is a sign that the items carried on the plane are valuable."

Nobody else in the room could understand what we were talking about, and I felt my pulse race. Mrs. Chiyoda. Would she risk her successful career as a tour operator to steal from a guest?

"Where were you tonight?" I asked.

She glared. "At the hotel all evening, resting. If you don't believe me, ask the waiters in the restaurant who served me!"

"What are you all talking about? I need to take my incident report," Brian Hunter said.

The things the young night manager asked were all straightforward—when was I in the room, when was I not, when had I last seen the kimono? Brian asked me for a receipt to show the kimono's value, which of course I didn't have—just the short note, handwritten in Japanese, that Mr. Shima had written.

"I can translate," Mrs. Chiyoda said grandly, and she read it. She shook her head when she was done reading it.

"It describes a very old robe belonging to a museum, but it doesn't say exact age or value. I cannot begin to guess value—that is not my expertise—but I can think that nobody should have given such valuables to a young person to carry. Antique kimono are irreplaceable cultural treasures."

"Right," I said coldly to her. "Can't we move on and get in touch with the police?"

"What I'd like to do first is interview the maid and the maintenance superintendent to your floor—they'd be the only ones with master key cards to your room," Mark Leese said.

"As Mrs. Chiyoda pointed out, this is a very valuable item," I said. "We can't let time pass and for it to slip farther away. Starting immediately, I'd like the police to

conduct intensive searches of luggage at all the airports—Dulles as well as Reagan National and that one
closer to Baltimore."

"Miss Shimura, I know you're from a different country," Mark Leese said. "Unfortunately, in the U.S. of A.,
the police wouldn't put out an APB on a missing
bathrobe."

I saw Brian Hunter's mouth quiver, and then it came—
the laugh. He thought the whole idea of an all-points
bulletin for a young woman's bathrobe was hilarious.

"I keep telling you that a kimono is not a bathrobe,"
I said between gritted teeth. "Now, I've got a question
for you. There were two times today that the entry code
to my room didn't work. Each time I had the key card
recoded to work. Once it was recoded by a woman
called Julie, and then, most recently by you, Brian."

Brian nodded. "I remember that."

"At the time you said something that I remember very
clearly. You told me that there were a number of guests
having problems with their key cards. I want to know
their names."

"Ma'am, we prize confidentiality for our guests—"

"Let me put it another way, then. Exactly how many
requests did you have about entry problems with Room
410?"

"I'm sure just the ones you made—"

"How can you be sure? I mean, how can you be sure
that the person asking for entry to Room 410 was always really me?"

"We don't give out key cards without asking for ID.
It's hotel policy."

"You forgot to ask for my ID—"

"No, I didn't!" Brian was tugging at his goatee as if
he'd become extremely nervous. He knew that I knew.
But he wouldn't admit it in front of the security officer.

A cellular phone hanging in a case attached to Mark Leese's belt sounded a high, shrill beep. "Yeah. No kidding. We're in 410. See you." He hung up and grinned at me.

"Well, I have good news. Your passport's been found in the area where we recycle scrap paper. I guess you must have dropped it in your room and it was accidentally thrown away."

"I'd never drop something as valuable as a passport," I protested, shutting up when Hugh put a restraining hand on my arm.

A moment later there was a knock on the door. Mark Leese opened the door to a maintenance worker in a horribly stained uniform who handed him a small red booklet with a flourish.

"Found it in the recycling Dumpster. It was pretty close to the top," the man said.

"What amazing work!" I said. "Were you also looking for the kimono?"

"Sure. They told me to look for a robe, but I didn't find one. Anyway, why would it be in paper recycling? Something made of cloth would have gotten mixed up in laundry."

I watched Mark Leese turn over the pages of the passport with a frown.

I said what I'd been thinking since I first saw the passport in the maintenance worker's hand. "It's not my passport."

"How'd you know?" The security officer shot me a suspicious glance.

"Japanese passports are red. American ones are blue."

Mark Leese nodded. "Yes, unfortunately this isn't yours. But it's good we found it."

"Why? It's not as if you can give it back to the owner."

"What are you saying?" Mrs. Chiyoda interrupted. "Of course he will give the passport to me, and I will give it to the correct member of my tour group!"

"You can't give it to Hana if she's not here," I snapped.

"How did you know the name on the passport?" Mark Leese demanded. Every face in the room turned to me.

I looked at Hugh, and he shook his head ever so slightly. I remembered belatedly that he'd urged me to keep Hana's name quiet for the time being. I'd spoken without thinking because I wanted to confirm my suspicion.

"Hana is a friend of mine," I said, making a slight exaggeration. "She was supposed to meet me earlier today and she never showed up. Her roommate and I are a little worried about her whereabouts. In fact, we searched the mall for her between seven and eight-thirty this evening."

"It's just midnight! Don't worry," Mrs. Chiyoda said, giving me a phony smile. "Some of our ladies like to stay out quite late."

"You're *sure* you never saw this passport before?" Mark Leese asked. "You're *sure* you didn't have this Japanese woman's passport and accidentally drop it in the recycling?"

So he suspected me, all because I'd known the name on the passport. If he thought I was dishonest, he might think there had never really been a bride's kimono in my luggage—he could think I was concocting a theft in order to make money from an insurance company.

"I'd not seen the passport before," I said, my voice cracking. "I just sensed that since Hana Matsura's missing, she might be in trouble—"

"Please don't worry," Mrs. Chiyoda repeated to me. "Our girls occasionally stay out so late that they don't come back till morning. It is the excitement of travel in America. I'm sure that Matsura-san will be very glad that her lost passport was found so quickly. My thanks to the excellent work of your hotel staff." Mrs. Chiyoda nodded to Mark Leese and Brian Hunter. Then she turned to me. "Please get some sleep, Shimura-san. It will be a long day tomorrow at Potomac Mills."

"I'm not going. I've got to work." Though I would have gone in a flash if that mall had a boutique that could replace the kimono I'd lost. But this was the twenty-first century, not the nineteenth, and the fabric of the day was polyester, not Japanese silk. And I was no longer in Japan but America, where things moved more quickly and dangerously than I'd remembered.

11

When I peered at the clock radio the next morning and saw it was seven-thirty, my first smug reaction was that I'd adjusted to the U.S. time difference. A half minute later the events of the previous evening came back. It was around one A.M. when our tense gathering had broken up and I'd walked Hugh Glendinning to the hotel lobby to say good night. He had looked at me for a long moment and asked, "Do you want me to stay?"

"Of course not! You know how I feel about you—I mean, how I *don't* feel about you." I was blushing, giving myself away.

"Forget it, then. I just thought you might be nervous about security. Do you think you'll move out tomorrow?"

I shook my head. "I'm not particularly afraid for myself. And I know I've got nothing left to steal—not unless the thief is into vintage clothes, which I doubt, because my own wardrobe was left untouched."

Hugh cracked a smile. "Every cloud has a silver lining. I'll go off now, as my day tomorrow is quite demanding. I could meet you for dinner, though. Call me, if you'd like that."

He'd put the ball in my court, but before I had a chance to volley back, I had to deal with meeting Allison to discuss my outlines and then figuring out whether to tell her, as well as the Northern Virginia police, about the stolen kimono. The more I thought about getting police help, the warier I felt. I knew that the police in my mother's hometown of Baltimore—just forty miles north of where I was—couldn't even solve 50 percent of the city's homicides. I could only imagine how little energy would be devoted to a hunt for a kimono that belonged to a Japanese institution. If I reported the theft to the police, the only certainty I could count on was that Mr. Shima and his cohorts would hear that I'd fallen down in my courier duties within my first twenty-four hours of service. Furthermore, the kimono exhibition hadn't yet opened at the Museum of Asian Arts. The Morioka Museum might decide to remove all their kimono because of the theft of the one that the Museum of Asian Arts hadn't been willing to protect. Then I'd have Allison Powell furious with me, too.

No, I decided, it wasn't time for the police yet. If there was a chance that I could quietly get back the kimono from Hana, or whoever else had taken it, I'd be saved. The Morioka and the Museum of Asian Arts would never know. At least, that was my theory.

I couldn't dial my parents for advice because it was only four-thirty A.M. in California, so I decided to damn my budget and call Takeo Kayama in Japan. In Tokyo it was early evening. I called the country house first.

Japanese phones ring differently: they have a soft, fast, and high-pitched trill. I was overcome with homesickness as I heard the sound of the ring. If I'd stayed home I wouldn't have lost the museum's kimono. I would be starting off my morning with a nice long run, followed by a morning of shopping in antiques galleries or reading some of my trade magazines. How peaceful my old life had been.

When nobody picked up, I decided to try the city apartment where Takeo occasionally stayed during the week. Again, the phone rang with the same trill, and I felt as homesick as before.

"Yes?" Takeo said briskly, picking up the phone after the sixth ring.

"I'm so glad that you're there, I've got a big problem—"

"Rei?"

Didn't he recognize my voice? I answered crossly, "Yes, I'm calling from my hotel."

"Oh. I was just about to go out."

"Out? You never go out!" Was it my imagination, or was there the sound of someone else's voice in the background? A woman's voice. Well, it was probably his sister. Her apartment was next door to his.

"Natsumi and I are going to the engagement party for a family friend. But you can tell me quickly what's going on."

"Okay. I really just have one question. If you were responsible for something precious that belonged to another person, and that precious item disappeared, would you tell the person immediately or try your best to find it before confessing about the loss?"

"Is the person in question Japanese?"

"Yes."

"You lost my safety charm, didn't you?" There was accusation in his tone.

"No, no, it's still in my carry-on bag." I was irritated that Takeo was so wound up about his silly amulet. "One of the Morioka kimono that I brought was stolen from my room. I reported it to hotel security, but I haven't done anything about the police yet because I think there might be a chance I can get it back. That is, if the person I suspect of taking it actually took it."

"Oh, no. That sounds complicated—"

"It's a complete disaster. It turns out that because this kimono was never listed on the Museum of Asian Art's loan receipt, it might not be insured against loss. It's worth fifty thousand dollars at least—not to mention that it's a one-of-a-kind piece that can't be replaced."

"Rei, I'm sorry. That's such bad news—I wish I could help you, but I've got to go out right now."

"Just answer my question first. Do you think the Morioka people would be more disturbed if I don't go to the police immediately?"

"I don't know. Theft is quite disturbing to the Japanese psyche, maybe because we have so little of it here, and everyone thinks it's done by foreigners. It's really unfortunate that the treasure was stolen in the U.S."

"Ironically, I think it might have been a Japanese thief."

"Who would believe you? The Morioka is a conservative Japanese institution. I suspect they'll describe the crime as something done by the Americans against the Japanese."

"Oh, my God." I thought it had been bad when the Japanese media had caught me in a clinch with Takeo, but this would be far worse. It could set back foreign relations between the two nations.

"I'll call you when I get a chance," Takeo said. "Try to keep your spirits up."

He'd hung up before I could reply with similar good wishes. What a strange conversation. Still, he'd confirmed what I thought about not telling the Morioka the bad news too early.

I had a quick room-service breakfast of a bagel and juice, then picked up my note cards relating to kimono and prepared to head down to the hotel's business center. I still had to work up two lecture outlines for Allison. I looked at the clock and saw that it was not yet eight A.M.—the scheduled time of departure for the office ladies' trip to Potomac Mills. There was one last thing I could do before going downstairs.

I called Room 401, and a soft voice answered in Japanese. Kyoko, I thought, judging from the hopeful tone.

"Hi, it's Rei. Did Hana come back?" I said, sensing the answer.

"No. I'm very worried." Kyoko's voice quavered.

"Well, maybe she's en route. It must have been a really fun night for her," I said sarcastically, thinking about how hard my own evening had been.

"Rei-san, what about your meeting with the lawyer? Is everything all right now?"

"Not really," I said. "The kimono's still missing. By the way, I'd appreciate it if you keep that information private. I would be embarrassed if others knew of my misfortune."

"Of course," Kyoko said. "I'm not a gossip like Hana was."

I felt a sense of foreboding twist in my stomach at her use of the past-tense verb. It was as if Kyoko had decided Hana had died. "About Hana," I began. "Why don't you tell Mrs. Chiyoda that she's missing? You shouldn't have to go through this misery alone. She might have given Hana some tips on where to look for guys—you never know. She is the tour group leader."

"Yes, that's a good idea. Maybe I'll get a chance to speak to her before we leave for Potomac Mills."

I hung up with Kyoko and went downstairs to the hotel's business center, which was a conference room that had a couple of computer terminals, a printer, a fax machine, and Saundra, the hotel's gum-chewing "business associate."

"Do you want to check e-mail?" Saundra asked when I checked in at her desk.

Instead of snapping at her that I didn't believe in e-mail, I said, "I'd like to write something and print it out. Do you have a word processor or electric typewriter?"

"We used to have a word processor, but when it broke, nobody around here could fix it. Most guests know how to keyboard on the computers—we have both a Mac and an IBM compatible. Which do you want?"

"I'm afraid I don't know how to use either," I said, feeling stupid. How had I managed to go so long in my life without using computers? At home in Japan, I still used a word processor that I'd gotten secondhand from the office of the kitchenware company where I once taught English.

Saundra looked sadly at me and said, "With tutorial instruction—that means, me helping you—the fee is fifteen dollars per quarter hour. Once you get started, I'm sure you'll do fine."

She was right. It didn't take more than ten minutes for me to learn how to format, save, and print my work. The harder part was bringing in the two specific women and their clothing to illustrate the power that Japanese women had in fostering opulent kimono design in the Edo period—and to show how, with Japan's increasing wealth during this time, kimono styles, as well as roles for women, became more circumscribed. I'd thought this all through back in Japan, but putting it down on paper for Allison Powell's inspection was a bit unwieldy.

As I bluffed my way along, I thought that in a sense, what had happened with kimono design in the past was recurring with modern office ladies' shopping mania. Because Hana and Kyoko's fathers were solid providers, the girls were able to spend their own income on travel and luxuries. They would marry new providers, and if luck was with them, keep shopping. Hana had talked about escaping this routine with an overseas sex fling, but still, she was looking forward to a future as tightly bound in tradition as that of my Japanese aunt or my grandmother.

After two hours, I printed out what I had composed, signed the bill that Saundra prepared for me, and went up to my room to dress for Washington. Then I went down to the front desk, where Julie, the woman who had helped me with my key card the first time around, was checking in some new guests.

"I'm Rei Shimura. Yesterday I had a problem with my key card. I don't know if you remember," I began.

"Oh, yes, Miss Shy-myoore."

"Well, yesterday evening I reported a theft from my room. I don't know if you heard about it?"

"I saw it on the log that the night manager leaves for the next manager on duty. I'm sorry you're missing some items, but as you must know from the sign on your door, the hotel cannot be held liable for items guests claim are missing from their rooms."

"I see. How often does this kind of thing happen here?"

"Not often at all," Julie said, sounding defensive. "Most of our guests like to use safety-deposit boxes. I know I showed you one yesterday, but you turned it down—"

"The item that I had was too large."

"The kimono, maybe, but not the passport and plane tickets."

Brian had written a surprisingly thorough report, but Julie still didn't seem to care. I looked at the front-desk manager, trying to think how I could coax her into action. She seemed a rather prissy sort. I'd have to play on that.

"Yesterday, you quite properly asked me for identification when I told you that I needed my key card to be altered to get into my room," I said.

Julie nodded. "It's hotel policy."

"Brian mentioned to me later that there were a few other Japanese ladies having trouble with their key cards. Did you handle more key-card requests than the one from me?"

"Yes, if I remember correctly, I did. There were a couple of Japanese girls needing help, but it turned out their key cards were fine; they were just putting them in upside down."

"Do you keep a log of the guests who request help with the key cards?"

"No. It's a small enough matter, plus we know everything's safe because we check for ID each time we do it."

I nodded, thinking that Julie would be the last one to let a crook slip by. "Have you heard anything from maintenance or housekeeping about the kimono being found?"

Julie shook her head. "I'm sorry. It's red, isn't it? That would have shown up easily if it got mixed up in the laundry. But there's a bulletin in the employee area about it, so everyone's keeping their eyes peeled."

I skipped lunch because I was disheartened, choosing to walk the two miles to the West Falls Church Metro Station in my sensible low heels. I passed the length of the mall and thought how odd it was I wasn't seeing other people. All were enclosed in their automobiles, despite the fact that it was a sunny day in the sixties.

Hana had gone to the mall, and she'd never come back. Had she been kidnapped? I recalled the urban legend that swirls around every American shopping mall. It involves a kidnapper taking a child into a rest room and cutting and dyeing the child's hair just before an alarm is raised. The kidnapper always vanishes, and the child is always found. The story is scary enough to be titillating, but not so devastating that it would keep people from shopping at the mall.

I couldn't imagine that a woman as fit and young as Hana could easily be kidnapped, unless there was a weapon involved. It was easier to believe that she could have gone somewhere willingly with a one-night stand who had wanted more than sex. Something much worse.

I thought about Hana all the way into Washington, and then, as I got out of the Metro and started my trek to Kalorama, I moved on to the problem of how I'd tell Allison and Jamie about the kimono loss. In a way, they deserved to hear about it, because it wouldn't have happened if they hadn't rejected the *uchikake* for the exhibition.

A dark thought that had flitted through my mind returned. What if Jamie had raised the ruckus about not letting the kimono stay in the museum because she'd *wanted* it to be at risk?

It didn't seem likely, especially since she hadn't known that the bride's kimono was coming. Still, it was possible. By the time I reached the museum entrance, I'd decided to hold off telling Allison and Jamie what had happened. I would nose around them a bit longer and learn whether my suspicions were justified.

12

I arrived close to one so, unlike the previous day, the museum lobby was filled. I stood in line behind a half-dozen tourists paying admission at the reception desk. The tourists right in front of me had heard about the kimono exhibition from reading *The Washington Post* that morning and were disappointed that the kimono couldn't yet be seen.

"I'm sorry it's not open yet," I said, taking it upon myself to do a little public relations. "On Friday, when everything opens, I'll be delivering the lecture. I hope you'll come back."

"We were planning on going to the Smithsonian Friday," the first tourist said, still sounding annoyed.

"I think we can come back. Especially if it's a free lecture," her companion said.

After the two ladies had left, I heard Allison's voice behind me. "Rei, you seem to be taking over our receptionist's job."

"I thought I should explain the correct time so they'd come back," I said, my confidence suddenly faltering. "Was that wrong?"

"No, it's fine," Allison said, but from the way she was looking at me, I could tell I'd overstepped. I felt myself start to sweat under my tight-fitting vintage silk knit

Diane von Furstenberg wrap dress. I'd made an etiquette blunder in the country of my birth.

Upstairs in the curator's spacious office, Allison sat down at her handsome mahogany desk to read the outline I'd brought. I sat on a more standard-issue business chair—black rubber handles and a wool-blend upholstery—that was pulled up to a computer workstation made of melamine. Computer furniture was comfortable, but usually so ugly—yet another reason for me not to turn my Tokyo apartment into an up-to-date high-tech office.

The computer was on, and the screen in front of me filled with a jumble of advertisements, some of which were even blinking. So this was what the Internet was about: advertising. Buying things. I wondered what possible role it could play in a nonprofit museum.

I turned when I heard footsteps. Jamie had clattered into the room wearing a short black dress. Her feet were shod in unsexy Doc Martens, but even that couldn't disguise her long, beautiful legs. "Oh, hi, Rei." She was acting friendly, as if there had been no tension the day before. "Do you want to check your e-mail?"

"I don't have an e-mail address. Frankly, I don't know how you navigate your way past these blinking advertisements to get to e-mail."

Jamie laughed. "Funny that you say 'navigate'— that's the name of our software program. I could show you how easy it is."

"Jamie, it would be better if you went off-line so we can go into Word and revise Rei's outline," Allison said.

I glanced at Allison, realizing that she really was in a bad mood that morning. Jamie's face was pink with embarrassment, and I got up to let her have the chair in front of the computer. She moved about the plastic handle that I'd learned was called a mouse. Suddenly the page of advertisements vanished, and the screen was filled with something called eBay. In the brief time that it was up, I saw that it held a list of various antique furniture pieces with prices next to them—as if it were an auction site. Now this was interesting—auctions on the Internet? But Jamie made the Internet vanish and got busy typing descriptions of kimono.

"How long are you planning to take questions, Rei?" Allison asked, breaking into my thoughts.

"As long as you'd like," I said quickly. "I thought for the noontime session I'd talk for thirty minutes, and then spend about fifteen minutes doing kimono wrapping, during which time I could certainly answer questions. Does that sound good?"

"Sure. For the VIP reception, though, you shouldn't speak so long—twenty minutes would be perfect, with ten for question-and-answer."

"You both must be very busy with last-minute details for the reception," I said, trying to finesse my way into some hard questions. "How late did you work last night?"

"Are you talking to me?" Allison asked sharply.

"Um, well, I was curious about you both. I'm interested in the contrast between Japanese museum culture and the culture here."

"As professional employees, neither Jamie nor I clocks in." Allison wrinkled her nose, as if I'd made her think of distasteful pink-collar jobs.

"So how late did you work last night?" I repeated.

"Jamie left at five-thirty and I was gone by six. We leave before the guard sets the alarm, just to make things simpler," Allison said frostily.

Jamie bit her lip and said, "Allison mentioned that you were looking to do more research on courtesans and their kimono."

"That's true—and not only courtesans, but the

women who lived in the infamous Yoshiwara Pleasure Quarter."

"I was just thinking about books. When I was in school, I read a really lively and detailed text about life in late Tokugawa Japan written by an Englishman—Dunstan or something like that. It might have been called *The Sun Sinks* or something similar."

I paused and thought. It had been a long time since I'd read Tokugawa history. "It doesn't sound familiar. Is it recent?"

"Not in the slightest. It was published in the 1850s, and what I saw was a photocopy of the original text, which makes me think there were no reprints. There was a lot about kimono design in there; that's why we had to read it."

"So you're telling me about a good book that's completely unavailable?" That, or she was making a point of showing off in front of Allison.

"I don't know that for sure," Jamie said. "You could always check at the Textile Museum down the street, or at the Library of Congress."

"Perhaps I will. But can someone like me walk in and be allowed to handle the books?"

Allison sighed. "Rei, you're a guest scholar at our museum. Of course other museums will let you do research, once you sign a visitor's card. Just explain who you are."

I left the Museum of Asian Arts not quite sure what had happened. Perhaps Jamie was trying to throw me off her trail by offering me a supposedly helpful tidbit for my research. As I thought more about the name Dunstan, something snapped into my memory. There was a tombstone in the Aoyama Foreigners' Cemetery that belonged to Dunstan Lanning, an Englishman who'd somehow sneaked into Japan before the country allowed foreigners and had been executed by the Shogun government for disrespect. I could guess that what he wrote was hard-hitting and far from the topic of textiles, but now that Jamie had mentioned him, and Allison had heard her, I felt obligated to follow up.

The Textile Museum didn't have the book, so I decided to try the Library of Congress. It hadn't looked that far away on the map, but by the time I got there, I was thoroughly confused. Again, I was in for some grand architecture—this was a conglomeration of grand white buildings that looked like the last place anyone could borrow a book. I found my way to the Jefferson Building, and as Allison had said, all I needed to do was fill out a brief form in order to gain entrée to the collections.

The Asian Division turned out to be a vast area containing all kinds of books relating to Asia, predominantly in Asian languages but also in English. Towering stacks surrounded a long, grand reading room where I saw just a couple of men reading Chinese-language newspapers at long mahogany tables that were lit by lamps with old-fashioned green reading shades.

A librarian whose name badge made me guess she was from Thailand listened to my request, then checked the library's computerized catalogue.

"Yes, we have a book by Dunstan Lanning called *The Setting Sun,* as well as another book written twenty years earlier that is titled *A London Lad in the Tokugawa Court.* We also have a book written by a Japanese scholar in the 1950s that examines the life and death of Lanning."

I told her that I wanted to see all three books and settled myself down at one of the long tables, under the glow of an old-fashioned reading lamp's emerald-green shade. As tired and miserable as I felt about the missing kimono, opening these books, and reading quietly for a few hours, was a bit of an escape. It was a gentle way of delaying the reality of my need to report the crime to the Morioka Museum.

I had perfected a sort of speed-reading style in college, and this was the method I hoped to employ, given that I had such a short time to read *The Setting Sun*. The problem was that I had to be very careful turning its fragile tea-colored pages. After half an hour I realized that the book was a straightforward account of the brutality of the Japanese Shogun system; no wonder Dunstan Lanning had lost his life. At the same time there was an element of entertainment to the book, with references to the spending habits of some of the lords, especially on clothing. Ryohei Tokugawa's name appeared once, and it was mentioned that he received the bulk of his income from rice grown by farmers in the Kansai region. If Ryohei Tokugawa was a *daimyo,* as feudal landowners were called, he probably had lived in western Japan instead of Tokyo. I read on, but there were no further references to his life, and certainly none to his wife's.

When I'd finished with *The Setting Sun,* I opened Lanning's earlier book, which had a title that distinctly reminded me of Mark Twain's *A Connecticut Yankee in King Arthur's Court,* although of course, this book had been written earlier than Twain's—in 1830.

In this book, Lanning seemed more positive about the Tokugawas than he'd been in *The Setting Sun*. I read glowing accounts of splendid banquets and gentlemen's and ladies' robes, including a paragraph that nicely validated my theory that courtesans were the greatest fashion leaders of the time. Lanning wrote:

For the lass who has beautiful hair, complexion and composure, there is no greater fortune than to be in the

Floating World entertainment quarter. While the gates
are guarded, and the girls not allowed passage out,
there is no real desire to leave—who would seek to leave
the land of sweetmeats and delicious teas and silken
garments? In the case of ladies who are the favorites of
aristocrats, there is no limit to excesses allowed. A
young lady in the Yoshiwara Pleasure Quarter whom I
shall take the liberty of naming "Miss Love," is known
to be a favorite mistress of one of the most pleasure-
loving Tokugawa cousins. Miss Love has such an enthusiasm for fashion that she has brought about the
employment of two dozen weavers and embroidery experts solely responsible for her clothing.

I paused, and then read the words over again. Love.
The closest Japanese translation to that word was *ai*—
could Dunstan Lanning have referred to a woman who
was actually named Ai?
I read on.

On one memorable occasion, Miss Love had a finely
embroidered length of silk inscribed with poetic verses
by various aristocratic men of her acquaintance. After
the fabric had been covered by calligraphy to her satisfaction, she had it sewn into a kimono for herself. The
only person in the Tokugawa Court not charmed by this
robe of words was the courtesan's most special patron,
who was said to have flown into a jealous rage at the
thought of other nobles' hands touching the silk of a
garment worn by his beloved.

I felt my heart begin to pound as I thought about Ai's
red-and-pink *furisode* that I'd brought to the Museum
of Asian Arts. It was inscribed elegantly with several
lines of calligraphy. I knew from the notes given to me

by the Morioka Museum the name of each noble who had signed the robe.

I stopped myself. I was stretching a guess into a theory—a risky thing to do. But I had to admit there were bits and pieces that matched up. Fact one: Ai-san was the possible name of a young woman who lived in Tokyo, where she created a fabulous kimono wardrobe that was bankrolled by a Tokugawa family member. Fact two: In 1830, a woman called Ai, who owned a kimono collection more appropriate for a courtesan than an upper-class virgin, married a tea-shop owner in Osaka, a city in the Kansai region—territory under the influence of Ryohei Tokugawa.

"We're closing soon," a voice said in my ear. "Did you find what you needed?"

"Is there a way I could borrow these books? I haven't even gotten to the biography—"

The woman shook her head. "I'm sorry. But I think you might be able to find the biography of Dunstan Lanning at a good bookstore, since it's still in print."

"Thanks," I said, and rapidly began copying down the terrific passage I'd read about Miss Love. Then I resumed my work, no longer speed-reading, because I was desperate to catch another reference to Miss Love.

Dunstan Lanning was a great raconteur, but his stories certainly meandered. It wasn't until a hundred pages later that I found a reference to the Tokugawa lord's final gift of clothing to Ai—a splendid *uchikake* patterned with a *tsujighana* design of mandarin ducks, for her arranged wedding to a commoner in a distant town. "It was not that the Lord had tired of the lovely Miss Love, who was just entering her twenties—in this gentleman's opinion, the most graceful time in a woman's life. It was that the wife had grown tired of hearing admiring gossip about a lovely, younger lady who had more splendid robes."

This was it, I felt with a flush of excitement. Not only did I have a reliable account of Ryohei Tokugawa's mistress wearing a calligraphy-inscribed robe, I now had the evidence of the wedding kimono patterned with mandarin ducks. Ai Otani was the character Dunstan Lanning called Miss Love. When I returned to Japan, I could tell Ai Otani's great-great-great-grandson that he could be proud of his ancestor, indeed.

But just as I'd received the answer, I'd been given a new set of questions.

Why had Allison Powell selected a group of kimono belonging to two women who were rivals? If Allison actually knew the connection between Mrs. Ryohei Tokugawa and Ai-san, why hadn't she made it clear to me? Was it some kind of test of my own research abilities? And finally, if the two women at the Museum of Asian Arts were harboring secret knowledge about the kimono, why had Jamie told me about the Library of Congress, thus leading me straight to the key?

13

$\mathcal{I}$n the gentlest way possible, the librarian urged me out of the reading room at two minutes to five. I didn't mind. I had learned more than I expected about the lineage of the kimono I had been carrying. At this point I knew I should go back to rest at the Washington Suites, but I was too wound up.

I took a short taxi ride to Dupont Circle, and once there, I went straight to a place I'd noticed when I'd gotten out of the Metro earlier: Kramerbooks. There, I found a tenth-edition copy of the biography of Dunstan Lanning. The bookstore had a pleasant café, so I sat down and ordered a caffe latte. After all, it was six A.M. Tokyo time—I was just starting to wake up. As I was thumbing through my backpack looking for a pen to use for underlining important passages, my fingers touched Hugh Glendinning's business card.

I really looked at it this time. Under *Hugh Glendinning* it read, *Assistant Director, International Contracts.* The firm was called Andrews, Ferguson and Cheyne and was located downtown on I Street.

"Mr. Glendinning's office, Rhiannon speaking." A woman with a perfect BBC accent answered on the second ring. I wondered if the firm was the kind of place that thought British accents made good window dressing.

"I'd like to just leave a message for Mr. Glendinning to call me sometime, if he has the chance." I knew from experience that I could never speak to Hugh during the workday. He was always in meetings with bosses or clients.

"Is this Miss Shimura?" Rhiannon asked, pronouncing my surname perfectly.

"Yes," I said, feeling spooked. Had he told the office about me? How bizarre—how different from our time in Tokyo, where our cohabitation had been something we'd tried, quite unsuccessfully, to conceal.

"I've instructions to put you through immediately, madam. He'll be with you shortly."

Before I could react to this, Hugh's voice was on the line. "What's happening?"

What's happening? He sounded like a 1970s American sitcom. Is this what a few months in a strange country could do to him? I wondered if he'd gotten into Casual Friday dressing as well.

"Um, I'm calling because I decided I wanted to take you up on dinner."

"Great. I'm in conference right now, so let's make a quick plan of where and when."

"I'm in Dupont Circle right now."

"I can be there in, um, forty minutes. Meet me at the fountain in the middle of the circle, we'll go on from there."

I was left with some time to kill, during which I read a third of the biography of Dunstan Lanning. I was beginning to think Lanning was a bit like my friend Richard Randall—fawning when it came to matters of fashion, but at heart a genuine, honest person. Dunstan Lanning had been killed because he'd published an account of an aristocrat who beat an innocent peasant to death—a mention that could only have embarrassed the Shogunate.

I concluded my reading session thinking that Dunstan Lanning had been a fairly reliable narrator— unfortunately, too honest to save his own head. It was a miracle that his books had made it into print in England, and were waiting for me to find in Washington, D.C., 150 years after their original publication.

It was five thirty-five, and I needed to go off to meet Hugh. In the bookstore's tiny bathroom, I tried to freshen up, but somehow I had misplaced my last MAC lipstick. There was nothing I could do to improve myself except run a comb through my hair. What would Miss Love have done? Pinch her cheeks, maybe. Blacken her teeth with coal, for a fashionable smile.

I skipped both.

The fountain where Hugh had asked me to meet him was smack in the middle of Dupont Circle—literally surrounded by lane upon lane of buzzing traffic. Fortunately, there were some pedestrian walkways and stoplights, so I crossed, bit by bit, with the flood of humanity. Once I had entered the small park that surrounded a fountain, I marveled at this tiny, busy green space within the traffic maelstrom. Old men in shabby clothing were playing chess at tables, younger men were cruising each other close to the fountain, and there were a few toddlers jumping around under the supervision of rather hip-looking parents—the kind with tattoos and copies of the *City Paper* or *The Gay Blade* tucked under their arm. The scene was quite different from the park in Japan, where the old people performed tai chi, and the young families seemed to be dressed like department-store mannequins.

Hugh was already sitting on the ledge of the fountain. He was wearing dark wraparound sunglasses and talking on a cell phone. In other words, he looked like a lot of the American yuppies I'd seen in the Starbucks on Connecticut Avenue. I wouldn't have known him except for the gorgeously tailored suit in a soft, mushroomy color, and the fact that he was waving at me. I kept to an even pace, though a part of me wanted to sprint to him. By the time we were face-to-face, his phone was off and in his pocket.

"Aren't you a picture," he said, taking off his sunglasses as he looked me over. I'd walked quickly enough from the bookstore to get warm, so I'd taken off my light coat.

"What a strange thing to say," I said, my eagerness turning to reserve.

"No, I mean it. The dress. Isn't there a photo of your mother in it?"

While in Japan, Hugh had checked out my family photo albums. He'd thought that my mother looked a little like Catherine Deneuve and was canny enough to say it to her when she phoned me once, and he'd picked up. After that my mother had been very interested in Hugh, and when he left Japan, she had mourned along with me. But six months ago she'd decided Takeo Kayama was the next great hope. I suspected my aunt Norie had told her about his *Fortune* magazine ranking.

"Of course it's my mother's," I said, upset that Takeo had popped up in my head again, making me feel guilty.

"There's a good restaurant nearby called Obelisk, but it can be a bit chancy to get in at the last minute. We can try," Hugh said, leading me to one of the many crosswalks radiating out of the park.

"Could we do something . . . unfashionable?" I asked. "I mean, eat in a place that's low-key? I'm feeling a bit overwhelmed. After losing that bridal kimono, I found out some things today that are . . . incredible. I need to talk without distraction."

"Well, then, if your shoes don't bother you, how about walking a few more blocks to a little place in my neighborhood? It's good for drinks and those little Spanish dishes—tapos or however you say it—"

"Tapas!" I said. Hugh was always awkward when the language wasn't English or legalese.

As we walked along from Nineteenth onto Columbia Road, the atmosphere seemed to shift. The gracious old town houses were home to businesses with Spanish, African, and Asian names. I heard unidentifiable Spanish pop music spilling out of some doorways, and a band I liked, Cornershop, singing "Brim Full of Asha" from another. There were shops selling incense and newspapers and vintage electrical fixtures. I would have loved to explore, if I didn't have so many problems.

"You really live in this neighborhood? What is it called?" I asked Hugh. This was a significant change, since Hugh had chosen to live in one of the most expensive, foreigner-occupied apartment buildings in West Tokyo.

"It's called Adams Morgan. It used to be very posh at the turn of the last century, but then it fell off. In the 1980s, immigrants from Africa and Central America started a great restaurant and club scene going on Eighteenth Street. Then the yuppies moved in all around." Hugh gave me a self-effacing grin. "I arrived too late to be able to afford to buy property, so I'm renting the second floor of a house on Biltmore Street. This neighborhood is like Notting Hill without Julia Roberts and Mexico City without the altitude problem. I quite like it."

"It's not your style, though. I thought you'd live in The Watergate or somewhere else similarly fancy and convenient—"

"No more cost-of-living allowance for me. Those

glory ex-pat days are over, Rei. I shop for provisions at Price Club and buy my clothes at that all-American mall near your hotel."

"I never dreamed you'd join the rest of us plebes. After all, you've got such a nice title on your business card."

"It's not 'partner,' which is all that really matters." Hugh raised his left eyebrow, a neat trick of his. "Anyway, less pressure is nice. It gives me the chance to leave work before seven, which almost never happened in Japan."

Hugh waved me into a plain glass door labeled EL RINCON ESPAÑOL. The owner beamed at him when he walked in, and the waiter called him by his first name. Within a minute we were ensconced at a cozy table with a carafe of a zesty Rioja between us. A short while later the waiter brought a savory pancake of egg and potato, a bowl of mushrooms marinated in garlic and wine, and slivers of a salty hard white cheese with some crusty rolls.

"This is so good," I said, relaxing for the first time all day. "I was looking forward to coming to America to eat all the ethnic food I can't find in Japan, but I've been so upset about things that I forgot to have dinner last night and lunch today. I'm behind schedule."

"That's awful, because you're even thinner than you used to be. We're going to have to finish up with a chocolate mousse at the patisserie on the corner. It's the best kind of chocolate with the essence of hazelnuts."

"Mmm. Well, it's true I want to eat chocolate every day that I'm here. I'm trying to undo the dulling of my palate from all those lousy Lotte bars."

Hugh smiled at my reference to the most popular brand of Japanese chocolate, which was usually the only option in Japanese shops. He knew me so well—

better than Takeo, I realized suddenly. Takeo and I had
never shared a chocolate bar together, because he wasn't
fond of sweets.

"So tell me what's happening, Rei," Hugh said, after
we'd both eaten a dinner's worth of snacks.

"This is the thing. I knew four of the kimono that I
brought over belonged to the wife and daughter of one
of the ruling Tokugawa families. The other four kimono—including the bride's kimono that was stolen—
belonged to a woman called Ai Otani who was alive
during the same time. Jamie—she's the conservator at
the museum—suggested that I look for a specific book
that talked about life under late Tokugawa rule. It was
a rare book, she said, but I might find it at the Library
of Congress. I did find it there, as well as an earlier
book by the same author with some really amazing information." I saw I had Hugh's rapt attention, so I
went on. "Ai Otani, the one with the really fabulous
kimono, was probably the mistress of Ryohei Tokugawa. And the other kimono that I brought—a very
nice, but typically matronly kimono—belonged to Ryohei's wife. She apparently forced Ryohei to drop the
mistress, and I'm guessing he was the one who
arranged the marriage between Ai and a tea merchant
in Osaka."

Hugh was silent for a minute. Then he said, "You're
going to give a great lecture tomorrow evening. I'm
sorry, but there's no way in hell I'm staying away."

"Okay. Just don't speak to me, and it should be fine."
I winked at him, then got serious again. "Don't you see
how strange things seem? If the Museum of Asian Arts
had made it clear that they wanted me to bring the kimono belonging to a wife and the mistress of an important lord, and talk about their lives, that would have
been easy to understand. But they never said the ki-

mono belonged to a pair of romantic rivals. I don't know if they were testing me, to see if I would find out. If Jamie hadn't given me the tip, I would never have known the truth—and just how awful the loss of the bridal kimono is."

"What's happening with that?"

"Well, as you might have guessed, the hotel staff hasn't found it."

"Did you report it to the police?"

"Not yet. I want to have a chance to check things out with Hana, the Japanese girl I mentioned to you. She's simply got to come back tonight, since the tour leaves tomorrow morning."

"What? You mean to say the office ladies arrived on a Monday night and are leaving on a Thursday morning?" Hugh looked at me incredulously. "They don't even have time to get over their jet lag."

"Well, the whole purpose of the tour was shopping. You don't need more than two days to shop this region. On the way back, they're stopping on the West Coast to go to a mall in southern California. Two days there, and then they'll be back in Tokyo on a Sunday, ready to go to work the next day."

"What if Hana remains on the lam?"

"Then I'll have good reason to believe she robbed me. I'll assume that she's traveled on to another place using my passport, and that she plans to sell the kimono. I was thinking that it might actually be easier for the police to track her if I get them in gear *tomorrow*. She could very well have used my name to obtain her seat on a plane, and that kind of information could be accessed by the police—"

"Rei, you're stalling. I don't understand."

I looked at Hugh. How well he knew me. "I'm not in a rush to do it because . . ." I paused, realizing that

Takeo's advice was the chief reason I'd not yet let the Morioka Museum know about the theft. I didn't want to go into the topic of Takeo Kayama with Hugh.

"Because you're nervous?" Hugh finished for me.

"That's part of it. The bride's kimono wasn't insured, so they might choose to hit me up for its value, since no insurance company's going to pay them. I don't even know what the value is. I imagine they can charge whatever they like, especially after I give my talk and reveal that Ai Otani was a much more interesting figure than previously thought."

"We don't know what they'll do until they have a chance to respond," Hugh said. "Don't lose sleep over that point."

"How can I not lose sleep when I'm still on Japanese time? Anyway, this evening with you has made me feel better, but once I leave this restaurant, I have to face reality. I'll call the Morioka Museum." I drained my wineglass regretfully. "I probably should go home now."

"You're in no state to be walking about in the dark," Hugh said. "Let's go around the corner to the patisserie, and then I'll drive you back to Northern Virginia. Don't worry, I'm safe to drive. I've only had one glass."

I wasn't safe to ride a private form of transportation with Hugh Glendinning at any time of day or night—I knew that from past experience.

"I want to take the Metro," I said. "It's always faster."

"I'll walk you there, then." Hugh put money down on the table and waved good-bye to his restaurant friends as we left. "Chocolate first?"

"I changed my mind. I'm not hungry," I said glumly.

"I can't believe how badly your visit is turning out. I'm really sorry."

"Yes, I'm sorry, too," I said, not looking at him as we

walked along. Seeing Hugh had screwed everything up. Because he'd come to my room, and I hadn't felt comfortable talking there, I'd left the kimono unattended. And though that in itself should have made me furious with him, spending time with him was stirring up all kinds of old romantic memories that I wanted to forget.

"I'd better put you in a cab," Hugh said. "You're obviously too tired to walk."

I pushed away the five-dollar bill he tried to give me when a cab pulled up the instant after he'd waved for it. "I don't want anything more from you, okay? I shouldn't even have accepted those tapas."

Hugh put the money back in his pocket and said, "Go to the Woodley Park Metro: it's the closest station. You shouldn't pay more than four dollars."

I got in the cab and told the driver to go to Woodley Park.

"I heard that already. I will not cheat you, okay?" The driver sounded as if he had African origins—he was a foreigner, just like me.

I turned around in the cab as it started to move, to see which way Hugh had gone.

He hadn't moved. He'd stayed in place, watching. He had the same expression on his face that he'd had the previous evening when he'd stretched out his hands to me and I'd stopped him.

A car moved in behind us, and then I couldn't see him anymore.

14

Jt was time for the See America Travel tour to move on to California. The next morning the lobby was buzzing with talk about shopping at the Beverly Center as the office ladies loaded their suitcases onto a series of luggage trolleys. I kept my eye out for Kyoko, who hadn't answered her phone when I'd called the room. Finally, at five minutes before the planned time of departure, she appeared, dressed in a Burberry raincoat over jeans.

"There you are, Rei-san," she said. "I tried to telephone your room a few hours ago."

"Sorry. I accidentally had it off the hook." I'd kept on telephoning the Morioka the previous night, and hanging up in fear after one ring. At last, I'd fallen asleep with the receiver on my pillow.

"I reported Hana's absence to Mrs. Chiyoda, and she has made a call to Hana's emergency contact number—her parents. I guess they'll decide what to do next." Kyoko paused, then continued in a lower voice. "I want to tell you something else. It's about Hana's luggage. One of her suitcases is not in our closet, I realized. I think she might have gone traveling."

"Why didn't you tell me this earlier?"

"I was too distracted to realize it. Then yesterday, when you suggested I look at the things in our room, I

noticed that there was only one suitcase of hers left behind—the empty one she'd intended to fill with shopping. She took away the suitcase with her own clothes."

This news—that Hana had split with her luggage, the
perfect way to carry the kimono—made me all the more
anxious.

"Kyoko," I said, "if you see Hana on the plane, or in
California or back in Japan, will you please call me?"

"Of course. I know that you're worried."

"Yes, I am. But please don't let her know that you're
contacting me. I want it to remain—private."

"Why?" Kyoko asked.

"I don't know how to say this without upsetting you.
I don't have any proof, but—"

"Oh dear! Are you thinking she was involved—
took—the kimono?"

I studied Kyoko. Her face looked worried but not
tense. If she had taken the kimono herself, she was
doing a masterful job of appearing innocent.

"Perhaps," I said. "What do you think?"

"The bus will be leaving in five minutes!" Mrs. Chiyoda broke into our conversation.

"I don't like to think that Hana would have done
that . . . but I don't know. I promise to call if I see her.
And we should talk again, when we are both back in
Japan," Kyoko said as Mrs. Chiyoda started dragging
her suitcase off.

"I'd like that," I said, but they were already too far
away for her to hear.

J watched the tour bus pull away and felt wistful. The
office ladies were going for a couple of days to Los Angeles and then home to Japan, where things were safe,
where everything worked. I was stuck in a country that

was supposedly my homeland but had brought me nothing but trouble. On top of it, I no longer had a passport or ticket to help me exit.

I turned from the foyer and began the walk back to my room. Julie, the blonde who was the daytime front-desk manager, was smiling and waving at me. "I have something you're waiting for!"

I rushed toward her and said, "The kimono?"

"Well, according to the contents slip on this overseas express package, there are three." She smiled brightly. "Funny, isn't it? Most people come here to buy things. They don't have them sent from Japan."

So Aunt Norie's kimono had arrived. I took them upstairs, realizing that I'd almost forgotten I was going to give a speech in a few hours. I was going to have to get dressed without anyone around who could help me. Kimono dressing was something I'd regularly practiced since I was fourteen—but still, it was a lengthy, challenging activity.

In my room, I slashed at the tape on the outside edges of the box with my nail scissors—angry at the fact I was going to unwrap a modern kimono, when all I wanted to have was a particular old one. But once I got the lid off the box, time seemed to stand still.

The first kimono Aunt Norie had sent was a rich reddish orange—the color of cayenne pepper. I unfolded the kimono and found it had graceful sleeves that stretched almost to my ankles. Norie must have worn it before she married and switched over to more appropriate shorter-sleeved robes.

This red kimono, handwoven out of a sumptuous *rinzu* silk, was decorated with *yuzen*-dyed cranes rising up from the hem. Cranes were a symbol of good luck and of long life, often, but not exclusively, appearing on garments worn by brides. The *obi* she'd sent along as its companion was a black silk brocade woven with red, orange, and yellow octagons.

The second kimono was subtler—a gold-and-cream-patterned *shibori* tie-dyed silk. I closely examined the tiny, puckered, irregular circles forming the shapes of different flowers and leaves; there was very slight variation, which told me the work had been done by hand. The *obi* was red-and-brown-striped silk overlaid with a pattern of gold rondels.

The final kimono she'd sent was a mossy green, about the color of Hugh Glendinning's eyes. A scene of the moon, stars, and long autumnal grasses was etched in gold and black along the left front hem; the same theme was reprised at the kimono's shoulders. The coordinating *obi* was black, with a repeating pattern of teahouses woven in gold.

In addition to the kimono and *obi*, Aunt Norie had included brand-new gold-and-black thong slippers, two pairs of *tabi*—white superfine cotton socks with a separation for the big toe—and an underrobe for each kimono, one cotton gauze half-slip and undershirt, small clips, and a dozen assorted sashes and waist-tying devices that would give me a properly cylindrical shape. I was familiar with all the underkimono apparatuses from my kimono school course, but there was one final element that surprised me: a bizarre ponytail elastic holder that was completely covered by short wispy lengths of black hair—hair that felt quite real to me as I fingered it. I experimented in front of the mirror and, lo and behold, found that tucking my short lengths of hair into it resulted in the illusion that I had more hair than I did—enough to make a nice low bun at the nape of my neck. It was a great device—I could see using it in my daily life when I wanted to change my look.

I spread out the red kimono on my bed and put the others back into their box. As I did this, my hand touched a card made of *washi* paper and decorated with golden ribbon. It was written in *hiragana*, the phonetic alphabet that I could read.

> Rei-chan:
> Packing these kimono for you, I was overcome with a rush of nostalgia. I wore the red one to a dance where I met your uncle; the green one to a very important *ikebana* exhibition; and the gold one to a wedding. I enjoyed these kimono, and I hope that you will, too. It is crucial that you wear the kimono as tightly as possible; I know that you are a girl who loves most of all to be comfortable, but please try your hardest to wrap the kimono so it makes a slim line. Remember the size and shape of your obi bow will reflect on you. As a woman of twenty-eight, you must wear a bow that is not extravagantly girlish. You must wear makeup, but it should be powder and a light, pretty lipstick, and very natural-looking mascara. Please practice the essentials of good kimono posture: straight back, with shoulders relaxed and chin down. And most important, walk with small steps, and your toes pointing inward. There is no point in wearing a kimono if you are going to walk like a man.
>
> —Your loving aunt

I smiled for the first time that morning. It was like having my aunt in the room. Between the lines, I could hear her saying: *This evening is important. Even though you may have troubles, you must hide them away. Stand straight, because you will be watched, and you will be listened to.*

I stayed in the hotel room all day, using the time to harass the front desk every other hour about their fruitless search. Then I began a search of my own, calling airlines to see if anyone named Rei Shimura had traveled to Japan or California. When a few airline employees were suspicious enough to ask why I wanted to know, I answered straightforwardly that my passport and ticket had been stolen. Most of them said they couldn't help me and that I should call the police. All Nippon Airways did confirm for me that my ticket had not yet been turned in. They'd take custody of it if anyone presented it at a counter.

"Take custody of her, too. Don't let her get away if you see her," I said. I hadn't received any word from Kyoko about whether Hana was on the See America plane or not. I wondered why she hadn't called; maybe there had been interference in the airspace, making a call impossible. Or if Hana had shown up, there had been no way for Kyoko to call me without being noticed. In any event, I would have to wait for news.

I wanted to discuss these new worries with Hugh, but I figured he was annoyed enough with my behavior the previous evening not to want to speak to me. I doubted I'd see him at the lecture in the evening. I had told him that I wanted to be on my own. Now I was alone, and it didn't feel good.

I gave myself a full hour to dress in Norie's kimono. Everything went on carefully, in the prescribed arrangement: first the silk socks, then my own best silk lingerie, covered by a thin, gauzy cotton undershirt and half-slip, followed by a luscious green silk underkimono, which I fastened around my waist with a snug braided cord.

Once that was on, things got more tricky. I slipped into the red kimono and pulled the left side snugly over the right; then I pulled the thirteen-foot-long *obi* sash around my waist and tied it almost, but not completely, tight. The next part was inserting a slightly curved rectangular piece of cotton-covered plastic underneath the front of the *obi* and then pulling the sash totally snug. Japanese women sometimes joked that this technique was like an instant diet, because it constricted the waist so much. I always felt skinny when wearing kimono, though when I looked in the mirror, I could see that I didn't look that way at all. I could have exchanged my 110-pound body with my aunt Norie's 130 pounds— and you couldn't have told the difference if we were in kimono. The robe, and all its trappings, took over a woman's body—redefined it into something that was no longer sexual but highly decorative.

Kimono could be sexy, I reflected as I folded the *obi* into a smooth, tailored style that Aunt Norie often wore, then checked the result in the full-length mirror. To wear a kimono for seduction meant draping the back of the collar enough to reveal the nape of the neck in an enticing manner and tying the kimono loosely enough to reveal the underrobe, or a bit of the rich lining, when you walked. I knew these intimate ways to wear kimono, but I would never have dreamed of trying any seductive moves at the Museum of Asian Arts.

At the very end, I slipped into the *zori* sandals. They were about a size too small for my feet, but that was correct. It would keep them on tightly and foster the mincing gait that was part of kimono dressing.

At the Metro station, I began the slow ride down the escalator to the platforms, trying to act as if it was completely normal for a woman to be catching a subway at five P.M. dressed in a kimono. For the first time since I'd arrived in America, I was being stared at—by women and men both. As I waited on the platform, a young man sidled up to ask the name of the restaurant where I worked.

Instead of taking offense, I gave a short pitch for my free public talk at the museum on Friday. My train came and I shuffled on, my toes pointing neatly inward, aware that I had already stepped into the footprints of the alien woman I'd be for the evening. I would be gracious and calm. I would present the full glory of the world of kimono and, for a few hours, forget about the nightmare of the missing kimono.

From Dupont Circle, I cut through the side streets over to S Street. It was dusk, so some of the turn-of-the-century town houses had their windows lit, and I could see charming domestic scenes: a woman chopping onions in a cheerful red-and-green-tiled kitchen in one house, a man lying on his sofa reading the newspaper in another. As I proceeded toward the museum, the houses became even grander; many of them were diplomatic residences. These house windows were more likely to be covered with chintz draperies than open for my inspection, but I caught a few glimpses of shimmering chandeliers and handsome furniture and paintings. Washington was an interesting place—so much more aesthetically pleasing than the area around Nation's Place mall. If only I'd stayed in some little bed-and-breakfast in Dupont Circle, someplace where a sharp-eyed, quick-fingered office lady would never have ventured.

I took a couple of deep breaths as I approached the Museum of Asian Arts. Major Andrews, the guard I'd seen on my first night, opened it with a flourish. I moved through the crowded lobby and up to the grand staircase, which I climbed carefully. Museum employees were running up and down the stairs around me, carrying things, talking on cell phones. I'd never seen the place as busy as it was tonight.

"Rei! Oh, how wonderful you look!" Allison came swinging out of her office in a calf-length dark blue-and-purple *shibori* tie-dyed silk dress.

"Thanks. You look great in those colors."

"I don't feel great," Allison said. "It's been a very stressful day. The chef wanted to substitute California roll for grilled eel—can you imagine? If we served California roll, people would think we just ran out to the supermarket for the buffet."

"Really," I said. "Actually, I've had a stressful day and night, too."

"Please tell me after it's all over, dear. I just want to get through our talk in one piece. Now, don't worry about a thing—your slides are in order, your notes are at the podium. Right now people are having the first drinks and walking through the exhibition, so they'll be all excited to hear your comments about it. At six, Dick Jemshaw will give the opening remarks, and then I'll follow with my pitch, and then you're on for the last half hour. Ciao, darling, I've got to finish up a few last details. I'll look for you near the side of the stage when I'm finishing my remarks."

I went downstairs and saw that in the few minutes we'd talked, a great number of people had arrived. About half the American guests were in smart business attire; the rest were fashion mavens wearing the Issey Miyake and Rei Kawakubo style of excessively baggy clothing, as well as artsy types in vintage Japanese *haori* coats and indigo cotton vests. The Japanese-embassy guests had their own distinct look: the men were in dark suits, the ladies almost all in very fine kimono, but none in red like me. My stomach tightened under the rigid plastic board that helped my *obi* keep its shape. Should I have worn the softer gold or green? Would they think I was *iroppoi*—too bold and colorful? Would they sense immediately that I was twenty-eight and should have found a husband, and a quieter kimono style, three years ago?

I wandered into the gallery where the kimono were on display. As I began making my way through to check that all the labels were right, Jamie came up to say hello. She was wearing a long-sleeved black lace shirt with slim black trousers and black patent-leather pumps that made her look even taller, and thinner, than she was.

"What do you think?" Jamie asked, sweeping her hand toward the kimono in the gallery.

"It looks beautiful," I said. "When did they go up?"

"Well, I was done with vacuuming them by four-thirty, but hanging the kimono and checking the labels took a while—I think Allison and I worked till eleven. Major Andrews was bummed out having to wait so long for us to leave, and I was worried I wouldn't make it to the Metro before it shut down for the night. Fortunately, I got in."

"Sounds like a rough night."

"Yes, you should be glad you chose a freelance career instead of a museum job. You could set your hours the way you like—and make good money." There was a slight bitterness to Jamie's voice, and I could imagine what she was earning as a young museum professional.

"Actually, Jamie, I'm not rolling in money. I cleared fifteen thousand during my first year. I still have trouble knowing that I'll make my rent—it's a very difficult business." I was thinking about telling her how I was now responsible for the loss of the uninsured bride's kimono, but I held off. I couldn't say anything before I spoke to Allison—it wouldn't be correct.

"I'm sorry. I didn't mean to be rude about your job. It's just that—sometimes it's so hard here." Her back was to me, and she was hugging herself.

I walked around to face her, and I saw that she appeared to be on the verge of tears.

"What's going on?"

"Oh, just personal stuff. Once we get through tonight, it should be better." Jamie sniffled and looked at her watch. "The presentation's started. Shouldn't you be in there already?"

"I suppose so," I said, a brief stab of stage fright gripping my stomach. "By the way, I want to thank you for that tip about Dunstan Lanning's book."

"Oh, did you get something useful for the lecture?"

"I'd say so. I want to talk to you about it later."

There had to be four hundred people downstairs now—I could barely make my way into the gallery, where folding chairs made of gilded bamboo had been placed. Dick Jemshaw was making his opening remarks. He delivered something that sounded as if it had been canned ten years ago, speaking of his happiness to be opening an exhibition that would bring together two great democracies, and how, through appreciation of past traditions, we would all build toward a secure future. Dick thanked Ambassador Miura for being present, and the ambassador himself, flanked by two guards, came forward to acknowledge the applause and accept a certificate framed in kimono silk. Dick closed by citing Honda Motors for its generous sponsorship of the exhibition.

Allison ascended the speaking platform and thanked the museum's associates, donors, and friends. Then she began her comments by saying how unfortunate it was that Western society did not understand until recently that objects worn or used in daily life could also be works of art. In Japan, she pointed out, there was never a difference in status between a kimono artisan or a painter—both were celebrated. The Japanese understood from the advent of their civilization that artistic and useful items could be one and the same. The kimono was one of the world's greatest art forms, and the Edo-period robes on exhibit in the galleries were a tribute to a lost age in which beauty and idealism reigned supreme.

Even though Allison wasn't saying anything particularly compelling, she was a good public speaker. Her voice carried beautifully, and she smiled and made eye contact, using her hands gracefully to make emphatic points. I could see that a lot of people in the audience approved. When she moved on to introduce me, her voice kept the same caressing tone.

"Rei Shimura has come to us from Japan, where she is chief executive officer of her own firm devoted to the restoration and sale of Japanese antiques. In addition to searching out antiques for private clients, she has sold important Japanese decorative art pieces to some major Japanese museums and temples. She's also published articles in the journals *Daruma*, *Arts of Asia*, and *Guide to Ceramics*.

"We asked Rei to share with you a few of the most notable treasures from the kimono collection at Tokyo's esteemed Morioka Museum. Tonight, Rei will talk about Edo-period kimono designs for women. Please join me in welcoming our lovely, honored guest."

I moved forward to the podium, thinking I had not been so nervous in a long time. Allison shook my hand, beamed for the cameras that were clicking, and then walked off the stage. I adjusted the microphone down to my height just as Hugh Glendinning stepped into the room's doorway.

I hadn't wanted him to come, but he was there. He smiled at me rather tentatively. I gave him the tiniest nod and felt a strength pass between us. No matter how crazy the last few days had been, I was in charge of my talk.

It would go well.

It had to.

15

"Good evening to everyone, especially His Excellency Ambassador Miura and Madame Miura. Just like the languages I'll speak tonight, the kimono is of two worlds. It was born as a simple garment worn by farmers, but graduated into a garment worn by the upper class. Today it is a garment so expensive and special that it is usually worn only on special occasions."

I glanced around the room and saw significant numbers of people chatting to each other. If I didn't catch their attention now, they might very well wander out of the room.

I touched what I was wearing and said, "I selected this kimono to wear for you tonight because I want to communicate the fact that the kimono is more than just a historical outfit—it's a living symbol of social identity." I smiled at Allison, but she looked back rather cagily—what I was saying hadn't been in the script. "So, I'm curious about your skills of detection. Can anyone here guess what the style of kimono I'm wearing says about me?"

For a few painful seconds there was no reaction. Finally a Japanese woman raised her hand. She was wearing a dark green kimono and wore her salt-and-pepper hair in a smooth bun. Her eyes were sharp, and had a sparkle that made me feel I was in for something.

"Shimura-san, I would be honored to make an analysis," the Japanese woman said in English. "But please turn yourself around. I noticed something strange earlier and would like to see it."

The crowd stirred—this was interesting to them, but suddenly I was struck with paranoia. What was wrong? Had I sat on a wad of chewed gum? But slowly I turned, hoping for the best.

"Yes, it is a most interesting situation. Miss Shimura's kimono is red, a happy color that young ladies wear mostly for special occasions. The scene of cranes hand-painted on the robe's hem is a classic motif, though the style of painting is a bit—what is the word, nostalgic?"

"The robe belongs to my aunt! It's actually thirty years old!" I stage-whispered in Japanese and then English. This brought a tiny ripple of laughter.

"Now, the situation that is confusing is the *obi*," the woman from the Japanese embassy went on. "The *obi* is a sharply contrasting pattern to the kimono, which was more common in the old days than the new, which makes sense if the kimono belongs to Miss Shimura's aunt. But what seems strange is the *obi* knot. Why has a young unmarried lady not worn her *obi* tied in a fancy bow? Miss Shimura has chosen the sober *obi* style of a wife. It is not possible to be married and single at once—at least not in Japan."

Now the crowd was roaring. I laughed, too, but inside I was cringing. The simple truth was that I knew that while single women were certainly entitled to wear the simple bow, it wasn't what people expected. In the interest of making a bow without any possibility of its falling apart, I'd decided to copy something I'd seen Aunt Norie do.

"You caught me," I said, smiling as best I could. "You figured out that I am an unmarried girl who yearns to be otherwise." As the crowd laughed again, I stole a quick glance in Hugh's direction, but he was no longer in the doorway. Either he'd left because he was embarrassed for me, or he'd found a seat. I couldn't worry about it. I continued, "This painful dissection of my sartorial style brings me to the topic of Edo-period kimono. I've brought a collection of *kosode*—the robes that are ancestors to the modern kimono—from one of Tokyo's greatest museums. This is a collection that has never been seen outside of the Morioka Museum, and what's special about it is that the pieces belong together—they tell a story of two women, who shared good taste as well as a passion for the same man. One would get him; one wouldn't. But who would be the victor when it came to style?"

I clicked the remote control for the slide projector and showed the first slide: the red *furisode* decorated with palace curtains, clouds, and fans. The crowd had quieted down; I could see they were interested. Even Allison Powell was smiling.

"Images of the Floating World; palace curtains that close lovers off from those who pry; clouds, to carry bodies to the point of ecstasy; fans, to hide coyly behind, or to relieve the overheated." I knew I was dramatic, but this audience, most of whom had already enjoyed a few glasses of wine, seemed receptive. "This kimono most likely belonged to Ai, a lovely and highly intellectual woman living in the pleasure quarter of Tokyo between 1820 and 1827. Ai's chief patron was Ryohei Tokugawa, a cousin of the Shogun. Ryohei paid for Ai's fine clothing collection, almost all of which she was intensely involved in helping design—although, of course, the weaving, embroidery, appliqué, and sewing were carried out by professional craftsmen. In this kimono, the patterns on the fans were executed by *shi-*

bori, a painstaking tie-dyeing technique. After that, she commissioned a renowned painter to *yuzen*-dye the curtains and fans on this kimono and asked three court nobles, including her lover, to inscribe original poetry in calligraphy on sections of the robe. The results were breathtaking enough to have framed as a hanging scroll, but Ai had no intention of doing anything so wasteful. She had the cloth made into a *kosode* for herself."

I smiled at the audience. "You see, a woman's worth was judged by her clothing. A smart, high-class woman couldn't read *kanji;* she couldn't be an artist or hold any kind of job. But she could commission beautiful clothing—paid for by her *shujin,* the word that means both husband and master. In the Edo period, wealthy wives and mistresses sponsored a renaissance in extravagant clothing design."

I went on for fifteen more minutes, talking about each kimono from the Morioka and the theories behind the design preferences of both the Tokugawa wife and Ai. I tried to pay equal attention to both women, but as I began the question-and-answer portion, people seemed fascinated by the idea of Ai. As I was retelling Dunstan Lanning's account of how Mrs. Tokugawa had forced her husband to give up Miss Love, I heard a loud voice in the rear of the room. Someone was interrupting before I was finished. I stopped talking and realized that it was a Scottish voice: clear, loud, and frantic.

Hugh Glendinning was speaking to someone at the door. I couldn't catch all of what he said, except for the last two sentences: "Where's the guard for the kimono gallery? We need someone there now!"

I wanted to drop my microphone and race to the gallery when I heard the urgency in Hugh's voice. I was wearing kimono and *zori,* though, which made that kind of physical impulsiveness ridiculous. Furthermore, since I was the speaker, I was in danger of inciting pandemonium.

So, into the microphone, I said, "I'd like to forward the request we've overheard for added security patrol to the kimono galleries. After they've gotten to their posts, you'll have plenty of time to get in there, too, and look at the kimono. Please take the time to visit the reception line in the foyer with Ambassador Miura, and don't miss the glorious food in Pan Asia. I'd suggest that you move to these places slowly, since there are so many of us here. Thank you again for your enthusiasm."

I stepped down, hearing the applause but concentrating on what was going on outside the room. The kimono gallery was across the foyer and up a few stairs. I could barely keep to my aunt's prescribed kimono waddle; it wasn't doing me any good against the dozens of people crowding the way.

There were two guards at the entrance when I reached it, and a quick glance revealed that all the Morioka kimono were hanging in place. Hugh was in the back corner, speaking rapidly to Allison. I started toward them, then stopped, remembering that I was supposed to barely know Hugh. I took a deep breath. The Morioka kimono were safe. My speech was over. I'd wait to hear what happened.

I went back into the foyer, and a waiter said, "Are you Miss Shimura?"

I nodded.

He pressed a glass into my hand. "Someone wanted me to give you this."

I thanked him and took the glass of champagne, with its base wrapped in a paper napkin. The napkin had been scrawled on in large, looping handwriting I recognized as Hugh's. I unfolded it to read: *I'll meet you on the Spanish Steps and explain.*

The Spanish Steps were a charming, thoroughly impractical flagstone stairway two blocks north of the museum. They started up high on S Street and ended low on Decatur Place. I'd seen them from the second-floor window in Allison and Jamie's office.

Hugh hadn't given me a time, so I kept an eye on him throughout the evening, feeling somewhat relieved that we had a plan. It turned out that the talk had gone better than I'd thought. At least a dozen people pressed business cards on me, hoping to meet later for consultations. I'd forgotten how forthcoming Americans were—I glowed in their friendly enthusiasm. The embassy crowd was nice, too. After I'd finished my glass of champagne and chatted with a few more guests, I saw Allison trying to catch my eye. I made my excuses and went to her.

"You were charming," Allison said. "I wasn't sure what you were doing at the beginning, but it worked out fine, though I wish you hadn't said anything about the kimono gallery at the end of your talk—"

"But I was worried! What happened there?"

"One of our guests sounded a false alarm. He thought a guest was moving too close to the kimono. This kind of thing happens all the time; it's really nothing to get in a tizzy about. Anyway, by the time the guard arrived, the troublesome guest had gone away."

"Why wasn't a guard in the gallery in the first place?"

"We told them they could go one by one to use the rest room or take whatever break was needed while everyone was listening to the lecture. Later on it would be too busy for that. I'd arranged to have Jamie in there while they left, but obviously, she must have had to step out for some reason."

"Don't you think your insurance company would want to have guards in the gallery at all times?"

"Relax," Allison said sharply. "There's no reason to worry about insurance that you're not even paying for."

I put my glass down on a Korean chest that I probably shouldn't have touched—or so I guessed from the way Allison's eyes lingered on my hand. I picked up the glass again and said in a tight voice, "There is reason to worry. You've got to have security in there at all times. Do you remember the bridal kimono you didn't want to keep in the museum? The one you said I had to take responsibility for? Well, it was stolen from my room."

"Oh," Allison said, her face seeming to pale. "Oh—"

"Yes, it's awful, isn't it?"

"It's—appalling news. But tell me, why did you risk leaving the kimono in your hotel room? I told you to find a safe location!"

"The only safe location I had access to was a hotel safety-deposit box, and the kimono was too big. I was going to ask you for an alternate suggestion, but the kimono never survived the night."

"There's no need to point fingers," Allison said coolly. "I empathize with you, and I'm sorry. Sorry that I didn't explain more to you about the minimum standards of care one employs when carrying museum pieces. I just didn't know. Sometimes you seem sharp, but other times, a little inexperienced."

I felt myself start to choke up. No, I wouldn't let myself lose control in the gallery the way Jamie had been on the verge of doing.

"I'm going out for a little while," I said, turning away.

"But we need you in the receiving line!"

I shook my head. "You asked me to deliver a lecture. I did that already. What I do now is up to me—just as the security of the kimono collection is up to you."

I clip-clopped quickly in my sandals up S Street to the top of the Spanish Steps. I looked down the charming, irregular staircase, and under the glow of a dim street-light, I saw Hugh waiting. His body was shrouded by shadows and his head was turned away, as if he were studying the row of beautiful houses on Decatur Place.

"Hugh, I'm here!" I whispered loudly as I started down the steps. He raised a hand in greeting, and I hurried a bit faster.

In the canon of Japanese ghost stories, there are plenty of accounts of demonic spirits who manifest themselves in beautiful human forms and seduce, but later destroy, the innocent or silly person who falls under their spell. I'd felt a surge of goodwill when I saw Hugh earlier in the evening, but now, as I took tiny steps down the steep flight, I felt some trepidation. Maybe it was because of the fog, and the way the steps reminded me of those that were shown in an advertisement for *The Exorcist,* the 1970s horror movie that had recently been rereleased.

"Rei?" I heard Hugh's voice coming from the wrong direction. What was going on? I stopped my descent down the steps for a second.

"Wait for me," came Hugh's voice again. It really was like a ghost story; his voice and quick footsteps seemed to be behind me. I turned around and saw Hugh. I whipped my body back in the other direction to gaze down the length of the steps. The person who'd been waiting for me had taken off. He ran a short distance down the street, and at the same time a truck that had been parked with its lights off suddenly started. There was a slam of a door, and the truck lurched off in the darkness.

16

"Did you see that man waiting for me?" I said just as Hugh caught up to me on the steps.

"Yes. I was wondering if you'd brought someone with you," he said.

"No. I came out a few minutes ago and I saw the man—person," I amended, since I really didn't know. "When I said your name aloud, the person seemed to acknowledge me, but somehow—I didn't want to go down. I can't figure out why I was spooked—or if the person was a man or a woman, for that matter." I was thinking about how Jamie had disappeared from the museum. She was close to six feet tall and had been wearing pants—with an overcoat on, and turned away from me, she could very well have resembled a man. Maybe she'd been waiting for me because she wanted to confide in me about her troubles at the museum—or because she had some other plan. No. I was being paranoid.

"It was a rotten idea for me to suggest that you come out here, in the dark—I swear, Japan spoiled me in that regard. I'm accustomed to feeling safe at night in big cities when it really isn't."

Takeo had said America was dangerous, but I hadn't expected to be at risk. But here I was, burglarized two days previously, and now almost lured by a stranger pretending to be my boyfriend—ex-boyfriend, I corrected myself. I asked Hugh, "Do you think anyone knew you wanted to see me at the Spanish Steps?"

"I wrote the note on a napkin at the bar. I suppose there must have been twenty people behind me waiting for drinks—any one of them could have seen. Plus I tipped a waiter ten bucks to make sure you got it—that could have attracted attention. I'm sorry, Rei."

"Let's just get off these steps," I said. "We'll finish this talk elsewhere."

"Where do you want to go?"

"Anywhere but here."

"My flat's about twenty minutes away—"

"No!" Just as with his car, I didn't trust myself to enter Hugh Glendinning's apartment and emerge unscathed. "I'd—I'd rather go home. Maybe you can walk me to Dupont Circle?"

"Better than that—I'm going to ride the Metro back with you. After what happened tonight, I don't want you out of my sight." Hugh had his arm around me as we began walking, and though he'd set off at his usual pace, he quickly slowed to accommodate my snail-like pace because of the constricting kimono.

"Sorry about the kimono," I said, shaking off his arm. The way he was touching me made me feel more like a doll than I wanted.

"It's gorgeous," Hugh said. "But it seems very difficult to walk."

"I'll manage. Anyway, why don't you tell me everything that happened since I saw you in the auditorium. I started talking, and then you left, for some reason. What was it?"

"I wanted to zip into the gallery to take a quick look at the kimono so that I could get more out of your lecture. When I got there, I saw there was only one person in the room—a guy who looked rather like a Japanese salaryman, but with bizarre behavior. He was looking inside the sleeves and necklines of the kimono, and all around the backs of the installed pieces, crawling on the floor, even looking up the skirts. I don't know if he had a fashion fetish or something more criminal in mind. He didn't know I was there until I coughed, and then he took off."

"He must have been casing the room," I said, feeling completely shaken. "Thank goodness you interrupted him."

"I wish somebody had caught him. Later on, at the reception, I told Allison in great detail about what I'd seen, but she seemed much more annoyed with me than anything. She thinks it was just a fellow from the Japanese embassy making sure everything was safe. I said, if you show me the guy you're talking about, I can tell you if he's the one, but she bluffed and said she'd get a reception attendance list from the ambassador's secretary tomorrow. I said there might not be any kimono left tomorrow if she waited that long, and then she said I was taking my position on the advisory committee too seriously."

"Well, I think she's negligent. Perhaps I should try to speak to the director of the museum—what's she called? We haven't been introduced."

"Her name is Marina Billings, and I've met her only briefly. I'd hope that she'd take the museum's security more seriously than Allison seems to do. But she's not around tonight—she was summoned home by her child-minder. Her young son had a high fever or some awful thing—I can understand why she left," Hugh said.

I rolled my eyes. I'd forgotten his reverential attitude toward families—it had been a sore point with us a year ago. Hugh had wanted children, marriage, the whole nine yards—or whatever was the equivalent figurative measure in Scotland.

We'd hit Connecticut Avenue and were now walking in the midst of many people dressed far more casually than we were. People stared at me in the brilliant kimono, then skipped over to Hugh in his trendy butterscotch silk viscose suit. We didn't fit in here any better than we had in Japan. Forget children and marriage, I thought grimly. Nobody would believe it.

The ride down the Dupont Circle escalator, I'd learned from my previous travels on it, was a long one, and quite steep. I held tight to the right-hand side and tried to look anywhere but where I was going.

Hugh was right behind me, and he kept talking through it all. "This is one damnably scary escalator ride. Going up isn't bad, but going down—well, I hate it."

"I think escalators are better than stairs," I said. "I survived a fall down the stairs at Ebisu Station a few months ago."

"How in the hell did that happen?"

"A man hit me. But that's a story for another time. Talk about something pleasant."

"Well, I think your talk went brilliantly. You've grown more confident in public, and your Japanese language skills have skyrocketed."

"A year will do that," I said, thinking about how my time with Takeo had changed me. So many things were better—yet why wasn't I happy?

Hugh had turned his attention to his wallet. "Hey, I've got nothing smaller than a twenty, and I don't want to jingle like Father Christmas for the rest of the night. Can you spot me a few small bills?"

"Sure." I gave him a five.

"Thanks." Hugh slid the money into the machine and

got his Metro fare card and change during the time I was still figuring out how to add value to the fare card I already had. I'd been using the same one for the last three days. He waited for me, and then we rode another escalator to the train platform that said SILVER SPRING. A train pulled in just as we got there, so we boarded and found two seats together.

"Well, I spent some time today looking into your legal situation," Hugh said, watching me lower my body onto the seat next to him, staying a good foot away from the seat back because the *obi*'s bow prohibited my resting.

"I hope it's good news."

"Well, it's a bit of good and bad. I called Metropolitan Insurance to find out if it was possible to buy protection for a museum item from overseas that had accidentally traveled without insurance. They said it could have been arranged."

I exhaled as much as the tight *obi* would allow me. "So Allison could have helped me out . . . but she didn't!"

"All she needed to do was write a letter, fax it to the Morioka for a signature, and then on to the insurance company. It would have meant the museum's registrar assigning it a temporary loan number as well."

"The registrar is away. I guess Jamie would have done it." But why not?

"The good news is that *you* probably can't be held responsible for the kimono's loss."

"How's that?"

"Mr. Shima lent you the kimono without bothering to check on the insurance situation. That's negligence. A judge would likely believe the fault lies with him and his museum's administration."

"A judge in America, perhaps. But what about Japan?" I asked anxiously.

My question got lost because it was time to rush out at Metro Center, along with the great wave of people making transfers. We made our way down the steps to the lower tracks, where the Orange and Blue Lines were. The platform was packed with rowdy teenagers, a few of whom pointed at me and did a weird side-to-side waddling motion. I wondered where they'd gotten it—some imported animated program? All I knew was that I must look like a joke.

When the train came, Hugh and I were momentarily separated in the crush, and when I boarded and slipped into one of two empty seats, a crying young woman sat right down next to me. Hugh took a seat across, mouthing, *Later*. Next to me, the girl blew her nose and wiped her eyes violently. It was hard to concentrate because the teenagers had a boom box that was blaring music that I hated.

The teenagers finally got out at a station called Rosslyn, leaving Hugh and me alone in the car. He held up two dollars in the air and beckoned to me.

"I meant to give you your change. Thanks."

"That's okay," I said, waving it off.

"You've been taking a lot of taxis, haven't you? Small bills are handy. Come sit with me and let's finish our business." Hugh looked at me entreatingly, so I nodded and went to him, tucking the two dollars securely in my *obi* so I could use them later to pay for my cab ride from the Metro station.

I said, "You said that the loss is the Morioka's responsibility. I don't think so—I practically got on my knees, I wanted the *uchikake* so much. Mr. Shima gave in because he was touched by my feeling. There's a proverb for it in Japanese—'when two hearts meet.' That's what happened."

"But would he risk his heart to put his own museum's

possessions at risk?" Hugh said softly, looking at me. Suddenly it felt as if we weren't talking about business anymore.

"It doesn't matter what risk he took. Mr. Shima can say whatever he wants to the museum director and insurance investigators because we were alone together in his office when I made the request. Mr. Shima could say that he *asked* about insurance, and I assured him that the kimono was covered. Or something like that."

"I see. You're worried he'll tell the story differently than you did? Perjure himself, if necessary?"

"Exactly. And please don't talk to me about this thing going to trial—it just makes me feel sick." I shuddered. "All I want is to get the kimono back from Hana. I don't want to prosecute her; I just want it back. If things stay quiet, the Morioka will never know the trouble I had, and there won't be any horrible stories in the Japanese media about my incompetence."

"If it's a situation where you can't eat lunch in that town again, you should move here—"

"Oh, what a great idea! Especially since Allison knows I am responsible for the loss of the bridal kimono. I'm sure she'll tell everyone else in the textile world."

"How does Allison know?" Hugh sounded aghast.

Looking down at my lap, I said, "I told her this evening. I was upset because she really didn't seem worried enough about the safety of the kimono on exhibit. I didn't want to see them vanish, too."

"So your loyalty was first to the kimono collection— and not to yourself."

"I just didn't want to add more losses to the tally I'm going to have to report to the Morioka Museum. It's such a mess."

I shut my eyes, but opened them quickly when I felt

the light pressure of Hugh's fingers on my wrists. When I gave him a curious look, he moved his hands up underneath the full sleeves of the kimono. Trust him to find the only form of access into the silk cocoon that covered me so snugly.

"This silk is amazing. Can men wear it?"

"It's called *rinzu,* and no, men don't usually have a reason to wear it, or touch it the way you're doing, for that matter." I began to wiggle away, but Hugh pulled me closer. Somehow, his fingers had traversed their way from the loose-fitting sleeves into the edge of the kimono's tight bodice. We were locked together, and I couldn't move without risking damage to Aunt Norie's precious garment.

"I'm sorry," Hugh said in my hair, not sounding that way at all. "I guess we're stuck."

"Wait a minute," I said. I took one of my hands off his shoulders and very lightly tugged around the top of the *obi* to release a bit of tightly wrapped kimono. Now there was more room, and Hugh slowly pulled his hands out.

"I've tried to be good. It's just that, well, you've looked so—untouchable—all evening that I couldn't stand it anymore. I've been dying to find out if you're the same woman underneath all the layers."

"I'm not," I said, finally ready to say what I should have said a while ago. "I've been meaning to tell you that I'm seeing someone in Japan."

"You're seeing someone?" Hugh looked at me with eyes that held a mixture of sorrow and tenderness. "Oh, my God. I had no idea that I buggered things so badly that you needed professional help."

"I'm not seeing a shrink. I'm seeing a man. A boyfriend." As his expression moved from pity to horror, I said quickly, "It started about six months ago. I'm quite—committed—to this man. Everyone thinks he's just right for me."

Hugh's face was now utterly grave. It reminded me of how I'd felt when I'd opened my suitcase and found the bride's kimono gone. After a few seconds, he said, "I know I deserve this. But to whom did I lose, another *gaijin* or one of your own?"

One of your own. It was the first time I'd ever heard him talk about my Japanese side in such a way, and it caused a sharp blaze of anger to rush through me. "Takeo's Japanese, as you can probably guess from his name. He loves Japan and plans to live there forever."

"So that's why you chose him—he loves Japan." Hugh had a mocking tone in his voice that I didn't like. "Forgive me for being blunt, but I think you'd be better off with someone who loves you more than a country."

"You're a terrible one to talk about love. You ran off to another continent just when things got serious. I don't know what's going on between us now, exactly— friendship, helping out, quasi-dating—but I'm sure that once I board the plane back home, you'll strike me from your mind again."

"Do you really think that?"

"Yes! And I hate what you did, bringing me here under false pretenses—"

Hugh sighed, leaning his head against the window. At last he spoke. "How many times can I can say I'm sorry for being a bastard? And I admit that it was manipulative for me to arrange for the museum visit, but I did it for you, not just for me. I wanted you to make some money and international contacts—"

"International contacts—ha! If that's your mission, why didn't you just give me a round-the-world ticket so I can meet all your exes? I think I'd collect a few stories that sound like mine."

Hugh didn't answer, and I felt a new fury. He wouldn't even look at me, now that he knew there was someone else in my life. As he stared out the window at the cars and trucks keeping pace with our train car, I knew he probably couldn't wait for the train to reach my destination—so, job done, he could turn around and go back.

Damn it, I thought, I would make him face me, face the woman I'd become. Going against everything I'd learned in kimono-dressing school, I clambered onto him, taking care only to fold up the front flaps of my kimono skirt so I had freedom of movement. I felt my half-slip begin to tear. Petticoats were replaceable, I thought as I grabbed Hugh's chin with my hand. "Don't you dare stop talking. I came too far, and at too great an expense, for you to shut up now."

The train stopped, and a canned female voice announced that we were at a station called Court House. Just like at the other stations, nobody got inside the compartment. Longing for the train to close its door and leave, I moved impatiently against Hugh. It was a rash move, because it aroused me. I moved again, remembering what it felt like to be up against him that way in bed. And as angry as I was, I longed to kiss him: a long, slow, remember-me kiss that would transform me from a girl wrapped too tightly in a kimono to the free spirit I once had been.

Hugh was looking at me now. His expression told me he knew exactly what was happening. Before I could open my mouth again to curse him, he'd kissed me.

I was jolted, both by the feeling of his mouth on me and by the movement of the train. It was a kiss that started out gently, tasting of champagne and soy and something good and indefinable.

"I never stopped missing you," Hugh said, moving

on to my neck. "I know it sounds like a line, but it's true. I can't be without you, I just can't—"

I couldn't bring myself to answer; I just wanted to stay melded to him. Hugh was kissing my mouth, my face, my neck, and I moved against him desperately, as if it were possible to make love through all our layers of silk and wool.

As we rushed down the center of Route 66, I was aware of nothing but the sound of the train and Hugh whispering, between kisses, that we belonged together, that I was going to give Takeo up, just as he himself had given up his old girlfriend. Now the floodgates were open, and I was saying things, too, but all I really could concentrate on was the feeling of his fingers in my hair, and his mouth on the tiny vee of skin that was all the kimono's neckline exposed. I was so angry, so joyful, so desperately aroused. I felt myself heading into a new place, one where the only kimono that mattered was the one that I wanted to take off.

"I'll go with you to your hotel," Hugh said, his hands caressing my bare legs under the kimono. "I have to stay with you tonight, please don't make me go away—"

"I won't tell you to go." As I kissed his mouth again, I felt something wet slide down and hit my mouth. Rain? No, tears. I was crying. It felt so right to be on Hugh's lap.

"I should never have left Japan. I was such a bloody idiot." Hugh choked as he whispered the words to me.

I glanced at our reflections in the window and was stunned by what I saw. Not only were we both crying, we were also departing a station whose name I didn't recognize. I'd gone too far.

"We missed the stop. I should never have trusted myself with you in a moving subway car," I added, almost wiping my face with the edge of my kimono sleeve before I remembered that it was Norie's. "We've—we've got to get ourselves organized and take the next train in the opposite direction."

"I can't wait that long," Hugh said, buckling up his belt, which I had no memory of undoing. "Let's just get out at the next stop and catch a taxi."

Takeo, forgive me, I thought as we got out at Vienna, knowing that he never would.

We practically fell into the lone cab waiting at the station. Hugh pulled me into his arms—it was as if the driver didn't matter at all to him, though I was aware of intent eyes reflected in the rearview mirror as Hugh stroked the silk of my robe, whispering to me how he wanted to do all the unwrapping himself, even if it took him half the night. His reaction reminded me of something I'd been told in kimono school—that one of the most supremely erotic experiences for a man was undressing a woman in a kimono. My same chatty mentor had said that for a woman, the feeling of breathing freely, when unclothed, after being so tightly wrapped, was divinely liberating— like making it to the top of Mount Fuji. I agreed with that point. Tonight I would find out all the rest.

Ten minutes felt like an hour in the taxi to the Washington Suites hotel. When we pulled up to the modest entrance, Hugh stuffed his twenty-dollar bill in the driver's hand and neglected to ask for change—something I had at least the sense to remind him of. The driver, deprived of a thirteen-dollar tip, scowled at me as I awkwardly made my way out of the cab. My kimono was helplessly askew. I must have looked quite disordered, I thought, when I set my first footsteps toward the front desk and Brian Hunter yelped.

"Miss Shimura? You're supposed to be dead!" Brian said with a tone of wonder in his voice.

"What do you mean?" Immediately my thoughts

flashed to the scene on the Spanish Steps, the man who'd been waiting. How had Brian known?

"The police said they found you."

"Where?" I asked, completely befuddled. Had they gone to the reception?

"Out at Nation's Place mall. They came to ask about you because they found a dead Japanese lady with two key cards from our hotel and a passport identifying her as Rei Shimura."

17

It had to be Hana. I sank down on the stiff little settee in the reception area that had been Kyoko Omori's favorite waiting place. All the good feelings in my body drained out, leaving me feeling sick. I realized I was crying after Hugh sat down next to me and handed me a soft cotton handkerchief from his pocket. He was still the only person I knew, outside of my Japanese aunt, who regularly carried a handkerchief.

"I'm sorry, darling. What a shock. Thank God you're alive . . ." His voice trailed off.

"But Hana's dead, and it's really my fault," I said, wishing for a minute that I *had* died. "Kyoko thought Hana was in danger, but I just kept reassuring her that it would be okay. What right did I have to do that? I knew nothing—"

"What's going on?" Brian Hunter interrupted. "Are you talking about that missing Japanese girl from the last tour?"

So Brian had been listening to us. I shook myself mentally and said in as normal a voice as I could muster, "Yes, I think she might be the one they found. Can you get the police to come back?"

"They left their card with Mark in security—I'll call him and say what you said, okay?" Brian seemed eager to please, for a change. I took Hugh's arm and took him over to the lobby entrance, where Brian couldn't hear our voices.

"Sorry, but I think our rendezvous is off," I said.

"Of course it is. But shall I stay and help talk to the police? Just in case you're nervous . . ."

"I don't want the police taking down your name during the interview. They're bound to go on and talk to Allison, and she'd figure out you know me quite well."

"True enough. Call me tomorrow, whenever you've got a chance." Hugh gave me a last long look but no kiss.

As I walked back toward the elevators by myself, I caught Brian Hunter staring at me.

"You're awful close to your lawyer."

"It's a long-term business relationship," I said crisply. "Have you called security yet?"

"Yeah. The same police are coming."

"You can send them up, but give me twenty minutes to change. All right?"

"Uh-huh," he said, but the way his eyes lingered on me as I headed up to the elevator made me uncomfortable.

Two officers were at my door thirty minutes later—a man and a woman, which relieved me at first, since I thought I could better explain to a woman everything I knew about Hana. Of course, it happened that the male, James Harris, was the one with more power—a homicide detective—while Lily Garcia was just a regular patrol officer.

Harris looked a few years younger than my father, with a head of thick, silvery hair and a lean body clad in khakis, a polo shirt, and a tweed jacket. He didn't look at all like my idea of a detective. Maybe it was because his gun was concealed. I assumed he had one, because Lily Garcia obviously did—it was holstered at her trim waist. She was a redhead about my age, but age was all we had in common. She had been stone-faced when I'd tried a tentative smile on her, then walked around my body, looking me over in a way I hadn't experienced since my first college fraternity party. It was positively rude, the way Officer Garcia's eyes X-rayed through the simple white shirt and jeans into which I'd changed.

The patrol officer said, "You look a hell of a lot like our Jane Doe."

"Not really. Her hair was a lighter brown than mine. Dyed," I added a bit unnecessarily, because I thought Lily's hair was colored, and I wanted to punish her a bit for the nasty once-over.

"Why do you think you know anything about the victim?" Detective Harris said, as if trying to avert a cat-fight.

I remembered that I wanted them there. "A woman in the Japanese tour group staying here disappeared. Her name was Hana Matsura. I believe she broke into my room and made off with my passport, plane ticket, and an antique bridal kimono that's incredibly valuable. I wonder if you saw anything near where you found her?"

The two exchanged glances. "Did you make a report about the theft from your room?" Detective Harris asked.

"I made a report to hotel security two nights ago." I paused. "How long ago was the woman killed?"

"The autopsy hasn't yet happened, but I'd guess within twenty-four to forty-eight hours, judging from the start of decomposition." Detective Harris looked at his colleague. "When's the medical examiner going to do it?"

"Tomorrow morning," Officer Garcia said.

"Can you tell me—where you found her?"

"In a Dumpster at the Nation's Place mall. She was carrying the passport and airline tickets in your name, plus two key cards belonging to this hotel. That's why we thought she was you," Harris said.

"Can I get the passport and tickets back?"

"Sorry, it's police evidence now. We'll give you a note that you can use to help when you apply to the correct agencies to get new documents. It shouldn't be a problem."

"Okay," I said slowly. "That's interesting that she had two room keys. Coded to her own room and mine, I bet. It's just like I thought—"

"Hold that thought," Detective Harris said. "I'd like to get out my tape recorder, Miss Shimura. If that's all right with you."

Hugh would probably have screamed no, but I saw no reason to be fearful. I was frankly relieved to be telling what I knew to people who had the power to do something about it. I told them everything—about how I'd been courier for the group of kimono, and shifted unexpectedly to sit next to Hana, who had been so friendly. Then I told them about Hana's disappearance and about how her roommate, Kyoko Omori, had casually revealed that Hana believed I was carrying something valuable right after I realized my kimono was gone. Finally I described the bizarre pattern of lockouts from my room, and how during those times, I figured that Hana had ample opportunity to search my room.

"Tell me again the reason that you didn't contact the police?" Detective Harris asked at the end.

"My first step was hotel security. They said they would look around for the kimono, and that if I wasn't satisfied with the outcome, I could file a crime report with you." I didn't want to reveal that I had been afraid that police involvement would lead to the Morioka

Museum's learning of my failure before I had a chance to discreetly get back the kimono.

"But there was more than a theft! We're talking about a complex situation with a woman who disappeared in a country that was foreign to her. You didn't think that was worth reporting?" There was a tinge of disgust in the detective's voice.

I knew that my face was embarrassingly pink as I answered in a shaky voice, "As I told you already, Kyoko and I originally thought Hana had run off with a guy for the night. The tour director encouraged us not to overreact. We all knew that if the story got back to her family in Japan, it might impact her wedding plans adversely."

"Back up for a second. Even though she was engaged, you thought she was looking for company?" Detective Harris asked.

"I said that to you already. I suppose he could be the likeliest one to have killed her."

"Did you ever see a man with her?" Harris looked at me intently.

"No, but remember that I never went to the mall with the group—that's where it would have happened." I paused. "I do have another theory. Maybe, instead of pursuing a guy, she decided that my kimono was the better bet. She could have stolen the kimono, run off toward the mall, and been intercepted by a robber who killed her and took it for himself."

"Are you sure you really lost your kimono? What about that garment laying on your bed?" Lily Garcia's voice sounded patronizing.

"What you see *lying* on my bed"—I stressed the verb she'd used incorrectly—"is a contemporary kimono that I wore earlier this evening." I was letting it air for the night, which was proper treatment before folding and wrapping it up in rice paper again.

My grammar lesson didn't seem to impress anyone. Detective Harris turned off his tape recorder, in fact. As he stood up to leave, I asked, "What about the identification of the body? Do you want me to look at her?"

"We'll check Ms. Matsura's passport—the one you say that hotel security has—for her emergency contact names, and see if that person will come. Usually, it's a relative."

"But her relatives are in Japan!" Didn't he understand what I'd said about Hana coming on the tour?

"So you're saying that you want to make the ID?" Detective Harris leaned against the door, studying me, as if to determine whether I was reliable enough for the job. It reminded me, in fact, of all those old job interviews at museums in Japan—job interviews I'd failed, they'd said, because I couldn't read *kanji*.

"It's not that I *want* to do it, but I feel obligated," I said tightly. "I'm the only person in this country who knows Hana—outside of Kyoko Omori, who was her roommate here, but went on with the others to California."

"California's not as far as Japan," said Lily Garcia.

"Do you have any contact information for the tour? Where they're staying in California?"

"I heard it's a Ramada Inn in Studio City. The tour director's name is Mrs. Chiyoda."

"Fair enough. We'll see whether we can get in touch with this person before worrying the parents unduly. Which reminds me, we didn't know anyone in town who could ID you, so we asked the San Francisco police to call on your parents. I imagine they're pretty worried."

"I'll call them," I said swiftly, fearing for the worst.

My parents' line turned out to be busy. I sensed that they were spreading bad news to everyone. After half an hour of futile attempts, I called the operator and asked her to make an emergency intervention.

"And what is your name?" the operator asked me.

"Rei Shimura. Their daughter," I added, in case she might mispronounce my name and confuse them.

When the operator interrupted my parents' phone call, I heard my mother arguing with a ticket agent. In fact, she was so caught up in bickering over the price of sympathy fare that she didn't believe it really was me. After the agent got off the line, my mother said, "Whoever this is, I can't talk to you now. I'm in crisis."

"Mom, this is Rei! I'm alive. The police made a mistake."

"You don't sound like my daughter." My mother sounded as skeptical as the last time someone at a Tokyo shrine sale had tried to suggest to her that some plastic lunch trays were really vintage lacquer.

"It's because you're upsetting me," I said, shaken by this cold reaction.

My mother stopped crying and said in a hesitant voice, "If you're really my daughter, you'll know the answers to a few questions."

"Mom, I can't believe you're going to give me a quiz." I groaned, but still, my mother went on.

"What did you do back in the eighth grade that was so naughty you were grounded for a month?"

"Um . . . I got caught selling the answers to the Japanese grammar test." A rash move that I'd thought would make me more popular, but hadn't.

"What's your favorite family dinner?"

That was a tough one, because my mother wasn't much of a cook. But I knew she was proud of a Chinese noodle dish she and my father had copied from a favorite restaurant in Palo Alto. "Dan-dan noodle."

"Hmm. That's my favorite, but not really yours. Now, what's your favorite place to pick up clothing?"

"Your closet, for all the I. Magnin leftovers."

"Oh, you *are* my daughter!" my mother exclaimed. "Toshiro, get on the other phone. Rei's on the line and she's alive!"

"Daddy, I'm so sorry for all the worry," I said, when my father's voice boomed out from the extension he had picked up.

"I never believed it was you! It couldn't be. I just allowed myself to have faith, and to hope—"

My mother interrupted, "I had my doubts, too. They said you were wearing black leather pants. I said, not *my* daughter! She and I have the same taste in clothes."

"We'll see her in a few hours and know if it's still true," my father said dryly.

"What do you mean, a few hours? I'm sorry, but I never made a reservation to come out—"

"Don't worry, sweetheart. The agent I was talking to is booking us on the red-eye leaving in three hours. So we'll see you in the early morning!"

"What—how did you decide to come?" I asked.

"The police asked us to come and identify whether the body they had was really you. Now we've got something much better on our plate. Sightseeing in Washington, a bit of shopping, and we'll get over to see your grandmother in Baltimore, of course."

I lay back on my bed and thought that I was quite lucky to be alive and to have parents who wanted to see me. I knew I had been guilty of shutting them out of my life in Japan. It wasn't fair to tell them not to come.

"Do you want to stay with me at the Washington Suites? If you really arrive tomorrow we'll have time before my kimono lecture the next day."

"I can't think of anything I'd like better, but does the hotel have available rooms?" my father asked.

"I'm sure they do, because a tour group recently left. Anyway, it's in a dud location, near Dulles Airport."

"We're flying into Ronald Reagan National Airport." My father made a snorting sound that told me exactly what he thought of the airport's recent name change.

"Great. You can take a cab from there." I told my parents that I loved them—and to have a good trip.

18

Thursday morning, I was dragged out of a dream that bells were announcing the closing of a subway car's door. I awoke with a start, realizing that I wasn't on a grimy platform in Tokyo but in a hotel bed in suburban Virginia. I shut off the clock radio blaring the Stone Temple Pilots' song "Sour Girl" and staggered into the shower.

As the water rained down on me, I felt lucky to be around to feel tired and sulky. I was alive, while a woman carrying my passport wasn't. I dressed in a favorite Pendleton plaid skirt, with a black sweater and matching tights, a schoolgirl look that seemed fitting for my first meeting with my parents in over a year. I called down to the front desk to find out where my parents were, but the front-desk clerk was too cautious to give me their room number. She did put my call through to them, though, and my mother picked up.

"It's me. Are you very tired?" I asked.

"Of course not, sweetie. Can you come up for breakfast? We're in 605. Daddy was getting ready to order some room service—there's a Japanese option that sounded intriguing."

I had noticed some of the office ladies on tour eating miso soup, rice, and pickled-bamboo-shoot breakfasts in the hotel restaurant, but it was the last thing I'd wanted to order in America. However, if my parents wanted to eat it, I'd go along with them. I was starting to get tired of bagels.

The door to Room 605 was slightly open, so I called out a cheery hello and walked right in. I stepped back in haste. A woman with a purple silk robe coming halfway off her shoulders was locked in an embrace with a man—an embrace that looked about as passionate as my own the previous evening. Suddenly the woman pulled her robe closed and turned to greet me. I blushed to see that the lover was my mother, with a lighter shade of blond hair than she'd had a year ago. My father looked more embarrassed than she at having been caught in the act.

"Sweetie, you're here so quickly!" my mother said, embracing me now in a way that was warm and motherly, despite the aroma of Shalimar. "I'm so glad to see you," I said, choking up. It wasn't just happiness at the fact that my parents were there; it was a sense of wonder that they were still enough in love to touch each other that way.

"Rei. You look so grown up." My father, who was dressed in a Norwegian knit fisherman's sweater, jeans, and Birkenstocks, came over to kiss my cheek.

"After twenty-five, women don't like being told they look grown up," my mother chided him.

"I don't mind that you think I look older. I'm glad to be a day older and still alive."

"Not half as glad as we are," my mother said, settling down on the rumpled king-size bed and gazing at me as if she couldn't get enough. "Now, instead of mourning, we'll celebrate. At that famous shopping mall!"

"You know, the body was found there. I hardly think it's the place to celebrate." I broke off, distracted by the sight of my mother, who'd slipped off her silk kimono and now crouched over her suitcase, sorting clothes, in nothing but a black Spandex teddy. She looked remarkably slender.

"Your body, Mom—what's the secret?" I asked, amazed by the sight of this fifty-five-year-old sylph.

"Pilates exercises three times a week," she said, sliding off the bed, her arms full of clothes. "I've been trying to get your father to do it, if only to strengthen his back, but he still prefers tai chi." She held up a shirt and looked at me. "Should I wear this? If it's going to be warm, I can wear it under my Cynthia Rowley suit. If it's colder, I'll do the Krizia knit sweater-jacket and pants."

"The weather's in the sixties—it's like Japan," I said. "By the way, did you bring a travel sewing kit? I tore the half-slip I need to wear again tomorrow."

"How big is the tear?" my mother asked.

"About thirty inches long."

"I think we should just get you another slip. My treat. I'd love to take you on a lingerie shopping spree," my mother said, slipping into a pair of stirrup-strap nubby wool pants that were far cooler than anything I owned. Her decorating business had to be going well—there was no way my father's university salary could support that particular pair of pants.

"Don't you think it will be difficult to find a slip that goes all the way to the ankle?"

"They'll have one at a bridal boutique. I noticed they have three bridal shops at the Nation's Place mall."

My mother had come in on a red-eye flight, been in the hotel two hours, and already she'd read through the mall's offerings. I rolled my eyes. "Okay, we'll go there. Today's a free day for me—the only possible item on my agenda is checking in with the police."

The doorbell chimed, and my father opened it to a waiter bearing a tray laden with two Japanese breakfasts and one grapefruit. I could imagine where the grapefruit was going.

"Since it is an established fact that you are alive, why are the police still interested in talking to you?" my father asked, arranging all our breakfasts on the Chippendale desk similar to the one in my room.

"A Japanese woman on the plane with me disappeared. I think it's quite likely she was the real victim." In between sips of the soup, which was comforting, despite not being as hot or as well flavored as what you'd get in Japan, I recounted the long story of Hana—as well as of the missing bride's kimono. My mother ate her grapefruit and finished the rest of my Japanese breakfast during the time I was talking.

At the end, my father shook his head. "In my years practicing psychiatry, I have noticed how terrible things shadow certain people. A woman who is raped once is raped again. A man who was beaten as a child beats his children."

"I don't know if there was any kind of trauma in Hana's past," I said.

"It's not poor Hana that I'm thinking about." My father looked pensive. "Why is it that ever since you've gone to Japan, you have repeatedly been touched by death? It worries me that even on the way home to us, there is a death and you are involved. I think—never mind. You don't want to hear."

"I'll tell her, then!" My mother's words rushed out. "We want you to come back to San Francisco. It makes so much sense! Take a little time to unwind and get back to a healthy inner space. You can join my Pilates class. And as far as work goes, maybe you can start some import-export thing between Japan and

California—Asian furniture, at the moment, is very hot."

"No," I said, my stomach tightening. "I can take care of myself, and more importantly, I have to take care of things with the Morioka Museum. I allowed their kimono to be stolen, and suggesting it was connected to something as horrible as a murder doesn't lessen its absence. Now I'm thinking the kimono might be in a Dumpster at the shopping mall, if the killer didn't take it with him. I've got to do what I can to get it back."

"Rei, a kimono means nothing!" my mother said.

"Look at you! Krizia this, Cynthia Rowley that. How can you say clothes aren't important?" I shot back.

"Well, I would gladly give up all my clothes if was a choice between life and death. As for you, sometimes I wonder."

I put down my bowl of miso soup and went to look at the cars glinting in the sun in the hotel's vast parking lot. "It's not just the bride's kimono that matters. It's honor, and keeping promises, and the loss of something that really belongs to Japan."

"The way of the Bushido," my father said softly. "How strange to hear it from your lips."

I turned back to stare at my father. He was talking about the samurai code of do or die—and that startled me. I couldn't abide the idea of samurai culture, both for the elitism that it advocated and the violence that it condoned.

"I'm not some kind of samurai person," I said. "I have no pretensions whatsoever—"

"Oh, you are," my father said, sipping from his soup bowl and smiling. "You are the eighth generation descended from a samurai who lost his arm in defense of his lord's castle. I find it fascinating that the strong character my parents wished for did not emerge in my brother or me, but in you."

My father's almost delirious ramblings turned into snores after breakfast. He was exhausted. So I did what my mother wanted; I took her shopping.

My parents had rented a Corolla. With my mother at the wheel and me as the chief navigator, we circled the mall, looking for a close parking space. Midway around the building, we approached an area that was sealed off with bright yellow tape that said POLICE LINE DO NOT CROSS.

"Let's stop here," I said immediately.

"There are no empty spaces here," my mother objected.

"I bet this is where Hana died. I want to get out, just for a minute."

My mother sighed heavily. "Well, I'll wait in the car by the curb."

I stepped out of the car and walked as close to the police line as I could. I could just see the edge of a Dumpster, but a corner of the mall kept it from being clearly visible. I ducked under the tape and went into the secured area, just far enough to get a clear view of the Dumpster. Now I could see it: about six feet tall, a dull green, with a generally grimy look. Japanese people, young women especially, felt strongly about cleanliness. Some office ladies even wiped off telephone receivers before speaking into them and wouldn't permit their mothers to wash their clothes and their fathers' in the same load. A Dumpster was a truly foul place for Hana to die.

There was a loading dock a few feet away from the Dumpster. I could easily jump up on it and then I'd have a clear view into the Dumpster. I knew Hana wasn't there anymore, but I was curious. Had they really taken out all the trash and combed through it for my kimono, as the detective had said last night?

I was afraid to look, but something greater than fear gripped me; it was a sense of guilt. I had been suspicious and angry toward Hana for the last couple of days, but now I felt her loss. As Detective Harris had hinted, I could have saved her if I'd immediately reported her absence to the police.

I walked over to the loading dock, ignoring my mother honking the car horn, and pulled myself up. Then I walked the few steps necessary to see into the container.

There was nothing inside. A few strips of crime-scene tape had been placed across it, apparently to discourage potential dumpers. The Dumpster looked dirty, all right, but I didn't see blood, or anything truly grisly.

I heard the honking sound again, and then the sound of a police siren. I whipped around and didn't see a police car but understood that one was near. I got off the loading dock fast, and instead of running straight back to my mother in the car, I went behind the loading dock, skirting around a building that wasn't visible from the road.

"Ma'am, can I see your license and registration?" A policeman was speaking to my mother.

"I know I'm not supposed to stop here, but I had to answer a call on my cellular phone," my mother said in her most stentorian tone—a decibel level once used to get me to clean up my room. "You see, unlike most people, I think driving while on the phone is dangerous."

"Crime scene . . . move on . . ." I couldn't catch all that the answering male voice said to her, because it was at a normal speaking level.

"You mean—it's not safe?" my mother shouted.

"Against the law . . ."

"Thank you for the information, sir. I'll just try to find a parking place and go into Off Fifth, the Saks outlet. I came here specifically to buy some *shoes*!"

A car door slammed, and the Corolla purred off. I waited a few beats, and a second car followed. Good. The cop was gone. Keeping close to the edge of the building, I began inching my way out of the service area. From where I was standing it was a good ten minutes' walk to the nearest entrance to the mall, a walk that I spent thinking about how stupid and pointless my investigation of the Dumpster had been. What could I possibly find, that the police hadn't?

Nothing, I had to conclude. All I'd accomplished was getting a clear picture of Hana's dismal final dumping ground.

"You almost died. And then, you almost got sent to prison," my mother said when I joined her at Off Fifth.

"Nobody gets put in jail for snooping." I swooped down to hug her slim shoulders. "The worst that could have happened is the cop would have yelled at me. But thanks for keeping me from that."

"I'm going to yell at you lots this evening. What do you think of this sandal? I can't believe I can even get a pair of Jimmy Choo sandals at a discount. Do you have any idea what these cost normally?" She turned over the shoe and showed me the sale price: $400.

"Mom, it's almost November. Why are you looking at sandals?"

"I'm doing some work in Las Vegas. Everyone wears open-toe there, as well as fabulous dark nail polish. I'm trying to fit in, just as you do in Japan."

"Can't you find a cheaper one?" I objected.

"Rei, if I bought cheap things you wouldn't enjoy wearing my hand-me-downs so much. Face it, expensive makes sense, especially if the two of us are going to share."

I left my mother to her own decadent devices, buying myself two far cheaper pairs of Aerosoles and one pair of Bottega Veneta T-strap heels. My mother wanted to pay for the stilettos, and I didn't protest when I realized how happy it made her. "This is my daughter," she said to the shoe salesman coming out of a storeroom with boxes up to his chin. "She does have a long foot, but at least it's not wide. Actually, she wears the same size that I do. We wear each other's clothes as well."

I ducked quickly into a sports shoe outlet to get myself a new pair of Asics, which were cheaper here than in Japan, where they were made. I was also pleased to find a tiny MAC makeup boutique, where I meticulously inspected all the new colors, and wound up buying two new frosted shades along with three of my favorite old colors. Then I joined my mother at St. John, where she reminisced with the sales clerk about buying the ladylike suits over the years. St. John had gotten a little bit edgier. We found a creamy belted cardigan with a fake fur collar and a coordinating skirt that looked businesslike yet felt incredibly cozy.

Shopping, the way my mother and I were doing it, was not about practicality, but sheer pleasure. I had judged Hana a shallow person to spend all her money on clothes, but now I could understand it a little better. It was an exhilarating feeling to be able to buy dreams like this—the dream of being a bit taller, because of the stiletto heels—and perhaps slimmer, after I'd run a hundred miles in the new Asics. The suit from St. John made me feel like a New Age Holly Golightly, and the lipsticks . . . well, I had to admit they made me think of kissing.

We couldn't stop shopping. At BCBG, I found a slinky red dress of a velvet and Lycra mixture that my mother pronounced fine for a "little evening," whatever that meant. She also insisted on a simple turquoise silk slip dress from the Nicole Miller boutique. I couldn't imagine where I'd wear it, but my mother said she could. The Nicole Miller transaction took five minutes, about the amount of time she had to strip me down, slide the dress over my body to see if it fit, and throw her Visa card at the sales clerk.

"I didn't mean for you to buy me so much," I said to my mother, but she pooh-poohed me as we went on to Escada, where she decided she had to have a winter-white pantsuit in the window for herself.

When I pointed out that its merino wool fabric would be very difficult to keep free of stains, my mother said, "I barely eat anymore, so it will be safe with me. In fact, I'll hand it down to you in a couple of seasons."

"It's not my thing," I said darkly; I was beginning to burn out. "Hey, shouldn't we go to the bridal boutique to look for the half-slip?"

"Oh, you're American," the pretty female sales clerk said with a laugh. "I thought I saw you the other day. There was a girl who looked a lot like you, but she had an accent . . ."

I looked at her more closely. "Really. Tell me about the other person."

"She was Japanese, I guess, but had hair that was lighter than black. She was wearing a cute quilted coat—Barbour, I think they're called—with black leather slacks. The girl sticks in my mind because she asked me to show her a coat that was typically Amer-

ican. Can you imagine?" The clerk wrinkled her
nose.

"Typically American?" I pondered that for a minute.
"Did she use those words?"

"She told me she wanted a typical American coat. She
said a plain coat that was like what everyone wore. I
told her that Escada was actually a German label, and
our clothes are quite expensive and worn by discerning
clients worldwide. If she wanted American, she should
go to the Gap."

"Of course," my mother soothed. "Escada is classic,
but the clothes are so well made that they could hardly
be called typical."

As my mother and the sales clerk went back to discussing my mother's new suit, I stared out the window
at the crowds of shoppers. Hana had been in Escada,
looking for a coat to disguise herself. Was it because she
wanted to get away with the kimono—or was she hiding from someone else?

19

I had the impulse to go around the mall to more stores to find out whether a fashionable Japanese woman had been looking for ordinary clothing. My mother revolted, though. She said that what I was doing was morbid, and that I should take my mind off things and just shop.

"Mom, you're more Japanese than the Japanese," I scolded.

"Hmm. How so?" she asked as we struggled to fit all our boxes and bags in the backseat of the Corolla.

"It's the shopping—your uncontrollable desire for small luxury goods. I watched the way your eyes lit up when you found those sandals at a price that was still stratospheric. You thought you had found a bargain, and you were in bliss."

My mother smiled serenely. "You know, your father has commented on my hobby recently, and I gave him this explanation. I deserve what I wear because I work hard for my clients. In fact, I'm considering this a working vacation, since I'm going to the Washington Design Center this afternoon to look at some new sources. Do you want to come along?"

"I'd better first check whether the police have called.

I might have to go look at the body of the woman who was found."

"I wish you wouldn't. Like Daddy said, it's not healthy for you to repeatedly encounter death scenes. I don't understand why you wanted to poke around in that Dumpster, either."

My mother dropped me off at the Washington Suites. Before going to see my father, I lugged eight shopping bags to my room and checked my voice mail. Detective Harris had indeed left a message. My pulse quickened as I heard his recorded voice ask me to call him back. I dialed the number he gave me—it must have been a cell phone, because he answered it himself, immediately.

"Ms. Shimura, I'd like you to come in for a chat. Do you have time this afternoon?" he asked, sounding completely businesslike.

"Yes. I'll get something to eat first and then I'll be there." I knew that if I saw Hana's body on an empty stomach, I was liable to get sick. "Is the medical examiner finished with the autopsy?"

"Mmm-hmm."

"So, how was she killed?"

"I can't tell you that until the investigation's complete."

"Oh. I was just wondering if she was killed in the Dumpster—or killed somewhere else, then brought there." What I needed to understand, though I didn't have the guts to say it, was whether there was a psychotic American serial killer stalking the hotel, in which case I would be getting myself, and my parents, out posthaste.

"Let's talk in person," Detective Harris said, which made me all the more nervous. It had to be really bad, if he wouldn't tell me over the telephone. "I can give you directions to the county police headquarters. It's about fifteen minutes away."

I went to my father's room to tell him the situation.

"May I come with you?" he asked immediately. "I haven't eaten yet. Maybe we can do that together."

"What about Indian food?" I was thinking about the plainest vegetarian dishes—rice, a bit of green peas, maybe some potatoes. I needed carbohydrates.

Our Nigerian cabdriver had grown up eating Indian food, and he recommended a south Indian vegetarian place on Chain Bridge Road, Fairfax City's main drag. From there, we could walk a couple of blocks to the police headquarters.

"I'm surprised you know where it is," I said to the driver.

"Oh, it is the largest building in the town. Fourteen stories high."

That didn't sound very tall by either Japanese or American standards, but when I saw the height of the building compared with the rest of Fairfax City, I understood what the driver meant. Fairfax was tiny, from the narrowness of Chain Bridge Road to the diminutive brick row houses that lined either side. It was a pretty little town loaded with small shops that I was sure my mother would have loved.

I paid for the cab. My father had offered, but I told him to take me to lunch instead. The food was fair—more authentic than Tokyo, but not bursting with the flavors of the Indian food I'd tasted in Singapore. Over *dosa* stuffed with potato curry and *idli,* we talked about how nice it would be one day to taste the real thing in its country of origin.

After lunch, it was a short walk across the road to police headquarters. The building's receptionist, an unsmiling young woman in a police uniform, asked to see ID from both of us after we'd passed through the metal detector. I opened my wallet and pulled out a few cards before realizing I had nothing. "My passport was stolen," I said. "Actually, that's the reason I'm here."

"No driver's license?" She seemed disapproving.

"It's at the hotel." I didn't mention that it was an international one—that would probably not have pleased her.

"Here, write down my license number for both of us. We're a family unit." My father smiled and held out his California license.

The woman must have caught my father's light accent, because she asked, "What country were you born in?"

I stiffened, as I always did when people tried to single us out.

"Japan," my father said. "But I have lived here for many years."

"She's from Japan, too?"

"No," I said briskly. "I'm an American citizen. Now, can I show you a social security card or credit card?"

After having me write down my social security number, the guard finally allowed us to take the elevator to the eighth floor. A set of locked glass doors faced us now. Inside them was a police officer, who pressed a code that allowed us to open the doors. It was all very secure. When I'd visited the police in Japan, it had been just like walking into a post office. This place, with its warren of cubicles, each with a computer terminal, and dull beige carpeting was more like a corporate office than my image of a police station.

Detective Harris came out to meet me. I noticed he didn't look happy to see my father. "Who're you?" he asked bluntly.

I was sick of the curtness of American officials, so I decided to inject a little civility. "Detective Harris, please meet my father, Dr. Toshiro Shimura."

"How do you do," my father began, but he was interrupted.

"What we're going to discuss with your daughter today is serious. You might not be comfortable hearing it."

"I've done forensic psychiatry, so not much can shock me," my father replied politely.

"Yes, he's pretty tough," I said.

The detective gave me a long look. "Let's get out of the hallway and into a conference room, where we can begin the formal discussion. My boss and some of the people from vice and narcotics will be joining us there."

Vice and narcotics. Maybe they thought Hana had been killed by a drug dealer. I felt the fear inside me melt into shock. I wouldn't have thought Hana would buy drugs, but she had been a curious person. Maybe she'd taken a risk, just so she'd have another wild memory before her wedding.

"Oh, good! A real police experience," my father said, rubbing his hands together.

Detective Harris snorted. "Don't say that I didn't warn you."

There were three other men and one woman in the room dominated by a long fake conference table. There was also a tall stand holding a television, with a video-cassette recorder. I wondered if things were so quiet around Northern Virginia that they watched movies on the job.

"Miss Shimura's here," Detective Harris announced as we walked in.

"Ooh. Well, look at her today," drawled a man wearing blue jeans and cowboy boots, feet crossed and up on the conference table. I flinched, because showing the undersides of one's feet was a very disrespectful act in Japan and a number of other Asian countries. I wondered whether my father was thinking the same.

"You her lawyer?" a second man asked, looking at my father's socks and sandals with a quizzical expression.

"Oh, no. I'm her father—"

"Her father! You've got to be kidding," said the only woman, whom I now recognized as Lily Garcia from the previous night. She seemed rowdier. I wondered whether it was because of peer pressure.

"So, this is your sugar daddy! Nice sweater," the cowboy said.

I was beginning to think maybe I should have brought a lawyer. No, Hugh was the wrong sort; his experience was with contracts, not police. I looked at my father and said quietly in Japanese, "They're being so rude. Would you like to sit out in the reception area?"

"Absolutely not," my father said in English. "I want to make sure you're all right."

We settled down in two chairs next to each other, and I gave my father's hand a quick squeeze.

"Okay, now that we're assembled, let's get started. Mind if we tape this?" Detective Harris asked.

"Go ahead," I said, thinking if I protested, the police group would have mocked me even more.

"Miss Shimura, I want to reinforce to you that my goal, as detective in charge of this case, is to identify the victim and apprehend a suspect as quickly as possible," Harris said.

I nodded. He had something up his sleeve, I sensed.

"However, it looks as if the case might not be a simple matter of a tourist death. I'm hoping that you'll be very honest with us today."

"Of course I'll be honest," I said. "I feel terrible that

I didn't talk to you earlier, when Hana might still have been alive. I'll try to think of anything and everything that could be of significance."

"Miss Shimura, are you sure that you want your father to be present?" Detective Harris asked again.

"Of course. Just because he was born in a foreign country doesn't mean he can't handle hard facts. As he told you before, he's a psychiatrist who has had experience with criminals."

"All right, all right. I won't beat around the bush," the detective said, sounding grim.

All of a sudden the people around the table were laughing hysterically. I exchanged glances with my father. This kind of behavior was very different from the sober Japanese police force I knew. Now I could understand the reason far fewer criminals were convicted in the United States than in Japan. The American cops were simply too busy laughing.

Detective Harris was snickering, too. "I'm sorry, it was a poor word choice. Seriously, folks, let's quiet down so Miss Shimura can hear the charges and respond. We're not going to get anything on tape this way."

"Charges," I said, feeling faint. "How could you charge me with anything?"

"At this point it's just a conversation. We want to hear what you have to say about your other job—the one that you never mentioned last night."

"Oh? Well, I guess there are so many things I've done to make a living for the last few years that I didn't tell you them all. I thought the situation with the death, and the theft of the kimono, was more important."

"Would you tell about your other jobs now?" the detective asked.

"Sure. I have a small business exporting Japanese antiques to California, and I write occasional articles on arts and antiques. In case you're wondering, I declare my income and pay taxes to the U.S. government on everything I do."

"But I don't suppose," the detective said, "you pay taxes on your income as a prostitute?"

20

"A prostitute?" I exhaled sharply. "You suspect that's one of my jobs?"

"Your main job," Detective Harris said evenly. "We aren't such country bumpkins that we don't know what a big-money industry prostitution is in Japan. What I wonder is whether you're here as a solo sex worker or as a representative of an organized-crime organization."

"This is absolutely crazy!" my father interrupted. "You cannot speak to my daughter that way. I want to make a complaint to a supervisor—"

"I'm the head of vice and narcotics." Cowboy raised a languid hand. "It seems to me that Detective Harris is doing a good interview. The dead Asian lady, whoever she may turn out to be, had engaged in sexual intercourse shortly before the time of death. Miss Shimura volunteered the information that she had a close friendship with this woman. Therefore, we suspect they both did the same kind of work."

"I didn't hear a Miranda warning, you didn't ask my daughter if she wanted a lawyer—" my father thundered on.

"She's not being arrested, okay?" Cowboy said. "As the detective said, this is just a conversation. An information-gathering experience. The more your daughter helps us, the easier it will be."

"I can't believe this," I said. "Yesterday, I went out to give a lecture at a museum. I came home on the Metro, learned that I was supposed to be dead, and I telephoned you to correct the misinformation. I'd never have called you if I knew you planned to frame me and poor Hana for something so obscene!"

"Ah, here's the first bit of your story that's lining up with ours. You rode the Metro." Cowboy's eyes rested on me. "Did you ever *ride*."

Suddenly I knew. My private moments in an empty train car with Hugh had somehow been witnessed—and misunderstood. I could explain my way out of it, but I didn't want to do it in front of my father.

I looked directly at my father and spoke to him again in Japanese. "It's not what you think. But I'd prefer to talk to them alone."

"Rei. Oh, my God." My father put his head in his hands, and his shoulders were shaking.

"I'm just going to find a place for my father to rest," I said, standing up and taking him by the arm. "I'll explain to you later," I said in Japanese. "It's not as bad as it seems—just a little bit embarrassing."

"I'll come with you," Lily Garcia said, as if I was going to try to escape. I gave her a withering look, but it didn't do a bit of damage.

"No, Rei, let me go alone. I'll wait for you outside the building," my father croaked.

When my father had gone, I sat down again. The loss of my father didn't make me feel any calmer. Knowing that my voice was shaking, I began to speak.

"I'll tell you what happened. Yesterday evening, I rode the Metro with a close friend. We kissed and hugged each other. We thought the train compartment was empty. I don't know who could have seen us, but we certainly didn't mean to offend anyone."

"You're right that nobody was in the train compartment. We found out what happened from videotape provided by the Metro police," Detective Harris said. "They've occasionally been using cameras on routes that have trouble spots. Officer Garcia, whom you met yesterday evening, reviewed the tape when it came in, so she recognized your face. Since then, she's done a thorough analysis of potential crimes committed by you and the john and brought it to the attention of vice and narcotics. Good work, Garcia."

"Thank you," she said gruffly, and I could see how much the praise meant to her.

"I heard Virginia was a conservative state, but it's simply outrageous that two people can't kiss on a train without being called in by the police," I protested.

"Well, Ms. Shimura, you did a hell of a lot more than kissing. We've got a recorded image of you taking your payment up front from the client, followed by a discussion of what service you'd provide, followed by your performance of said service, followed by the two of you dressing and leaving the train at Woodbridge Station."

"I did none of those things!"

"Let's run the tape," one of the cops at the table said. "The guys in vice said it's pretty damn hot."

Lily Garcia worked the VCR controls, fast-forwarding through the teenagers boarding the car at Metro Center. I couldn't even see myself, the car was so full of teenagers. There was no sound to accompany the video, but I clearly remembered the music that had been playing.

"Those teenagers are the ones you should be after, not me. They were playing a boom box really loudly. Nine Inch Nails. It was a real assault on the ears—"

"Yeah, yeah. Playing audible electronic equipment carries a two-hundred-dollar fine. Now, prostitution . . . that gets you up to a year in jail, a twenty-five-hundred-dollar fine, or both."

I watched the kids leaving the train compartment at Rosslyn. Now the camera, which had to have been mounted fairly high, and close to the back of the car, showed the train compartment with just Hugh and me in it. I was sitting on one side of the compartment, Hugh in a row across the aisle.

A minute passed very slowly. I saw, for the first time, how Hugh gazed at me for a while before he said anything. Then I saw his hand holding up two bills.

"It was left over from the money I lent him for a fare card. Just two dollars," I added.

"Oh, yeah? Since when do Japanese girls lend money to male American strangers?" the vice and narcotics chief in cowboy boots asked.

"He's not a stranger to me," I said stiffly. I decided not to correct the misinterpretation of Hugh's nationality, or give his name. The last thing I wanted was for Hugh to be hauled in. I could predict what would happen; his law career would fall apart, and he'd be thrown off the advisory committee at the museum. Not to mention that he was at risk for jail time—just as I was.

The video continued, and I watched myself turn around to look at Hugh beckoning me to take the money. It was clear that I'd refused the money at first. Then I walked slowly down the aisle, holding the edges of the seats for balance as I went. Officer Garcia froze the screen on an image of me sitting down next to Hugh and tucking the money in my *obi*.

"There you see it. Ms. Shimura accepts payment from john. The next thing we're going to see is their discussion of the terms of the service to be performed."

At this point all one could see were the backs of our heads, though occasionally Hugh's beautiful beaky nose showed as he turned to face me, all the while talking earnestly. I remembered that we'd been discussing how terrible it would be for my career to report the loss of the kimono to the Morioka Museum. Then I watched with a sinking feeling as Hugh began fiddling with my kimono sleeves, working his way up into the kimono until our bodies were pressed tightly together. Officer Garcia fast-forwarded through the short, unhappy conversation I'd had with Hugh about Takeo, to the time when I lost control, climbed on Hugh's lap, and yelled at him just before he kissed me.

The camera had caught only the back of Hugh's head and his shoulders, but it showed my face and upper body well. I had to admit that I was moving against Hugh in a way that was erotic. The ecstatic expression on my face added to the illusion that we were doing something X-rated. I knew that I should feel sickened, but the sight of Hugh and me so deeply involved was fascinating. Had I really reacted so strongly to him? I could see my lips moving, speaking to Hugh. I now remembered what I'd been saying.

The scene ended with the videotaped image of me in tears—you could tell from the slow river of mascara running down one cheek. By this point I did not look anything like the fancily dressed young miss who had gone off to give a museum lecture in a formal kimono. I looked like someone who'd been through a war.

Hugh and I got to our feet. I watched as I tried desperately to smooth the lower half of my kimono, which had loosened, and Hugh buckled his belt. After we left the train compartment, Lily Garcia put the video on pause. There was a smattering of applause.

"Our very own Emmy Award nominee for prime-time drama." The cowboy vice chief grinned and said, "If you don't mind my saying, it looks like you really enjoy your work."

"I do mind you saying, and it most certainly was not work. You're like a bunch of Peeping Toms, watching me with a man I care about strongly. And there's no way you can possibly argue that it's sex, because you didn't see a single exposed body part! If I'm guilty of anything, it was poor judgment about sitting next to someone I find very hard to resist."

"Awesome speech," Cowboy commented with a grin that revealed a gold tooth. "Still, I don't believe a word. Does anyone here?"

Everyone shook their head.

"Let's move on," Detective Harris said. "I want to establish Miss Shimura's real link to the dead woman. I have a little theory," he said, looking closely at me. "It's that you and Hana were in the same line of work, and you killed her—or you know who did. Maybe she took your kimono because there were drugs sewn into it. That's why you asked the hotel staff to get it back for you, but weren't too quick to contact us."

"You've got it all wrong," I said, feeling hollow. "Hana wasn't a prostitute. She'd come to the U.S. intending to have a fling with someone—but it was entirely for pleasure, not for pay. I tried to talk her out of it, because I thought it could be dangerous—now I know I was right."

"Miss Shimura, have you ever been arrested?" Cowboy asked in a fake conversational voice.

"Of course not," I snapped. "I've never even gotten a traffic violation."

"Well, there's something we have here in the judicial system called a plea bargain. You squeal, you walk. Or at least you don't do quite as many days in the big, bad American jail. There are some prisons with pretty tough chicks in them. Chicks who'd want to do a lot more than kiss and embrace."

"Plea bargains are something I will deal with later, when I'm in court, not sitting around a conference room with you and your rude friends having a so-called conversation." I was so angry now that I'd regained a bit of courage. "I came here because I wanted to help you identify a woman who died. You seem to put that pretty low on your list of priorities."

"Consider this," Detective Harris said. "Since you weren't straight with us about things from the get-go, that makes your credibility as a witness less than stellar. We're going to attempt to get the ID made by the woman who was supposedly rooming with Hana Matsura."

"Kyoko Omori," I said. "But she's in California, about to go home to Japan—"

"We found her. She's now in the process of arranging a flight back to Dulles. She'll get in this evening. She's bringing a man who says he was engaged to marry Hana. He's coming from Japan via L.A."

I shook my head at that. "What about Hana's parents?"

"Whaddaya mean, what about her parents? Not everyone is able to travel when they get news about a possible death in the family."

"I can't believe her parents didn't come. That's so—unloving," I said, thinking about my own parents coming to see me. Suddenly I was reminded of my father waiting downstairs. "I've got to go."

"You know the drill, Miss Shimura. Don't leave Virginia without telling us."

"I'm just talking about going downstairs to see my father. You gave him a terrible shock when you unfairly accused me of a crime."

Detective Harris said, "Well, if you're innocent, you can always bring in this guy you say is your close friend."

"I won't. He has a right to privacy—"

"I thought you'd say that," Detective Harris said, without smiling. "It's the standard excuse given."

"You won't believe anything I say. I shouldn't have bothered opening my mouth."

"Yeah, should have kept those luscious lips zipped on the train," Cowboy said. "That's where you made all the trouble for yourself."

I found my father sitting on a bus-stop bench on Chain Bridge Road.

"What did they say?" he asked anxiously.

"Oh, not too much," I lied. "Like I told you, it was a simple misunderstanding. They have these cameras in the Metro sometimes, and the camera photographed me sitting close to someone—a friend I hadn't seen in a while." I was striving to make everything sound as cool and non-sexual as possible. "Because of the differences in our gender, and my style of clothing, it aroused the police's interest. You see, not many women travel the Metro wearing kimono. They thought I was an illegal alien."

" 'Prostitute' was the word they used. But I knew it couldn't be true—just as I received terrible news yesterday and couldn't believe it."

"I didn't want you to see the video. Not having seen it myself, I had no idea what they would present me with. As it turned out, the video was accurate; it just showed a little hugging and kissing—about as much as you and Mom did this morning," I added, to reassure him.

"So, what's your friend's name? Was it someone you knew in college?"

"I didn't know him in college, but I've known him for

a while—a couple of years." I paused. "The less I say about it the better."

"Rei-chan, that doesn't sound good."

"It's just that—there are some complications in my personal life. I'd rather sort them out myself."

My father gave me a long look. Then, in a gentle voice, he said, "You know, even though we've been together for a few hours, I realize that I haven't yet asked you how you are. I wonder if you're sleeping well at night."

"No. How can I, with the murder and the kimono theft?"

"What about money? Do you seem to be spending more than usual?"

I goggled at him. Did he know about the shopping spree my mother and I had gone on? Then I thought a little more and realized that my father was probably checking for psychiatric mania. My uncharacteristic promiscuity must have made him worry.

"I'm not doing anything out of the ordinary, Otosan. I am suffering stress, but I'm also aware that stress is part of life, and things are bound to improve."

"I don't like to meddle in your life, Rei, but I wonder if I could meet this—friend—of yours. I don't think all the blame for the incident should rest on you. He was a partner in it as well."

"I prefer that he keep a low profile—it just makes good sense," I said. I couldn't possibly tell him the other reason I wanted to stay away from Hugh. I'd realized it when I was watching the video of Hugh rapturously kissing the base of my throat while I mouthed words that I'd never said to Takeo. *I love you.* The feeling had been buried so deeply inside me that I thought it had gone away. But it had just been lying dormant, like a virus buried in the spine, waiting for the right time to reemerge. I was in crisis, so I was back in love with Hugh.

21

Back in Room 605, my mother was lying on the bed, paging through catalogs she'd picked up at the Washington Design Center.

"So, did you have fun?" she asked.

I exchanged glances with my father. To my surprise he said, "It was all right."

"If you'd come with me, you'd have had a better time. Did you do what you hoped for: identify that poor dead girl?"

"No. The police said that Kyoko Omori, the woman who was Hana's roommate, is flying back to do it. She'll have Hana's fiancé with her."

"Oh, dear. Her fiancé. He must be devastated," my mother said.

"What I'm wondering about," I said, "is why her parents didn't want to come. You decided to travel the instant you heard a woman had been found dead with my identification in her pocket."

"People react differently to shock," my father said. "I wanted to come so I could prove to myself it wasn't you. Your mother wanted to come because she couldn't bear the thought of you being alone and dead, without us there to care for you. I imagine Hana's parents might be so stressed by the idea of death as well as foreign travel that they feel unable to fly."

My parents' endless concern—even after knowing what the police thought of me—touched me so much that I felt weepy. I struggled to control my voice as I said, "I'm grateful to you for being willing to come see me. I only wish I could live up to your expectations. Unfortunately, I don't think I can."

"Rei!" My mother was rushing toward me, arms open, as I backed toward the door.

"I need some time alone," I said, trying hard to control my voice. "I have to go to my room. I'll see you in a few hours."

Allison had called, leaving a message that she hoped I felt all right after my untimely departure the previous evening. The message was recorded around one P.M. I figured that meant the rest of the Morioka kimono collection hadn't been stolen. There was also a terse message from Hugh. Where was I, and when could he see me again.

I called Hugh back at work, and again the receptionist with the Miss Moneypenny voice put me through immediately.

"Are you with someone?" I asked when he said hello.

"No, I'm just doing research. Can you come to see me? I'm missing you terribly."

"Not at the moment. I'm afraid things are really bad. I went to see the police, and instead of talking to me about Hana, they presented me with a videotape from the time we were riding in the Metro."

"We changed trains in Metro Center." Hugh paused, and I could sense him thinking. "Was the videotape from before or after?"

"After. What's really awful is that the cops think we engaged in an act of prostitution. I mean, I was the prostitute and you were the client."

"What a load of rubbish! That kind of accusation will never stand up in court. I'm sorry you went through this alone, but now that it's over, take a hot shower and don't let it bother you—"

I wanted to shake him. "The camera caught an image of you offering me money. I sat next to you and took it, and then the rest happened. Tell me, why were you buckling your belt at the end? I don't recall doing anything really X-rated."

"You unbuckled my belt because it was getting in the way of your, um, movements. But nothing really raunchy happened. It was a snog, not a shag."

"Good," I said, wondering what the police would make of his bizarre British slang. I didn't think it would help us.

"Does the camera show much of my face?"

"Actually, you lucked out because the camera mostly caught the back of your head. Not a hair out of place," I added sourly. "And they're clueless about your identity. They've somehow assumed you're an American guy called John, and I haven't done anything to change that misconception."

"How d'you think that came about?" Hugh sounded almost amused.

"Well, when I tried to explain that I'd given you the money for a fare card, they said why would someone like me give money to a strange American. And later one of the officers said that I accepted payment from John."

"A john. That's the word for someone who solicits prostitution."

"Really? I guess I've been out of the country so long I don't know all the slang."

"It's an old word, Rei." I heard Hugh chuckling on his end.

"I don't think they can arrest me, or they would have

done it earlier. Still, unless you want to have an embarrassing interview with the guys in blue, I think you should definitely stay away from me. Besides, things are crazy here. My parents arrived and Hana's roommate Kyoko is coming back tonight to look at the corpse—along with the guy Hana was planning to marry. If the police hammer at her with the same accusation of prostitution that I received, she'll be completely mortified. I can't imagine what he'll think—"

Hugh snorted. "I can. He'll think he walked onto the set of a Junzo Itami comedy."

Despite my unhappiness, I half smiled. I'd taught Hugh about all the best modern Japanese cultural references. It was tragic, though, that Japan's greatest comedy director had dropped to his death from a high building a few years earlier. Rumors swirled about the tragedy, but nobody really knew for sure whether it was murder or suicide. Well, I wouldn't let false rumors shadow Hana's reputation. She hadn't been a prostitute. I'd make sure that was known.

My parents and I wound up eating Tex-Mex that night. It was a compromise because all three Shimuras had different ideas about the best place to eat. My mother wanted to try Kinkeads, while my father wanted to eat at Asia Nora. I was the lone voice for Austin Grill at the Nation's Place mall, and because it was closest, I won.

My mother groused the whole time that Mexican food wasn't worth eating anywhere east of California, but my father and I ate our enchiladas and smiled at each other. The place was definitely a big chain, but the *mole* was terrific.

When we returned to the Washington Suites, there

was a slight commotion at the front desk. A young Japanese couple was trying to check in. Brian at the desk was shaking his head repeatedly, as if he wouldn't accommodate them. When I caught sight of a familiar suitcase and a Burberry raincoat, I knew to hurry over.

"Kyoko-san! You're back," I said, taking in her worried face. She looked at least five years older than when I'd last seen her.

"Rei-san? I can't believe you're still here." Kyoko's face now held a hint of suspicion.

"Yes, my assignment is not done. And now my parents are here, too."

"Oh, your parents! I must not disturb you." Kyoko glanced in the direction that I waved and made a slight bow to my father and mother.

"Don't worry about them," I said. "Have you been to see the police already? If not, there's something I've got to warn you about. They think we're a couple of—"

There was a slight coughing sound coming from someone nearby, and I looked over to see the slim Japanese man who must have been engaged to Hana. He was just as Hana had said: five feet ten inches tall, and he looked fairly nice, with his hair cut in the super-short style that was now fashionable, and wearing a North Face jacket open over a soft red sweatshirt and khakis. He looked good, like the healthy, energetic Japanese male models in advertisements for cars, or houses, or banks.

"I'm sorry. You must be . . ." I stopped, unable to remember his name. He'd formed a very small part of my airplane conversation with Hana.

"Watanabe Yoshiki," he said, bowing slightly. "You can call me Yoshi."

"Shimura Rei." I introduced myself, putting my last name first, as he'd done. "How I wish we were meeting

under happier circumstances. Hana-san would be
touched to know that you'd traveled so far for her."

Yoshi ducked his head, but didn't say anything. I
wondered how close he'd gotten to her. Their introduction had been arranged, but they had been dating. Staying in love hotels and singing karaoke were the main
activities I recalled Hana mentioning.

"We go to see the body tomorrow morning," Kyoko
said. "And then we hope to fly back to Japan in the
evening. However, it seems we can't even get rooms
here. I didn't think to book the hotel in advance. I was
just so confused and troubled, it was all I could do to
find a flight."

I wondered if she'd paid her own way for the last-
minute fare—or if Hana's parents had helped her pay.
Somehow, the situation of Kyoko and Yoshi, the friend
and the fiancé traveling to make the ID, seemed even
more sad.

I tried to get back to the issue of shelter for Kyoko
and Yoshi. There was a Holiday Inn nearby, but I also
sensed that going to an unfamiliar hotel, at such a trying time, would be hard. I could give Kyoko my room;
moving into my parents' suite wouldn't be that difficult
to do. But that still left the issue of where Yoshi would
sleep.

"Let me introduce my parents," I said, suddenly
mindful of my mother and father in the background.
My mother smiled and said hello in Japanese, which
made Kyoko gasp with admiration. My father spoke
Japanese to them, too. I suddenly found myself struggling to recall whether I'd explained to my parents
about Yoshi having been engaged to Hana, since my father was talking to both young Japanese as if *they* were
a couple. Yoshi didn't seem to notice, but Kyoko's complexion had pinkened.

I went to the front desk and asked about the room situation. Brian Hunter, who was looking just as waiflike and wasted as ever, muttered there was a single room available as well as a "family suite," which was essentially two bedrooms joined by a bath. For both rooms, the prices were more than double what we'd paid as part of the tour.

"You know, this is really an emergency situation," I said.

Brian blinked rapidly and said, "It's because of the dead lady?"

"Uh-huh. It's really bad publicity for the hotel, don't you think, that a guest died nearby, and the parties who've come to cooperate with the police can't even be sheltered?"

The young clerk nodded and went into the back room to consult with someone. He came back and offered a 30 percent discount on the suite, and 10 percent off the single room.

I joined Kyoko and Yoshi again to explain the choices of rooms. "One of you could easily take my room for the night—it will only take me a few minutes to move into my parents' suite, where I can take the couch. On the other hand, you could stay in a two-room suite, though I think that could be a little bit awkward—"

"I wouldn't want you to have to go to the trouble of moving your things," Kyoko said. "Maybe Mr. Watanabe can take the single room, and I'll stay in another hotel."

"This is my first time in America. I am nervous alone. I don't mind sharing the suite, if she is willing."

"Of course you should do that," my father said. "It's best to stay together!"

"Very well, then," said Kyoko, sounding miserable. "Mr. Watanabe and I shall check in."

My parents and I followed the two of them to their suite, which was on the same floor as theirs, and after seeing that everything was in order, we said good night.

"So, what was the reason you wanted them to split up? Rei, it seemed a bit unkind," my father said when he, my mother, and I were back in Room 605.

"Dad, they're not a couple. Yoshi was engaged to Hana. It's totally inappropriate for him to share a suite with Kyoko."

"As inappropriate as a public display of affection on a subway train?" my father asked coolly. "I think not. And no matter what the prior circumstances were, I sensed those two needed to stay together."

"Misery loves company, you mean?" my mother said.

My father shook his head. "There were a number of subtle cues that showed the existence of a relationship: the way that Yoshi paid for the room entirely on his charge card, and carried all Kyoko's baggage himself. The two were holding hands when we came into the lobby—she dropped his hand when she saw you, Rei. Didn't you notice?"

"Oh, no!" I hadn't seen what my father had taken in so quickly. Well, he was a psychiatrist who'd done lots of therapy with patients who had troubled relationships.

"Anyone for a nightcap?" my mother said, opening the mini-bar and taking out a small bottle of Bailey's Irish Cream.

"If there's milk," I said, settling down on the small couch in the suite's sitting area.

It was almost eleven, and I knew I'd need something to help me sleep. As my mother and I sipped our creamy cocktails, my father went into the bathroom for a soak. Like many Japanese, he was addicted to the ritual of an evening bath.

"Just so you know—your father told me what the police said you did on the train. I understand it was just a heavy make-out session or whatever you call it these days," my mother said, curling her stocking feet up under her on the couch. They kept a shoes-off household, as I did, wherever they went.

"You both must be very disappointed in me," I said, concentrating on her pedicured toenails rather than her face.

My mother sighed. "If it was a new friend you'd met at a bar or someplace like that . . . yes, I guess I would be. But your father doesn't think it's the case. He thinks it's an old friend. And I have a hunch who it might be."

"Really," I said.

"It's Hugh, isn't it? The older brother of that crazy Angus person who stayed with us for a little while two summers ago."

"What makes you think that? It's an awfully long stretch from Scotland to Washington. Not to mention that you've never met Hugh—"

"I know he's in Washington. He called us up a few months ago, wondering if your last address was current. I told him yes, but that you had moved on and had a new boyfriend."

"How could you?" I said, mental wheels turning. Hugh had seemed so surprised when I'd mentioned Takeo. Had that just been a show?

"Well, when you told me you were coming to this area to give a lecture, it was all I could do to control myself and not suggest you look him up. What a remarkable coincidence that you did meet, and on the subway at night—"

"There had been a few previous meetings. I *meant* not to see him, but that turned out to be impossible." The Bailey's had loosened my tongue. "Each time I see him all the old feelings come back."

"Well, I would never presume to tell you the choice to make, but some people would envy your situation. Personally, I think it's good for men not to be overly sure of themselves and their chances."

"Is that why you told Hugh not to contact me?"

"Absolutely. I knew what he'd done to you—he'd left and stopped calling. He needed to know that you'd gone on to better things, which, in a sense, you have. Let's face it—how many millions of Waspy lawyers are there—versus flower-loving Japanese men who happen to have a *Fortune* 500 rating?"

"Mom, that's so shallow! You remind me of that book that tells women who date that they have to follow a bunch of silly rules."

"Darling, I'm old enough now that I make my own rules. And my rule is, if my daughter refuses to let me meet her boyfriends, I'm going to make my judgments based on the few details she leaks. I happen to be predisposed to prefer men from Japan. Can you blame me?"

"I'm glad you're happy with Dad. But the truth is, Takeo is very different from Dad, and I don't know that I'll ever get to introduce you. He doesn't like to travel to the States, and he's not even very social in Japan."

"What? That sounds crazy. Some of our most wonderful reports on him were from Norie."

"Well, that was the old Takeo. The new one likes to stay home and eat corn-and-octopus pizza." I couldn't bring myself to confess what the rest of every date entailed. "Now that you know everything about my love life, are you still interested in hearing what I have to say about kimono? The lecture's set for tomorrow at noon."

"You mean—you're allowing us to go? You'd said something on the phone, but I thought you were likely to change your mind."

"Of course I want you there. Maybe you'll get a chance to talk to Allison Powell, the curator. I want your opinion of her."

"Oh, really?" My mother leaned in, already interested. She loved giving opinions, and like most daughters, I usually didn't welcome the opportunity.

"There are things about her that are really odd. She's a little too casual about the issue of the kimono collection's safety. Because of that, we had an argument at the VIP reception."

"How awkward," my mother said. "Well, maybe I can try and smooth things for you a little bit."

"It's not that I want you to make things better for me. It's just that I think you could do a more accurate reading of Allison because you come from the same place."

"And where is that?"

"Wellesley. You're class of 'sixty-eight and she's class of 'seventy." I'd taken in the framed diploma on the wall the first time I'd been in Allison's office.

"I see," my mother said. "All right, I'll speak with her. But the real reason I'm going is to see you shine."

22

"Let's eat downstairs," I said to my mother when I called them the next morning promptly at eight. I was in the mood for something other than a bagel. Pancakes, maybe, or a fried egg with a side of vegetarian sausage.

"Sweetie, it's five A.M. for us. Can you give us a little more time to sleep?" my mother groaned.

"Okay. I'm sorry. I'll see you later." I called Kyoko and Yoshi's suite next. "Are you two ready for breakfast?"

"Um, uh, maybe in a little while." Kyoko sounded distracted.

I got to the business I didn't have the opportunity to broach the previous evening. "I've got to warn you about something before you meet the local police. They have a crazy notion that Hana was a prostitute and I'm in the business. It makes me worry they might ask you, too, about that kind of work."

"But I know nothing about that—that kind of work—"

"Of course you don't. I wanted to warn you so that you could be ready to handle them."

"What—what do I say back?" Kyoko sounded panicky.

"Just be your own gentle, natural self. I know that

you'll be able to convince them—but you probably shouldn't mention that you're sharing a suite with Yoshi. They might interpret that unfairly."

"Oh, dear. Now I wish I'd never agreed to come. I wish the horrible time was over—"

"Let's think of something to make up for it afterward. Would you and Yoshi be my guests for dinner tonight?" I asked.

"I'd like it very much, if it's not too much trouble."

"Not at all." After I hung up, the phone rang again. It was Hugh, asking how the last night had gone.

"Fine," I said. "Kyoko and Yoshi got in. They're sharing a suite."

"Hmm," Hugh said. "Sounds as if they're rather friendly."

"Yes. My father thinks deeply friendly, if you know what I mean."

"Oh, that's intriguing." I could sense Hugh smiling on his end. "Your parents should be rested by now. Let's all have dinner tonight."

"Well, I've actually just promised to entertain Yoshi and Kyoko."

"Let me come along. Please."

"But you don't speak Japanese. I think you'll be bored."

"I don't care what language you'll speak. Come on, Rei. I'm aching to see you."

"One question first. Did you speak to my mother on the phone a few months ago?"

"I guess I did. She was pleasant as usual and had lots of questions about young Angus. Why?"

"She told you that I had a boyfriend, didn't she?" I paused. "That means you already knew about Takeo when you started feeling your way up my kimono sleeves—"

"The truth is, she didn't provide many details, so I

privately decided that this so-called boyfriend could not be a serious one. And when you didn't mention Takeo after I brought up my dream on my first night, I knew I'd guessed right."

"What unbelievable arrogance. Was the dream about me in the kimono even real?"

"Of course! Rei, I may be an arrogant bastard but at least I'm honest—and completely uncreative. I couldn't fabricate a dream like that one. That symbolic kind of stuff is completely *your* territory—"

"Thanks very much, and let's drop it. Now, on to our evening. Make a reservation for four—I'm thinking Italian. Japanese people usually like Italian food." I wouldn't mind some decent gnocchi myself.

"I know just the place." Hugh sounded happy again. "It's a very fashionable northern Italian spot in Georgetown that has a chef with the hands of an angel. Lots of fresh snappy flavors to start, then lush creamy sauces, and finally, chocolate desserts so dark and dense that you'll—"

"Hugh, someone else is calling me. I've got to take it."

"I'll pick you all up at seven. Bye, darling."

I clicked over to the other call. It was Allison Powell. "Rei, I'm just calling to check that you remembered the noon lecture is *today*."

"Of course," I said. "I've been meaning to say that I was sorry for the way I left the museum the other evening."

"Oh, it's all right. Those big evenings can be stressful. And I want you to know that the kimono collection is still hanging safely. No attempts at robbery. Mr. Shima walked through this morning, and he said he was satisfied with the security arrangement."

I caught my breath. "Are you talking about the registrar from the Morioka?"

"Oh, yes. I should have told you that right away. When you told me that you'd lost the bridal kimono, I called the Morioka Museum to offer my condolences. They were a little surprised to hear it from me instead of you. I said that surely you'd tried to reach them, but must not have been able to get through or leave a message."

"When did Mr. Shima arrive?" I asked, feeling doomed. I'd been thinking about how I was going to break the news to him. Now it turned out that he already knew.

"Yesterday evening. He called from Dulles Airport, asking where he should stay, and I told him to come to the Sofitel, where we could arrange a discount. We're going to try to pay for his lodging ourselves out of the Honda grant, since he really did go to quite a bit of trouble. Apparently he wasn't even on duty at the museum this week, but the people we spoke to managed to reach him by cell phone, and he immediately volunteered to come and see what he could do to help."

"How diligent," I said, feeling as if I was in a bad dream.

"Yes. He's due at the museum this morning at nine, and I assume he'll stay through your lecture. He'll want to talk to you, I'm sure."

I was pacing my room in my kimono undergarments when my parents finally came to see me. It was ten o'clock.

"Did you eat something?" my mother asked.

I shook my head. "No. I had some bad news . . . so I forgot to eat. I haven't even had morning coffee."

"Well, let's place a room-service order before we do anything," my mother said, getting on the phone to order three Japanese breakfasts plus an extra cappuccino for me.

"Do you feel comfortable telling us what happened?" my father asked.

"Well, I spoke to Allison, the curator from the Museum of Asian Arts. She telephoned the Morioka Museum and told them that I'd lost the bridal kimono. The museum is concerned enough that they sent their registrar, Mr. Shima. He arrived last night."

"Probably on the same flight as Kyoko and Yoshi," my father said.

"I'm scared that he'll think I stole the kimono. He's probably going to check with the police to find out if I even bothered to file a crime report. And then, if he contacts the police who know me, he'll get a glowing report on the kind of girl they think I am."

My telephone rang, and I hesitated to pick it up. I didn't want to talk to Hugh in front of my parents.

"Aren't you going to answer it?" my mother said, making a move toward the telephone herself. I snatched it up. It was Kyoko Omori.

"I'm sorry to disturb you, but I had to tell you the sad news. I'm calling you from the Virginia Medical Examiner's Office." She carefully said the last four words in English.

"Oh?" I waited.

"Yoshi-san and I both recognized her—there was no argument. But oh, how she was killed! I cannot imagine anyone would be so inhumane."

"How?"

"Well, they wouldn't explain, but from the body, we could tell. There was a knife stab into the center of her throat. An instant death. So ruthless."

After I murmured a few words to Kyoko that I doubted offered much comfort, we hung up. Then I sat down, thinking.

An instant death, so ruthless, so—*historical*. A stab

through the throat in a position that caused instant artery damage was the way a samurai wife was trained to kill herself should her husband take his life or be killed. In the old days, aristocratic ladies carried knives tucked into their *obi*. Today, the ceremonial knives are worn like a fashion accessory on a Japanese bride's wedding day, tucked into the cord that binds the *obi*.

In the twenty-first century, there was no longer a threat of hostile warlords, but there was an increasing threat of divorce. A woman carrying a knife at her waist on the day of her wedding was declaring to the world that she'd rather kill herself than have her marriage dissolve. I considered it unlikely that the average American criminal would know about this stylized suicide method. Whoever killed Hana knew something about Japanese history—either an outsider's scholarly perspective, or an insider's cultural one.

My mother helped me put on the gold-and-cream *shibori* kimono, but it turned out that my father was the one who could tie the perfect *obi* bow. From the memory of helping his cousin, he said, which led my mother to rib him a bit. The bow he tied for me was a bona fide single woman's bow but rested at a cockeyed angle, the kind of bow that he thought was right for someone in her late twenties. I liked it.

We got into the car to go to the museum at ten forty-five, but hit a bizarre slowdown on the Roosevelt Bridge. There was no accident or construction to pass— just a long stop-and-go period, during which my parents debated where to go to lunch while I obsessed over my lecture notes. I was planning to do a version of the same talk I'd delivered at the museum opening, but with the addition of wrapping a kimono on a mannequin.

It was eleven-forty when we reached S Street, so I had my parents drop me off at the museum before they parked. Allison Powell was standing in the rear of the museum lobby, talking with a dark-haired man a little bit shorter than she. From the back, he could be anyone, but I knew that most likely it was Mr. Shima.

"Hello," I said, hesitant to break into their conversation but knowing that I had to.

"Oh, hello, Rei. It's good you're here. This is the Japanese embassy's cultural attaché, Mr. Morimoto."

I bowed to him, murmuring the polite words of introduction. So, my forthcoming humiliation in front of Mr. Shima would be delayed—just slightly.

"We at the embassy are very sad, and worried, to hear about the loss of the important cultural property."

I came up from my bow to meet Mr. Morimoto's thoroughly somber face. Oh, my God. I hadn't thought a late-Edo-period kimono could possibly be designated an Important Cultural Property—an item held in such reverence by the Japanese people that it was registered with the government. Mr. Shima had said nothing about this to me, and now the piece had been lost.

"I am very sad and worried, too," I said. "I filed reports about the theft with the hotel security and the local police. I'm praying that they'll be able to recover the kimono."

"My office, as well as that of the consul, would like to be involved. Can you come to the embassy for a conversation when you're done with the talk?"

Great. Another conversation with authority figures that would no doubt end in my incriminating myself. "Fine," I said.

"If you can bring your own travel insurance papers, that would be most helpful."

"I—I didn't carry them today. I was just focused on the lecture—"

"We have the loan agreement, which includes details of insurance on the back. Would that suit you?" Allison said.

Mr. Morimoto shook his head. "That's not what I need to see. I'm interested in Miss Shimura's traveler's insurance."

"I'll be glad to talk to you about it later. Right now I'd like to get settled at the podium. Is Jamie around? Maybe she can help me." I'd not forgotten how upset Jamie had been the night of the reception—and how she might have been the one waiting for me at the foot of the Spanish Steps.

"Jamie isn't here today," Allison said. "But since the crowd today is smaller, you'll be speaking in the kimono gallery and we are going to have to eliminate the slide show."

"What?" This was a major change in plans.

"Well, there's not enough free wall space to use a screen. However, you can use the actual *kosode* on display to illustrate your points."

"I can't touch them, though," I said. "Do I still have a mannequin to demonstrate kimono dressing?"

"Yes, it's there along with a kimono and *obi* from our collection."

"Ooh, I'd better see what they're like." I bowed slightly to Mr. Morimoto and made my escape.

Allison had not been exaggerating when she said today's audience was smaller. There was no crowd whatsoever. Despite the write-up in the *Post,* I counted nine people in the gallery, and some of them were walking around and looked as if they weren't staying for the lecture.

Where were my parents? I wondered as I went to the small table and chair that had been set up for me. I laid down my notes and looked at the kimono and *obi* hanging on a lacquered stand, and an underrobe already in place on a mannequin. The kimono garments were all early twentieth-century pieces—nothing special. I guess that was what they trusted me with now.

At two minutes past noon, Allison appeared in the gallery, flanked by Mr. Morimoto and Mr. Shima, who looked at me with such a stern expression that I felt like running and hiding. He sat down in the first row, next to Mr. Morimoto. The two were talking in voices so low I could hardly hear anything, though the words "hotel" and "police" floated out. Obviously Mr. Morimoto was telling him about the kimono theft.

Allison strode up to the microphone, which was completely unnecessary, given the size of the group and the space, and spoke. "On behalf of the Museum of Asian Arts, I want to welcome you to the opening of a very exciting exhibit which brings together some of the most precious kimono from our own collection as well as that of the Morioka Museum, one of Japan's foremost museums."

As Allison went on, she seemed to be holding off on introducing me, yet she was waxing rhapsodic about the Morioka. She went on for almost five minutes, using material that had been lifted from the outline that I'd shown her.

It was twelve-ten and Allison was holding forth on how the sleeves of a kimono illustrated the wearer's status in society when my parents quietly entered the gallery and took seats. Now there was a total of ten in the audience.

I looked at Allison one last time and stepped slightly to the side. Why not give her all the space she wanted? She was the curator. There was no way that I could possibly interrupt her.

How much could the Japanese men in the front row follow? The two of them sat with faces as mild looking yet heavy as the great bronze Buddha in Kamakura. The rest of the audience didn't seem to realize anything was amiss. Why should they? After all, Allison hadn't mentioned that I was going to speak.

Finally, when it was eighteen minutes after twelve according to the clock on the wall, Allison hyperventilated and said, "We have with us a guest today—an American of Japanese heritage who has a special interest in kimono. Rei Shimura has generously offered to demonstrate how a kimono is worn. Feel free to make a quick demonstration now, Rei."

My father was looking completely puzzled. My mother was ticked off; I could tell from the way she was tapping her Bally pump against the floor as if she wanted to decimate it. I had twelve minutes to give my talk, and Allison had just spoken about my demonstrating.

If you discounted my parents, Allison, and Mr. Shima and Mr. Morimoto, there were just six who had come for the kimono talk. Six people—a pretty negligible group. But I recognized the two tourists who had come the day before; the ones I'd told about the date of the lecture, who'd in fact come back to hear it. The ladies were beaming at me as if I were Santa Claus. I couldn't let them down.

"The kimono," I began, in a voice that cracked. "On a surface level, it's a bit like a shroud—a way to conceal a body in a tightly wrapped length of silk. The kimono erases breasts, waist, and hips. It's hard to imagine such a garment pushing women forward." I paused. "Wearing this kimono today, I realize there are only two actions I can do comfortably: Stand. Or kneel."

There was an intake of breath. Someone, somewhere,

got the message that I knew Allison was trying to subdue me.

"But the kimono, despite all of its layers, can also be seen as an empowering garment. The amount of nape of the neck—or the inner lining that you reveal—tells a lot about the kind of woman you are. And in an odd way, the garment is democratic; it looks as lovely on a sixty-year-old woman as it does on her five-year-old granddaughter. I won't tell you about the subtle differences between Edo-period *kosode* and today's kimono: Allison Powell already did that in her inimitable fashion. What I do hope to show you is how, as we wrap a kimono, we enfold ourselves in layers of culture and tradition."

I began dressing my mannequin. I explained how important it was to flatten out the bust line, how buxom women would strap their chests down for the sake of a clean line. I talked about how there had originally been a series of three kimono worn on top of each other, but that most modern women wore two. Then on to the main kimono: in its fabric and design, themes of nature were important, but it was crucial to wear a robe that anticipated the coming season rather than simply stated what happened. In Japan, longing and waiting were everything.

At some point in my talk, I saw my father start to smile. Out of the corner of my eye, I saw Allison rapping on her watch. I kept wrapping my mannequin; I'd barely gotten to the *obi*. I was now explaining the messages sent by the various bows. My six listeners seemed deeply fascinated. I demonstrated the complex turtle bow, which drew appreciative sighs from my mother and the two tourist ladies. The turtle was an intense feat, with a beautiful result—it made scarf tying look like child's play.

"Can I answer any questions?" I asked at ten after one. The lecture should have been over at one, but I was determined to deliver my planned program.

"How much does a kimono like you're wearing cost?" one of my tourist friends asked.

"This was a one-of-a-kind, custom-made design from the mid-sixties. Then it might have cost the equivalent of five thousand dollars, but for the same design custom-made today, I'd guess it might be ten to twenty thousand dollars, depending on the stature of the artisans involved. Interestingly, once a kimono has been purchased, its value decreases dramatically. There's no market for used contemporary kimono like the one I'm wearing, because Japanese people don't feel comfortable wearing garments that belonged to other people. The only used kimono that can be sold for high prices are those from the Edo period and earlier," I said, with a wave of my arm to the kimono in the gallery.

"How can *anyone* buy a kimono that costs so much?" the tourist continued in a disbelieving tone.

"Young women don't usually pay for them. Their grandmothers do, especially if it's a coming-of-age kimono that a girl wears to visit the family shrine at age twenty. It's quite common for a Japanese girl to be given a choice: her grandparents will pay for her college education, or for that over-the-top kimono. Look at the robes on display in here—what would you choose? What really lasts—silk brocade, or your essay on *Beowulf*?"

There was a subtle ripple of laughter. I fielded half a dozen more questions, and even though I saw Allison waving her hands like an umpire at a baseball game, I made sure that I answered every question. After all, if people didn't want to hear me talk, they could leave.

At the end of it all, I received a tiny round of applause. Only eight were left—my parents, Mr. Shima and Mr. Morimoto, Allison, and three museum visitors. After the people got out of their chairs, Allison came up to me with a horribly false smile and said, "Well done."

Her praise couldn't be fainter, I thought. "Thank you. I was surprised to hear you using a lot of points from my outline in your introduction. Is that why you wanted me to show you the outline ahead of time?"

"No." But Allison at least had the good grace to blush.

"I know you!" my mother said, interrupting our tense moment. "You were at Wellesley. I was Catherine Howard from the class of 'sixty-eight."

"Allison Lancer Powell, class of 'seventy," Allison said, smiling at her. "I didn't know there was another kimono lover at school."

"Well, it's not my life's work. But I admire Japanese fabrics because I work as an interior designer."

"Good for you. Perhaps I can talk to you a little about our museum's advisory committee. It's a group of professionals from the area who give us input and direction on our programs—"

"I'm quite busy with the board of trustees of the Japanese Museum in San Francisco. That's where I live. I'm only here to see my daughter, Rei."

Allison looked from my blond mother to me in confusion. The resemblance was not obvious—especially when I was dressed in a kimono. I knew I looked more like my father, who was at the moment making a covert inspection of Mr. Shima and Mr. Morimoto. I hadn't had a chance to tell my father about the Japanese cultural attaché, and I guessed he was wondering if Mr. Morimoto was another representative of the Morioka Museum.

"Rei has done an outstanding job given the challenging circumstances," Allison said.

My mother kept smiling, but I had a sense that she

was scrutinizing Allison. She'd been close enough to overhear what I said to Allison about her appropriation of my lecture outline.

Mr. Morimoto cleared his throat. "We are sorry to be taking you from your parents, Miss Shimura."

"What's that?" my father asked sharply. "There will be no taking of my child anywhere! She is a U.S. citizen living in America. She cannot be deported."

"It's all right, Dad," I said quickly. "Mr. Morimoto is the cultural attaché at the Japanese embassy. He'd like to show me around at the embassy down the street."

"I'd like to accompany you," my father said in Japanese. He must have wanted to present them with the picture of a protective family.

I'd learned the hard way that it didn't pay to go into unknown situations with my father as a witness. "Daddy, I'd rather go alone. Why don't you and Mother have some lunch. I can catch up with you here in a couple of hours."

"I'll be happy for you to be my guests in the museum's restaurant," Allison said, surprising me.

"That would be lovely—if it really isn't too much trouble," my mother answered with a smile.

"When you are free, we shall be here, waiting for you." My father looked reprovingly at Mr. Morimoto, as if to warn him that he'd storm the embassy if I wasn't released.

"Don't worry. It won't be like yesterday," I said.

"Did you have some problem yesterday?" Mr. Morimoto asked as we walked out of the museum together.

"Well, we were discussing some rather unpleasant news with the police. It turned out that a Japanese woman tourist carrying my passport was murdered. This is the woman who in all likelihood had the bridal kimono—"

"Please hush," Mr. Morimoto said. "This is for discussion within the embassy walls."

So they wanted secrecy, I thought as I silently walked with the two men down S Street to Massachusetts Avenue. There was no hustle and bustle in this part of Washington, unlike Dupont Circle and Adams Morgan. Nobody could have heard us, and now that we weren't talking, the silence was heavy and awkward. But it was their choice, not mine.

23

The embassy of Japan was, to my eyes, the most imposing of a long row of embassies on Massachusetts Avenue. It was not a matter of height or ornamentation; it was just that the long, cream stucco building looked as if it had been built to Japanese specifications, not converted from something originally meant as a private home. Unlike the other buildings, it looked as if it had always been an embassy rather than a home—in large part because of a striking series of tall, thin windows that gave it a Frank Lloyd Wright aura of streamlined elegance.

Inside the embassy, I didn't have to sign in because I was being escorted by Mr. Morimoto, but I did have to pass through a metal detector. Then the diplomat ushered me into a room that felt like a large white box. There were no windows or pictures, just a long rosewood conference table that reflected the glare from the harsh fluorescent lights overhead. The chairs around the table were made from steel and plastic. The only other object in the room was a telephone. Still, I imagined there was a tape recorder, and maybe even a camera, hidden within the room's walls. That was why Mr. Morimoto had wanted me to wait to speak.

Someone was waiting for us already—a young Japanese man who looked me over carefully and nodded without smiling. He was introduced to me as Mr. Yashiro, from the office of the consul. The three men sat on one side of the table. I sat on the other, recalling how I'd sat in a similar arrangement at the Morioka Museum.

"We understand that you're an American citizen, Miss Shimura, who has lived in Japan for some time. Which language would you like to speak?" Mr. Yashiro asked in English.

"I'd rather speak Japanese," I said. "And before I answer your questions, I'd like to say to Shima-san how very sorry I am about what has happened. I will explain to you exactly how the kimono was stolen from my locked room."

"You know? This was something you witnessed?" Mr. Yashiro responded instantly.

"No, I mean to explain everything that came before." I tried to stay calm. I must have tripped over my Japanese—I'd have to be careful and use simple language, words that couldn't be misinterpreted.

I told them everything. I narrated how I'd kept the boxes close to me on the plane, even carrying them into the rest room; how I'd told Hana they were just souvenirs for my parents, but that she'd been disbelieving, and intrigued enough by what I was carrying to mention it to her roommate later on. I described how I'd carried the kimono as a group to the museum and was stunned to learn that the museum couldn't accept the bridal kimono. I went on about how I'd hoped to put it in the hotel safe, and when that didn't work out, that I planned to find a safe, locked storage place elsewhere.

"But you didn't store it safely anywhere. Why not?" Mr. Shima asked at the end of my monologue.

"Well, because that very night it was stolen, either during a short outing I took to, um, a shopping mall, or during the twenty minutes I took to get a cup of tea downstairs. I called the museum that night but didn't get a reply. In the time since, I've done a lot of thinking. I believe that the woman I met on the plane is the most likely thief. My theory seems even more likely to be true since her dead body was found along with a key to my room and my passport."

"But no kimono," Mr. Morimoto said.

"That's right. Whoever killed her must have taken it. It was the most valuable thing with her." I paused. I wanted to say what I'd been thinking about Allison and Jamie possibly being involved, but I knew they wouldn't believe it. They would regard Allison as an honorable person because she'd called Mr. Shima to alert him about the missing kimono.

"Miss Omori has just returned from Los Angeles to identify the body of the victim," Mr. Morimoto said.

"Yes, I know. She checked into our hotel again. Are you going to interview her and Mr. Watanabe?"

"I was with Miss Omori and Mr. Watanabe today when they went to see the body," Mr. Yashiro said. "We talked to each other then."

"What do you think of the police handling of this situation?" I asked, thinking that the police might finally have some motivation to look for the kimono, since a diplomat had taken an interest.

"What do *you* think?" Mr. Yashiro turned the question on me.

"They seem very interested in finding a solution to Hana Matsura's murder, but they don't have an accurate understanding of her character. Also, I'm sad to say that I think they're not going to search for the kimono at all."

"We know that you spoke to them at their headquarters," Mr. Shima said. "It was very shocking when they said you are part of the Floating World, and you had no good answer."

I took a deep breath and said, "They have no more understanding of the Japanese Floating World than of the proper way to eat rice. They're trying to make me a scapegoat, because they don't want to look for a thief."

"What's your personal insurance situation, Miss Shimura?" Mr. Yashiro asked.

"None," I said. "The goods I was carrying over were already insured by Metropolitan, the museum's insurance carrier. Usually, I have travel insurance when I buy plane tickets using my credit card, but this time the ticket was paid for by the Museum of Asian Arts."

"A free trip? Very nice for you," Mr. Morimoto commented with a slight sneer.

"Have you filed any insurance claim for the bridal kimono?" Mr. Yashiro persisted.

"As I just explained to you, I didn't make an insurance plan for it because I believed that it was covered with the group of other kimono traveling. The only reports I've made are to hotel security, who informed me that the hotel can't pay for items missing from rooms, and to the police."

"So there's no money coming to you?" Mr. Morimoto asked.

"None at all. If I had it, of course I would give it to the museum."

Mr. Shima said, in a low voice, "There's no point. That *uchikake* is irreplaceable."

"I know. I can only tell you how sorry I am that it was stolen. I try so many times, in my mind, to think of what I could have done to save it."

"I wonder if you did save it," Mr. Yashiro, the consular officer, said. "I wonder if you caught Miss Matsura in the act of taking the robe from your room, and committed an act of such savage defense that you killed her. During the fight, the robe was probably ruined. You knew you could not return it to Mr. Shima, so you reported it stolen."

I caught my breath. Mr. Yashiro's fantasy was straight out of an old samurai drama. Did he really think I was capable of killing? Was he watching to see if I showed the right, or wrong, reaction?

"If I killed Hana in my room, how could I have discreetly moved her dead body out of a crowded hotel and all the way to a shopping-mall Dumpster? I would have had to take a taxi. Blood and guts would have been everywhere. The police would surely have me locked up by now."

"Police must have all evidence in hand before they make an arrest," Mr. Yashiro said. "I'm sure, given your previous encounters with the law, you know that."

The embassy must have located the Japanese media accounts—the things that Richard had mentioned a few weeks ago when we had lunch at Appetito. I'd brooded then that my slightly colorful past would have kept the Morioka from seeing me as a worthwhile art courier. Now I had more to worry about.

"So, I've been around a few people who passed away, but the Japanese police never charged me with a crime; in fact, you could argue that I helped out in their investigations."

"Needless to say, what has happened here is more serious than anything before," Mr. Yashiro said. I wondered if he'd trained as a lawyer—he was really good at intimidation.

I tried to seem cool by leaning back a little in my chair. However, I couldn't proceed beyond fifteen degrees because of the big *obi* bow centered in the middle of my back.

I sat up straight again. "It would be easy if you could blame it all on me: what a clever way to wrap up the sad story of a lost national treasure and a dead young woman. If this happened in Japan, you could have had the police hold me in prison for days without a warrant."

"What's the point of what you are saying?" Mr. Yashiro sounded bored.

I'd been speaking Japanese, but now I switched to English. "This is my country, and I know my rights. One of them is the right to due process. I've given you some very useful information, but apparently, you've already made up your minds. All I can say is that if you remain trapped inside your tiny box of stereotypes, you'll never find the kimono."

Because of my attire, I couldn't storm out. I rose awkwardly from my chair and made a slow, awkward exit because of the tightness of the kimono and the flopping *zori* on my feet. Despite my appearance as a traditional Japanese girl, I couldn't mask the woman I'd become during my lean and desperate years in Japan—and, even more unsettling, the woman the American police, and Japanese government, suspected I'd become.

My parents were buying Hmong Christmas-tree ornaments in the gift shop when I found them. I assured them that nothing disastrous had happened during my time at the embassy, and that I was ready to go back to the hotel and change my clothes. I was tired of being a Japanese doll.

My mother started talking to me about Allison Powell as soon as we hit S Street.

"Rei, she's *divorced*," my mother said.

"So what? Aren't three-quarters of my friends' parents divorced?"

"This is *quite* a divorce," my mother said. "Her husband was some muckety-muck at the World Bank. She used to live right in Kalorama. But he got the house—to live in with the second missus. I got the feeling that she's very frustrated and short on cash. She could very well have needed that bridal kimono for more than aesthetic reasons."

"I don't know how she dragged out so many personal details," my father said. "I can't get so far with some patients after six months."

"I can't believe it either," I said. "Allison was very casual and impersonal with me."

"You're her junior, sweetie, but we went to school together. When I was going into my unconventional marriage, my own mother once came to me, waving the Wellesley alumnae magazine, asking why I couldn't just marry a nice American banker like the other girls were doing. The alumnae note she was pointing to was about Allison, ironically."

I bit my lip, thinking of my conventional Scottish lawyer, the one who'd suddenly turned into the bad catch—the dangerous one, the one who made my heart ache. Who would have known?

"Rei, I think your mother should have married James Bond," my father said. "The way she conducted covert intelligence on this woman was so disturbing that I felt I had to leave. I spent the rest of the time looking at Korean pottery."

My mother beamed. "After you left, darling, we had some wine and got even deeper in conversation. I told her all about how disappointed I was that Rei had chosen to work in Japan, where things are so difficult. Allison said then that she was very sorry she hadn't been able to keep that bride's kimono you lost—I mean, that was stolen."

"She said that I lost it?"

"Yes," my mother said after a moment's reflection. "I think she said it was a lost kimono. Anyway, she told me the bride's kimono hadn't been insured under her museum's policy, so it seemed as if you might be held responsible for the loss to the Morioka. She was feeling around, I think, to see if Daddy and I would be willing to help you financially. She was worried for you, she said."

"I don't think I'm in that much danger," I said, steadfastly refusing to think about the tense conversation at the embassy of Japan. "You see, the museum in Japan released it to me without bothering to check about insurance. A lawyer told me that that could be counted as negligence on the Moriokas' part."

"A lawyer?" my mother said, looking at me closely.

"Okay, it was Hugh. But the important thing you've found out for me is that Allison must have heard from Mr. Shima that the Morioka Museum may sue. Even if I win the case, as Hugh thinks I might, it would be a disaster for my reputation. I could hardly work in Japan again."

"Oh, really?" my mother said, a gleam in her eye. "Then you'd have to work here! If you don't want to be so close to Daddy and me in California, your grandmother has enough connections to help you find a nice job in Baltimore or Washington. Why don't you come with us to Baltimore for dinner this evening? There's plenty of room at Grandmother's for all of us to stay overnight."

"Sorry, but I committed to taking out Kyoko and Yoshi this evening, since they're all alone and have been through such a nightmare." I didn't mention that Hugh Glendinning was coming along. I wanted to make it sound like all work and no pleasure.

"That's very thoughtful of you," my father said. "You can see your grandmother later during our visit."

"Great," I said, feeling faint. My solo trip to the United States was turning out to be full of friends and relatives. How ironic it was that as the well-wishers closed me in a tight embrace, I had never felt more alone.

24

Kyoko and Yoshi were in the lobby talking to Hugh when I came downstairs a few hours later. They seemed to be doing all right. I watched Hugh, his head cocked attentively as he listened to Yoshi, never interrupting. Hugh had spent two years as a lawyer working inside a Japanese company; he couldn't speak the language, but he knew how to handle himself.

Yoshi was wearing a jacket and tie, just like Hugh. Kyoko wore a sober black dress that I doubted had come from the mall. I had decided on the red dress from BCBG. Red, I figured, would hide Italian food stains, and worse.

"Very pretty," Kyoko said, sounding wistful as she looked at me. Yoshi's eyes passed over me without a reaction—typical good manners for a Japanese man. Hugh liked the dress, I guessed from the way he looked away from it quickly—as if he might get burned.

"I don't think it fits well. In fact, perhaps I should change," I said to Kyoko, suddenly nervous that I'd gone too glam.

"No, no! Please don't go to any trouble. Your friend Hugh-san was telling us that we need to get to the restaurant on time, because it is very popular," Kyoko said.

"I am very fascinated by Italian food," Yoshi told us.

"One of my hobbies is cooking pasta sauces. We received a pasta bowl as a wedding present . . ."

"Really?" Hugh said, smiling at the two of them.

"I think Yoshi-san means that he and *Hana* received the bowl as a gift. It's unusual to get presents instead of money at wedding time in Japan—isn't it?" I asked. Hugh was acting as if he'd forgotten that Yoshi was Hana's fiancé. I didn't want to be cruel to Yoshi, but I was interested in what his reaction would be. Kyoko, I could tell, was feeling sad—but I didn't know about Hana's ex.

"Yes, it is unusual," Yoshi said. "But between friends in the younger generation, presents are becoming more common."

A mundane response, devoid of emotion. Did Yoshi merely have good Japanese manners, or was he completely cool about Hana's death?

"Shall we go to the car? It's parked just outside," Hugh said.

"Let's go," I agreed, thinking that while Yoshi seemed calm over the pasta-bowl comment, Kyoko appeared slightly shaken. I was beginning to realize that my proposed double date, made up of four people who should not be dating—by any society's rules—was going to be awkward.

"Yoshi, why don't you sit in the front seat, since it's your first time in the U.S. I want you to see the sights as we enter Washington," I said, sliding in next to Kyoko in the backseat of Hugh's black Lexus.

"Nice car," Yoshi said, settling in next to Hugh without further ado. It was common, after all, for men in Japan to take the best seats in the car. "This interior is quite similar to the Toyota Windom."

"The Lexus is the same car as the Windom, just renamed to suit American taste," Hugh said, sounding happy again. "I drove a Windom in Tokyo, so I decided to lease something to remind me of the old times."

Yoshi and Hugh continued their conversation about cars, and I recalled how Hana had told me that Yoshi loved driving. Her parents thought they drove all night, when in reality, they stopped at a love hotel. Hana and Yoshi were both attractive, with healthy sexual appetites—why had they decided to have an arranged marriage? And why would Hana cheat on this man?

The music Hugh was playing over the stereo made me feel like moving—something I'd never heard before, a mix of the symphonic dance club sound that I loved overlaid with what seemed to be old recordings of American gospel. It was provocative, mournful, groovy, and upbeat all at once.

"What are you playing?" I asked Hugh.

"It's Moby's last album, *Play*," Hugh said.

"You haven't heard Moby before? His music is popular in Tokyo clubs," Yoshi said.

"I guess I don't get out much anymore," I said, feeling sorry for myself. Then I looked over at Kyoko, sitting silently and staring out the window, and felt the weight of her much heavier grief take over.

"It's been a hard day for you," I said to Kyoko.

"Yes, a very hard day. Coming out with you tonight and listening to music is a good change."

"Since we can't really talk about it over dinner—can you tell me some more about the autopsy?" I asked Kyoko in a low voice.

"We each went in separately to see the body. I went first. After I came back with the answer, the police told Yoshi that he didn't have to look, after all. The identification had been made. But Yoshi said that he had traveled so far that he wanted to know for himself."

In conversation with me, Kyoko was calling him

Yoshi, not Mr. Watanabe, as she'd done the night before. Had something changed since they'd shared a suite?

"How did he handle the viewing?" I asked. "Did he break down?"

"Not at all. He handled things well. Even when the police tried to ask if he was something called a pimp—absolutely ridiculous! We both showed our business cards, and that was that. After we came back to the hotel, Yoshi telephoned Hana's family to give them the news and hear what they want done. He was quite firm about wanting to do this himself."

"What did her parents say?"

"Mrs. Matsura cried. I could hear it clearly, even though Yoshi was the one on the telephone. Then Mr. Matsura took over the conversation. He requested that we make the arrangements to bring the body back on the plane. The medical examiner's assistant told us that after Hana's parents send a fax asking for her body's release, she will be treated by a mortician and packed in dry ice and put in a special box. We will have that box as extra baggage when we fly back."

A special box—just like the one that held the antique kimono. How ironic. I said, "This all sounds terribly expensive."

"Well, it's strange. Mrs. Chiyoda must have felt badly that this happened on her tour, because she gave me the ticket to travel. Yoshi paid for his own ticket, I know. It wouldn't be fitting for him to do anything else—especially since he's not going to be marrying into Hana's family, after all."

"I still don't understand why the Matsuras didn't come. Wouldn't they want to know for themselves that their daughter had really died?"

We were on the Roosevelt Bridge at this point, and

had been traveling at a sedate sixty miles an hour, when Hugh suddenly dropped to forty.

"What's going on?" I abandoned thoughts of Hana's family for a moment.

"A car has been tailing us for the last ten minutes. I'm trying to see if it's there for a reason."

Kyoko and I both turned around and looked at the bright blue compact car that had braked to avoid hitting us but remained on our tail.

"Hugh, you're paranoid," I said, but still felt a little uneasy.

"Isn't that a Geo?" Yoshi asked. "What a funny car to be making a chase: it's not capable of very high speeds. Hugh-san, why don't you take the next exit and see if they follow after?"

"I'm going to go downtown first and then circle back to Georgetown," Hugh said. "I've got to warn you, I don't know all the roads, and Washington's a damn difficult city to navigate. It makes Tokyo look like Disneyland."

"Disneyland is actually outside of Tokyo," Yoshi said. "It's a crazy place. Very crowded."

I kept my eyes on the blue car. Yes, it had no intention of passing us. I wished I could see the face of the driver, but in the dark, it was impossible to tell even how many people were in the car.

"I wonder if it's car-jackers," I said.

"Hope not," Hugh said, sliding into the fast lane and speeding up to seventy. Then, driving from one lane to the other on the northbound side of Constitution, he wove between vehicles and took a sharp left onto Seventeenth Street. A few more turns and the blue car was not with us anymore.

"On to Georgetown," Hugh said, sounding confident again.

"Well done," Yoshi congratulated, but I didn't say anything. I felt as if I'd come close to disaster and been pulled away at the last minute. We shouldn't have gotten away, but we did.

The Italian restaurant was called Café Milano, on Prospect Street in Georgetown, the almost too-cute-to-be-real neighborhood where many of the streets were still paved with rosy old bricks. Georgetown's large town houses, built in the early nineteenth century, were maintained with a fastidious fervor, with gleaming brass knockers on the gaily colored doors, and the window boxes overflowing with geraniums and chrysanthemums.

Still, there was an edge to the neighborhood—as Hugh began a careful backward swing into a tight parking spot on Thirty-third Street, a man in a soiled Bob Marley T-shirt and army pants emerged out of nowhere, halting the endless traffic in the road with an upheld hand.

"Do you see that man? He is going to help you!" Yoshi said.

"Damn, he's going to want a parking fee," Hugh muttered.

"What parking fee? This is a public street," I said.

"It's a very Washington thing. There are opportunists who see people trying to park and extort money from them."

"Maybe we shouldn't park here," Kyoko said uneasily as I opened the door next to me and got out. By now, the man was complacently leaning on the hood of the car. I made to walk past him, but he spoke.

"Nice car, baby."

"Thanks," I said tightly, although of course the Lexus wasn't mine.

"Thanks isn't enough, baby."

"We found that spot by ourselves."

"I stopped traffic for you." The man grinned nastily at me, showing a gold tooth. "I stopped a big Mercedes SUV that would have rear-ended your sorry little butt. Now, my normal service fee is three bucks, but for Chinese folks, it's four."

"We're not Chinese," I hissed, hoping that Kyoko and Yoshi hadn't heard his racist comment. They'd gotten out of the car and were standing on the sidewalk with Hugh outside the modern red-brick building that housed the restaurant.

"Rei!" Hugh beckoned to me. "Come over here, I'll give you the money."

"Lady, as far as I can see, you weren't the driver. It's up to your husband what he's gonna give me." The man advanced on me, so there was less than a foot of space between us.

For some reason, the man's casual misreading of my national origin and marital status made me just as angry as his assumption that we were going to pay because we were afraid. I'd endured too much crap for the last day and a half, a time when I was dressed like a doll who could barely walk. Tonight, I was wearing Lycra. I had mobility.

"Go bother someone else," I said, and turned away from him just as Hugh came barreling into the street to retrieve me. A stream of profanities followed us all the way to the entrance of the red-brick building where Yoshi and Kyoko stood anxiously waiting.

"Why in heaven did you do that?" Hugh asked me in a low voice as he gave all our coats to a coat-check person. I could see from the looks of a few patrons' faces that they'd seen what happened. They were shaking their heads and looking at me with sympathy. But not Hugh.

"I lost control, okay? I'm sorry to ruin the evening,"

I said, mindful that Yoshi and Kyoko were probably worried about the prospect of another murder.

"It's all right, Rei," Hugh said, but I could hear from the strain in his voice that he really didn't think so. "Let's just go in before we lose our table."

"I'm glad Rei-san is all right, but is that a typical thing for the American street? Dangerous men asking for money?" Kyoko asked Hugh.

"No," he answered, flashing her a reassuring smile. "But after all we've gone through on this ride, I think we deserve a drink."

When we finally sat down, and I had a chance to gaze around Café Milano, I knew instantly why Hugh had chosen it for Kyoko and Yoshi. It was Italian design heaven. The walls were decorated with silk ties framed like artwork, and the tables and curved bar were packed with more examples of European fashion. Women in well-cut little dresses and men with intensely stylish suits—or cashmere turtlenecks and leather pants.

"Eurotrash heaven," Hugh said, following my eyes. "But the food's absolutely delicious—simply done, yet stunning."

"Just reading this menu is exciting," Yoshi said. "I think I will try the ravioli Max Mara with cheese, artichoke hearts, and prosciutto inside."

"Max Mara is a clothing label, isn't it?" Kyoko asked.

"All the dishes are named after Italian fashion designers," Hugh said, smiling at her. He'd chosen the perfect restaurant. Kyoko and Yoshi could tell their friends they'd done more than purchase designer labels—they could say they'd eaten them, too.

"Would anyone like to drink wine?" Yoshi asked when the waiter appeared.

"I'd love some," I said gratefully. "Would you honor us by choosing the wine, Yoshi-san?"

"All right." Yoshi took the wine menu eagerly in his hands. At last, he selected a Vini Spumante. Hugh seemed startled by the choice but gave the order to the waiter. I wondered if Italian sparkling wine was very expensive. Hugh had told me ahead of time that he planned to pay for the whole meal, and knowing how hard it was to try to split checks in Japan, I agreed in principle. Kyoko didn't drink anything, but Hugh, Yoshi, and I shared the bottle. It was a delicious wine—bubbly and sweet enough to set off the salty appetizers that arrived a few minutes later.

"You made a wonderful choice, Yoshi-san. Do you know a lot about wine?" I asked.

"Oh, no, hardly! It's just that we don't have choices like this in Japan. It's easy, with such a fine list, to pick something enjoyable."

"But how did you know which wine to choose?" I persisted. I hadn't thought he was prosperous enough to indulge in regular wine buying in Japan. I knew I wasn't—even though I loved American and European wines, all I could afford was Japanese beer.

"I read magazines," Yoshi said. "They have recommendations that I try to remember."

"Choices are difficult, aren't they?" Hugh said. "I personally think the hardest choices to make are about relationships."

Kyoko drew her brows together as if she were perplexed.

"'Relationships' means the situation between two things, or two people. Boyfriends and girlfriends, or husbands and wives," I explained, shooting Hugh a warning glance. I couldn't tell what he was up to.

"I've been wondering, Yoshi-san, about how these arranged marriages work," Hugh said.

Kyoko said coldly, "I thought you were Rei-san's special friend."

Now it was my turn to blush. "Well, I do think of Hugh as a friend, but the locations we live in make it impossible for anything greater to occur. Also, as you can tell from our argument when parking the car, we are two very different types."

Yoshi drank a little more of the sparkling wine and looked at Hugh. "I wouldn't recommend arranged marriage for you. I don't think you have the right personality."

"And you did?" Hugh drank the last of his glass of wine, and with a subtle movement of his hand summoned the sommelier. This time he and Yoshi put their heads together and ordered two different Tuscan reds. I knew what Hugh was doing—trying to open the floodgates of communication with the help of alcohol, something that was done frequently among colleagues after work was finished in Tokyo.

"I'm a busy person," Yoshi said. "I could try to meet girls myself, but it would take a long time to find one who is right for me. An agency makes things easier. Hana was the eleventh girl I'd met with, so I guess I had become fairly tired of the process. Still, she seemed great. You never met her, but, well—she was something."

"I talked to Hana about the arrangements on the plane," I said, smiling at Yoshi. "She was willing to stay at home, but she wasn't a housewife type, was she? It probably appealed to you that she enjoyed travel and international culture."

"That's what I noticed when we first talked," Yoshi said. "But in the end . . . well, I was a little worried. The surface was beautiful, but I think she was a little bit high-strung. I wasn't sure she should go on this trip, but Kyoko-san thought it was a good idea."

Again, a hint of intimacy. I looked at Kyoko and said, "Why did you say that?"

"Well, she, ah, wouldn't be able to shop so freely

after marriage," Kyoko said, looking daggers at me. "Yoshi-san called me to ask me to take special care of Hana during the trip. I feel especially terrible because I shirked my responsibility."

"I'm a little confused. You two sound as if you've known each other for a while," Hugh said, deftly introducing the issue I'd wondered about.

"Of course. Kyoko is my cousin. Didn't you know?"

"No!" I said, staring at them both.

"This is the situation," Yoshi said easily. "Kyoko's mother is my mother's younger sister. We grew up a few miles from each other. We've been very good friends since birth."

"But I thought—you were Hana's friend from work," I said to Kyoko, who had been staring at her capellini Benneton.

"Only recently. Yoshi is the one who told me the news about the engagement. Then I made it my business to learn more about Hana," Kyoko said.

I paused, thinking of how I could phrase the next question. In the end, I decided there was no subtle way to do it. "Kyoko-san, did you ever give Yoshi your opinion of Hana's character?"

"No, I didn't. It isn't my business. I'm a little—please excuse me for a moment." Kyoko got up swiftly and walked toward the back of the room. I guessed she was going to the ladies' room to compose herself.

Yoshi said, "Kyoko-chan didn't tell me anything important until the plane ride over here. I guess she felt she needed to speak at last, because hearing about things from the police would be shocking."

"What did she say exactly?" I asked.

"She said that Hana had been looking for a temporary playboy. She did the best she could to keep control of Hana's movements. Rei-san, I understand you also tried to help. But it didn't work, unfortunately. The police told us there had been signs that she had relations with someone before she died."

"I didn't like what she was doing," I said. "I wouldn't have wanted to be you, left behind in Japan, not knowing."

I'd spoken spontaneously, and after the words had come out, and Hugh's face had gone ashen, I realized why I'd been so angry about Hana's campaign. I was talking about myself, revealing what it had felt like finally knowing, after having seen a magazine photo, that Hugh was spending his nights pleasurably with another woman on another continent. At that time I'd wanted to kill him. Had Yoshi felt the same about Hana?

25

Kyoko eventually came back, and not another word was said about Hana. Dinner was excellent, everyone agreed. Hugh and Yoshi had both devoured sautéed lamb chops with mushrooms over a mint risotto, while Kyoko nibbled on a Milanese-style breaded veal chop served with a tomato salad. The homemade mozzarella cloaking my eggplant-filled *mezzelune* pasta had seemed like a comforting blanket, but it couldn't smooth over the uncomfortable feelings that had surfaced for me.

I savored a giant chocolate truffle and tried to recall what the point of the dinner date had been. I'd hoped to figure out whether there was a legitimate reason to suspect that Kyoko and Yoshi had caused Hana's death. What seemed clear, at least from the story they'd presented, was that the cousins were close, but Kyoko had felt constrained to conceal from Yoshi his bride's shortcomings. Whether Kyoko had loved her cousin enough to kill Hana to prevent her sullying him seemed out of the question. Still, I thought there might be something just a little more passionate in her feelings for Yoshi than what one would typically feel for a cousin. Japan had no laws against first cousins marrying, either.

We left the restaurant around eleven, walking around

the corner to the place where Hugh had parked the car. As soon as we got in, a car stopped behind us, clearly waiting for the spot. Hugh began steering the Lexus out into the street, but before he'd gone a few feet there was a twisting, sinking movement.

I hadn't put on my seat belt yet, so I fell against the passenger door, and Kyoko, in turn, fell on top of me. She felt heavy and strong, I noticed immediately. Stronger than she looked. I imagined Hugh and Yoshi were also losing their balance in the front seat, but a quick glance in their direction showed they each had a lap shoulder belt.

Hugh stopped the car, even though it was at a crazy angle on the street. "Sorry, friends. I must have a flat tire."

"Don't worry. If you have a spare, I can change the tire." Yoshi had already unsnapped his seat belt and was making movements to get out of the car.

"I'll do it myself, because I'm the idiot who must have gone too long without checking the pressure."

The car behind us was honking, because it wanted to get into the space we'd vacated. However, the angle at which Hugh had stopped on the street was blocking it in both directions. Now was the time that Bob Marley could have made himself useful, but as he wasn't around, I jumped out into the street and directed the traffic myself.

Hugh had gone around to join Yoshi in looking at his right front tire. He held a small flashlight to it, as cars were slowly inching by. The male driver of a huge Ford SUV took the time to roll down his window and yell, "You're blocking the road, fools!"

I didn't answer him, and neither did Hugh. There was an expression on Hugh's face that told me this might not be a simple case of popping on a spare. He was crouched down by his left tire now, running a hand over its surface. Then he moved to the back and examined the other tires.

"What is it?" I said, going out to join him.

"All four tires have been slashed. We're going to have to call for a tow. "

I explained the situation to Yoshi and Kyoko, who looked grave.

"Do you think . . . the man who wanted money for parking did it?" Kyoko asked.

"Probably. Me and my big mouth," I said.

"What does that mean?" Kyoko asked.

"It means I shouldn't have said what I did. And I should have given him what he demanded."

"No, I should have given the money," Yoshi said. "After all, you and Hugh have done so much for us. Dinner was a delicious experience."

"I'm a little worried how long we'll have to wait," Hugh said. He'd gotten off the phone and slowly driven the car to a space in front of a fire hydrant—the only area on the street he could move into so that traffic could travel in both directions. "Friday night is a busy time. Yoshi, I think I should put you and Kyoko in a cab back to the hotel."

"That's fine, and we have plenty of money to cover the fare," Yoshi said. "Kyoko told me that she was rather tired. And how about you, Rei-chan?"

Everyone looked at me.

"I'll stay with Hugh for now and make it back later after the tires are fixed." I flagged down a taxi, got Kyoko and Yoshi inside, and gave the driver specific instructions on how to reach Washington Suites.

It was ten minutes later when I returned to Hugh, who was talking to a cop who was writing out a parking ticket.

"It's not his fault!" I bleated. "The car was vandalized, with tires slashed. We had to pull over somewhere, out of the path of traffic—"

"As you're hearing, sir, this lady is recounting the same sad story. We're expecting the towing company any minute," Hugh said. But no amount of explanation worked. The policeman kept writing while steadfastly ignoring us. At the end, he handed Hugh a ticket with a flourish.

"Fifty bucks," Hugh said. "As the Americans say, easy come, easy go."

"I'm sorry. I'll pay you back," I said when the policeman had left.

"What do you mean? It's not your fault. When you told me what that guy said to you, I wished I'd gone after him."

"About being Chinese?"

"No, about being married to me." Hugh rolled his eyes.

"Hugh, I—I wonder if it was necessarily that Bob Marley guy who did it."

"Who else could it be?"

"Kyoko was gone from the table for a long time."

"Why would she do a psycho thing like slashing tires?"

"I don't know if she was thinking about doing something to hurt you. Perhaps it was a message to me, for being so nosy and obnoxious."

"Or what about the car that followed us?" Hugh asked. "I thought I lost it, but who really knows?"

"I'm scared." It was the first time that I'd said it aloud, because I'd felt I didn't even have a right to that emotion in the beginning. After all, millions of Americans had suffered car thefts, home break-ins, and muggings. When the bride's kimono had vanished, I'd thought of it as a terrible thing to happen, but not a vi-

olation of my own safety. Now—with the death of
Hana, the unknown person waiting for me at the Spanish Steps, and the phantom driver—I had to take the situation more seriously.

Hugh took my hand in his. "I am, too. But I don't
want to give in to whoever did this. We'll figure out
who did it and—oh, look, our salvation is here."

The tow truck arrived with blinding white lights
flashing on top of its cab. Now traffic was seriously
snarled. With a backdrop of honking, Hugh took care
of the business quickly, tipping the driver twenty to deliver his car to a particular car-repair place in Adams
Morgan. Then we were alone.

"Should we take the Metro?" I asked, thinking that I
might not even be able to make it back to Northern Virginia before the line shut down at midnight.

"There's no Metro in Georgetown. I guess it's supposed to keep out the riffraff."

"Well, that strategy worked well," I said sarcastically.

"Yes, look at the two of us," Hugh said. "A couple of
daft foreigners who've broken the law twice in the last
forty-eight hours. Not to mention evading a possible
charge of prostitution and solicitation."

I laughed then, for the first time all evening. "So,
what do you want to do?"

"How about listening to live music somewhere? I can't
offer Moby, but we could probably hear a jazz act."

"There's a good place for music here," I said, thinking there was no point in running for the Metro after
all, especially since I didn't really want to go to the
Washington Suites. "I went there in college once. It's in
an alley."

"Blues Alley," Hugh said, smiling at me.

The club was two rooms, equally dim and smoky, and
packed with even more people than Café Milano had

been. These patrons were serious music lovers who
bobbed and swayed and called out cheers to the volup-
tuous woman with long, rippling hair and skintight leggings who was singing on a small stage. She was called
Charmaine Neville. Hugh had never heard of her, so I
told him about the better-known Louisiana band called
the Neville Brothers. Together, we decided she was
probably a sister or cousin to them.

"What kind of Scotch do you have?" I asked when
the waitress came around to the small table we'd managed to find. The best bet was the Macallan, so I ordered Hugh's neat and mine mixed with water. When
the waitress left, he said, "Why did you order something so strong? You know I don't drink that much anymore."

"After everything you've done for me tonight, the
least I can do is buy you a drink," I said. There was another reason I'd ordered the whiskey. I wanted to go
back in time, to pretend I was a year and a half younger,
at a strange bar in the Japanese Alps, tasting Scotch for
the first time at the behest of a man whom I was attracted to, yet slightly afraid of. The fear was gone
now—but the attraction wasn't.

Hugh didn't touch his drink; he seemed riveted by
Charmaine Neville singing an old standard about infidelity and emotional anguish.

"She's got a powerful presence," Hugh said, taking
off his jacket and loosening his tie. "Now, I want to
hear what happened at the museum today. How did the
lunchtime lecture come off?"

"The lecture was a disaster, but fortunately very few
people were there to witness it. Afterward I got strong-
armed to go over to the Japanese embassy, where I was
questioned by some bureaucrats and Mr. Shima, the registrar from the Morioka Museum, who interrupted his

vacation to come out and help handle the crisis. It's just awful. They don't trust me at all, it's clear."

"So . . . the blue car," Hugh said. "It could have been the embassy of Japan, or the police."

"Police or diplomats wouldn't slash our tires," I said.

"No, of course not," Hugh said, but he didn't sound particularly convinced.

Charmaine Neville was now singing a song with a chorus about a man who had the right key but put it in the wrong keyhole. Couldn't she give the theme a rest?

"I need some air," I said to Hugh. I got up and made my way through the crowd out the club's exit to the tiny alley. There, I leaned against the old brick building and breathed deeply of the cold night air.

Hugh joined me a second later, carrying our coats over his arm.

"Here." He offered me my coat. I slipped it around me.

"I wish that place had room to dance," Hugh said, taking me into his arms. I was wearing the stiletto heels my mother had treated me to, causing our bodies to come together in a way that was undeniably sexual.

"This feels terrible," Hugh murmured into my hair.

"How can you say that?" I moved in closer.

"I don't like the idea of infidelity. Listening to her sing about it . . . and having you in my arms now feels wretched. Yet I must admit I've never felt more aroused."

"It kind of reminds me of the very first time, in the Japanese Alps."

Hugh shook his head. "I don't feel that way. Then I'd only known you a short while, and I wasn't in love with you yet. It's not like it is tonight."

I looked down, feeling my cheeks get hot.

"Tell me again where your parents are right now." Hugh said.

"They're spending the night in Baltimore," I said.

"You sent them off, eh?"

I laughed. "No. They wanted me to come. I mean, t
go along with them—"

"I'm the one who wants you to come," Hugh said
and from the way he looked at me, I caught his mean
ing entirely.

Georgetown traffic is bad on the weekend, but if yo
stress the urgency of the situation and promise to ti
well, amazing things can happen. Our cabdriver zig
zagged across yellow lines, made illegal turns, and eve
cruised through two red lights to reach Adams Morga
in about ten minutes. Hugh didn't touch me in the tax
at all, just kept his eyes on me, which was all the mor
maddening.

His apartment was inside a handsome old tow
house: red brick with black shutters. We walked in th
front door, and as Hugh fiddled around for somethin
in his pocket, I gazed through another door to the build
ing's hallway, which was paved in turn-of-the-centur
red and black octagonal tiles.

"Shite. I must have given my entire key ring to th
towing company," Hugh said, looking at me gravely. "
have no other key to the house handy."

"No. You couldn't have done that to me, on a nigh
like this—"

"Well, I'm on the second floor. I probably could climl
the fire escape and get in through my kitchen window."

Just how many times would we break the laws o
Washington that night? I walked outside with him to a
small garden, where a motion-detector spotlight cam
on to illuminate us and a few bushes of late-bloomin
white roses. It was impressive that roses could be aliv

in late October, I thought as Hugh swung himself up on a cast-iron ladder that ended six feet above the ground. He climbed to the second-floor landing, where he fiddled with a window before looking sheepishly at me.

"I left it locked."

"What do you want to do? Is your landlord in the building?"

"Landlady. The last thing I want to do is rouse her at twelve-thirty." He paused. "I might have to break it. Can you throw me up something to use as a tool?"

"She won't hear a window breaking?"

"Not if it's done right." He was stripping off his beautiful jacket. I fished around in my backpack and came up with a portable umbrella. I tossed it up to him, watching it spin in the air like a martial-arts weapon.

Hugh caught the umbrella and wrapped his beautiful dark green suit jacket around it. Then, getting extremely close to the window, he tapped it. When nothing happened he hit it harder, and I heard the sound of breaking glass. As the glass shattered, a warning went off inside me. If I entered Hugh's apartment, I was going to cheat on Takeo. There was no question about it.

Hugh stabbed the umbrella upward as a sign of victory. Then he got to the task of clearing a large enough hole to insert his hand and open the lock. The window was pushed up, and he dove through just as a telephone inside started ringing. I heard him grab the phone and start talking.

"Yes, yes, it was I, Mrs. Weisburg. I'm all right, and I'm so sorry. Just an accident with a glass of champagne. Cristal, actually—Cristal champagne and broken crystal, heh-heh. I'll bring a bottle to you tomorrow. Get some rest, and again, I'm so sorry about waking you."

After Hugh hung up, he looked out the window

again and motioned for me to go around to the front of the house. I nodded, taking off my shoes as I entered the house. I didn't want Mrs. Weisburg to hear me enter the building.

"You are so outrageous," I whispered to him as he tiptoed down the staircase of his building and quietly opened the vestibule door.

"You're worse," he whispered back, before pinning me against the wall, lowering his head for a long, lazy kiss.

"Let's go up," he whispered, leading me by the hand to the second floor and through an opened door to an apartment that was older than any place I'd ever lived in, I could tell from the small fireplace sized just right to burn coal, the divided windows with wavy glass, and the lavish Georgian Revival moldings running around the ceiling. The fireplace and moldings were painted a creamy alabaster, but the walls were a bold, electric blue.

"Whatever happened to your beige tastes?" I asked, looking with confusion at the rest of the room. There wasn't much furniture—nothing except a stereo, stacks of books, a leather sofa, and one *tansu* chest that had been in his Tokyo flat.

"Don't even think of giving me your opinion tonight. At present, there's only one room I want you to decorate."

His vast bedroom was painted a rusty ocher color that I liked a little better than the blue. It held his familiar sleigh bed, neatly made up with plain white sheets, and an antique Biedermeier armoire that he must have bought recently. His bedside tables were computer boxes; he'd made a simple attempt at decoration by throwing a monogrammed hand towel over each one. As I looked around, Hugh lit some candles and disappeared for a moment. He came back in carrying a vase of yellow and cream tea roses that looked as if they were from the garden. His flower arrangement was awkward, to say the least—each stem trimmed to the same length and overstuffed in the graceful Waterford vase, with leaves and odd bits of twig underneath the waterline. This carelessly made bouquet was the antithesis of spare, elegant Japanese *ikebana*. Takeo would have cringed at it, not to mention the sight of me sitting on the sleigh bed, pulling off my stockings so recklessly that they snagged.

"I picked these for you the other day," Hugh said, setting the flowers down on the left side of the bed, the side where I customarily slept. "That's why they're a bit shabby. I hoped you would have made it here earlier, but I didn't want to rush you."

"I waited too long," I said, and without further delay pulled him over me.

Hugh was the same—and different. Touching his body was like retracing my way across a familiar landscape, but knowing it was the last time I might make the trip filled me with urgency. I sensed Hugh felt the same; his mouth moved over me with a hunger that reminded me of the way I'd devoured chocolate, cheese, and wine at my first meal in Washington.

I couldn't make up my mind which way I wanted him. I wanted him every way: on top, behind me, underneath. I didn't know that I'd scratched him until I saw a smear of blood from my fingertips on his sheets. By then it was too late; I was coming, and that was all that seemed to matter.

"That was insane," he whispered, rolling to my side sometime around two in the morning. For the first time I heard more than the sound of my own breathing.

"I know. Was it what you expected?" I whispered back, suddenly sensing what it must have been like to have to make love to me in so many positions. I'd stretched him to his limits—I hadn't wanted it to end.

"Well . . . I've dreamed about this so long, I didn't know what to expect. You delivered every fantasy, I guess . . ." Hugh trailed off, sounding unsure.

"But not the tenderness," I said. "It should have been more focused. I worry—I worry that you didn't come."

Hugh sighed. "How could I, knowing that it's going to end? I can't find joy in another man's woman. But don't worry about me. It was perfect sex otherwise, wasn't it?"

I rolled over and looked at him in the dim light that came from the one candle that hadn't flickered out. "What if I don't go back to him?"

"Of course you will," Hugh said, sounding weary. "Someone fluent in Japanese, who can fit in the way I never could."

"But you fit *into* me like nobody else—"

"So I'm a great lay. Thanks. That really warms my heart."

"Come on, Hugh. Give me a break." I kissed around his chest until I could feel the faint heartbeat. Then I continued my travels down a trail of gingery hair that ran along his chest.

"What are you doing, Rei?" Hugh whispered as I moved below his navel—as if he were shocked.

"Loving you," I said. And I did.

26

The morning after, with Hugh. In Japan, it usually meant us lying together, me dozing against his chest, thinking halfheartedly about bringing tea to bed, while he talked on the cell phone, telling his secretary at Sendai Limited that he'd eaten bad sushi the previous evening and wouldn't be in until at least noon.

Late Saturday morning in Adams Morgan I awoke with my body curled against Hugh's back, hearing a telephone ring, just like the old days. Hugh picked it up, mumbling something. Then he handed it to me.

"It's for you."

"Hello," I muttered, completely irritated. Who in the hell knew I was sleeping at Hugh Glendinning's apartment? Even if Yoshi and Kyoko suspected he was more than a friend, I didn't think they'd actually track him down through the Washington phone book, especially since I hadn't mentioned his last name.

"Rei." A man was pronouncing my name in the way that only Japanese did—with a soft *R*, that was somewhere between an *R* and an *L*. Since the guy had used my first name, and not my last, I knew it had to be a friend.

"Is this Yoshi-kun?" I asked in Japanese, adding onto his name the casual, affectionate suffix used for young men and boys. *Kun* was the word to use with a guy when *san* felt too stiff—just as *chan* was used for women one was close to.

"Who's Yoshi-kun? Your third boyfriend?"

It was Takeo, loud and clear and furious. The connection was so good that you couldn't even tell it was a long-distance call.

"Oh, hi, *Takeo,*" I said, putting stress on his name and punching Hugh lightly, to make sure he got the point. I wanted him to leave the bed, to give me at least a modicum of modesty. Instead, Hugh was regarding me with the lazy, contented expression of a man who had just had a night of great sex—and expected more of the same.

"*Oh, hi, Takeo.*" Takeo mimicked my American accent perfectly. "Hi to you, Rei Shimura. It's ten o'clock on a Saturday morning. Instead of being at your hotel in Northern Virginia, area code 703, you're in the 202 area code, which I know means Washington, D.C. Why is that?"

"How nice that you called. How did you get this number?" I bluffed, while thinking about how horribly fast everything had unraveled. I wasn't cut out for this kind of thing. I could barely balance on a pair of *geta* sandals. Why had I thought that I could balance two men?

"I called your room, and a woman picked up. A strange woman, with an American accent—"

"Hey, that could be important! What did she sound like? It might have been the kimono thief."

"Don't try to distract me with any bogus stories about kimono thieves. It was your mother."

"You're sure?"

"She said her name was Catherine Shimura, and she was hanging up clothes of yours that you had thrown about carelessly. I didn't know you were staying with your family."

"They came to support me in my time of crisis," I said, keeping my eyes on Hugh, who had gotten up, put on boxer shorts patterned with smiling faces, and started to pull himself back and forth on a rowing machine. A loud squeaking and grinding ensued as he rowed faster and faster. His face was red with exertion or anger—maybe both.

"Well, your mother told me to try you at this number. Hey, what's that sound? What are you doing, Rei? Don't tell me you're in bed with that fellow who answered the telephone."

"That noise is not from a bed, it's a rowing machine."

Takeo exhaled suddenly. "Hold on. You're at a gym?"

"You could say that," I said, looking around Hugh's bedroom. There was a squash racket propped up against the wall, along with a few cans of balls.

"Oh." Takeo burst into warm laughter. "Oh, Rei. Of course. I should have figured that's why a man answered the telephone. He's a trainer or something."

"Something," I said. Hugh was still rowing and glaring at me.

"Great. I brought my running shoes. I wouldn't mind working out for an hour to help fight the jet lag."

"Jet lag?" Suddenly my head was spinning. I lay back and stared at a sweet antique electric light fixture on Hugh's ceiling. I had to center, to get my bearings. What Takeo had just said about jet lag made me very nervous.

"Yes. This is the part you're going to be very happy about. I'm at the Hotel Sofitel on Connecticut Avenue. I thought about how sad you'd sounded the last time we spoke and decided that you needed me. I traveled even though I didn't have my safety travel charm. I got a seat on the last night flight out of Narita yesterday afternoon—and now I'm here."

*   *   *

I agreed to meet Takeo in an hour. After I hung up, I put my head in my hands and moaned, "What am I doing?"

"Getting ready to take a shower with me," said Hugh, who'd finished his exercises and was stripping off his boxers to go into the shower. "Come on. It's a nice big old-fashioned shower, with a shower head out of the side of the wall that will hit you in a place I think you'll adore—"

"Oh, shut up," I said, but I went in the shower with him anyway, not wanting to waste any time. I had to remove the scents of smoke and sex. A horrifying thought hit me: what if Takeo wanted to make love when I reached his hotel? I couldn't do it now—maybe not *ever.*

After we got out, I dried myself with the soft towels I remembered so fondly from Japan. Then Hugh shaved and I rummaged through his armoire.

"What are you looking for? Maybe I can help," he called cheerfully from the bathroom.

"Something to wear," I said.

"And you think I'm a ladies' size four?"

"I was thinking I could borrow one of your Marks and Sparks T-shirts and a pair of sweats or leggings or whatever."

"Sports clothes will look ridiculous with stilettos. Why can't you wear that insanely sexy red dress back to the hotel and get changed there? I'll give you a ride back after we pick up my car at the garage."

"I don't have time to make it back to the Washington Suites. I'm expected at the Sofitel in forty-five minutes."

"Sofitel. What are you talking about?" Hugh stuck his head out of the bathroom to look at me.

"Takeo was calling from there. He flew to Washington because he was worried about me."

"Oh, my God." Hugh walked into the room. He was still naked, and I carefully looked away from the parts I should never have gotten involved with again.

"So—so that's why I need to get dressed in fresh clothing. I can't possibly go see him in clothes from last night."

Hugh shook his head. "I don't believe you! You told me last night you were thinking of giving him up. Now you want me to lend you my clothes so you can go and meet your lover all nice and fresh, as if nothing ever happened between us. Well, forget it. I'll do anything for you but that."

He was right, of course. I had hinted to him that I might give Takeo up. Not meeting Hugh's eyes, I slipped back into the underwear and dress I'd worn the night before. I knew Hugh's reaction was a taste of what might have greeted Hana if she'd made it back to Yoshi alive—and he'd figured out how deceitful she'd been.

I said good-bye to Hugh, but he wouldn't respond. I went downstairs as quietly as possible, regretting that I'd never even gotten a chance to see the whole apartment. At the corner of Columbia Road and Eighteenth Street I had a quick cup of coffee and a vegetarian *empanada* from a stall called Julia's.

Forty minutes till I was due to meet Takeo. I paid the bill and started looking for clothes. Where was Nation's Place mall when I needed it? All I could find were silky Indian saris and Indonesian tie-dyed T-shirts. Finally I found a shop with cheap blue jeans for sale in the windows and some Central American shirts and accessories inside. I wound up with a scratchy but warm embroidered wool shirt, a pair of Wrangler jeans in a size actually meant for teenage boys, and beaded black leather moccasins. I went out the door looking like the coffee-advertising icon Juan Valdez without the sombrero, for forty-five dollars plus sales tax.

Now I had to figure out the Metro. When I asked someone on the street for advice, I was shocked to learn that the Sofitel was a five-minute walk. Takeo was staying so close to Hugh's that it was scary.

Why had my mother given Takeo Hugh's number? How did she have it handy, anyway—had she been carrying it around for months, waiting for the right moment to mess up my life? Outside the Sofitel, I walked around the corner and found a telephone booth. I dialed the Washington Suites and asked to be put through to my parents' room.

My father answered, which shook me slightly. I was ready to rail at my mother for giving out Hugh's number, but what could I say to my father about the situation? He'd been through enough at the police headquarters. I couldn't bear for him to guess I was involved in a sexual situation again.

"Daddy, it's Rei. When did you get back from Baltimore?"

"Two hours ago this morning. We know you never came home last night, and frankly, we're a little concerned."

"Is Mom around?"

"She's in your room hanging up some clothes she brought back for you from her mother's cedar closet in Baltimore. She's been there since nine-fifteen or so. If you'd rather talk to her than me, why don't you call her there?"

I sensed the hurt in my father's voice. "Um, no, that's okay. Please tell her that I'll be back in the mid-afternoon. Until then, I request that neither of you tell anyone where I might be, no matter who they say they are."

"What do you mean?"

"I'm just taking care of a little business," I said. "I'll explain more later. And by the way, Dad, I didn't intend to stay out last night. It happened sort of spontaneously."

"As spontaneously as your encounter on the Metro," my father snapped.

"Would it make you feel any better knowing that both times I was with the same man?"

"No father likes the idea of his daughter spending the night with any man. At least not until she's married."

I sighed. Despite his work as a psychiatrist specializing in adults with relationship problems, he was still a dyed-in-the-wool Japanese father.

"I'm sorry. I'll get back to the hotel sometime in late afternoon. I'll take you to dinner tonight." I hung up before he could say anything else.

The Sofitel was a pretty hotel—old, with fantastic rococo moldings all over the walls and ceilings. It was small, though, and I felt the eyes of the staff on me as I walked over to the elevators wearing my odd Central American fashions. Sailing up, I smoothed down my hair—I had forgotten to comb it after getting out of the shower, so I now probably had a bed-head look.

At the third floor, an Asian man got in and I moved to the back of the elevator, giving him the right amount of space. I studied the panel showing the floors, dreading the moment when it would stop on the sixth floor—Takeo's. As I was watching the light panel, I had a sense that my companion in the elevator was scrutinizing me.

I knew my clothes were odd, but were they really too informal for the hotel? I looked straight at the man and caught my breath when I realized it was Mr. Shima.

Suddenly I remembered what Allison had said casually about him staying at the Sofitel.

"Hello," I said uneasily. Even though he'd last seen me looking very conventional in a formal kimono, he obviously recognized me.

"Hello." He sounded just as wary as I. "So, you came to see me?"

"Yes," I said after a split second of thought. *Of course* he'd assume I'd come to him for a private meeting. That must have been why he said so little in the meetings with Allison and the Japanese-embassy people.

"I think we should talk downstairs," he said. "There is a lounge."

We rode up to Takeo's floor, but I didn't get out, and when Mr. Shima pressed the button to go down to the lobby, I thought briefly about whether Takeo would worry about my being late. Maybe.

We got out of the elevator and visited a bar about a thousand times prettier than the one in the Washington Suites, all warm wood, gleaming brass, and French patterned upholstery on the chairs.

Mr. Shima gravitated toward a table in the corner, which seemed appropriate to me. I walked toward it with him, then made a show of hesitation.

"I just remembered a phone call that I have to make. Do you mind if I take a minute to do it?"

Mr. Shima frowned. "Whom do you need to call so urgently?"

"My, ah—" I didn't know what to call Takeo anymore. "Never mind. I don't mean to take too much of your time. We'll talk now, and I'll call later."

Mr. Shima nodded stiffly, and he sat down in the seat of power, the one with a view of the hotel's entrance. I sat across from him, with my back to the entrance, thinking it was probably for the best. If Takeo came by, he might not recognize the back of me—certainly not in my wild woolen shirt from Ecuador.

Mr. Shima seemed to be studying the shirt with a very critical eye. I wondered if his interest in textiles included traditions other than Japan's. I looked down and saw in horror that one of the simple wooden buttons had come undone. There was a gap in the shirt that revealed a healthy amount of skin and the lace that edged my teddy. Mr. Shima must have realized I'd caught him peeking, because his face flushed and he spoke rapidly.

"I notice that you're wearing an example of Peruvian folk embroidery," he said quickly.

"The label inside says it was made in Ecuador," I said, because I didn't want to let him off for looking at me as if I were the prostitute everyone seemed to think I was.

Mr. Shima shook his head. "No, no, it cannot be. It is Peruvian. Please check the reference book titled *Folk Textiles of the Andes* if you want to know more."

"I've never heard of the book," I said, firmly buttoning up the gaping shirt.

"Don't you believe me?" Mr. Shima sounded quietly furious. I was reminded of his mood the very first time I'd met him, when I'd tried so hard to be accepted as a possible courier for the Morioka collection.

"It's not that. I'm a little confused about the change of topic. I thought you'd want to talk about the lost *uchikake*. You traveled so far, at such short notice, to address the crisis."

Mr. Shima nodded, but didn't speak, so I went on. "What has the museum asked you to do over here?"

"The top priority is to bring back the *uchikake*, in whatever condition it's found—and at whatever cost. But to do that, I need to hear from you what really happened."

"I've been telling my story over and over again, but you saw what happened yesterday at the embassy. I had a sense that no matter what I said, the diplomats didn't want to believe it. They had a preconceived idea of me—just as you did."

"I'm afraid I don't know who you really are," Mr. Shima said coldly. "When you examined the kimono with me, you displayed a sympathy to history that I liked. But what I hear now is inconsistent."

"The thing that the embassy people were hinting at—my involvement on the edges of some arts-related crimes in Japan a few years ago—isn't quite like it sounds." I took a deep breath and thought how best to go on. "I once helped the police locate an Important Cultural Property that had been stolen, and some other times supplied evidence that led to the arrest of some murderers. In light of my past experience with criminal types, I have some ideas about who might have wanted the bride's kimono."

"Please tell me."

Again, I hesitated to bring up Kyoko Omori—I really liked her, I was beginning to realize. "Well, I'm most suspicious of the museum staff here. I tried desperately to get Allison Powell to let me keep the kimono safely in the museum, but she refused to take it. She knew that I was keeping the kimono with me at the Washington Suites, as did her museum's conservator, Jamie Stevenson."

"But a museum employee—I've never heard of one committing a crime."

"The museum's not that well run. During the opening reception, the guards left the room with kimono, and a potential thief was found closely examining the room's security system."

"What?" Mr. Shima's calm expression faltered. "Miss Powell never told me such a thing."

"Of course she wouldn't. I've talked to her about my concerns, but she's not been very receptive to the idea of strengthening security—perhaps because of her own interest in taking more of the Morioka kimono collection for herself. I know she's going through some tough times financially. It sounds hard to believe, but one never knows."

I'd hit home, because Mr. Shima was silent for a minute. Then he said, "I might have to take all the kimono back with me. We can't knowingly leave the kimono in a dangerous situation."

"I agree. But if you take the things back early, would it violate your loan agreement?"

Mr. Shima sighed. "I don't know. To tell the truth, Miss Shimura, I'm not very good at understanding written English."

"Just as I'm not good at written Japanese," I said, appreciating that he was opening up to me. "I've got a copy of the loan agreement. I'll show it to your contact at the Japanese consul, if you like."

Mr. Shima nodded. "Thank you, Miss Shimura. I must say that I've been worried about things—and you. This conversation today has relieved me a little bit."

"We're on the same side," I said earnestly. "I can help you as long as you'll hold off on judging me the way the others all have."

"My opinion has changed," Mr. Shima said. "And I want you to think well of me, too. I want to write down the name of that Latin American textile guide for you." He took a pen out of his breast pocket and then pulled out an old receipt and began writing on the back: *Folk Textiles of the Andes. Ferrera and Dubin, Oxford University Press.*

"Your English writing is quite good," I said, tucking the receipt in one of the pockets of my jeans. "By the way, how long do you expect to be in Washington?"

"As long as it takes to find an answer about the whereabouts of the kimono. How about you?"

"The same," I said. When we parted, he bowed to me, and I gave him a bow in return that was respectfully lower than his, but not too low—just in case he really had been interested in what was underneath my shirt.

27

Since I was late, I decided to telephone Takeo with an explanation from the lobby telephone before approaching his room again.

"Where are you?" he asked plaintively.

"I'm in the reception area. I've just had an important conversation with Mr. Shima. I'll tell you about it when I get upstairs." It was true. I had a strong feeling that he wasn't going to sue me, after all.

Takeo opened the door before I even had a chance to ring it.

"I saw you coming through the peephole. Wow, I can't believe what you're wearing."

"It's weird, isn't it? I think I look like Juan Valdez—"

"Who's that? And will you help me find one for myself?" Takeo swept me up into an embrace and kissed me thoroughly—so thoroughly I had no chance to pull back, or even think about who I'd been kissing a few hours earlier. He felt good, actually. I felt a rush of affection for Takeo, followed by an immediate wrenching at the thought of Hugh, alone in his apartment, his dream of a romantic reunion with me shattered.

"I thought you weren't into conspicuous consumption," I said when I had a chance to break for a gulp of air.

"I'm not. But what you're wearing is so simple and rough. I like it very much."

"It's itchy—"

"Do you want to take it off?" Takeo ushered me into his room and bolted the door.

I glanced around at the room's decor—simple, classic, a room dominated by a king-size bed with the sheets turned back. "Um, I'd rather just get caught up. As I was saying before, I finally had a private talk with Mr. Shima. I think he understands that I'm not a bad person and together we can do what the police here won't do."

"What about me?" Takeo sounded oddly petulant. "I came here to offer help, that I could, but I wonder if you have time to accept it."

"I don't think it's fair to ask things of you when you're still exhausted from jet lag."

"Let's start simply. You'll stay here the rest of the afternoon and then we'll have dinner."

"I'd like that, but my parents are in town, and I have to entertain them."

"Why is that? Couldn't they wait till you went to California?"

"They thought I was killed. When it turned out I wasn't, they wanted to come anyway to spend some time."

Takeo shook his head as if he couldn't believe a word I was saying. "I'm slightly dehydrated, so my brain's not fully working, but it sounded as if you said your parents thought you were killed."

I used the time that he spent pouring us each a glass of Evian water deciding what I *couldn't* say. I couldn't tell him that the Northern Virginia police and Japanese embassy suspected me of prostitution, and I omitted the story of the double date for dinner with Yoshi and Kyoko, even though I thought the encounter had raised some issues about Kyoko's possible guilt in

Hana's murder. I wasn't ready to tell him about Hugh, either.

"It sounds like a lot of trouble—trouble that can't simply be solved by paying for the kimono," Takeo said at the end of it all.

"Oh, no. And I wouldn't expect you to offer to lend me the money—"

"That's good," Takeo said with an unmistakable shudder.

"Okay, I think the best plan for this evening is for my parents and me to pick you up for dinner. In the meantime, I've got to take care of some business back at the museum and then go home—I mean, to where my parents are staying."

"What kind of business?"

"Well, the museum hasn't paid me yet. I know you don't like to think about money, but I've got to, if I'm to meet my expenses here."

"Why can't I go with you to the museum?"

"Of course you can go," I said. "The one thing I ask, though, is that you look around by yourself while I do the talking with Allison. You know how nosy people can be about relationships."

Takeo sighed. "Are you embarrassed by how I look?"

"Of course not." I'd barely noticed what he was wearing because it was what he usually wore: black jeans and a black T-shirt. This look was fairly sexy and out there in Japan, but in America, it was so mainstream as to make someone appear practically invisible.

"Onward," I said, motioning to the door—and out we went.

It was a beautiful Saturday, I thought, as we walked through the streets of Kalorama toward the Museum of

Asian Arts. There were still no residents in the streets, but a good number of servants were bustling in and out of the houses, doing things like polishing brass door-knobs, trimming boxwood hedges, and washing cars.

"Look at them," Takeo said. "All brown-skinned. It's like in California—immigrants do all the work."

"Actually, it's just like Japan. I believe there are three Filipino servants who work at your father's house."

"Yes, but they're family retainers. They've been there forever. These people—I bet they just came off the boat and have no other choices. It's sad, really."

"A lot of these houses are embassies," I pointed out. "That one across the street, for example. It seems natural that the embassy of Myanmar would bring service workers from that country—"

"Myanmar? What a terrible regime! How horrible to have to pass the place that's a symbol of oppression of the Burmese people—"

And so it went, all the way to the museum. I reminded myself several times that Takeo's decision to fly to me on such short notice was a sign of deep commitment. With all the causes he cared about, he still had room for mine.

Inside the museum, I quickly paid Takeo's admission. The security guard recognized me and said I could go look for Allison upstairs.

"Take as long as you like," Takeo said. "After the kimono exhibit, I'll look at the Korean pottery."

"Thanks," I said, and hurried up the handsome spiral staircase to the administrative offices.

This would probably be my last visit to the museum. I'd delivered the kimono and the two talks, as agreed upon. There was nothing left for me to do. I'd figured out that Allison Powell was someone with whom I'd never get along. It was a shame I'd lost touch with

Jamie, though. I still wanted to know what she had to tell me—and if she was the mysterious person waiting at the bottom of the Spanish steps.

The door to Allison and Jamie's office was cracked open, so I knocked and waited. Nobody answered. I opened the door a little farther and saw the room was empty. The computer was turned on, though. I went and sat down in front of it, just as I had the last time. The envelope with my slides of the Morioka kimono was resting next to the computer. I slipped it into my pocket.

The computer screen said eBay on top. I remembered this was the auction site Jamie had been looking at the last time I was near the computer. The page seemed to be a launching point for searches for antiques that could be bought—things as varied as silver and Asian books. Was Jamie allowed to buy things for the museum this way—sight unseen? Or was she selling things?

There was a cursor blinking in an empty box, and the word "Search" next to it. Presumably you could type in something you were looking for, and the computer would find it. I got up and closed the door to the office. When I came back to the computer, I typed the word "kimono," and moved the mouse so the cursor hit "search."

Within seconds, the screen had changed. At the top, I read the startling message that there were 557 items containing the word "kimono" for sale on eBay. The first fifty items for sale were listed beneath.

I looked down the list, my eyes widening. There was such a long list, each followed by price, number of bids, and the date and time the auction for that item would be over. Most of the kimono were valued at around a few hundred dollars, but there were several for a few thousand.

Suddenly I had a sense of where the bride's kimono could have gone. I thought of the envelope of slides next to the computer. Jamie—or Allison, for that matter—could have scanned the picture of my bride's kimono for the eBay site in the hope of interesting buyers. I'd heard there were dozens of Internet sites where fine art was auctioned off—I'd never explored them before due to my nervousness about technology. I preferred to do things the old-fashioned way, in person. How stupid I'd been.

All at once I knew that I had to erase the signs of my snooping. But how? I moved the mouse around the screen, clicking on things, wanting it to go back to its original spot—but I only got deeper and deeper into the kimono listings. What could I do? Where was the off switch? I looked at the side of the computer monitor and saw a switch with a tiny light over it. I touched it and the screen went black. The kimono listings were gone, but then, so was the eBay page.

I couldn't be found in the office and held responsible—but I wouldn't put the slides back where they were, to be used for God knew what purpose. I'd give them back to Mr. Shima. In fact, I'd go right now. Just as I put my hand on the knob to open it, the door banged into my face.

"Allison!" I said as she started at the sight of me. "I was looking for you."

"Yes, the guard told me that. He didn't know that I was in the storage area."

We were completely alone on the second floor. I doubted anyone would hear if Allison pushed me out of the open, unscreened window in the back of her office, or did anything else to me. She was a large woman, and I knew that I was no match against her.

"I had a good talk with your mother yesterday. She

was a bit of a legend at school—I don't think she's changed much."

"She'll be glad to know that. In fact, she knows I'm here with you right now!" I added falsely.

"Why?"

"I don't know what you mean." In truth, I wanted Allison to know people knew where I was—that she'd be suspected if I disappeared.

"I mean, Rei, why did you come to see me?"

"This is a little bit awkward, but I realized that when I left yesterday, we hadn't settled anything about my payment."

"We ask our accountant to draft checks for that sort of thing just before the fifteenth of the month, which of course has already passed, but I've been so rushed that I forgot to give him the invoice. I hope you don't mind if I send you the check next month?"

I gulped. "Well, that would be a problem. My credit card's about to hit its limit because of some expenses." I was thinking about the shopping spree I'd gone on with my mother.

Allison looked at me as if she could guess what I'd done. "Can't you use your ATM card to get some cash?"

"My Japanese bank isn't part of any international networks. It's impossible for me to withdraw money here."

"Why don't you ask your parents for help over the next few days, and I'll do my best to see if I can get the check written next week. Don't worry that we're going to short you. We'll pay every cent promised in the contract, though I can't say you delivered exactly what was agreed upon."

"No," I said, reading the anger in her face. "I delivered more, and you didn't want it, and that screwed up everything."

"Well, I suppose you've got your own view of things, just as I do, and Mr. Shima does." Was it my imagination, or did she stress his name?

"Actually, Mr. Shima has heard the truth," I said. "I started telling him about the things that have gone wrong around here, security-wise, and he's considering withdrawing the *kosode* collection immediately."

"Exactly when are you going back to Japan?" Allison asked.

"Not for a while." I spoke aggressively because she'd made me very angry, and also because I'd heard someone walking in the hall outside the office. At this point she couldn't possibly murder me. "I can't travel because the person who stole the kimono stole my passport. It's now police property, and I haven't had the time to get a new one."

"I suggest you try to make the time for it," Allison said. "If you're worried about your hotel bill, you should try to avoid staying in this country for a longer period than planned."

"I agree, but outside of the Washington Suites, there's nowhere I can stay." An image of a narrow brick town house with a garden of yellow roses came to mind, but I pushed it away. I could stay at the Sofitel with Takeo, or freeload off my parents. I guess I did have a few options, but pride would keep me from ever using them.

"All right," Allison said, looking at me coldly. "I'll see what I can do."

"Thanks. I was hoping to . . . say hello to Jamie. Where is she?"

"I don't know. She takes the weekends off."

"She was gone yesterday, too."

"She didn't call in, which was a bit unusual, but I suspect she was tired from the VIP reception."

"Do you think she's okay?"

"Of course! If you really want to speak to her, why don't you call Monday afternoon? I might be able to tell you then what the accountant says about your check. But do call ahead instead of just coming here unannounced. It's so much easier for us if we anticipate you."

I knew I should just leave, but I couldn't. I felt humiliated, a typical sensation for me in Japan; though a Japanese person bent on shaming me would never have behaved as erratically as Allison did. It would have been a smooth and subtle operation. Despite Allison's velvet headbands and her Locust Valley lockjaw, she really had no manners at all.

"You remind me of someone," I said, looking hard at her. "At first I thought it was my mother, but that was wrong. You're like a man at a singles bar. At first, when you talk to a likely candidate, you're completely charming. But then, after she's serviced you, you treat her like a lowlife you can't wait to get out the door."

"How dare you say I'm a lesbian! Just because I'm a woman of a certain age, alone, doesn't mean I don't want to be with men again—"

"I'm not talking about *sex*. You used me because I look Japanese and fit into a kimono nicely. You didn't expect much of a lecture, because that would steal attention away from you. When it turned out I had something to say, that irritated you."

Allison sucked in her breath. "You sound as if I've treated you shabbily, when in fact I paid you more than the planned amount—"

"Money isn't everything. You made me assume personal responsibility for the Morioka's bridal kimono, when I know you could have worked out something with Metropolitan Insurance to ensure its safe storage here. Not that you run this place as tightly as you should—the lack of security is deplorable."

"Since when have you become an expert on museum security?" Allison demanded.

I shrugged. "You shouldn't have left any of the kimono galleries unattended during the VIP party. I bet you still don't know the identity of the Asian guy casing the galleries—let's just hope he doesn't come back."

"I don't want *you* back," Allison said rapidly. "Truth be told, my life has been virtually *ruined* by young women after master's degrees and the wealthiest trustees!"

Was she really talking about Jamie? Suddenly I recalled something my mother had said about Allison's divorce.

"Your ex-husband's girlfriend. She's younger than you, I guess?"

"Twenty-five last August, and from what I read in the *Washingtonian*, my husband celebrated by giving her a big party at Jean-Louis. I rather doubt she knew her appetizer fork from the dessert one; she came from nowhere—Nebraska or someplace like that—to Georgetown. I was dumb enough to give her an internship, and dumber still to let her stay over the holiday at my house, because she couldn't afford to fly home."

"I'm sorry," I said, and as the words came out, I really was. Unbidden, a picture flashed into my mind—of a wealthy Tokugawa lord and the two women who loved him. This time I thought about the first woman, his wife of many years, the one who wore exquisite, but properly subdued, kimono. This was the woman who had mothered his child, and watched helplessly as her husband fell in love with a younger, more beautiful woman.

I'd focused previously on the pain that the courtesan

Ai must have felt at being sent off to the boonies to marry a tea merchant. My sympathy had been in the wrong place. The real forgotten lover was Ryohei's wife—and the ultimate sad irony was that she'd been considered so unimportant that I hadn't found any record of her name.

I left Allison with regretful feelings about my insensitivity, though I still felt justified in my anger at her refusal to insure the bride's kimono. There still, of course, was a chance that she'd been involved in its theft. I had some questions about that for Jamie, but as Allison had said, she wasn't at the museum. I hadn't seen her since six o'clock on Thursday. Was she all right, or had the person who'd killed Hana gone after her, too?

I went into the museum's small hall, which had a pay telephone near the coatrack, and I did a little research on Jamie's home address. Then I realized I needed to retrieve Takeo. It was half an hour since I'd left him on the main floor. I found him sipping a cup of green tea in Pan Asia.

"This is the worst tea I've ever tasted," he said with a mournful sigh. "Why do Americans even bother?"

"Let's go outside," I said. "There are some things I want to talk to you about privately."

"What happened upstairs? Did you get the paycheck?" Takeo asked when we were walking on S Street.

"No. Allison gave me some song and dance about why it wasn't ready. I was disappointed, but at least I got something out of my visit to her office. She had left her personal computer showing an Internet site—an auction place called eBay. There were over five hundred kimono listed for auction there—I didn't have time to go through them at all. But I think it's worth checking if my bride's kimono is listed for sale."

"If so—why would the seller be checking auction progress from her work computer? It would call attention to her."

"Nobody at the Museum of Asian Arts is concerned about the bride's kimono—Allison is the only one who knows it was stolen."

"Who cares about eBay? I'm a little more concerned about the prospect that you might not get paid. Isn't that the whole reason you came here?"

"I want the money, of course, but now that I know the kimono's probably on some Internet auction site, all I want is to get it back for the Morioka. Hana Matsura's dead, most likely because she had the kimono, and now Allison's assistant Jamie is missing. That kimono needs to go back into storage at the Morioka—end of story."

"I can help you with that eBay site," Takeo said. "I've looked at it before. I once listed some rare back issues of National Geographic and they sold in a flash."

"Do you think you could check whether anyone listed the bride's kimono? The thief might very well not know the exact period, so you will have to search by physical description of the fabric, and stuff like that. I've got a slide I can give you." I opened the envelope and found the Morioka's slide of the bridal kimono. "If you can spend even an hour looking for auction sites, I'll never be able to thank you enough—"

"You will, tonight. After dinner." Takeo's smile was engaging, but I felt more miserable than ever before.

28

It was five o'clock, and my parents were drinking coffee in the Revolutionary Idea when I finally dragged myself back to the Washington Suites.

"Here she is!" my mother said brightly, as if nothing were amiss.

I sat down and looked coolly at her. "I apologize for being late. The business I had to take care of took longer than I'd expected. It was rather complicated, in fact, by the fact that you gave out Hugh Glendinning's phone number to someone calling my room."

"It was just an innocent guess," my mother said. "You weren't at home, but I saw your friend's business card in a prime spot near your phone. I only gave the number, not any name, to Takeo. I also said that I couldn't guarantee you'd be there, but the person answering might know your whereabouts—"

I cut off my mother. "How did you even get inside my room?"

"I asked the front desk for a key. They gave it to me when I showed identification proving that I was your mother. I had a copy of your birth certificate with me, because the police originally told me to bring it when I came to identify you."

"I wish you hadn't spoken to Takeo. He calle⟨ Hugh's apartment wanting to see me."

"Takeo Kayama is here?" My father's eyebrows ros⟨

"Yes. At the Sofitel. I promised him that I'd eat wit⟨ him tonight, but I want you two to come along. He⟨ tired from his travels, so he requested that we just ea⟨ downstairs in the hotel's French restaurant—I hope yo⟨ don't mind."

"Bring on the coquilles St. Jacques," my father sai⟨ smiling. "I'm glad to finally meet the young man Aun⟨ Norie has spoken about. And I'm sorry about our con⟨ versation earlier, Rei. I don't want to cause any mor⟨ misunderstandings."

"It's okay, Dad. I'm sorry, too."

"So we don't make any more mistakes, can you tell u⟨ whether Takeo is informed about your relationship wit⟨ Hugh?" my father prodded.

"No. He knows nothing right now, but I plan to te⟨ him at the right time."

"Does Hugh know about Takeo?" My mother ha⟨ picked up my father's trail.

"Unfortunately, yes. He practically threw me out o⟨ his apartment when he heard I was going to see Take⟨ again."

"I don't wonder. In light of today's socio-sexual cli⟨ mate—with the presence of HIV, hepatitis, and man⟨ other sexually transmitted diseases—it doesn't seem fai⟨ to submit one's partners to multiple risks." My fathe⟨ sounded like a more technically souped-up version of m⟨ lecturing Hana on the plane. Oh, how ironic it all was.

"We took precautions," I said, feeling even more hu⟨ miliated than I had when the police had called me ⟨ whore.

"Nothing's foolproof," my father said briskly. "Quit⟨ a few of my patients contracted AIDS even though the⟨

took precautions. The live virus causing HIV has been found in saliva. I doubt you had a dental dam inside your mouth all evening."

Of course I hadn't. I didn't even know what a dental dam looked like. I stared at the tablecloth, wishing I'd never come back to the hotel. My father had never talked about sex with me before, and he was doing it in such a graphic way. He was right about the threat of disease, of course—but with Hana dead, Jamie missing, and an antique kimono vanished into thin air, I hadn't been thinking practically last night. I'd yearned for, and gotten, satisfaction—a glorious feeling that had long since faded.

"It's not like in the old days, Rei," my mother said. "Men and women could have a little fun when they were dating, and if worst came to worst, you took penicillin. Daddy's made some good points, and if you don't mind a little advice from me, I see an easy solution to your dilemma."

"And what's that?" I asked suspiciously.

"Marry one of them. And after that, don't look back."

I shook my head. "You're just as old-fashioned as Dad, aren't you? I don't want to introduce Takeo to you. You'll scare him out of his mind."

"All right, so have dinner with him alone. At his *hotel*. I don't expect we'll see you again, because our flight back to California leaves tomorrow," my mother said, sniffing.

"Why are you leaving so soon?" Sure, I was irritated with my parents, but the thought of them leaving so fast, and in the midst of a fight with me, was distressing.

"I began to get the feeling that you'd rather spend your time doing other things than see us, so I called the airline and got us wait-listed on something leaving tomorrow. We didn't have forever to spend here, you know. Daddy's got to go to work on Monday morning, and I've got a show house committee meeting that afternoon."

"Well, in that case, I'll definitely have dinner with you tonight," I said glumly. "I don't know how I'll cancel Takeo, but I'll do it."

"No," my father said. "It's not fair to him since he's come all the way from Japan, and we would like to meet him. And I can promise for myself, as well as your mother, that neither of us will violate the confidentiality of our discussion. At least you were honest with us."

"All right," I said, calculating that if I drove into Washington with my parents, I would have to drive back with them, thus circumventing the issue of staying overnight with Takeo. It was a cowardly way out of things, but at least it would get me home.

"Now, there's one thing I ask of you," my mother said.

"Oh?" I asked cautiously.

"If we're going to a nice restaurant for dinner, you've got to change out of those clothes. I've never seen you look so much like—like the man in the advertisement for Colombian coffee. I don't know if this a trendy look or not, but it simply is not you."

To satisfy my mother, I wore the blue Nicole Miller dress she'd bought me two days earlier. I had raced through getting dressed in my room, because the telephone was blinking with messages—two from the police, who wanted to have another conversation, and one from the Japanese consulate. As I heard the cold, recorded voices ordering me to call them back, I sensed that what they had in store for me was bad. For the first time I began to think of fleeing. My parents could take me back to our house in California, where I could bury myself under the pink-and-green duvet that had been my favorite since childhood. But if I was going to do this, I needed to prepare.

I got out my driver's license from the hotel vault and tucked it into my bag just before my parents and I drove off to the Sofitel. When we'd picked up Takeo in his room, after the bows were made and polite greetings echoed by both my parents in Japanese and English, I explained to Takeo that my parents knew about the trouble with the bridal kimono, and that he could discuss what he'd found on the Internet in front of them. Takeo said— in his almost fluent English—that he'd gone through eBay and a half-dozen other auction sites to search for antique kimono, but not come up with anything that looked like the slide of the Morioka bride's kimono.

"The thief could be holding on to it—perhaps to put it up for sale after you've gone home to Japan, and the interest in the theft has died," Takeo said. "You'll need to keep checking in the future. You might want to get your own personal computer."

"That's a very good idea," my mother said, beaming. "I've been trying to get Rei on-line for the last few years. It would save me a small fortune in phone calls."

I rolled my eyes and said, "A computer. I can hardly think of a more enjoyable way to spend my check from the museum, if it ever comes to me."

"We Japanese don't like to talk about money," Takeo said, smiling at my parents and me. "I would much rather enjoy dinner with you."

Takeo had gone all out to make a good impression. He wore an elegant taupe velvet jacket over a black silk turtleneck and cream-and-black checked pants that I'd never seen before. He could have come straight from the window at Neiman Marcus, seeing how my mother gave him an approving once-over and winked at me.

Things were going pretty smoothly, I thought as we went through course after course of classic French food. Thank goodness there were things for vegetarians—I had a roasted portobello-mushroom sandwich. Takeo ate linguini with fruits of the sea while my father and mother satisfied themselves with steak frites, though they were busier with asking questions than with their food.

My mother wanted to know about the areas in Japan where Takeo had grown up; my father wanted to know about his hobbies. There was an awkward pause when my father asked what the two of us liked to do together, in our spare time.

"On a Saturday night, we might see a foreign film at Yebisu Garden Cinema, have dinner at Rei's aunt's house, and then end the evening dancing with a cross-cultural group of friends," Takeo ad-libbed.

"Oh, how lively!" my mother said happily. "It's good for Rei to get out like that. She's always been the introverted type."

"What?" Takeo asked, shooting an amused glance at me.

"They've known me from birth through graduate school, and I studied almost all that time. It's only in Japan that I relaxed enough to have fun." I stopped talking, remembering the missing bride's kimono. I couldn't imagine when I'd have fun again.

Takeo yawned heavily when we were having after-dinner coffee, so I insisted that I would see him upstairs to his room. "I'll be down in five minutes," I promised my parents.

"What was that all about?" he grumbled in the elevator. "You're twenty-eight years old. Isn't that old enough to spend the night with your boyfriend? Your father's a psychiatrist. I think he would consider it abnormal if you *didn't* stay up here with me."

"He's not that way at all, he's like a typical Japanese father! And besides, I have to drive them home tonight. Did you see how much they had to drink?"

"A small glass of wine each! Four people sharing one bottle of wine—pitiful! I didn't think it could be done."

"Well, I drank just a half glass, so I'm the designated driver. I'm sorry, Takeo. I have to go with them."

"You're not sorry." Takeo looked at me coolly as the elevator doors opened to his floor, and we got out.

"What do you mean? Of course I am."

"No, you're not. You've been avoiding me all day long." There was a bitterness in his voice I hadn't heard before.

"Okay, I agree that I've got—a problem. If you really want to talk about it tonight, I'll call you when I get back to the Washington Suites."

"Actually, I'm rather tired," Takeo said coolly. "Please don't call me tonight."

"But you were ready to have sex—"

"That involves a different kind of energy."

Takeo walked down the hall to his room, without a glance back.

29

"I love him. He's handsome, cultured, and obviously wild for you, my dear," my mother said as I drove her and my father out of the hotel driveway and south on Connecticut Avenue. Since I'd said to Takeo that I was going to be the designated driver, I'd felt the need to honor my word. The only problem was, driving on the right felt so foreign to me—I'd veered to the left by accident at the beginning of our journey and was finding it hard to live it down.

"Not only did he pay for the meal, he did it on a gold card," my mother continued. "He's financially comfortable, even though he's just your age. I can hardly believe it."

"He's using his father's money," I said. How different Takeo was from Hugh, who had gone to a public university on a scholarship and had spent a significant portion of his salary as a new lawyer paying for his younger brother's education.

"Catherine, I think we should leave her to make her own decision," my father was saying.

"What are you saying, Toshiro? Didn't you think he was wonderful? The two of them together just *belong*. Their skin color, their hair, the way they walk across a room."

I'd forgotten how my mother could get spun up with

a little wine. It obviously ran in the family. As for Takeo and me looking attractive together—it was true, to a limited degree, but that was so meaningless. His father would never approve, because I didn't come from the fabulously wealthy stratosphere that the Kayamas inhabited. I'd come from America, which was not good enough.

"It's not the old days, Catherine, when parents made decisions about love," my father said, breaking into my thoughts. "I offended Rei earlier because of my interference. I'm not going to trouble her again."

"Please don't talk about that. I have to concentrate on where I'm going," I said. I had meant to make a left earlier, but the turn would have been illegal, so now there was nowhere to go but into the traffic maelstrom of Dupont Circle—the traffic circle I'd had to cross when I met Hugh inside its center. It seemed as dangerous for drivers as it had been for pedestrians. There were traffic lights, and signs showing access to the streets that radiated out of the circle, but if you weren't in the correct lane a hundred feet ahead of each sign, it was impossible to find the way out.

I swore under my breath as I missed the lane that would have allowed me to continue on New Hampshire Avenue. Well, I'd just have to go around the circle again.

"Rei, sweetie, you should have allowed me to drive," my mother said. "I grew up here, practically."

"No, I needed to drive because I've got to make a brief stop somewhere before we go back."

"If it's that time of the month, there's a mini-drugstore in the hotel," my mother said.

"No, no, nothing of the sort. I want to stop by Jamie's place tonight for a quick visit." I exhaled with relief as I made the correct exit out of the circle and onto New Hampshire Avenue, heading northeast.

"A third man?" There was horror in my father's voice. "Rei, I know I just promised not to interfere in your life, but I'm worried there may be a biological reason for your change in sexual behavior. A more thorough psychiatric evaluation could be a help. We could just keep driving straight to either Sheppard Pratt or Johns Hopkins in Baltimore—"

"Why is it that whenever it comes to my sexuality, the Shimuras think I'm a depraved, mentally ill freak? Jamie is the museum's conservator, and she's female," I explained, trying to keep my voice from rising. "She's been missing for two days, and I've finally found her address and am going to check if she's all right."

"I'm glad to hear you're just seeing a girl. I wouldn't want anything to shake up the situation with Takeo," my mother said. "We'd be happy to visit your friend Jamie, as late as the evening is."

"It would be very nice if you could look for U Street," I said, though I was churning inside. The situation with Takeo was a disaster. I'd do anything to shake loose from it.

My mother located U Street but clucked her tongue as we drove east. "I don't like the look of this, Rei. There are hardly any cars around, and look at those poor people loitering on the streets."

I glanced in the driver's-side mirror to check out the people she was talking about. In the process, I noticed a dark blue compact car right on our tail. It looked like the one that had followed me the night before.

"Um, Mom, can you get the license number on the car behind us? I think it's the same crew that followed me yesterday."

My mother and father both twisted around to look.

"I can't make out the number, because there's mud on it, but it looks as if it has Virginia plates." My mother sounded more cheerful, all of a sudden. "The driver must be just like us: a tourist from Virginia who's taken a turn for the worse!"

Or, I thought, it might be my good friends from the police, following me in the hope of catching me with criminal associates. I continued on U Street, feeling just as scared as before. Jamie's address was only a few blocks farther east. I didn't want the driver behind me to see me go in—but I didn't want to give up, either. I had to know if Jamie was alive.

"I think we should go to a police station." My father's voice broke into my thoughts.

It was a reasonable idea—even though I distrusted the police—but there were no police stations marked on the Gray Line tourist map of Washington, just McDonald's restaurants. However, my mother remembered something about a police station on New York Avenue, fairly near the entrance to the Baltimore-Washington Parkway. My parents consulted and told me to make a right on Florida Avenue. From there, it was a straight shot through an increasingly dismal area of boarded-up houses, liquor stores, and pawnshops. At one red light, a woman wearing a tiny skirt and a short fake-fur jacket approached our car. When she saw our faces, she stepped back.

"I don't care if there's a police station up ahead: this is *not* where I want to go," I said, making a right turn on P Street. I'd been shaken by the glazed, sad expression on the woman's face.

"You should never have let her drive!" my mother grumbled to my father.

"She's got a license," my father shot back. "And I have to agree with her, Catherine, this neighborhood is not worth continuing to explore. We need to get back to an area with decent people, and shops and lights."

The blue car was still tailing us. I wished I had the gumption to shoot around the city the way Hugh had, but I wasn't behind the wheel of a Lexus with a powerful V-8 engine—I was in a Toyota Corolla. Furthermore, I didn't know my way around Washington. I'd never experienced a city like it—so many streets shooting out at sharp angles, so many circles, so many one-ways and left-turn prohibitions. It was a driver's nightmare. No wonder people kept recommending I take the Metro.

I saw a traffic circle ahead of me. Great. Another chance to go round and round and lose my bearings. I'd thought the roundabout would turn out to be Dupont Circle, but it turned out that it was a smaller circle that I hadn't been around before. Not many cars were in the circle, which gave me a bit of inspiration. I went around, switching lanes the way Hugh had done the night before, finally shooting off on P Street, the way I'd originally come.

"Where's the car?" I asked, glancing in the rearview mirror.

"It went onto Rhode Island Avenue, westbound. It was quite strange—the driver seemed to lose interest," my father said. "Maybe he wanted to find that circle all along."

"I bet the driver thinks we decided to retreat back to Northern Virginia. They're probably waiting for us at the Washington Suites parking lot. Well, they'll spend a boring hour there," I said, feeling my spirits rise.

Despite my parents' protests, I made a few more turns to get going toward the right part of U Street. I parked on Thirteenth Street, just around the corner from Jamie's apartment.

"Do you want to come with me, or stay in the—" I began to ask, but my parents were out the door and hurrying up the steps to Jamie's building. It was a dull gray town house with metal grates on all the first-floor windows.

"A quick hello, Rei, just to see if she's all right," my mother reminded me.

I didn't answer, because I had no intention of doing that.

The vestibule had a battered steel entry system with a long line of doorbells and an intercom. I pressed the button that said JAMES STEVENSON because that was the closest thing to Jamie's name. I checked my watch. It was ten.

There was no response, so I buzzed again. I heard a woman's voice say, "Go away."

"Jamie?" I asked.

"Who is it?" The tone of her voice changed from angry to curious.

"Rei Shimura. I just wanted to make sure you were okay—"

"I am."

"Could I—come up to talk to you about something?"

She paused, then said, "Okay. I'm on the third floor."

There was a buzzing sound, and I pushed the door open. I looked at my parents and said, "She wants me to go up."

"Then we'll go, too," my father said. "You can't expect your mother and me to stay outdoors in this city."

We trooped upstairs to Jamie's apartment, which had a big sticker on the door with an alarm company name. When she opened the door to us, I heard the telltale electronic chirp of a door sensor. This neighborhood, a half mile from where the prostitute had approached our car, must not be safe at all. I thought again about the blue car that had been tailing us. If its occupants really had been undercover police, it might have been a good idea to lure them to wait for us outside Jamie's building. But I hadn't thought of that—my instinct had been to shake them.

Jamie stood in an open doorway wearing a tank top and leggings that accentuated her fantastically lean shape. Her eyes widened when she saw my parents.

"We were all out together, Jamie," I said, and introduced them.

She nodded and gave a faint smile. "Please come in. The place is kind of a mess, I have to warn you. I wasn't expecting company tonight."

Jamie's apartment wasn't bad at all. There was a slight aroma from a cat litter box, and a chubby white cat sprinted into another room when it saw us. Overall, the apartment was a very pleasant one. I saw the remains of Chinese takeout on the dining table, and what a dining table it was—a round walnut one with ball-and-claw feet. The chairs surrounding it had antique needlepoint seats, and there was a magnificent Japanese triptych representing a procession of samurai hanging over the fireplace.

My mother murmured a few words of appreciation and went straight to the wall where a tapestry showing foxes and hounds was hanging. My father asked to use the bathroom.

"I hope he's not allergic to cats, there's a litter box in there—" Jamie said, after he'd left.

"Oh, no, don't worry. Can we talk privately in another room?" I asked her in a low voice. "My parents won't mind."

"You're sure?" Jamie asked as she led me into her bedroom—a small room dominated by a huge nineteenth-century four-poster bed. The canopy and matching coverlet were red silk. My gaze followed her as she went to the bed to straighten the coverlet, at the same time smoothly turning over a framed photograph on the bedside table so I couldn't see it.

"Have you been in bed the last few days?" In my efforts to see the overturned photo, I noticed a stack of books next to her bed. Right on top was Liza Dalby's book on the anthropology of kimono that I'd read in graduate school. Underneath that was a copy of the *Kama Sutra,* and below it, a small, old leather-bound volume that looked familiar.

"I was exhausted after the reception, so I stayed home for a bit," Jamie said, jerking me away from my snooping.

"I thought you might have been waiting for me at the Spanish Steps that evening. Were you?"

Jamie looked at me. "Yes, I was. But then your boyfriend came along, so I thought I better get going quickly. I know how these things are."

"What makes you think Hugh Glendinning is my boyfriend?" I asked, trying not reveal my panic.

"I sensed something strange in the restaurant. I mean, he was the one who had given your name to the committee, so he should have been friendlier, or more excited. So I hung around him during the reception, and it became clear. I watched him write the message about the meeting place. I wanted to speak to you before you got out there—to warn you. You told me that you didn't make much money, so I thought you were at risk for getting into the same horrible situation that I'm in."

Now I felt really sick. Was Hugh known around Washington as someone who preyed on penniless but pretty women? "Has Hugh ever come on to you?"

"No, no! I don't think I'm his type. I mean, he hardly notices me at all. That's why I was able to see him writing that note on the napkin."

"So tell me," I said, relief washing over me for an instant—only to be replaced with the worries I still had. "I noticed you've got a private security system, which is unusual for an apartment, and the apartment is listed under a man's name. Have you had—a problem with someone stalking you?"

"No. All that's because I don't want any break-ins. You've seen what the neighborhood's like, and my furniture's worth a lot. The security system and the guy's name on the mailbox is an ounce of prevention."

I nodded. "So, if you're not scared of a particular person, why were you so upset at the reception?"

"It's just—stressful working right now. Allison is demanding, and she also gets angry at the slightest thing. It's been that way since her husband left her for an intern."

"I heard about that. It must be hard for her—"

"Not just her," Jamie snapped. "Ever since the intern-president thing, it's been very embarrassing to be a junior employee. Especially if you're a woman. The way Allison's treating you reminds me of how she was with Sarah, our former intern."

"She was ticked off at me that evening, and it got even worse the next day, when I did the noon lecture. She used up most of my allotted time telling the audience things that had been in the outline I showed her. And she wouldn't let me show my slides. The lecture was a bust."

Jamie shook her head. "How strange. Allison can be resentful, but I can't imagine why she would deliberately sabotage an event at the museum. Any failure would reflect on her, wouldn't it?"

"I think she wanted to look good, and me to look like a disaster, to save face in front of the Japanese men in the audience."

"What Japanese men?" Jamie looked confused, and I realized that she hadn't heard anything from Allison about the theft of the bridal kimono. Interesting. Swiftly, I outlined what had happened.

"Oh, how awful!" Jamie said, hugging herself as if she felt chilly. "Please believe me when I say that I feel really terrible about what's happened. If only I hadn't pointed out that we already had a bride's kimono on display—I could have made room for your kimono, I should have been more open—"

It was true, of course, but there was no point in scolding Jamie. What was done was done. All Jamie could give me now was information.

"Who decided which kimono to request from the Morioka Museum—was it you, or Allison?" I asked.

"Well, we both looked at the slides. I view things from a conservation angle, so I wanted to get kimono in really excellent condition. Allison was after examples that showed a wide range of dyeing techniques and decorative motifs."

"If that was the case, how did you two wind up requesting only kimono that belonged to the two women who were rivals for the same man?" After I asked my question, I saw Jamie flush, so I pressed on. "You had to have known. You knew about the Dunstan Lanning book—in fact, you own it. Isn't that a copy on your bedside table?"

Jamie's eyes darted to the table. "I got it through an antiques dealer, and I knew it would have great stuff for your lecture. I couldn't just lend it to you outright, though, because Allison—well, I think she would have blown a fuse if I showed that I had some knowledge that she didn't. I have to say I'm stunned at how much you managed to pull out of your reading. I never realized that Ai Otani was the character Lanning called Miss Love."

"That kimono that was stolen was Ai Otani's wedding robe. It really is very important." I paused. "Anyone selling the bride's kimono could get a very good price, now that there's evidence that it's a Tokugawa relic."

"We're not in the business of selling things at the museum. We cannot appraise items because it's against our code of ethics—"

"Maybe you can answer a question for me," I said. "Why do you use the computer at the office to look at offerings on eBay?"

"You saw our computer?" She sounded startled.

"Yes, during the couple of times I was in the office."

"It's a research tool," Jamie said. "In addition to studying what objects sell for at big auction houses like Christie's and Sotheby's and Butterfield, we consult the Internet auctions. eBay's democratized things. They don't have a lot of fine things, but they are a good benchmark in learning what's out there, and how low its price can go. We use that kind of data when we make decisions about acquisitions."

"You've acquired quite a bit yourself." I looked around the bedroom. "You look as if you're an awfully good shopper."

Jamie flushed. "I like old American furniture. I work with Asian stuff all day. It's relaxing for me to spend my nights with the kind of things I grew up with."

The *kind* of things she grew up with. This meant her pieces weren't family heirlooms, but something else. How did a woman earning $20,000 a year, living in a cheap apartment in a borderline part of northeast Washington, live so extravagantly?

"I should get going. I promised my parents we'd only stop here for a minute," I said.

"So, are your parents here to help you pay for the lost kimono?"

"I would never ask my parents to cover my bills," I said tightly. "They came because a young woman was murdered, a Japanese tourist whom the police assumed was me, since she was carrying my passport. Hana had been missing for a few days before they found her. That's why I came here to see you. In my mind, you were missing. I thought the two situations might have a connection. I'm very glad that you're alive."

Jamie's eyes widened again. "You mean . . . that death of a Japanese tourist in Northern Virginia that was written up in *The Washington Post* today?"

"I haven't seen the paper, but I imagine so." I bit my lip. "One of the problems . . . the police think I might be connected with that death. In a bad way. I told them I was here at the request of the museum, but I don't think they quite believe me. I wouldn't be surprised if they visit Allison to ask her about me. If they do come to the museum . . . will you let me know?"

"Of course. Rei, when are you going back to Japan?"

"I don't know, exactly. I haven't done a thing about replacing my passport or trying to book another ticket. It seems hopeless, but I want to do everything possible to find that kimono."

"And lingering here keeps you near Hugh."

"That's crazy!" I said, but of course, it was true. I knew how the unconscious worked. I'd managed to see Hugh every day of my stay, despite my initial declarations of wanting to be alone, and the longer I was waiting for my passport, the more I'd continue to see him. Once I returned to Japan, it would be over. Life would once again mean working and living alone all week, and corn-and-octopus-pizza takeout with Takeo on the weekend. How did Jamie know so much about the way I felt?

Suddenly I had to see that bedside photograph that she'd turned facedown upon my entry in the room. When Jamie's fat white cat strolled out from under her fancy bed, I knew how I'd do it.

"Hah—choo!" I faked the largest sneeze imaginable and kept my hands over my face when I was done.

"God bless you," Jamie said automatically.

"Thanks. Um, this is a little embarrassing, but do you have a spare tissue? I need to make a major wipe-up. I didn't say this before, but I'm actually allergic to cats." The truth was that they made me nervous. You could say it was an emotional allergy.

"Oh, sorry! I'll just run into the bathroom and get you some tissue."

The instant she was out the door I flipped over the photograph. It was taken aboard a boat and showed a smiling couple: Jamie, wearing a bikini, with an older man in a Lacoste polo shirt with both arms around her, hugging her from behind. There was possessiveness in the man's gesture, though it looked as if Jamie didn't mind.

I'd feared all along that the photograph would show Hugh Glendinning. It didn't. Yet this was a man I recognized, whose hand had gripped mine a little too sensuously when we'd met.

There was no question about it. Even minus the business suit, I could tell that Jamie's boyfriend was Dick Jemshaw.

30

My parents were cuddled up close on Jamie's sofa when we rejoined them. My mother had her nose in a copy of *The Arts of Asia* and my father had his head on her shoulder, as if he were trying to catch a tiny nap. It was a sweet scene, and it tugged at my heart a little bit. My parents, long ago, had made the kind of choice that Jamie and I were both struggling with—and everything had turned out right.

"Time to go home. Thanks, Jamie," I said.

"I hardly helped at all. And look how tired your parents are." Jamie was looking at them, but she obviously wasn't thinking about what I was—she just saw a middle-aged couple slumped on her sofa.

My mother and father rose to their feet and said their good-byes, then the three of us hustled into the Corolla and locked all the doors.

"Do you know anything about an antiques dealer called Dick Jemshaw?" I asked my mother after we'd sorted out the directions and were heading back toward Virginia.

"I don't know a person by that name, but I saw a booth called Jemshaw Limited or something like that in the Washington Design Center."

"Did you look at the merchandise?"

"Oh, yes. Some English and American antiques, but most of the pieces on display were reproductions crafted out of old hardwoods—you know, the kind of thing that's being made in Asian countries for the U.S. market. A lot of the pieces were great looking and they would have fit my clients' budgets. It's not exactly my taste, though. If I were buying something made in Asia, I would want it to look Asian. Like your father," she said with a laugh. "And like Takeo."

"What about the furniture in Jamie's apartment? Do you think it could have come from Jemshaw Limited?"

"Hmm, that's interesting. I think pretty much all of Jamie's pieces are reproductions, but they're very good ones. I can't tell you for sure whether they were Jemshaw pieces because I didn't study his catalogue closely, but they seem to fit the general mood. Why do you ask?"

"Just curious, Mom. Thanks for your expertise." I was beginning to put together a theory. Dick Jemshaw, being generous to his young mistress, either lent or gave her items from his business. He might need to surround himself with the right furnishings in order to feel sexy. I myself had a serious fixation with Hugh's sleigh bed. Furniture mattered to me in a way that clothes mattered to other people.

If Dick Jemshaw's business focused on reproduction European and American furniture, though, why was he chair of the advisory committee for the Museum of Asian Arts? And how happy was Jamie with him as her partner? "Go away," she'd said when I'd buzzed her apartment. Now I recalled that when we'd gone to the museum's restaurant, she'd tried to avoid the table where Dick and Hugh had been sitting. Allison had pushed her to go—Allison, whom Jamie accused of being hard to work for.

Maybe Allison really didn't know about Dick Jemshaw and Jamie, but as I remembered her comment about women in their twenties falling into the laps of trustees, I thought that she had to understand the threat that a trustee's interest in her subordinate could pose to her own survival as curator of the museum.

I was in twenty-first-century America, not Edo-period Japan, I reminded myself. Women didn't have to sleep their way to high places.

But as I recalled the woman who'd been leaning into the window of a car on Florida Avenue, I brooded about the many forms solicitation could take. In a better section of northwest Washington, the girls might wear cashmere sweaters as comfortably as their Georgetown and Yale degrees. The client wouldn't pay with anything as crass as money—dinners in fancy restaurants and old furniture with the perfect patina would suffice. I liked these things myself, I was ashamed to admit.

It was midnight when we reached the Washington Suites. My parents and I parted and made our ways to our separate floors. There was a message on my telephone from Kyoko. She said that because of the funeral home's heavy schedule on Sundays, Hana's body would not be packed for travel until Monday. She and Yoshi were scheduled to fly home Monday evening. In the meantime, she wanted to know if I could escort the two of them to a museum on Sunday.

I slept fitfully until my telephone shrilled around seven.

"Hello?" I answered groggily.

"This is Detective Harris."

"Aren't you ever off duty?" I grumbled, thinking that

I should have let the call go to the hotel's answering service.

"For a case like this, I do what needs to be done. And if that means waking up a reluctant witness, I'll do it." He paused. "You sound like you were out late last night."

"Not so terribly late for us—but I guess it was late for *you*."

"What do you mean?"

"I'd thought you were the most likely candidate to have been tailing me from Virginia to Washington the last few evenings. Thanks for confirming my theory."

"If a car followed you, why didn't you go to a police station?" He sounded as skeptical as ever.

"What, and deliver myself into a nest of your classy friends? The ones who treat me like a twenty-first-century Suzy Wong?"

"Ms. Shimura, I don't know if you're being hassled by your pimp or someone else you have issues with, but if you'd like police protection, I can arrange it."

"I don't want a cop messing in my life, thank you very much—"

"Yeah, I guess it might cramp your style, going back and forth between your gentlemen—"

"You *are* following me!"

Detective Harris chuckled and said, "I don't need to follow you to know what you're doing. I get my information from a good source. And the information I've gotten has led me to ask you about your travel plans today."

"I'm not traveling anywhere. If your source mentions seeing me driving to the airport today, it's because I'm seeing my parents off. I won't leave Washington without the bride's kimono."

"Don't you think that kind of work is best done by professionals?"

"Sure. Except in this case, you've got a more pressing issue to deal with. Leave the little stuff, like a fifty-thousand-dollar stolen kimono, to me."

"The death of an innocent tourist is a tragedy—and my priority, as a homicide detective. If I'm able to identify a suspect, though, there could be every chance you'll find out about your missing kimono."

I paused to soak up what he'd just said. He now believed that Hana was an innocent tourist—Kyoko and Yoshi must have successfully restored her honor. That was good. Maybe there would be justice for me, too. "I understand your point," I said, in my most humble voice—the one I pulled out to bargain with dealers at the Tokyo shrine sales. "But don't you think that locating the kimono might lead you to either the killer—or someone who saw the killer? And I want to ask you something else. Does anyone in your headquarters know how to do research on the Internet?"

"Of course. We have links to the FBI and police departments and jails around the country."

"Well, I think you might find the thief or killer or whoever by hunting for the kimono at Internet auction sites."

"It's true that some of our guys have caught a few burglars in the past selling goods on-line. But it's always been more popular kinds of merchandise—TVs, Pokémon cards, what have you."

"I've got a color slide of the kimono that was stolen. I'd be willing to share it with you on a couple of conditions."

"Oh?"

"The first is that you'll actually try to do something about finding the kimono, instead of just giving me this second-priority business. And the other thing I want you to do is stop treating me like a hooker. It's really getting tiresome."

Detective Harris laughed. "I don't think of you as a woman who gets easily tired. You were at the Hotel Sof itel *twice* yesterday, according to our account."

"Well, if your source didn't tell you already, during the morning I had a chat in the lounge, with the registrar from the Morioka Museum, and later on, I had dinner with my parents and a friend who'd just flown in from Japan."

"You're very smooth—"

"I'm just being honest. Talk to my parents. Whatever But I'll tell you this—I'm going to be out of the hotel all day, so I need to know now if you have any interest in my slide."

Harris cleared his throat. "I do. I can come to get it now, if that's convenient."

For lack of inspiration, I dressed in the jeans I'd bought the day before and a taupe silk shirt my mother must have bought at Magnin's in the 1970s. It was a simple look, after all the dressing up I'd done to please Allison and my mother. But it was comfortable, and I didn't think it looked anything like what a prostitute would wear.

Detective Harris still looked me over a touch too long when I gave him the slide. I gave him a few last-minute ideas about auction houses where the kimono might have wound up, and then closed the door on him. needed to call Kyoko Omori and my parents to get on with the day. My parents' flight was scheduled to leave mid-afternoon, which meant we would have to head to the airport at one. When I mentioned that Yoshi and Kyoko wanted to go to a museum with me, they insisted on coming along.

"They want to see the Museum of American His

tory," I said to my mother. "I don't know if that's something you'd like to do."

"Sure. I haven't been to the Smithsonian Institutions in years, but I've always retained my membership. This means I receive a nice discount in the museum shops—I can help them buy souvenirs. And why don't you ask Takeo? After all, he's traveled so far and seen very little of you."

I dialed Takeo, feeling more dutiful than enthusiastic. He was not in his room the first time I called. It was only when I'd gotten downstairs to the Washington Suites lobby, and had met up with Kyoko and Yoshi at nine A.M., that I tried to call Takeo again, and he picked up.

"You mean . . . another group activity?" He didn't bother hiding the dismay in his voice after I explained about the trip to the Smithsonian.

"This is Kyoko and Yoshi's last day. We'll have plenty of time together in the future—" As I said it, I realized why I wanted to go on this outing. I was trying to find safety in numbers. Hana had been killed when she'd gone off on her own.

"I don't like groups. I want to wander around somewhere just with you," Takeo said.

The last thing I wanted to do. Briskly, I said, "Never mind. This was an invitation I extended to you out of courtesy."

"Can you come see me in the afternoon?" Takeo demanded.

"Maybe, after I've seen my parents off. Maybe that's the time we can spend talking. As I mentioned to you yesterday, something's changed in my life that I want to talk to you about."

"I know it! You've decided to go back to being an American. That's why you won't sleep with me anymore—it's a rejection of your Asian heritage."

"What a ridiculous idea," I said.

"Of course you deny it. You poor girl—I'm so sorry!" Takeo said, sounding completely sarcastic. "Maybe your psychiatrist father can help you with your pitiful frame of mind."

Totally fed up, I banged down the pay phone I'd been using and turned to Kyoko, who'd been hovering nearby with an anxious expression.

"My friend is not coming along."

"Hugh-san? What a shame."

I'd forgotten that Kyoko didn't know about Takeo. Well, there was no point in introducing the topic of a Japanese boyfriend who'd begun to hate me. "That's right, he can't come. Well, at least this way the car won't be too crowded."

Still, it was a tight fit with Yoshi, Kyoko, and me in the backseat. Kyoko and Yoshi both volunteered to take the tight spot in the middle, but as I was the smallest, and the daughter of the drivers, I felt duty bound to be there. My father drove and my mother pointed out landmarks, the same landmarks I'd pointed out two nights before, but that Kyoko and Yoshi were polite enough to pretend they were seeing for the first time.

"And here is the Washington Mall, a lovely system of rectangular park grounds that were designed in the early nineteenth century on a French model," my mother said. "The museums we'll visit are mostly bordered by Constitution Drive and Independence Avenue, but parking is always very tight, so we will park in the first spot we see."

"What do you think if I just park around here where it's less crowded?" my father asked, ever the practical one.

"Good idea," my mother said. "Oh, look, there's

something halfway up the block. A little small, but I bet you can squeeze in."

My parents were used to parking in the Bay Area, so for them, a spot with only a foot of space on each side was generous. Yoshi complimented my father on his skill. "Driving in America seems difficult, yet drivers seem greatly skilled. Rei's friend Hugh-san was able to swiftly drive away from a pursuing criminal. His reaction time is very quick and as daring as anything you'd see in the movies."

"What?" My father gave me an outraged look as we all got out of the car.

"It's not that he was a daredevil, Dad, it's just the same kind of driving situation that we were all in last night," I explained. "What would you prefer I do?"

"I'm starting to think that what's happening to tourist drivers in Washington is like the terrible rash of car-jackings a few years ago in Miami," my mother said. "I'll be glad when we return this car to the airport. Whatever you do, Rei, don't ride in any more private cars, and please don't expose your friends to them!"

"Mrs. Chiyoda, our tour group leader, said a shuttle bus or a taxi are the safest methods of travel," Kyoko said.

"Uh-huh. Mom, are you sure you know the way?" I asked, wondering how miserable this walk to the Museum of American History would be.

"We've got the Tidal Basin behind us, which means we're headed in the proper direction," she replied. "Things haven't changed that much in the last twenty years."

"Excuse me for interrupting, but I think we should be a few streets to the north," Yoshi said, holding out a tourist map.

"Yes, that's true," my father said. "Let's cut through on the next cross street to the north."

Yoshi and Kyoko liked this idea, because as we proceeded deeper inside the mall, the people watching got better. In addition to tourists like us, it was clear that there were real Washingtonians enjoying a Sunday-morning routine. We passed people sitting on benches reading newspapers and parents wheeling babies in strollers. There were runners, bikers, and walkers, too. But the mall really got its lively flavor from the impromptu groups of people playing team sports in different areas. We passed a huge group of men playing soccer, and mixed teams of men and women playing softball.

"Oh, look, isn't that game called rugby?" Yoshi asked as we continued along. "The game that is the favorite of Hugh."

"Who?" my mother asked pointedly.

"Who, indeed!" I said quickly. "Who likes rugby? I for one don't know much about it, but I hear it can be rather violent and dangerous. I think we should steer clear of the players."

"No, Hugh plays that game on the mall every Sunday morning. We talked about it in the car," Yoshi said. "I want to say hello, if you don't mind."

"Not a bad idea," my father said, surprising me until I realized he just wanted to satisfy his nosy impulses. As we walked along, I took heart in the thought that Hugh probably wouldn't notice us because the game was fast moving and intense. We came closer to the men, and it was clear that they were a tough lot. All were wearing rugby shirts and shorts, regardless of the chill in the air. Their hair was plastered with sweat, and they seemed hell-bent on rushing each other, butting heads and bodies, and kicking. How could Hugh play a game like this, and expect to make it safely into his law office every Monday morning? Maybe this was what he needed to do to escape from the tensions of his work. There was an ambulance standing by at the edge of the field, as if physical disaster were a routine occurrence.

I steeled myself not to look for Hugh, not to look at the group at all, despite the fact that Yoshi and Kyoko had chosen to stop at the side of a goal line and wave.

"I hope they don't get hit by the ball," I said. "Well, there's an ambulance waiting."

"Yes, you certainly couldn't count on me for help!" my father said with a grin. "My emergency training is so antiquated that I don't think I'm capable of doing more than putting a bandage on a knee. And I haven't done that for years—not since my daughter grew up."

"I wish a boo-boo on the knee was the only thing I had to worry about," I said.

"I do, too," my father said. "But I've sensed that you want to do all the bandaging yourself. You don't need me anymore."

"Oh, don't say that!" I reacted sharply.

"No, it's true. You're in a very dangerous situation, a case that the police seem unable to solve. I wish you'd let us take you home to San Francisco for a while. Your museum work here is done. You're uncomfortable spending time with Takeo. Why stay?"

"Because I have to make sure—" I broke off when I noticed that a big, mud-streaked man was talking to Kyoko and Yoshi—no doubt asking them to move away from the field. Then I saw a second man, muddy but leaner, with red-blond hair and a rugby shirt striped in blue and green that hung a little more gracefully than anyone else's. It was Hugh. He had stopped playing the game and had his hands cupped around his mouth as he called to them.

"Go to the side! I'll see you during break," Hugh called out. He was only about twenty yards away from

Yoshi, but I could tell that Yoshi hadn't understood what he was saying, because he waved with more gusto and began to jog toward Hugh.

Yoshi's spontaneous movement caused a general rash of swearing and catcalls among the rugby players. Why in hell was a bloody tourist coming onto their field?

"This'll teach him," someone with a rough Australian accent bellowed, and as my father and I gasped, the huge, hard rugby ball was suddenly hurtling through the air, right toward Yoshi.

As Yoshi had pointed out, Hugh Glendinning had fast reflexes. He barreled toward Yoshi, arms outstretched to catch the ball. He caught it, but not without his feet going out from under him. His body hit the ground, and he rolled over twice, then came to a stop.

31

"Hugh!"

I ran, hearing in the distance my parents calling me to stay back with them. There was a louder voice ringing in my ears: the voice of reason, the one screaming that if Hugh was seriously hurt it was my fault, because of whom I'd brought near the rugby game.

Hugh was lying flat on his back but with his legs twisted to one side. As I tried to get a better look at him, the other rugby players arrived and shoved me out of the way. I lost my balance and fell into the mud. It wasn't a hard fall, but enough to thoroughly soil my green wool coat—a vintage Pauline Trigère that my mother had handed down to me.

Yoshi's voice was behind me, mournfully saying, "I am very sorry, I am very sorry, I am very sorry—"

"Shaddup. He just needs to catch his breath," someone with an American accent said.

"Where are the paramedics?" I demanded of the huge, shiny man who had talked to Yoshi.

"We'll signal to them if they're needed. They're used to our play."

"Yes, it's not so bad as it looks. More a matter of little Miss Muffet falls from the tuffet," someone with a South African accent said.

"I think the man's right, Rei."

I heard my father's voice and looked up in confusion. I hadn't seen him in the crowd, but sure enough, he was examining Hugh. He was holding his hand, in fact, and moving it back and forth.

"I'm Rei's father," he was saying. "My name is Toshiro Shimura."

"Oh, Christ! I mean, oh, hello, Dr. Shimura. I apologize for my, um, condition. I'm not usually so messed up—"

"You're fine," I said to Hugh, feeling a great sense of relief flow through me.

"My clinically imperfect diagnosis is that he's had the wind knocked out of him. But he can certainly go to the hospital if he wants a work-up," my father said.

"I don't need to get any more worked up than I already am." From the way Hugh was looking at us all, it was totally unclear whether he was talking about being angry at me, or was frightened from the fall, or something else entirely. But he took hold of my hands and gingerly pulled himself up.

A cheer rose up from his rugby mates, who beckoned him back to the game. But Hugh shook his head. "I'm out on injury leave for the rest of the day, guys. Have fun."

"Can I meet you at the museum café in a half hour or so?" I said to my parents in a low voice. My mother had arrived in a swirl of turquoise pashmina and was determinedly smiling at both Hugh and me. Kyoko and Yoshi stood next to her, holding hands and looking very worried.

"I doubt that it will take her that long to sort me out," said Hugh, who was actually smiling back at my mother. "You must be Rei's mother. You look even better than in those photos."

My mother laughed—an anxious laugh that told me

he was trying to figure out whether he was sincere. My
father, too, seemed inclined to hang around and inspect
Hugh. He was willing to go only after a gentle comment
from Yoshi, who suggested that they should head
straight for the museum and meet up with me in a couple of hours. Yoshi, I thought, was turning out to be the
master of diplomacy.

"When I thought I'd finally lost you, I didn't know
what I was going to do," I said to Hugh as we walked
hand in hand along Seventeenth Street to where he'd
said his car was parked. I intended to drive him home,
have him change into clean clothing, and get him resting on his sofa with the ultimate therapeutic drink: a
cup of Darjeeling with milk and three sugars.

"Thanks for telling me. I only wish you'd told me
sooner."

"I thought you didn't want me to see me again—"

"I was just waiting for you to make up your mind."
When I didn't reply, he said, "You have decided, haven't
you?"

"Yes. But I'm not ready to declare anything, beyond
the fact that seeing you hurt was the *worst* feeling in the
world."

"So I guess we're still operating under the same de-
pressing circumstance." Hugh sat down suddenly on a
park bench, as if he didn't want to go any farther.

"Not quite." I sat down next to him. "I'm just taking
the time to figure out the best course for everyone."

Hugh stared across the street and said, "There's too
much pressure, isn't there? You're going through a trau-
matic situation with Hana's death and the missing kimono. You've also had only a few days to deal with the
idea of being with me. In the meantime, everything we

do is being witnessed by a gigantic audience—your pa
ents and Yoshi and Kyoko and Takeo, not to mentio
the cops and our unknown stalker friends. By the wa
do you know that guy, leaning against a tree and watc]
ing us? He's been there for the last five minutes."

About a hundred feet away, I saw him—a tall narro
figure dressed in a long dark coat. It was too far awa
to make an identification, but his hair was black an
thick in a way that could be Asian. He darted behin
the tree when I looked at him. I had a sinking feelin
that it was Takeo, who'd decided to find me in the plac
I'd said I was going to.

"How far is your car?" I asked.

"Halfway down the block. Do you have a genius R
Shimura strategy to get us away?"

"Just stay where you are and watch him. I'll com
back with the car and take you home. He won't hav
time to react."

Hugh looked at me oddly but went along with th
plan. As I'd thought, the man trailed me, staying fa
enough away that I couldn't quite identify him, whic
was frustrating. I clicked the remote that unlocked th
Lexus at the last possible minute and got in and quickl
drove down the street to collect Hugh.

"We should circle back and see what he looks like,
Hugh said after he settled into the passenger seat.

"I don't want to know. At this point I just want to ge
you home, put your hands around a nice warm cup o
tea, and return to my parents in one piece." I made a lef
turn straight onto the left side of the road, as I woul
have done in Japan, but quickly corrected myself befor
I could be a danger to anyone. It was a good thing all m
Washington driving experiences had occurred late a
night or early in the morning when few cars were on th
road.

"Do you think the guy watching might be Takeo?" Hugh asked.

"Yes. He knew I was going to come to this area this morning, but he didn't want to accompany me."

"Why not? Have you told him about me?"

"I don't know why not. And I've wanted to tell him, but he's a little resistant to conversation these days."

"I see," Hugh said, looking hard at me. "But he's not resistant to other kinds of activities, I bet."

"I'm not sleeping with him—nor with you again," I said, keeping my eyes on the road. "All it does is confuse things."

He sighed heavily. "I'm sorry about what happened in my flat, then. Because of it, you must think all I cared about was pleasure."

"But isn't pleasure why we have relationships?"

Hugh's face, under the mud, had flushed bright red. "Actually, you're the most, er, satisfying partner I've had—but perfect sex doesn't make happy endings. I've figured out that a good union depends on achieving happiness together in more ordinary parts of life. Sports, work, going out to dinner with friends—"

"I agree," I said, finally catching what he meant. "It's because I was afraid of losing the chance to start my own business that I wouldn't go away with you."

"That—and my bossiness," Hugh added. "I made you bend to my life, and that was wrong. Now I think I should have just let you choose a flat for the two of us and adapted to your lifestyle. As you know, I'm not overly fond of green tea—but I'd drink my tea greener than the grass stains on your coat if you'd let me follow you back to Japan."

"Don't talk to me like that now," I said, fighting back tears of joy. "I'm liable to have an accident."

Hugh laughed. "I'll shut up, then. Just accept the fact,

Rei, that you and I both were meant to drive on the left hand side of the road."

I parked Hugh's Lexus near the corner of Biltmor Street, close to where he lived, and walked him up to hi apartment. Hugh took his shower and I made a pot c tea. It was my first time in his kitchen, a pleasant enoug room with old wooden cabinets, and a black-and-white tiled floor and a stove and fridge from the 1940s. I wa stunned to see hanging on the wall above his toaster over a series of framed photos—old, grainy black-and-whit paparazzi pictures of a girl on the run that had appeare in the *Asahi Shinbun* and other Japanese newspaper some years ago. There I was, exiting his apartment build ing in Tokyo in the dated Talbots suit I wore to my ol job teaching English, and in another shot wearing slinky Azzedine Alaia dress as I left the Tokyo America Club with another man. On the fridge, I saw that he' clipped out a brief mention from *The Washington Pos* about my upcoming lecture. So this was the article tha I'd heard about. I read through quickly and saw wit shock the date given for the lunchtime lecture was Octo ber 18—Wednesday of the next week coming up. N wonder there had been so few people when I'd spoken o Friday, October 13. It had all been due to a typing error

I finished making tea and brought the clipping out t the living room, where Hugh, in his favorite old ter rycloth robe, was resting.

"Did you notice the *Post* got the date of the lectur wrong?" I asked as I handed him his mug.

"I was too distracted to read the fine print. There wa a mistake?"

"Yes, a serious one. The paper says the lecture is nex Wednesday. I wasn't even scheduled to be on this side o the world next Wednesday. I wonder—I wonder if the mistake was intentional."

"You mean—someone at the *Post* has it in for you? Listen, half the politicos in Washington will make that claim, but I hardly think you need to worry."

"Not someone at the newspaper. I wonder if Allison sent out a press release with a wrong date because once she met me she realized I wasn't good enough to do the job—"

"No, no!" Hugh said, smiling. "That notice went in to the paper four weeks ago. I know the press release was correct because I made sure that I read it. Dick Jemshaw faxed me a copy."

If Hugh had asked for a special favor relating to my lecture, Dick Jemshaw might very well have an inkling that his interest was more than professional. This brought up something else I wanted to hash out with Hugh. "How well do you know Dick?"

"He's been friendly to me. Lunch together that one time you saw us, and drinks with some other people from the advisory committee another evening. That's about the sum of our contact."

"Is he a client of your firm?"

Hugh shook his head. "I don't think he's got any legal troubles."

"And you don't owe him client confidentiality? That's good. Now I can ask you what I really want to know. Did he ever talk about having a girlfriend?"

"Not at all! He's a married man. Twenty years in or something like that."

"Married men can have girlfriends."

"Yeah, just like single women can have multiple boyfriends. Don't hit me, darling—all right, I do recall that Dick has an eye for gorgeous young women, including you, but is having eyes a crime?"

"What about Jamie, Allison's assistant—you know, that tall, pretty blonde who was with me at lunch that day?"

"He's never brought her up. Do you think they're seeing each other?"

"I'm positive of it. I saw a picture of them together at her flat, which, by the way, is furnished with very lovely furniture that is quite likely from the line he sells at the Washington Design Center."

"Are you saying that I could furnish this flat with Dick's generosity if only I asked for it? I'm a tall, pretty blond. A few people have said so anyway." Hugh's eyes twinkled.

"But what could you deliver in return? You're a sexy man, but would Dick care?" I said, smiling. "While you figure it out, I have to go back to get my parents off on their flight to California. I was thinking about leaving with them, but I've changed my mind."

"But they're leaving without me getting a chance to know them! Why don't I dress and come with you to the airport?"

"There isn't enough room for all of us in the car they rented. I'm sorry. But I'll see you later."

"I could drive the Lexus, maybe take Yoshi and Kyoko so you have more time with your parents—"

"We're going to have so little time there, and it all sounds a bit too overwhelming. I'll stop back and see you later tonight." I made a move to pick up the muddied coat that I'd discarded, then stopped. "I can't wear this in front of my mother. She'll be distraught."

"Well, better borrow my Barbour. I'll take your soiled coat to my favorite dry cleaner and have it back for you day after tomorrow."

Lending me a jacket was a small gesture, but one that I knew meant everything. He trusted me. He wanted me to come back.

"I love you," I said. It was the first time I'd said it to him since the Metro ride.

"Great," Hugh said, sounding grumpy. "When are you going to do something about it?"

J came back to the museum early enough to need to round up the tour group—as I'd come to think of my parents, Yoshi, and Kyoko. The foursome was looking at the collection of first-lady dresses up on the museum's third floor.

"Rei-san! Did you buy a new coat?" Kyoko asked.

"No. I borrowed this from Hugh." On him, the coat was short, but on me, it was almost knee length. I shrugged a bit deeper into its quilted, lightweight warmth. It smelled like Hugh—a mixture of Grey Flannel cologne and his own body scent.

"That coat is like Hana's," Kyoko said.

"Hana's was black. This coat is brown," I said, realizing I'd made a mistake in wearing it. Kyoko, who had seemed fine during the morning, had wrapped her old cloak of misery about herself.

"Rei doesn't look like Hana," Yoshi said. "Any more than Mrs. Shimura would resemble Nancy Reagan if she wore that lady's red evening gown from the museum."

My mother laughed. "I wonder if I should take that as a compliment."

"Of course," Yoshi said. I looked at him thinking how he'd seemed to recover from Hana's death. He'd been quiet at first, but bit by bit, he'd emerged as a cheerful, rather mischievous man. I found myself wondering if, despite the tragedy, he felt free. Perhaps he'd escaped a path that hadn't been the right one.

"Is Hugh lying down?" my father asked me.

"No," I said quickly, lest he be trying to figure out

whether I'd gotten into bed with him again. "I made him some tea, and then I left him. He said to tell you to have a good trip, and that he's sorry he wouldn't have a chance to see you again. I couldn't see how we could all fit in that compact rental car."

"Oh, sorry for the confusion. Yoshi-kun and I are not riding in your rental car," Kyoko said. "We want to give your parents the chance to say good-bye to you privately. Anyway, we've taken a lot of your time."

I made arrangements to call Kyoko and Yoshi that evening, in case they wanted to go out in Washington one last time, and then got in the car with my parents. I looked around as I got in, checking for the dark-haired man who'd seemed to be spying on Hugh and me earlier in the day. He wasn't there, and again, I thought of Takeo Kayama. Maybe he was at his hotel innocently working on his laptop computer. On the other hand, he could have followed me to the mall, and learned the worst.

32

It was one o'clock, and nobody had eaten, but dropping the rental car off was a priority before we did anything in the airport. My parents had hoped to simply leave the keys in the car, but it turned out they had to go inside and sign some papers because they'd forgotten to refill the car's gas tank.

I felt bad because I'd been the one who'd necessitated so much driving around—and it seemed there really was a problem with the bill. My father told the clerk the bill was clearly four hundred dollars over the fee he'd been quoted upon arrival.

"This total is completely wrong. I didn't come in on the eighth, I came on the twelfth. You're overcharging me."

"But our records show you did come on the eighth. You signed a contract at that time—" the agent said.

"May I see that," my father demanded. The agent handed the paper to him with a smug expression. I wondered if this was some kind of scam they played all the time.

"Here, it shows it clearly. This contract doesn't even say Shimura on it. Can't you look up Toshiro and Catherine Shimura?"

After a while everything was settled to my father's satisfaction, and I thought privately that it was a lucky thing indeed that no accident had occurred when I'd been driving the previous night, because I'd never been listed as a driver on the rental agreement. In my seven days of bad luck, I had to remember to think of the small victories.

"I think we did pretty well," I said to my parents after we'd walked from the car agency to the main terminal. "You thought I was dead, but I'm alive. We were chased, but nobody caught us. Mom's luggage was overweight, but we still had it accepted."

"Now, if only we had food in our tummies. Darling, is there anything you can eat at McDonald's?"

"They have more than that here," my father said, carefully studying the airport map. "Starbucks. Au Bon Pain. Ruby Tuesday—or is that a jewelry store?"

"I think it's hamburgers," my mother said. "Definitely off-limits for Rei. While you two go to the gate with the carry-ons, I'll get some bready things from Au Bon Pain."

Au Bon Pain. I meditated on the chain's name as my father and I found uncomfortable little seats in the American Airways gateway. *Good bread. Good pain.* As much as my parents had brought me trouble, they'd flooded me with love. And the hard thing was that, whenever I said good-bye to them, it never meant a few months. It would be a year or longer.

"You look sad, Rei." My father spoke in Japanese, the language we only occasionally spoke together.

"It's just that I'm wondering about when I'll see you again," I answered in English. I was more nervous about making language mistakes with him than with anyone in Japan.

"Soon, I hope." My father switched back to English, as if defeated. "Aren't you stopping in San Francisco on your way back to Tokyo?"

"I don't know when I'll go. I'm a bit hesitant to return to Tokyo given the debt that I owe the museum—"

"We can help you with money," my father said. "Whatever that Japanese museum asks—well, we'll get a lawyer to look at the situation first. Maybe Hugh can help. He seems quite capable."

"But you hardly met him," I said. "It was under the worst possible circumstances!"

My father looked at me. "Yes, and your recent escapades are all the kinds of things a father never wants to hear. But when I saw the expression on his face, looking at you . . . well, that was all I needed to see. I understood."

"You really think he's fine?"

My father looked at me quizzically. "Judging from that question, it sounds as if you're not so sure."

I put my head in my hands. "It's—very serious. He wants to live with me on my terms, in Japan if necessary. But what would our future be? If we had children . . . they'd only be a quarter Japanese. What would that be like? How could they cope socially?"

"What if you can't bear children?" My father used the challenging tone that was familiar to me, in times of crisis, all my life. But this was one of the oddest things he'd ever said to me. *Can't bear children.* I didn't like it.

"Are you telling me . . . you know something about my medical history that I don't know?"

"Of course not. I'm just saying . . ." My father trailed off and bowed his head for a second. The coldness inside me grew. Then he faced me again, gravely. "Your mother and I hoped to have three or four children. We understood that because of the way genetics work, some children might appear more Asian and others more Caucasian. We didn't care if our children didn't match.

We were excited to start our family. The problem was, it didn't happen."

"What do you mean, it didn't happen?" I asked, feeling even more confused.

"All the children died." I could see my father's eyes start to water. "Your mother had four miscarriages, three in the first trimester, and one at the end of the second. To some people, the babies might have been fetuses, but for your mother and me, they were real babies. Babies we lost."

"Oh, my God," I said, feeling tears sting my eyes. How sad I was now for never knowing. As a child, I'd been silently angry with my parents for what I assumed was their lack of interest in having more children. I'd thought that because I was a bad daughter, they decided not to have any more. I'd never suspected that I'd had these ghostly brothers and sisters.

"During the years this was happening, I sometimes thought that if we'd each chosen a partner from our own countries, we would have had children that lived. It was as if, by mixing our cultures, we were trying to achieve the impossible. The idea made no medical sense—but looking at the flocks of children on either side of the family, it seemed that those who picked similar partners succeeded in reproducing. When your mother became pregnant with you, we had no hope. We didn't have a nursery prepared for you until the last minute. And then you made it.

"We'd wanted an energetic team of children, and we wound up with one. One perfect girl—as bright, exasperating, and loving as all of them could have been together. You were our Japanese girl. Or at least, my family said. You had the Japanese coloring and hair— but your mother swore you had her cheekbones, and her figure."

I wiped my eyes and managed a small smile. It was true that I had gotten my mother's body. How else could I fit so well into her old clothes?

"I don't know how to tell you this any more directly, my daughter," my father continued. "Race means *nothing*. All the scientific studies back me up on this—people are better differentiated by things such as earlobe shape than the color of their skin."

"I think I know what you're saying—"

"Takeo Kayama is no more predisposed to being a loving husband and father than Hugh Glendinning. In fact, the opposite might very well be true."

"But they look so damn right. Like Colefax and Fowler. Osborne and Little!" my mother said.

I jumped, and turned around to see my mother standing behind me, clutching paper bags of food. I wondered how long she'd been there.

My father sighed heavily. "Catherine, do you mean to say you think it would have been a better idea for you to marry some white person?"

"No, of course not! But how can I help preferring to see Rei with Takeo? Almost everything about him is familiar and beautiful. It's true that he doesn't talk much and seems a bit moody, but I'm sure Rei will perk him up—"

I stared at them, thinking the situation was both funny and pathetic. Each of my parents preferred a different boyfriend. They were clearly looking for memories of each other in Hugh and in Takeo. And now I found myself wondering if I'd fallen for my two lovers in an unconscious attempt to replicate the two parts that had made me. I should walk away from the two men if I really wanted to get my head on straight. Start over, clean.

"*Boarding,*" the PA system said. "*American Airlines*

flight boarding to San Francisco now. First class and preferred customers—"

"Are you going on? I know you're business class," I said.

My mother enveloped me in her soft pashmina and the scent of Shalimar. "The hell with business class. We're not anything but your mummy and daddy."

My father joined the embrace, and I cried against both their bodies. "I wish I could spend more time with you. I'm just getting to know about things. Daddy told me about the babies you miscarried."

"Oh, sweetie, I don't like to brood on the past," my mother said, weeping.

"I'll explain why I told her," my father said, picking up the shopping bags my mother had dropped. "Catherine, we really do have to go. The sooner we're off, the more quickly Rei can finish some very important business."

There was a Metro station right at National Airport, so I was able to travel quickly to Dupont Circle, where I rode up the long escalator, for once wishing the ride would never end. My plan was to go to the Sofitel, where I'd sit down with Takeo and talk. I'd tell him the truth that he deserved to hear.

Inside the hotel, I called up to his room and asked him if I could come up.

"I'd rather talk to you over lunch. Let's meet in the bar," he said.

"Good idea. I'll go in there now and start looking at the menu." My mother had forgotten to give me a croissant at the airport, so I was starving. I found a nice table near the front of the restaurant so Takeo would get a glimpse of the city beyond the hotel's glass doors. He had hardly been out of the hotel, I realized; just to the Museum of Asian Arts. What a terrible trip. And I was going to make it worse.

I would offer to pay the lunch bill, so I emptied my jeans pockets to check out my financial situation. I had about thirty dollars—not a fortune. I would eat French onion soup with a roll—to leave enough money for Takeo to order something nice. From now on, though, I was going to coax him into the streets of Dupont Circle and Adams Morgan to eat more cheaply.

I put away the money and was left with a piece of paper that I planned to throw away—the note Mr. Shima had given me about the book of Central American embroidery. I doubted I'd ever look for it; as I began to crumple the paper, I saw what was typed on the back. The paper he'd given me was a receipt for a rental car; he'd rented one from the same agency, Swifty, that my parents had used. The specifics of the order were too light for me to read, but the receipt made me think. Mr. Shima was the rare Japanese tourist who was brave enough to rent a car. Why? Was it to see local sights, or to follow me?

Since Takeo still hadn't arrived, I jumped up from the table and hurried to a side hall near the rest rooms where I'd seen a pay telephone. When I called 411, the operator asked if I wanted the number for Swifty at Reagan National Airport or Dulles. Dulles, I said firmly, because that was where international flights landed. But when I reached the rental agency, asking if they had rented a car to a Mr. Shima, there was no record of a customer by that name. They suggested that I check Reagan National and the Baltimore-Washington International airports.

Feeling irritated, I dug around in my pockets for more quarters. Damn, but this was inconvenient. I struck out with Baltimore, wasting fifty cents, but when I reached Reagan National I had some satisfaction. Yes, a Mr. Shima had rented a Geo Prism on October 8. When I asked the car's color, the person on the phone confirmed that it was blue.

I hung up, wondering how I was going to get the answer to the most important question of all—had Mr. Shima rented a car, and followed me, upon orders of the Morioka Museum? Or was this a task he'd taken upon himself?

My credit card was about to hit its limit, but maybe I could manage one last long-distance call. It was the middle of the night in Japan, though; I'd have to wait until eight that night to make my call to the Morioka Museum. This time I'd ask for the man at the top, Mr. Ito, and lay out all of my suspicions.

"Rei, there you are!"

Takeo jarred me from my thoughts by taking me by the shoulders and turning me away from the telephone. "Oh, hi. Sorry, I had to phone someone."

"Well, let's eat now. My stomach's totally empty."

"Okay," I said, putting the receipt, which now had new telephone numbers scrawled all over it, back into my jeans pocket. "But you know, we don't have to eat here. Maybe we can get out of the hotel and eat somewhere less formal."

"But I like the food here. There's a salmon plate that I've been thinking about ever since you called."

In the dining room, I tried not to blanch at the price of Takeo's lunch entrée and the bottle of California Chardonnay he ordered. I ordered onion soup with a glass of tap water on the side. A platter of rolls was set out between us right away, so I had something to do with my hands as I began my awkward conversation.

"Takeo, I want first of all to thank you for coming to

Washington. I'd hoped, from the very start, that you'd come along to keep me company. I didn't expect my parents and—everyone else."

"It's been a hard trip," Takeo said, looking slightly impatient as the waitress served me the onion soup, and then served him his poached salmon topped with tomato-and-basil sauce.

"Yes, the trip has been full of unexpected things," I said, after the waitress left us and he'd had a few bites. "On my first day here, I was having lunch at Pan Asia, the restaurant inside the museum, and I met an old boyfriend."

"Oh, really? You mean someone your father's age?" Takeo laughed at his own joke.

"No, I mean old in the sense that I used to know him. His name is Hugh. I told you a little about him before."

"Oh, of course," Takeo answered, sounding relaxed. "Hugh Glendinning, the lawyer you used to date. How bizarre that he's here. Well, coincidences do happen."

"It turned out that it wasn't really a coincidence. Hugh is part of the museum's advisory comittee—sort of a high-powered volunteer group," I explained, when Takeo raised his eyebrows at the English-language term I'd used in our Japanese conversation. "Apparently he suggested me as a possible lecturer on kimono. The museum doesn't know that he knew me personally. And I wouldn't have taken the job if I'd known Hugh suggested me."

Takeo chewed his salmon, then spoke. "Well, I don't see why you're so worried about my reaction to this. It's unfortunate that this favor from an old friend resulted in so much bad luck, but you can hardly blame him for that."

"I'm not blaming him. I'm blaming myself." I took a scalding mouthful of soup, followed by a sip of cold water. This course of revelation was truly painful. "Takeo, I slept with him. I feel really terrible about it—"

"Why? Listen, I know I'm a little more liberal than others about these things, but I believe your past belongs to you, and I don't really care to know about it. What counts is that we're together now. I'm not talking about marriage, or anything old-fashioned like that, but I like having you as a girlfriend. It's good, isn't it?"

"You're not listening!" I said in frustration. "I'm trying to explain that I did it last Friday night. Here, in Washington. I'm so sorry, I had no idea this was going to happen—I never meant to deceive you, but it was like a *tsunami,* a giant wave of feeling that came back. I think . . . I think I'm in love."

After the torrent of words, I fell silent. Takeo's complacent expression was gone. He understood.

"Don't talk about love," he said in English. "The correct term is 'cheating.'"

"I understand that it was a terrible thing to do." I stared into the murky brown depths of my bowl of soup, too miserable to eat another spoonful.

"I want to know exactly what you want," Takeo continued in his new, cold English. "Is it forgiveness, or a convenient good-bye?"

"I don't know what I want. I just felt that I had to be honest with you—"

"How can you possibly talk about being honest and good after what you've done? That slut who was killed—yes, I can understand why she did it, and how she was punished. But you, a girl with a doctor for a father—I can't believe it! Aren't you ashamed of what you've done to your parents as well as to me? To think that your contaminated body could have—touched—mine yesterday, if we'd gone to bed—it makes me want to vomit."

He was obviously very upset, and he'd had a glass and a half of wine. I had to treat him carefully. In my calmest voice, I said, "Takeo, I am ashamed of myself. Yes, I did something that my father, and most of society, wouldn't approve of. But I won't let you talk about Hana like that. She deserved to live just as much as you and I do."

"I know you thought I'd marry you someday, but it will never happen. Thank God that I found out about your true character now. To think I had to fly halfway around the world to learn this!"

After Takeo finished his short explosion I realized how quiet the restaurant was. About half the tables were occupied, and everyone was looking at us. A waiter in a black jacket was headed our way.

"I don't want anything," Takeo said in loud, angry English. "Go away."

"Sir, there's a problem with the noise," the waiter said sternly. "Your conversation is disturbing the other diners. You'll either have to lower your voice or leave."

"Lower—and you're talking about me? Nobody is lower than this woman here!" Takeo flung his hand up to point at me, knocking over the bottle of wine.

Diners gasped, and the room stayed still.

"I'm very, very sorry," I whispered, feeling my body start to shake. I stood up and removed from my pocket all the dollars and change I had and put them in the center of the table, hoping it would cover the meal, and put on Hugh's coat. All I wanted to do was flee.

"Go back to him!" Takeo yelled in Japanese, following me into the lobby. "I'm going out, too. After I'm done, you'll know never to treat anyone like this again."

"Are you all right, miss? Do you want me to call the police?" The waiter had followed us into the lobby.

"No!" I said quickly. "I think it's going to be fine. We're just saying good-bye right now."

"I hope you enjoy knowing that I'm going straight to the museum, where I'll tell them all about the trick that you and your boyfriend pulled: the expense-paid trip to Washington, just so the two of you could screw." Takeo had switched back to Japanese, perhaps because he wanted to make sure he could use the most clear, and vulgar, language possible. "After Allison hears the truth from me, I doubt you'll ever get paid."

Takeo didn't have a coat, but he ran out the door into the cold, turning in the direction of Connecticut Avenue—the route to the Museum of Asian Arts, which I'd taught him the day before.

33

There seemed to be a collective sigh of relief from the hotel's patrons at Takeo's grand departure, but I had no time to relax. I had to move. I couldn't let him catch Allison without me there to explain. At the same time I didn't want to go after him all by myself. Takeo had been so angry—he scared me.

I dashed back into the restaurant, noticing, as I went, that Mr. Shima was sitting at a table having lunch by himself. His stunned expression let me know he'd heard all that Takeo and I had said to each other.

The waitress was just starting to pick up the money I'd left on the table as I reached it. "Oh, I'm sorry but I need a couple of quarters back to make phone calls, and the fare card and that little paper. I'm sorry." I turned to the other diners and made a sweeping bow that included Mr. Shima. "I hope I didn't ruin everyone's meal. I'm leaving now."

I ran out of the restaurant and back to the pay phone in the hotel's hall.

"Miss, maybe you should call 911, which is a free call," the waiter persisted. "Or if you wait a minute, I think our concierge can call a women's shelter—"

I waved him off. I was already dialing Hugh's number. It rang four times and then a recorded message came on. "It's four-thirty," I said into the telephone. "I'm about to leave the Sofitel to run over to the Museum of Asian Arts. Takeo's already on his way there to see Allison Powell. He's going to expose us. Please come to the museum, if you can, because I'm really—scared." I hung up, knowing that it could be hours before Hugh heard the message.

I left the hotel in the opposite direction from the one that Takeo had gone. I knew that California Street would lead me in the same direction as the museum. I would have to find a cross street that went all the way through to S Street. Takeo had about a two-minute lead on me, but he was walking. If he didn't take a taxi—and I ran—I could beat him.

It was Sunday afternoon, which was to my benefit, I thought as I began to labor on the uphill section of the run. Allison probably wasn't working. Still, Takeo knew the administrative offices were located upstairs, since he'd seen me go there the previous day. If the museum was open, he would locate someone to whom he could shout his ugly story.

It was seven minutes to five when I sprinted down Twenty-third Street and to S Street. To my left lay the museum, and to my right was the path that I guessed Takeo would be taking—or had taken. I could just make out the figure of a dark-haired man walking briskly. He was too far away for me to see his face, but I guessed it was the same person who'd been watching me outside the museum. Takeo, perhaps. Or maybe not. Takeo could already have made it into the museum.

I didn't waste any more time wondering but sprinted the last twenty yards to the museum. Major Andrews practically jumped on me as I swung open the heavy door.

"We close at five," he said. I looked beyond him to the receptionist, who was pulling out the cash box from her desk and was making all the obvious signs of closing up.

"I'm sorry, I just need to go in to the administrative offices—"

"Oh, you're the kimono lady. I didn't recognize you in those clothes."

"Is Allison here today?" I panted.

"Yes, it's not a normal day for her to work, but I did see her earlier. I don't know if she slipped out the door already, because I'm in the process of closing the galleries."

"Did a Japanese man enter the museum? In the last few minutes, I mean?"

"Yeah, I saw a guy like that check in five minutes ago," the guard said. "He didn't want to pay admission at first, but we straightened him out."

"Thanks," I said, my spirits sinking. "I know you're closed, but can I just take a quick peek around to find him, and then we'll both leave?"

"Yeah. I'm going to go into the west side of the building, to close those galleries, so if I see him there, I'll tell him you're looking for him."

As soon as Major Andrews had left the foyer, I quietly hustled up the staircase, glad for my rubber-soled shoes.

Allison's office was empty, with the computer, photocopier, and lights turned off. I didn't see a purse or any other signs of her, but I decided to go down the hall to check the doors to the other offices of museum staff— the people I'd never really gotten to know. Now I wished I had—if they heard, in the last few minutes, Takeo's interpretation of my relationship with Hugh, they'd think the worst. But they didn't seem to be around. I didn't see any museum staff except for the guard. Perhaps all I had to do was get Takeo out of the museum and calm him down.

I was about to start downstairs when I overheard a commotion in the vestibule.

"But I'll just be a minute! I must speak to Miss Allison Powell immediately." It was Takeo, his voice loud and clearly furious.

"You'll have to wait till tomorrow morning, sir. She's not here, and the museum is closing."

"I won't be here tomorrow. I can't spend another night in the city, not after what she's done—Rei Shimura, that tramp!"

"Sir, the lady was here, but she's gone out. I need you to do the same."

So the major had fibbed to save me. How good of him, I thought with a rush of gratitude as I listened to some more sputtering from Takeo. Then I couldn't hear him anymore. The guard must have successfully thrown him out. Perfect. I'd wait just a few minutes, to allow Takeo to walk a sufficient distance from the museum, and then I'd emerge.

I could hear the guard whistling a cheerful, old-fashioned song called "Anchors Aweigh." If he was whistling, he clearly hadn't understood the awful things Takeo had said. So Takeo wanted to leave—I didn't think it would be possible for him to get on a flight that evening. He'd probably wind up at the Sofitel for one last night.

I wondered if Takeo would call my parents in California to scream at them about me. Fortunately, they were still in the plane, so I could call them ahead of time to warn them. Takeo might call Hugh, too—he had his number, and probably had figured out that I really hadn't been at a gym Saturday morning.

Mindful that this museum was probably the only place in Washington where I could get away with a free phone call, I went back into Allison's office to call

Hugh. He was still out, so I left a message saying that I was about to leave the museum, and that Takeo had been thrown out of the lobby. I'd explain in more detail later.

I hung up and started down the staircase, seeing the receptionist was no longer at the front desk. As I reached the bottom of the stairs, I was stunned to hear a chirping sound. A bright red light flashed on a security keypad next to the main door. It looked like a higher-tech version of the security system in Jamie's apartment, I realized as I drew closer to read the message on its face.

ARMED—ALL SECURE

The museum's alarm was on.

I had the awful thought that perhaps the museum guard, when he spoke to Takeo, really did believe that I'd left the museum. After all—I'd told him I'd only be five minutes. Now, if the alarm was on and the guard no longer around to help me, I was trapped.

What a mess. How could I extricate myself? Jamie, I thought suddenly. She might know which codes I could press to get myself safely out of the museum—and then rearm the system against intruders.

I found Jamie's number on a list in the unlocked top drawer of the receptionist's desk. I dialed it, and Jamie picked up on the first ring.

"This is Rei Shimura. I'm in a really bad position." I paused and tried to get ahold of myself. My voice had been wavering like a scared little girl's. "I accidentally got left behind in the museum—and the guard locked the doors and armed the system!"

"Oh, no! How did that happen?"

"It's a long story. But I'm standing here, staring at a keypad by the front door that says the system is armed and all secure. How can I get out? I promise that if you tell me the code I'll never pass it on to anyone else!"

"Rei, that code is so classified that only the museum director and our two full-time security guards know it. I always leave before they punch it in."

"What can I do?" I was feeling frantic.

"I can't call anyone from security to come back for you because it's so irregular, they'd have to report to Allison. The fact that you're in there, alone after closing, would only make things worse. She doesn't trust you. She called me this morning after the police called her. She told them she believes that you reported that kimono stolen but actually *gave* it to your parents to take to California to sell—that's why she's checking eBay all the time, looking for the evidence."

"I think I know who's got it, Jamie, and I'm sure he doesn't know much about eBay—"

"Rei, that's really interesting, but I've got to go. Did you hear that click on my line? It means I've got to buzz somebody in."

"Is it Dick? Do you think he knows the code?" I asked desperately.

"Of course he wouldn't have it. He doesn't even work for the museum. And—and I don't know why you think he'd be coming to my apartment!"

"I saw the photo in your bedroom," I said.

"Oh!" She was silent for a minute. "Okay, it's true. I'll tell you about it later. But don't call me again—*please*. At least not until after ten."

"After ten? What do you suggest I do with my time until then?"

"Lie down on that couch in our office. Read some journals, make some coffee, whatever. Just be sure to clean up after yourself. You can sneak out after the museum opens tomorrow. I'll help you do it."

Jamie clicked off, and I held on to the phone, unwilling to let go of my lifeline to the outside world. Then I heard a second click.

I hadn't heard that sound since the days my mother used to check which teenage friends were calling me—the right ones or the wrong ones. I remembered the tell-tale click, and how furious it had made me. Hearing the click now made me terrified. Someone was in the museum with me. Someone listening in, who didn't want me to know.

I had thought that I'd overheard Takeo being thrown out of the building, but perhaps he'd come back when the guard was closing up the different galleries. But if Takeo was crazy with rage, why would he tiptoe around, listening in on the phone?

Something else nagged at me. What was it that the museum guard had told me when I'd come into the museum?

I pictured myself running up the steps into the museum and asking straightaway about Takeo—no, asking the guard more generally about a Japanese man. Yes, the guard had said. A Japanese man was looking around in the galleries.

I got up quietly and walked over to the pair of windows set on either side of the massive door. Through the window on the left, I saw it: a blue Geo Prism parked halfway up the block. I hadn't noticed it during my frantic run to the museum. In the slight bit of light that came in from the window, I pulled out the car-rental receipt and looked at it again. The writing was so faint, but it looked as if the date the car had been rented was October 8. October 8—a full two days before I'd arrived on the plane with Hana.

Mr. Shima had been in the United States even before Hana had died.

My fledgling suspicion—the one I'd wanted to share

with Jamie—was now confirmed. And suddenly my worry about setting off an alarm seemed quite trivial. In fact, sounding an alarm might be a very good idea.

I tugged at the knob to the front door, but it wouldn't move. I stared at the two additional locks over the knob. This was what was keeping me from exiting; they were the kind that required keys, and none was in sight.

I could search through the receptionist's desk, but that was locked. And the sound of my trying the door must have carried, because I heard the quick click of footsteps above. Mr. Shima was on his way down.

I remembered the museum's layout, which was a blessing, since it was dark and there were few lights on. I walked quietly to the left, entering the hall that led to the north galleries containing all the textile collections, including the special kimono show. I recalled an exit in the back of that side of the building.

I'd made it into the first kimono gallery just as the other person started coming down the stairs. It was no longer at a fast clip—it was a stealthy one. That bought me a few more seconds but also made it clear that he wanted to catch me unaware—to trap me.

Beyond the room holding the Museum of Asian Arts' kimono lay the second gallery of kimono—the treasures from the Morioka. The emergency exit sign was clear—I'd been right about a door in the back. But now I was worried that it, too, was locked. If I got there, and couldn't get out, I'd be trapped at the back of the museum.

Something I'd read about differences between women and men came to me. The male reaction to stress was fight or flight. The woman's reaction was to stay and try to achieve safety. I could do that, maybe. I could hide until I had a chance to get back to the phone and call

911. Then again, I might accidentally set off a motion
detector near something valuable, and I wouldn't even
need to call 911.

I took a second to survey the kimono gallery. The
Museum of Asian Arts' large, padded ivory silk kimono
was hanging on a large T-stand, about five feet six
inches high. I knew how much the kimono had been
revered by Jamie—maybe it had an alarm on it, an
alarm that would save me.

I put my hands on it, and nothing happened. Damn,
damn. But then again—this was the biggest kimono in
the exhibition. That was an advantage in itself, and I decided to use it.

Making one last frantic check over my shoulder, I
slipped inside the kimono and held its front lapels
closed, hiding myself quickly just as I heard the sound
of footsteps on the tiled floor of the museum's lobby.
The sound disappeared after a few seconds, and I
guessed the person had gone to search the museum's
south wing, which housed the galleries devoted to ceramics and works on paper.

I debated whether there was enough time to run
out and make a phone call, but decided no, just as the
footsteps came back, growing louder as they crossed
the lobby floor. Then the footfalls were soft and
close.

He was in the kimono gallery. I kept my eyes on the
gap between the kimono's hem and the carpet and saw
a flash of black. Black shoes, slightly worn down at the
heels. Mr. Shima's shoes—I'd noticed them when I'd
first met him at the Morioka.

I swore silently at myself. Why hadn't I asked the car-
rental agency the *date* of Mr. Shima's rental? If I'd figured things out back at the Sofitel, Detective Harris and
his colleagues could already have tracked Mr. Shima

down. I'd lost another chance when I'd been on the
phone with Jamie and I hadn't revealed Mr. Shima's
name. Jamie could have told the police what I'd said in
the event I disappeared. Not that they'd ever find me
healthy and whole. I had the feeling that what Mr.
Shima had meted out to Hana would be my punishment
as well.

34

Mr. Shima had moved past me and into the back gallery, the one with the kimono from the Morioka. I couldn't hear him anymore, but I didn't dare peek from the garment. He could be standing anywhere, looking anywhere. Waiting.

Now I understood how clever the registrar had been. He'd known my itinerary and must have arrived in Washington two days earlier than I—enough time to be thoroughly rested for the job ahead. Because he had a rental car, he could get around easily. He must have looked for the kimono in my room when he knew I was out. He would have gotten in when Hana had opened my door. I bet he had forced her to leave the hotel with him in his car. He'd taken the kimono from her, and then killed her and dumped her body.

There was no risk to this theft, I thought with bitterness. Mr. Shima would go on with his job as the Morioka registrar, since there was no shadow of scandal or blame on him. The kimono theft had happened overseas, so it would automatically be the fault of Americans. The amount that Mr. Shima would earn on an overseas kimono sale might be $50,000 to $100,000. A nice sum, but not large enough to draw special notice at his bank. Then again, $100,000 wasn't so much money. A hun-

dred thousand dollars—was that sum worth the risk of
committing murder?

From the next gallery, I heard a soft sound—the
whisper-soft noise that silk makes when it is folded. Mr.
Shima was going to steal the entire kimono collection.
Maybe it hadn't been his original plan, but now he had
the opportunity. And unfortunately, if he decided to
take all the kimono in the show, he'd eventually unwrap
the bride's kimono that was sheltering me.

So, Hugh's dream had been a premonition. I was
wrapped in the bride's kimono that he had dreamed
about, and the man in black was near. I would never
know what the dream had really meant to Hugh, but I
knew for myself that the man in black was a represen-
tation of evil: the kind of evil that would snuff out the
life of a young woman who was in the way, and a second woman who knew too much.

I took a few breaths to calm down. I was spinning
into an irrational state. If the fire door at the back of the
museum could be opened, Mr. Shima would surely leave
with the goods. That would be an ideal situation, since
I could call the police, who would later catch him with
everything at the Sofitel or one of the airports.

I concentrated every bit of my energy on listening.
The whisper-soft sounds of the kimono collection being
folded continued. Then the folding stopped, and his
footsteps walked softly along the carpeted gallery floor.

Suddenly I couldn't hear him anymore. Had he quietly walked out through the other gallery and to the
back door? I wanted to weep with anxiety. And then, as
if in answer to my absolute misery, I heard the tinkle of
breaking glass, and then the museum's alarm began to
ring. It roared with the kind of fierce, ominous sound of
Japanese sirens warning residents that an earthquake
has taken place.

To me, the sound was welcome. I understood that Mr. Shima had done what I'd hoped for: he had broken out of the museum.

I'd been clutching the inside of the kimono so tightly that my arms had cramped, so as I emerged from the protective tent of the bride's kimono, I took a moment to stretch. I rotated my neck with relief, turned around, and froze.

Mr. Shima was still there.

He was standing perfectly still and watching me. I glanced at him, and at the pile of neatly folded kimono in the corner of the room.

"You're wearing her coat? But how . . ." he murmured, looking at Hugh's Barbour hanging loosely on me.

I opened my mouth to speak, but no words came out. He must have thought I was in Hana's coat. He knew what Hana had been wearing. I'd been right in my guess that he had killed her.

"For once you have nothing to say. I'm surprised," Mr. Shima said.

The alarm continued to bleat, and I found myself marveling at the Japanese registrar's calm. Didn't he understand what the alarm meant? At last my voice came back, though I had to struggle to speak in Japanese. "Um, do you hear the alarm? It means the police are on their way."

"No, they aren't. The alarm company will telephone this place, to make sure the siren didn't go off by accident. Because of your nice American accent, I'll have you answer the phone and tell them not to worry. Won't you?"

"Yes," I said, because my eyes were on something that Mr. Shima had slipped out of his pocket. It was a small dagger with a mother-of-pearl handle. A bride's knife—the kind that was still tucked into an *obi* as a decoration.

Mr. Shima stroked the knife, looked at me, and said, "I need the receipt. I saw you put it in your pocket earlier today."

It wouldn't do to make him angry. I handed the receipt over, and he put it in his pocket. "Thank you. I was careless to give it to you the other day."

"My father would say—he'd say it was the unconscious working," I said.

"What?" Mr. Shima sounded distracted, as I'd hoped he would.

"Unconsciously, you feel bad about what you did. You wanted to be caught. And as you heard earlier, I've already told someone about when you really arrived here. You won't get away with anything."

"The girl you were talking to is no problem. My partner will handle that." Mr. Shima broke off because the phone had started ringing, true to his prediction.

"Not yet," he said as I started for the phone. I stopped and let him wrap an arm around my body. Then we moved as one to the reception desk. He sat down on the receptionist's chair, jerking me down so I was on his lap. It was horrible being close to him like this, especially because I could feel the unmistakable sign of his arousal. So violence excited him as much as the prospect of stealing.

"When you pick up the phone, you must answer 'Museum of Asian Arts,'" he instructed, and I nodded, feeling the edge of the bride's knife on the nape of my neck. "Do it now."

I picked up the phone and said in a shaking voice, "Museum of Asian Arts."

"Darling, is that you?" Hugh was on the other end.

Mr. Shima was sitting very close to the receiver—I wasn't sure how much he could hear.

"Yes," I said.

"We set off the alarm by breaking a window . . ." Hugh's words were hard to hear because of the static coming from his cell phone. "Takeo . . ."

"What's going on?" Mr. Shima hissed in my ear in Japanese.

"The museum is closed right now," I said stiffly. I wanted Hugh to sense that things were not right.

"Did you hear that?" Hugh sounded excited. "Takeo and I met . . . rough going at first, but okay now—"

"Thank you for calling, sir. I must end this call," I said as woodenly as possible.

"What? Oh, I get it, you don't want the phone to be tied up in case the alarm service phones . . . so stupid about these things—"

"Not at all," I said. I used those words because I didn't think they'd trigger any suspicion from Mr. Shima. To the Japanese ear, it was a common, innocuous phrase that meant "you are welcome."

"What did you say?" Hugh paused, sounding a bit uncertain for the first time.

"Not. At. All," I repeated emphatically. Mr. Shima was holding the receiver and listening in at the same time that I was speaking.

"You're not okay," he said.

"Not at all," I repeated.

"Ah, I think I get it—"

"I urgently request that you call during regular museum hours, when someone else can assist you," I said, flinching as the knife nicked my neck. I was too frightened to feel pain—all I felt was a trickle down the back of my neck and Mr. Shima's arm tightening around my diaphragm.

"What's going on?" Mr. Shima whispered into my ear in Japanese. "Who's on the line?"

"The caller is not dangerous to you. He just wants to know what hours the museum is open," I said back to him in Japanese. Then, into the phone, I said, "The museum *lobby* opens at ten daily. Closing hour is five. Do you understand?"

"I think so. Ah, what is the price of admission?"

"Admission is five dollars, but as our kimono exhibit from Japan's famous Morioka museum is so *cutting edge,* an additional donation is requested—a very sizable, significant amount."

"Right," Hugh said. "I will make the greatest contribution I possibly can. Is there anything else I should know about the exhibit?"

"You need to clear the line of this stupid caller so we can take the call from the alarm company," Mr. Shima said in swift, angry Japanese. "If you don't hang up now, I'm going to cut through the back of your neck. Do you understand?"

Tears came to my eyes. Even though Hugh could probably overhear Mr. Shima muttering to me, he wouldn't have any inkling of how terrible the words were.

"I must tend to business here," I said stiffly. "Thank you for calling the museum."

I hung up the receiver.

"Who was that?" Mr. Shima looked at me closely.

"Like I said, a caller to the museum—"

"Well, we've got to hurry now. That call should come soon, and I'll need you to take it. I've changed my mind about what you'll say to the alarm company. You will say that you're going to kill yourself."

"What?" I looked at him, shocked.

"It makes perfect sense. You were going to be exposed as the kimono thief, and you'd just lost the respect of your Japanese boyfriend. Good reasons to die, *neh*?"

"You think I'd slit my own throat?" I asked.

"Of course not! I wouldn't let you hold the knife. I'll do it myself. We'll wait two more minutes to see if the alarm company calls. If they don't, we'll just go ahead with business."

"Why don't we just leave?" I asked, thinking if I got outside, at least I'd have the chance to run. Even if Hugh had called the police, it would be a while before they arrived and could figure out how to enter the museum. It had already been five minutes since the alarm had gone off and no company representative had called.

"I will. After the police arrive and are concentrating on examining your lovely body," Mr. Shima said with a slight laugh.

"I still don't understand why you stole your institution's kimono in such a roundabout way," I said, determined to distract him from the two-minute countdown.

"I'm not removing these textiles—I told you that already. I am interested in getting your fingerprints on them so it looks like you were the one who wanted to steal them."

"So if you don't want these kimono, why did you take the one from my room?" I said, walking back into the gallery at the prompting of the knife blade he held between my shoulders.

"I wouldn't have had to even take it from your room if it hadn't been for that stupid girl. She was there first and complicated everything."

"What time of day was it?" I asked, because I still wanted to know.

"The early evening. You'd gone downstairs with that man, and after I'd followed you and gotten a sense that you'd be a while, I went upstairs with my special tools. I was surprised to see the door was slightly ajar—quite delighted at my good luck. I went inside and got right to work, but then she came out of the bathroom—a vulgar young woman with a lipstick in her hand—"

"My MAC lipstick," I said, hardly able to believe it. So that was where my missing stick of Rage had gone.

"I don't know. I can tell you that when we struggled, some of it touched the kimono, and that's when I became very angry. To damage something that our museum had cherished so carefully for years!"

"So you killed her then?"

"No, I had to convince her to leave the hotel with me. I did that with the aid of the very knife at your neck, Miss Shimura. And when we got outside, to a quiet place, I found that it worked just as well as the ancient samurai thought it would."

We'd reached the stack of kimono, and with Mr. Shima holding the knife in front of me, I sat down, awkwardly, and began doing as he said—touching each kimono, pressing my hands firmly along the front of each garment.

"The kimono—you liked it, but it was because of more than the fabric," I pondered aloud as I methodically imprinted my hands along the silk. Detective Harris had mentioned smuggling drugs in the kimono. Now I recalled how, at the X-ray machine at Narita Airport, the security officials had wanted to look in the box. An interesting shape, or shapes, must have appeared on the screen.

"There was something hidden inside the garments," I said, thinking out loud. "Something else from your museum. But because the customs broker helping me was a pro, he was able to finesse things at the X ray so they wouldn't bother opening the package."

"Oh, really? If the goods were there, why didn't you see them when you opened the package?"

"An *uchikake* has a very deep hem. In the Edo period,

when so many people weren't allowed to show their wealth, they wore their jewels inside the kimono, sometimes sewn into the hems," I said.

"The Morioka doesn't have jewels," Mr. Shima said.

"True, but it has a priceless *netsuke* collection." I looked at him, and knew that I was right to have guessed that small ivory figurines, once worn as ornaments hanging off kimono, were the most sensible objects to smuggle out of the Morioka Museum. They were more valuable than kimono because there was a much bigger market for the exquisitely carved ivory.

"Never say priceless. *Netsuke* are easier to sell. My American contact has a waiting list filled with the names of people who don't ask questions, just pay."

"Dick Jemshaw," I said, just as the phone began to ring.

"You're right again, Miss Shimura, but there's no more time to chat. You're going to answer the phone, and act confused, but make up something if they ask you to give them the password. Then I want to hear you say you're going to kill yourself. If I don't hear you say those words, you know what I'm going to have to do."

I understood. I moved at a quick pace toward the ringing phone with Mr. Shima right behind me.

Mr. Shima picked up the receiver and made me press my face close to his so he could hear what was being said on the other end of the line. I prayed it wasn't Hugh again.

"Museum of Asian Arts." My voice came out in a whisper.

"This is Mr. Jones calling from Professional Sentry Services, the company that has a contract with the museum. An alarm went off and I'm calling to check what the situation is. Is everything all right?"

I looked at Mr. Shima. He was nodding emphatically. "Yes, everything's fine."

"And who are you?"

Again, he nodded and mouthed the word "Shimura."

"Rei Shima—Shimura," I said, as if I were merely stuttering. If there was a tape of the call, maybe someone would figure out later what I'd been trying to say.

"Ms. Shimura, we don't have you listed in the computer as a museum staff member qualified to sign off on security concerns."

"Um, it must be because I don't normally work here," I said, looking anxiously at Mr. Shima. He smiled. It was all going according to his plan.

"Just give me the password, and then I can sign it all off."

"Let me see . . . I'm trying to remember. It's been a while since it was given to me." I paused. "Something about . . . cats, no, I think it was something about dogs. No, it was Japanese history—"

"It's easy to forget. Do you have it written down somewhere?" The alarm company employee was entirely too accommodating—not very good for a security company that should be on the lookout for thieves, I thought. But that was beside the point. I had a minute more to talk before Mr. Shima killed me.

"Why don't you try to think really hard, run through what seems most likely to you," the security-company man suggested.

"Chippendale," I said, knowing that there was no way in hell that it could be right.

Mr. Shima was so physically close that I could feel his head nodding alongside mine.

"Chippendale . . . that's not right. I can give you a hint, if you can tell me the museum curator's mother's maiden name."

I almost laughed. The ultimate irony is I knew Allison's maiden name—Lancer. But not her mother's.

"Howard," I said, giving my mother's own name.

"What's that? I couldn't quite hear you."

"The alarm is so loud. I'm really sorry I set it off," I said miserably, trying to speak louder. It did make it hard to hear the voice on the other end of the line.

"Don't worry! It happens to many of our clients. Can you spell the maiden name for me?" Could the alarm-company guy be so stupid that he was willing to believe whatever word I made up? If so, nobody would ever come to look for my dead body that night. The only thing I could think of doing to delay was misspell the word. "Okay, I think it's H-O-W-A—"

"I didn't hear the third letter, can you repeat it all again from the start?"

"H-O-W—"

I fell backward as Mr. Shima gave a sudden jerk. Oh, God, this was it. He was stabbing me. No, he'd just fallen backward. Because I was on his lap, I fell, too—but in the next moment strong hands seized me under my arms and yanked me over the table.

"You okay?" asked a man wearing a baseball cap and black T-shirt with the word POLICE on it, setting me down on an antique Chinese chair that I knew the museum didn't want anyone sitting on.

"How—How—" I broke off, not sure whether I should keep spelling my mother's maiden name, or whether I should ask what had happened. "How did you get here?"

"We got the message from your friends outside—the ones who set off the alarm in the first place," the man said as he snapped handcuffs onto Mr. Shima. "Because of the information you relayed when they called you, we were able to guess that you and the suspect were downstairs near the reception area, and that the suspect was armed with a knife."

I wasn't going to have to explain my way out of anything, I thought with amazement, as I heard the SWAT man give Mr. Shima the Miranda warning. After he'd finished, the warning was repeated by a Japanese man I vaguely recognized from the Japanese embassy.

Mr. Shima was crying, but I didn't feel sorry for him. He'd killed Hana and thrown her in the garbage, just because she got in the way of his *netsuke* smuggling operation. And he would have killed me.

"After you get your medical done, we'll see you downtown," the SWAT man said to me. "In the meantime you might as well catch a ride downtown in the black Lexus parked outside. You got a couple of friends in there who are very worried. They seem like out-of-towners, though—you think they'll be able to find their way around town?"

"A couple of friends?" I repeated faintly. "You don't mean—one Japanese and one Scottish?"

"Yeah, exactly that. Two good-looking guys with strange accents, both very concerned. They're the ones who set off the alarm in the first place."

"I see." This was an etiquette situation that neither the American nor Japanese experts could tell me how to handle. But as my mother would say, it was the kind of problem more than a few women would like to have.

35

Hugh hugged me first, wordlessly. His face was as wet as mine. Then Takeo took me in his arms, dry-cheeked, but murmuring an apology that I thought I'd never hear from him.

"I can't believe this," I said to them both as I stepped back and regarded the improbable sight of my East-West boyfriends standing together. "Because you talked to each other, you wound up saving my life. After I was so hard on both of you—"

"You were never awful," Hugh said as I slid in next to Takeo in the backseat of the Lexus. It seemed the right place to be.

"You were torn between two men and two countries," Takeo said softly. "I see it now."

As Hugh drove, the two of them described how things had played out. Hugh had retrieved the phone message I left at his apartment, and gone to the museum, only to find it shut with an irate Takeo pacing in front of its door, convinced that I was still inside. It had been Takeo who had gotten on Hugh's shoulders and thrown the rock that broke a museum window, setting off the alarm; and Takeo who had been standing close to Hugh's cell phone, taking in the brutal words that Mr. Shima was whispering in Japanese. By the end of the short, disjointed communication, both men knew that Mr. Shima was with me, and I was in serious trouble. So Hugh did what he did best: organize. In the space of a few minutes he'd gotten the 911 dispatcher to put him in touch with a SWAT team.

At the police station, I was questioned separately from Mr. Shima, and the name Dick Jemshaw must have come out in both conversations, because the police roared off to his house in Bethesda. And two hours later, when I was going over my statement for the umpteenth time, I heard the good news that the bride's kimono had been found at Dick Jemshaw's home—along with a collection of fifteen *netsuke* that had been sewn into the hem.

Takeo, sticking to his word, left Washington the next day for Tokyo. It was the same flight that Kyoko and Yoshi were taking, so he and I saw them at the gate at Dulles. Kyoko and Yoshi were very social and talkative at first—so giddy, almost, that I was beginning to think they might finally be comfortable with the idea that the two of them belonged together. When they saw the way that Takeo and I were looking at each other, though, they quietly made their way off to Starbucks for a few final purchases.

"I know that saying I'm sorry can't make up for what I did to you," Takeo said as we stood side by side, watching out the window at the runway. Two baggage carts had just arrived at the plane. "What I said yesterday in the restaurant was unforgivable. Then I led you to a place where you almost lost your life."

"What you said to me in the hotel represents a bad five minutes. It doesn't replace all that happened in the last year, since I met you."

"I'm glad you had a good last year," Takeo said.

I didn't answer immediately because I was watching through the window some action on the runway. Four baggage handlers were transferring a long black box covered with a thick layer of plastic tarp into the plane's hold. Hana. I was seeing her again at last.

"Why do you look so sad?" Takeo asked.

"It's Hana. I think her coffin just went into the plane. I'll always choose to believe that she went into my room to try on makeup . . . not to steal the kimono. Anyway, if she'd truly stolen the kimono and gotten away, she'd still be alive. A human life is worth so much more than cloth. Or *netsuke*."

"Dick Jemshaw was the one who was going to sell the *netsuke,* you said to the police last night. Do you know whether he confessed to being involved in the murder, too?"

"The police told me that Dick Jemshaw admitted asking Mr. Shima to smuggle the stolen *netsuke* for him in exchange for fifty percent of the profits. Then Mr. Shima had his—complication—with Hana, and he told Dick. Dick told him to get rid of the body . . . so he did know. So he's an accessory." I thought of how Hana had talked to me about accessories while we were on the plane—what a weird, alternate meaning of the word applied to Dick Jemshaw. At the same time I knew that it was very lucky for Jamie that the police had found the *netsuke* at Dick's house, and not her apartment—where I had worried they might be. The only mystery I hadn't figured out was who had slashed Hugh's car tires. Mr. Shima swore he'd lost our trail and not gone into Georgetown, and Kyoko hadn't done it—at least, according to the Café Milano staff who'd seen her go into the rest room and then straight back to her table. My final conclusion was that the vandalism on the Lexus had been done by the parking intimidation expert in the Bob Marley T-shirt. There would never be a way to prove it, of course. And even I had to admit that this kind of crime was small potatoes compared with what had happened to Hana.

I shook myself and went back to the topic that interested Takeo. "Dick Jemshaw will probably serve five to ten years in prison—at least, that's what Hugh thinks."

"Hugh's a good thinker," Takeo said softly. "He's perfect for you."

"I wouldn't say perfect." I felt as awkward about the situation as when I'd first walked out of the museum.

"We had time to talk when we were sitting in his car and you were trapped inside. We both were going crazy knowing that you could die. We talked about nothing but you. And I realized that I want you, but I do not have the same kind of attachment that he does. I'm just so different—I can never live your way. Or his. All the people you want to see, the places you want to go. You have so much heart, so much energy."

"It sounds as if you've given up," I said, feeling sad again.

"It's not giving up—it's facing reality. In my own irresponsible way I do love you, but I never felt like saying it, because I wasn't sure. After my behavior yesterday—well, I think you understand how hellish I would be to live with. But I'll be around in Japan, if you ever change your mind and come back."

"Of course I'm coming back. I'm going to get my passport straightened out this week—"

"Take your time deciding. You should explore some business possibilities here, and see what it's like to be with someone who loves you enough to want to marry." The last few words Takeo seemed to choke on. I knew how hard this was for him.

I took Takeo's hands in mine. "I'll never forget this."

"I know. But would you do me a favor and please leave? I want to compose myself before I get on the plane. The longer you look at me, the closer I come to breaking down."

I left the gate in a haze of tears, understanding that there could be no happy ending for Takeo, just as there hadn't been for Hana, or Yoshi, or Kyoko. Americans had been affected by the kimono scandal, too. Jamie, I knew, was quietly miserable, even though I had reassured her privately, during a quick phone conversation earlier that morning, that I didn't bear her any grudge. I remembered how my reputation had almost collapsed because of a stupid, reckless moment on a Metro train. Jamie was twenty-three and deserved to go on with her life, to make better choices.

Allison Powell had taken a sudden leave of absence from the museum, which meant that Jamie would temporarily assume her responsibilities. I suspected Allison's leave might become permanent, because it was now widely known that she'd been warned of a risk to the kimono exhibition but hadn't beefed up security. Jamie had said to me that Marina Billings considered me the one who had saved the museum's collection from a devastating crime while all of them had been too distracted to notice what had been going on. The museum's director would go on to repeat her flattering quote for reporters from *The Washington Post, Washington Times,* and *USA Today,* not to mention the various television networks.

Marina wanted me to deliver my kimono lecture again on Wednesday, the date that a harried editorial assistant at the *Post* had mistakenly typed in as that of my speaking engagement. Given the avalanche of publicity the exhibition had received, and the extra speaking fee I'd receive, I said yes. After all, I still needed to do some souvenir shopping—a Versace belt for Richard Randall was high on my list.

I was relieved that the two men who had been distrustful of me at the Japanese embassy had sent flowers and a note congratulating me on great personal bravery. And then, from Japan, the Morioka Museum's director, Mr. Ito, faxed a letter of thanks for saving the museum's collection. He and Mr. Nishio and the Japanese police were beginning a full-scale investigation of their holdings in case Mr. Shima had been pilfering museum storage for a while. Mr. Ito added that he wanted to have a talk about my doing more work for his museum, after I'd returned to Japan and had a chance to think things through.

I wasn't sure when I'd go home, because I still hadn't made any effort to replace my passport. In the meantime I was living like an exhausted young woman who had too few pennies in her pocket. It would take another twenty-four hours for the museum to come through with a check for me, so, from the airport where I'd dropped off Takeo, I decided to take the Washington Suites' free shuttle bus back to the hotel. There, I packed up my goods and said good-bye. Brian Hunter took a Polaroid snapshot of me in the lobby and asked me to autograph it.

On the outside, I was solvent, but inside, I was a wreck. I'd been close to death before, but the extended time with Mr. Shima had been more disturbing than anything I'd experienced. He'd cut the back of my neck with a bride's knife; the cut had been fairly deep, it turned out, deep enough for the female plastic surgeon to warn me that I might have a scar—not that a scar on the back of the neck was any kind of problem, she'd hastened to add. I wouldn't go through the trauma that women did who'd had their faces, or breasts, disfigured.

It wasn't until after Takeo had kissed me good-bye at the airport that I thought about how the nape of the neck was considered the most erotic part of a Japanese woman. If I wore a kimono again, I'd have to pull the collar snugly against my neck, hiding the ugly marks. I was going to have to call my aunt Norie about it before I went home—I knew she'd cry when she saw my nape.

Feeling somber, I shuttled my suitcases on the Metro and then trudged from Dupont Circle to Hugh's apartment, letting myself in with the extra key that he'd given me. Hugh had gone to work for a few hours but would be back by supper. It was good to have a few hours to myself in the late afternoon, in an apartment with old gas-electric fixtures that shone with a cozy glow. I unpacked the beautiful dresses and the suit my mother had helped me buy, and hung them in a small section of Hugh's closet. I stored everything else in one drawer, so that it wouldn't seem as if I were moving in.

I'd stay for a little while, just long enough to have a sense of peace and happiness again. I'd said as much to Hugh the night before, which he'd spent holding me tightly in my old room at the Washington Suites. Hugh had repeated that wherever I wanted to live, he'd follow—but only at my invitation.

I smiled to myself, thinking that the greatest luxury in the world surely was the gift of unconditional love. The promise of a quiet evening with Hugh slipped around me as softly as the finest *rinzu* silk.

Now it was five o'clock, and I lit a fire in the living room and poured myself a small glass of sherry. I was almost completely unpacked. The only things I couldn't find an obvious place for were the three long rectangular packages that belonged to Aunt Norie—the kimono she'd lent me. Now I opened up the rice-paper covering to examine the last kimono, the one that I'd never worn, made of the green silk that reminded me of Hugh's eyes. As I looked at it again, I decided that the green was just as close to the color of the moss Takeo cultivated in his garden in Hayama. Green, the color that had proved to be more significant to me than any other.

I took a shower, taking care to protect the area of my neck that had been taped. Then I began dressing. First came new, shimmering peach-colored lingerie and the half-slip that my mother had bought me. Over that went a gold silk underkimono, which was followed by the various waist ties, and then the green kimono, more sashes around the waist, and finally the *obi*. I spent the next fifteen minutes in front of the armoire's full-length mirror tying the black-and-gold *obi* with a wide and splendid bow. Then I rotated the sash so that the bow rested on the proper place in the middle of my back. I tied orange and gold *obi-jime* cords over the *obi* as the final decorative flourish.

I was almost done. Standing sideways so I could see the back of my neck in the mirrored armoire door, I adjusted the back collar of my kimono. The tape over my injury showed, but I found I didn't mind it as much as I'd thought. The mark was a symbol of a rite of passage—a passage to a stronger identity. Now I knew that I didn't need to stand alone to be strong.

I perked up my ears at the sound of a key opening the vestibule door a flight below. Hugh bounded up the stairs, softly singing "Honey," a song I'd been getting to know. He sounded better than Moby, but I guess I was biased.

Hugh was moving quickly, but I wanted to beat him. Before he could reach his front door, I'd unlocked it.

The World of Sujata Massey

Look for these riveting mysteries by
Sujata Massey,
starring Japanese-American sleuth
Rei Shimura.

The Salaryman's Wife
Zen Attitude
The Flower Master
The Floating Girl

THE SALARYMAN'S WIFE

Rei Shimura is a 27-year-old English teacher living in one of Tokyo's seediest neighborhoods. She doesn't make much money, but she wouldn't go back home to California even if she had a free ticket (which, thanks to her wealthy parents, she does). Her independence is threatened, however, when a getaway to an ancient castle town is marred by murder. Rei is the first to find the beautiful wife of a high-powered businessman dead in the snow. Taking charge, as usual, Rei searches for clues by crashing a funeral, posing as a bar-girl, and somehow ending up pursued by police and paparazzi alike. In the meantime, she manages to piece together a strange, ever-changing puzzle—one that is built on lies and held together by years of sex and deception.

"Sly, sexy and deftly done."
People magazine "Page-Turner of the Week"

ZEN ATTITUDE

With her own antiques business and live-in Scottish lawyer boyfriend, Rei Shimura finally has a life to be proud of in Tokyo. But when Rei overpays for a beautiful chest of drawers, she's in for the worst deal of her life. The con man who sold her the tansu is found dead, and like it or not, Rei's opened a Pandora's box of mystery, theft, and murder.

Only Rei sees the tansu as the key. It will take a quick wit, fast feet, and, above all, a Zen attitude for Rei to discover what a young monk, a judo star, and an ancient scroll have in common and why her own life hangs in the balance.

"A gifted storyteller."
USA Today

THE FLOWER MASTER

Life in Japan for a single Californian woman with a fledging antiques business isn't always fun, but when the flower arranging class Rei Shimura's aunt cajoles her into taking turns into a stage for murder, Rei finds plenty of the excitement she's been missing.

Surprisingly too many people have a reason for committing the crime—including her aunt. While struggling to adjust to the nuances of Japanese propriety, trying to keep her business afloat, and dealing with veiled messages left under her door, Rei sifts the bones of old skeletons to keep her family name clear—and her own life safe from an enemy with a mysterious agenda. If Rei doesn't want to be crushed like fallen cherry blossoms, she's going to have to walk a perilous line and uncover a killer with a dramatic flare for deadly arrangements.

"Sujata Massey is at her masterful best."
Lisa Scottoline

THE FLOATING GIRL

Rei Shimura is finally beginning to feel as if Tokyo is home. Now a writer on art and antiques at the *Gaijin Times,* a comic-style magazine aimed at affluent young readers, Rei's latest assignment is a piece on the history of comic book art. During a weekend of research and relaxation at her boyfriend Takeo's beachside house, Rei stumbles upon the perfect subject: an exquisite modern comic that reveals the disturbing social milieu of pre-World War II Japan.

Rei's story, though, evolves into something much darker. One of the comic's young creators is found dead—a murder that soon takes the tenacious Rei deep into the heart of Japan's youth underground. Immersed in the investigation, she finds herself floating through strip clubs, animation shops, and coffeehouses to get the true story—and save her own skin.

"Rei is one of the most complex female protagonists around . . . Another must-read."
Booklist

Watch for Sujata Massey's new hardcover,
The Daimyo's Daughter
Coming soon

Antiques dealer Rei Shimura is in San Francisco visiting her parents and researching a personal project tracing the story of 100 years of Japanese decorative arts through her own family's experience. Her work is interrupted by the arrival of her boyfriend, lawyer Hugh Glendinning, who is involved in a class action lawsuit on behalf of aged Asian nationals forced to engage in slave labor for Japanese companies during World War II. These two projects suddenly intertwine when one of Hugh's clients is murdered and Rei begins to uncover unsavory facts about her own family's actions during the War. Rei unravels the truth and finds the killer, and at the same time learns all about family ties and loyalty and the universal desire to avoid blame.

Immerse Yourself in the Beauty and Mystery
of Seventeenth-century Japan

Exotic, Thrilling Stories by
Laura Joh Rowland

Author of *The Samurai's Wife*

"Nearly impossible to put down."
Washington Post Book World

SHINJŪ
0-06-100950-4/$6.99 US/$9.99 Can
The evocative, gripping thriller set in the heart of
romantic medieval Japan that introduced memorable
detective Sano Ichirō.

BUNDORI
0-06-101197-5/$6.99 US/$9.99 Can
"Bundori is terrific."
New Orleans Times Picayune

THE WAY OF THE TRAITOR
0-06-101090-1/$6.99 US/$9.99 Can
"Like Umberto Eco's classic,
The Name of the Rose...excellent."
Booklist